LIV'S SECRETS

ARMINLEAR

ISBN (paperback): 978-1-956450-50-7
(eBook): 978-1-956450-51-4

Library of Congress Control Number: 2022951609

Armin Lear Press Inc
215 W Riverside Drive, #4362
Estes Park, CO 80517

LIV'S SECRETS

A NOVEL

JANET LEVINE

ARMINLEAR

To My Great Grandparents
Eliyahu Meier and Rosa Rosenberg who in the 1870s
encouraged their Sons and Daughters to emigrate from
Lithuania to the sunny shores of South Africa

AUTHOR'S NOTE

As there may be misunderstandings of unfamiliar South African terms, the words in bold below explain the different nuances.

African(s) = Black South Africans (singular/ plural)

Afrikaner(s) = singular/plural—White South Africans descended from the original Dutch settlers in the early 1600s. Intermixed with descendants of French Huguenots who settled among the Dutch Boers (farmers). They brought with them grape vines from famous French vineyards and that is why today South Africa has such a renowned wine industry. The settlers bastardized High Dutch into what we know now as the language Afrikaans, always with an "s" at the end. These Afrikaners were the originators of apartheid. Afrikaans is a guttural language that sounds something like German.

Afrikaans = bastardized (dialect) of Dutch. I can converse very easily with Dutch speakers from Holland and especially Flemish speakers from Belgium who also developed a bastardized form of High Dutch.

Boers = Afrikaans word for farmers. Used to describe Afrikaans-speaking settlers. In contemporary South Africa used derogatorily to describe the small group within the Afrikaner population, who still cling to apartheid dogma.

Most (but not all) Afrikaners of Dutch descent have a "van or Van" in their last name. It means "from." Those of French descent have a "de or De or Der" which also means "from" or "of.". Some have both! Like the last name "Van Der Merwe". Think of New York City and the early Dutch settlers who bought Manhattan from the native people with 61 guilders of trinkets. Roosevelt, Van Buren, many others are descendants of those Dutch settlers, as are the names of many streets in Lower Manhattan. USA and SA share a similar early settler history.

There are many other White South Africans who are not Afrikaners, we speak English which is the lingua franca of all South Africans—Black and White. My antecedents share the fictionalized story of Helmut and Gittel, and the early days of the Weisz family when they arrived in Johannesburg. (For instance, the Yeoville home still stands and serves now as a synagogue and community center. The brothers did own a milling business.)

Growing up my family and I only mixed with English speakers in Johannesburg. I have distant relatives who were farmers and they spoke both English and Afrikaans. Non-Jewish White English speakers are descendants of the 1820 British settlers who landed when Britain ruled the Cape Colony as part of the British Empire. There are eight African languages spoken, plus English and Afrikaans. English is the language of all commerce, medicine, law, and academia. On the famous gold and diamond mines the various African speakers from different areas developed *fanigalo*, a mix of rudimentary English, some Afrikaans and the more common African languages like Zulu and Tswana. This became the lingua franca for Black migrant miners speaking different languages and their White mine bosses.

During the apartheid regime (1948-1994), White children were divided into English and Afrikaans medium schools K-12. For 12 years I learned Afrikaans as a second language and took a minor in Afrikaans at university. I was already involved in politics and wanted to understand and speak fluently the language of the Afrikaner oppressors. My Afrikaans counterparts had 12 years of English as a second language. That is why we all can speak a modicum of mixed English and Afrikaans

In the dormitory townships, Africans had only four years of compulsory education, the basic minimum of United Nation standards for reading, writing and arithmetic. They were taught in Afrikaans. Afrikaners are the only Afrikaans speaking people in the world. South Africa is a polylingual country for which I am grateful. Listening to African people speaking their native language allowed me to appreciate the music in languages because I don't understand the words. I do speak a little Zulu.

WEISZ FAMILY, AND OTHER MAJOR CHARACTERS IN THE NOVEL

Weisz Family:
Patriarch Moishe Weisz m. Leah Beinash in the 1850s in Lithuania Their children in birth order: Helmut, Gustav, Wilhelm, Rae, Trudi, Max, Leo
Helmut m. Gittel Feinstein: two children, Bernard and Sally. Bernard married and had two children and lived in Palestine later called Israel. Sally never married. Helmut remarried Golda.

Gustav m. Fanny: two sons, Jacob and Maurice. Gustav remarried Gertrude: one son, Harry

Wilhelm had a son, Micah and a daughter Beatrice.

Max never married, no children

Rae m. Moishe Lieberman: no children

Trudi lived with Fritz Benjamin, no children

Leo m. Jane Goldman: one daughter, Olivia. Known as Liv. Liv m. John Ivans, one daughter, Marion.

Rosie Lann and **Daniel Molefe** feature in Liv's life

Jaco Malan is Liv's confidante and ally

Hennie Van Niekerk is her nemesis

Mendel Beinash and the Beinash cousins.

The Minthof family: Patriarch Rafael, his son, Jacob, Jacob's three children Paul, Miriam and Bluma, all feature in the Weisz saga.

The Moekena family: Abel, his wife Kelihiwe, Alfred, Moses

Noteworthy historical **figures in the saga** are Robert Mangaliso Sobukwe, Hendrik Frensch Verwoerd, Helen Suzman, Alan Paton, David Pratt, Albert John Luthuli, Laurie Gandar, Benjy Pogrund; President Paul Kruger, President Louis Botha, President Jan Smuts, President Chaim Weismann. (See short Biographical Notes at the end of the book).

Liv's Secrets is a work of historical fiction. I have taken slight liberties with the articulation of ideas by these figures, for plot development.

MAP OF SOUTH AFRICA 1960

Plettenberg Bay is 230 km (145 miles) south west of Port Elizabeth

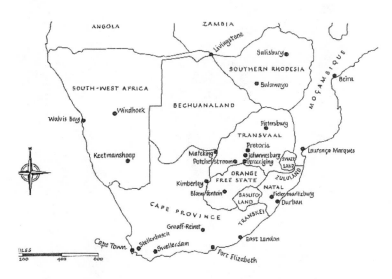

Map entitled "South Africa and Adjoining Territories. Provinces and Principal Cities" on page 86 from South Africa: A Study in Conflict ©1965 by Pierre van den Berghe. Published by Wesleyan University Press. Used by permission.

PREFACE

They discovered a land filled with golden promise, promise of wealth and peace, a land bathed in warming sunshine, whose wealth derived from Black men toiling at great depth to unearth the precious metals laid down over millennia. They arrived to live in South Africa a little over a hundred years ago, mainly from Lithuania, Latvia, Poland and Belarus, those early members of South Africa's Jewish families, to live in the promise of that shining southern land. Later, descendants of those early pioneers, pirouetting and intertwining their own lives with the lives of their families, danced to the throbbing beat of South Africa's drums, a sound of promise often threatening to whirl out of control, a dreidel run amok. Around and around, in ever-widening circles, touching more and more lives, a hundred years later that promise, now molten in the cauldron of conflict, scorched other generations. The heat of promise in meltdown.

2010
LIV

I'm eighty-eight years-old now, born in 1922 into a century of strife and struggle. Most days I feel every one of those eighty-eight years. I'm not sure how old Methuselah is, but certainly that's as old as I feel. Other days, especially if I can venture out into the refreshing, morning air and onto the back porch to drink my first cup of tea for the day, I feel younger. Almost as I was, so many years ago, before this creeping, physical decay, diminishment of teeth and eyesight, white hair thinning, everything drooping, dark spots, lines and wrinkles, and my skin like crepe or fish scales depending on the light. Catching a glimpse of myself in the mirror, I panic.

Who am I looking at?

Now, even with two hip replacements, I shuffle step. I use a stick or two sticks or the walker or Sibongile's arm.

Sibongile lives with me. Certainly, the house accommodates

two people. I call her Sibby, a worthy companion. Trained as a nurse, she prefers caring for old people. Hospital jobs at places like Johannesburg General are difficult for a young person. In her twenties, a post-apartheid woman, confident and vital, she often sings softly and sometimes more loudly, her voice as smooth as melted chocolate.

I love my garden even though I can't walk farther than the rose border. When I do, I'm scolded for walking alone. Sometimes we walk to the swimming pool and sit under the honeysuckle and wisteria loggia. The birds sing to one another; Africa is filled with song.

Although my memory and mind fade in the present, I remember. I remember the past, enough to fill a book . . . my life contained in a book. But the time was long passed that I had the physical strength to write about all those lives, a hundred years or more of lost lives: ghosts and secrets, secrets and ghosts: Nomzie, Natalie, my father. Much more than memories will die with me. All that will be left are photo albums and letters. Burn the letters, I urge myself, maybe they tell too much. But no one will read them. When I'm gone, they'll be tossed with all the other clutter.

Those albums and letters are filled with my memories and ghosts. My memories are more real than the daily trudge through my circumscribed life. Gnarled arthritic hands were a "family souvenir," older relatives used to tell me somberly when they couldn't lift anything and moved slowly. I didn't understand then, but now I do.

A decade ago, someone gave me a gift to Ancestry.com. Ancestry.com results confirmed, in a general way, what I already knew. I am a hundred percent Eastern European Jew, most likely from Lithuania—Riga or Memel—but, maybe as well, Latvia, Belarus, and Northeastern Poland.

When I turned eighty, the entire extended family gathered for a reunion at three rental villas on Majorca. We were over fifty people . . . the last time we were all together.

One of the younger children, a bright adolescent, remarked when I shared with the group the Ancestry.com results. "I bet you know a million stories from Eastern Europe?"

I nodded. "Yes, I do. Not a million but many. My own, and stories of my . . . let me see . . . your great-grandparents, my grandparents, my parents."

"You should tell those stories to a historian. People collect oral history. I'm sure if you inquired, someone from one of the universities will be interested. For instance, kids today learn about the Holocaust that way. Before they go on a field trip to somewhere like the Holocaust Museum in DC, survivors your age, even older, come to school to talk to them. At these museums they watch videos and testimony of other survivors."

We learn history from survivors' horrific nightmares? Is this all we have to share? Nightmare stories. Our century was one of struggle and strife. Perhaps I've lived too long? I'm forgetting the beauty of life; I'm forgetting the joy, the love, and the surprises.

"You are right," I replied to Adam, my young interlocutor. "That is a good idea. I do have many stories. People should know what I know. I'll tell my stories to someone at the university. I'll leave the record to you. One day soon, when I die, they'll be your family tales to do with as you wish."

I kept my promises. I told my stories to an oral historian. I've left my record for other generations.

Older each year—I've lived here for four years now—I'm slowly fading away in *Loeriebos*, my home I love so. *Loeriebos* is named after the loerie, a brilliantly colored bird from the Knysna forests, and its soft-grey colored cousin, the Transvaal loerie.

Like so many other South African Jewish families, mine are scattered—England, Israel, Switzerland, Australia, Canada, New Zealand, Costa Rica, and of course, America. I am one of the last of my direct family of Weiszes in South Africa.

When I spoke to the young woman, the oral historian from Wits University, I started my stories in the year 1960. Such a pivotal year on so many levels—personal history, family history, and, certainly the most consequential year in South Africa's troubled history.

1960
LIV

On a warm but rainy summer's night, about forty people sat in the elegant living room of a Johannesburg suburban home listening to famed author and political leader, Alan Paton. He explained the implications and pitfalls of the latest apartheid government legislation. After his presentation, the guests moved to the bar area and chose wine or beer. Then they broke into smaller groups to chat.

Liv stood alone in the center of the room, uncertain which small knot of guests to join. Surprising her from out of the group gathered on a side of the room, a woman moved in her direction.

She looked older as she approached than at a distance—in her mid-thirties, maybe a little younger than Liv, maybe somewhat older, with fine lines wrinkling her eyes and evident around her generous mouth. A little taller than Liv, and sturdy. Or what is called statuesque, Liv mused.

"Rosemary Lann. Hope you don't mind me introducing

myself? I'm new in town. You look approachable." With a polite smile on her face, the stranger held out her hand.

Approachable? Me? Liv thought and smiled back. Pleasantly surprised, she shook hands, Rosemary's hands cool and smooth to the touch.

"Liv Weisz. Do I detect an English accent?"

"Yes, I'm from London. I'm visiting for a while, seeing friends and family, and enjoying the sunshine and warmth. London is miserable at this time of year." Rosemary Lann smiled almost warily. "Everyone calls me Rosie."

"Do you know Alan? This is a semiprivate gathering."

"Oh no, I came with someone who knows him." Rosie looked around the room for her companion. "One afternoon last week at the bookstore in Hillbrow, I talked with him. We were standing at the shelf of South African authors and seeing my interest, he asked if I would I like to hear Alan Paton speak. I accepted then and there."

Liv nodded. Of course, she wanted to hear Alan Paton speak. Who wouldn't? Ever since the publication of his novel *Cry, The Beloved Country,* he's become an icon. Along with General Jan Smuts and the often-banned Nelson Mandela, Paton headed the list of South Africa's most internationally well-known crusaders against apartheid.

"A true honor to hear him," Rosie continued. "I'd so disappoint people at home if I passed over this chance. And you, why are you here?"

Liv nodded at their host. "Special invitation. Jaco's a good friend. I know Alan and his family a little—"

An acquaintance greeted Rosie and interrupted their interchange. While they talked, Liv studied Rosie. She had shining blue eyes, elegant profile, peaches-and-cream skin under a head of long, fair hair with a reddish tinge, insouciant with a hint of shyness. Rosie was well-named . . . an English rose.

"I'm sorry. I didn't mean to interrupt you." Rosie turned to Liv again and their eyes met. Rosie looked away.

Liv wondered if Rosie was nervous or cautious? Probably both. "Did you tell me . . . no, I don't believe I asked you. What do you do?"

"Oh, I write. I'm a journalist . . .freelance." Rosie's voice dropped to a hesitant whisper.

Liv found her attempt at evasion irritating. "Then, if I may ask again, what do you do for a living?"

Startled at the bald question, Rosie replied hesitatingly. "Oh, as I said, I write. Freelance journalism."

"Ah, a mystery woman. Good for you. I adore solving mysteries."

Rosie shrugged. "And you, what do you do?"

"Touché." Liv laughed. Indeed, that was part of the question of her life with no discernable answer. A question so complex, she couldn't unravel although she'd tried many times. She chose the safest route to an answer, and said, "Oh, I guess you can call me a philanthropist. I do good deeds . . .and I garden . . . and I collect books. Africana and now exiled, Black writers. I'm a mother."

In essence, this was true. Liv accepted a wine glass from the waiter circling the room with a tray of glasses and Rosie took another. Animated now, she gave Liv a speculative look. With a sardonic lift of an eyebrow, Rosie asked, "Then, if I may ask again, what do *you do* for a living?"

Letting the question fade, Liv's mind raced. What do I answer? I'm a member of the idle rich? True, but also not true. What does Rosie see? The same face that stares back at me in the bathroom mirror every morning. Dark curly hair, dark eyes (my best feature, people tell me), a straight nose, thin lips usually pursed in habitual concentration. Edgy energy (hard for me to stay still), skin tanned from the summer sun. Rosie, a journalist, was no doubt cognizant of details.

Liv felt like moving away. *Why am I engaged in this exchange anyway?*

Unsettled, she said, "I'm sorry, I don't recognize your name. I can't say I've read any of your work."

Maybe Rosie was a member of the idle rich, too? Her accent placed her in the British upper class. Despite her irritation, she intrigued Liv. "Lunch, maybe, soon? Phone me."

In nodding silence, Rosie moved to accept the calling card twirling in Liv's fingers. Liv bypassed Rosie's outstretched hand and with casual ease dropped the card into a pocket of Rosie's lightweight rain jacket.

"I would like—" Rosie's words shriveled in the high-pitched sound of police whistles and scuffling noises at the front door. A khaki-uniformed policeman pushed Pauline, their hostess, into the living room and five burly men in plainclothes followed them. Everyone froze.

"SB—Security Branch," Liv whispered standing close to Rosie. "Secret Police."

"*Almal stand stil! Geen praat nie!*" The policeman bellowed his order in Afrikaans. Liv sensed Rosie's bewilderment and inching even closer to Rosie, looked straight ahead and whispered a translation for her. "Everybody stand still! No talking!

Jaco moved with deliberate strides to the front of the silent group, who watched him with stark intensity, alert to the urgent threat. He stretched out a hand. "Do you have a warrant to enter my home like this? To manhandle my wife?"

"You must be Advocaat Jacobus Malan? *Nie,* Advocaat, as

you know, no warrant needed." The policeman continued. "The Liquor Act says no liquor to be served at mixed gatherings."

His guttural accent jarred Liv's ear. Jaco gestured to his guests and returned the policeman's stare. He asked, his voice laden with sarcasm. "Do you see any alcohol?"

At the first police whistle, the savvy group had dumped wine and beer into vases and shoved glasses under chair cushions and behind books on the many shelves lining some of the walls. For a moment their eyes met, and Liv read the shock and mute appeal in Rosie's glance. From the angle of her arms, she intuited that Rosie still held her glass behind her back.

Counting on being unseen, Liv slid her own hand behind Rosie and encountered her clammy fingers on the glass. With urgent but steady movements, she loosened their grip as she pried the glass away. With care she slipped it into a tall, empty, woven Venda basket on the side table behind them. She trusted her action remained soundless. Was she the only one who could hear the slight scratching sound as the glass nestled into the basket? Liv squeezed Rosie's fingers to reassure her, but her cold fingers lay limp in her grasp. Liv let her hand fall and they did not glance at one another.

Everyone in the room avoided each other's eyes. One of the men from the cadre of plainclothes police stepped forward.

"Meneer Malan." His clipped accent marked him as the one in charge. "We apologize for the inconvenience. We are looking for Mr. Alan Paton. We have information he is here tonight giving a talk. You know very well, Meneer, for Mr. Paton to speak at mixed gatherings where there is alcohol is illegal."

Jaco raised an eyebrow. He spoke in his soft, courtroom drawl. "I ask you again, my friend. Do you see alcohol here?"

The policeman's voice remained even, but a tightening line

emerged along his jaw. He scanned the room. "No, I don't see any, but I'm not a fool, I can smell it. One day soon, Meneer, we will have the Unlawful Organizations Act and be without need for these other regulations."

Had they all crossed a line too far? Another of the all-important questions troubling Liv of late—crossing which line was one too far? *I'm in so deep, there is no turning back now. Or is there? There were always alternatives, other ways to deal with dilemmas, except in death and taxes. Death and taxes sounded ominous. Is risking my life part of the tax my family owes this country?*

"Mr. Paton was here," Jaco almost cooed, his smooth voice breaking into her thoughts. She made a conscious effort to be present. "Our guest, and he came to meet these people. He is quite famous you know, and many people want to meet him. His recent award . . . his book . . ." Jaco let the sentence drift into silence.

The man smiled with contempt. "Mr. Malan, you patronize me. His book is scandalous, *'n skandal*. He is not a true South African. He tells traitorous lies in his book." He goaded Jaco into indiscretion.

Watching Jaco's face, Liv saw he almost enjoyed the chess game. Her heart pounded even faster now in fear for him. Jaco moved his king. "Be careful, Meneer. Slander is still on the statute books in this country. You can't go around calling people 'traitorous' without proof." He held up his hand, silencing the officer. "According to the law, works of fiction are not deemed traitorous."

The man turned away. "*Kom manne! Hy is nie by die huis nie. Ons is klaar met hierdie mense.*" Once again Liv translated for Rosie. "Come men! He's not in the house! We are finished with these people!"

The security police vanished into the night. Only after the car engines faded in the distance did anyone move.

Limp with relief, Liv hugged Jaco, and over his shoulder she saw Rosie fingering the calling card in her pocket.

Ten days later, Rosie came for an afternoon visit. Liv, flanked by French poodles, one white and one black, welcomed her to *Loeriebos*. Dressed in casual, light-brown, wide-bottomed slacks, topped by her signature, open-necked, ivory-colored silk shirt and an oversized straw hat shading her eyes, Liv stood in the gravel circle in front of the house talking to a gardener who held a rake over his shoulder. Liv waved to Rosie.

When Rosie opened the car door, she sniffed the air as the pervasive and pleasant eucalyptus scent enveloped her. Liv saw her admiring gaze—evident as well in many other visitors—alight on the gray-and-brown peeling bark of the tall, slender, eucalyptus trunks surrounding three sides of the house.

"Welcome to *Loeriebos*."

The gardener walked away, and Liv strode toward the car, obedient dogs at her heels; Rosie, an English rose, indeed. You simply need to look at her, my response to her the night of the Paton meeting was exactly right.

Rosie smoothed the skirt of her pink-and-white shirtwaist dress highlighted by a wide, white leather belt. Her open-toed sandals exposed her winter-white feet while her blond hair glistened like a golden aura.

"Hello," Rosie responded with familiar shyness. "I'm a little scared of dogs but these seem well-trained."

"Meet Edith and Marcel. Yes, well-schooled and a little older now so more sedate."

Rosie faced the front of the house. "What a beautiful old house."

"Thanks. The original farmhouse burned down over there by the pond." Liv pointed in the direction of a copse of oak trees. "Originally this land worked as a farm with several tobacco drying sheds occupying the site. I commissioned an architect to convert that space into this house. I wanted to save the old bricks, supposedly cast here on the farm over ninety years ago. Local earth tones blend into the landscape. I love the purple and reddish hues."

"How dramatic with those white thunderhead clouds as a backdrop."

"Yes," said Liv. "Those are Highveld clouds. They form in the summer."

"Highveld?"

"Oh, of course, you don't know yet. The Highveld is all the land in the interior of South Africa, a vast plateau. Johannesburg is at the altitude of six thousand feet. The Lowveld, especially on the eastern part of the country is at sea level, and along the northeast coast of the country it is subtropical. There is a two-thousand-foot drop from the Drakensberg escarpment. That's where the Kruger National Park was established.

"But come inside. A cup of tea, a cold drink?"

"No thanks, I'm fine."

Rosie appeared ill at ease again. Why? Perhaps as simple as she's shy? An introvert? A private person?

Once inside, Liv watched Rosie observe the original, yellowwood floorboards, the antique furniture, Persian rugs, and the dark wood grandfather clock ticking solemnly in the hallway. Then Rosie spoke in a more normal voice. "This is all so lovely."

"The grandfather clock is a family heirloom. No one else in the family wanted it. A wedding gift to my Papa Helmut and his wife, Gittel, from the legendary Sammy Markus. Fits in here as I've gone for a traditional old Cape Dutch style. My family owns a house in Plettenberg Bay something like this one." Liv noted Rosie's blank look. "Near Knysna . . . the Garden Route."

Rosie nodded in recognition and Liv continued. "Knysna, the center of the Eastern Cape coast. Been the center of the indigenous timber industry for almost two hundred years now. Controlled cutting only. The forests are all national parks. The whole area is the place of my heart."

Liv, with a sensuous touch, ran her hand down one side of the stately grandfather clock. "Stinkwood, such an inappropriate name for such beautiful wood. When first cut it exudes a rank odor."

She could have relayed more about the furniture and house, but Rosie obviously only tried to show interest. They walked along the passageway toward the library.

During the visit Liv noted approvingly how reverentially Rosie handled the Olive Schreiner first editions, as well as first editions by Black writers, also historical Africana texts, even a few manuscripts. Rosie interested her.

They agreed to meet again, in Hillbrow, Rosie's temporary home territory.

That evening after Rosie's visit, as she loved to do when home, Liv stood next to the swimming pool and watched the day drift into dusk—a gouache of color and light. She listened attentively for the hadidas as they winged their way to their roosts, calling and answering. Then, she walked the dogs.

They moved on the long driveway before cutting off onto a path through the long veld grasses. Liv imbued her appreciation for the land and the buildings. In the late afternoon sunshine and shadows, the house she loved never looked more charming, more inviting. She read its moods in different lights. She understood the whisperings of the century-old eucalyptus trees standing guard. Beyond them she merged with the blue sky and the drifting, white shapes of fantastic galleon-like thunderheads.

Liv often wondered from where arose her love of the veld, wild grasslands, gardens and gardening. Papa Helmut loved the wild places of South Africa since he first arrived in Ramoutsi from Riga in Lithuania in the 1890s. He introduced Aunt Sally to them, and in her turn, she and a much older by then, Papa, introduced Liv to many of those places, too.

1960
LIV AND DANIEL

The week following the afternoon visit with Rosie, Liv sat in the sunlight streaming through the large lead paned windows, reading newspapers in her library at *Loeriebos*. She heard the phone ring in another room and Daniel's voice, "Hello, Liv Weisz residence. Daniel Molefe speaking."

During the long pause that followed, Liv's heart fluttered, A call emanating from the Security Branch? She settled when, with no concern, Daniel hummed a catchy phrase from the latest Miriam Makeba and Jerusalem Epistles' album. No doubt the caller never expected to hear an educated, male, African voice. After a muffled response to which Daniel replied, "Yes, this is her residence. Please wait while I find her."

Liv saved him the trouble. She entered her study where they were working, and smilingly, Daniel held out the receiver. "Someone for you."

He exited, allowing Liv the privacy she always requested

when she was on the phone. Since childhood, she hated people overhearing her conversations.

Rosie had phoned, she said, wanting to arrange a day for their Hillbrow lunch. On the day Rosie visited *Loeriebos*, Liv had suggested this get-together, but now she regretted it. Further involvement with Rosie added complications to her already too-complicated life. Liv explained she was engaged in an urgent project and would phone Rosie soon.

Replacing the receiver, she turned to the draft she and Daniel currently worked on. On one side of the document ran the complete *Freedom Charter*.

THE FREEDOM CHARTER

As adopted at the Congress of the People, Kliptown, on 26 June 1955, we, the People of South Africa, declare for all our country and the world to know the following:

South Africa belongs to all who live in it, Black and White, and that no government can justly claim authority unless it is based on the will of all the people;

Our people have been robbed of their birthright to land, liberty, and peace by a form of government founded on injustice and inequality;

Our country will never be prosperous or free until all our people live in brotherhood, enjoying equal rights and opportunities;

Only a democratic state, based on the will of all the people, can secure to all their birthright without distinction of color, race, sex, or belief;

And therefore, we, the people of South Africa, Black and White together equals, countrymen and brothers adopt this Freedom Charter;

And we pledge ourselves to strive together, sparing neither strength nor courage, until the democratic changes here set out have been won.

The People Shall Govern!
All National Groups Shall have Equal Rights!
The People Shall Share in the Country`s Wealth!
The Land Shall Be Shared Among Those Who Work It!
All Shall Be Equal Before the Law!
All Shall Enjoy Equal Human Rights!
There Shall Be Work and Security!
The Doors of Learning and Culture Shall Be Opened!
There Shall Be Houses, Security, and Comfort!
There Shall Be Peace and Friendship!

THESE FREEDOMS WE WILL FIGHT FOR,
SIDE BY SIDE, THROUGHOUT OUR LIVES,
UNTIL WE HAVE WON OUR LIBERTY!

Aiming to inspire younger people in the townships, on the other side of the page, Liv had drafted several brief paragraphs on the importance of the *Freedom Charter*. The ongoing struggle, she wrote, remained resolute in adherence to the document. Pamphlets now circulated through clandestine channels despite many of their campaign leaders at the Kliptown Congress banned, placed under house arrest, or imprisoned. Many others were found guilty of treason. In her annotations Liv emphasized that the first demand—the people shall govern—captured the impetus for the struggle. As she wrote, she always remembered how carefully

Sobukwe laid out arguments to support the demands in the *Freedom Charter*.

Daniel was translating her work into appropriate African languages.

They continued to work in Liv's study to complete the pamphlet on the *Freedom Charter*, soon to be distributed once the leadership pinpointed the actual day of the onset of the protests. After they both approved the proof copy, Daniel leaned back in his chair, folding his hands behind his neck.

"You've never told me. You were at Kliptown?'

"Yes."

"I'm curious. What was it like to be there? To be there when the *Freedom Charter* was adopted."

He smiled with characteristic, disarming charm. Liv remembered five years back to that dry, winter's day in Kliptown, a dusty "gray area" in no-man's land between Johannesburg and Soweto, when she sat uneasily among three thousand delegates and affiliates of the ANC.

"The truth . . . five years ago I wasn't yet in the movement, so it felt strange to be there. Recently divorced, casting around for something to throw myself into. Jaco invited me to tag along. The event was like nothing I'd experienced before. I didn't know where I belonged among all those people or even if I did belong. After Sobukwe spoke ululations filled the air. Women's voices joined together like huge flocks of birds greeting the dawn. Always thrills me."

Liv fell silent. All her life she recognized the exhilarating energy running though her like a wash of warm water—adrenalin—when she calculated the odds but still plunged into risk. She craved that rush when at Kliptown—being afraid but moving into the fear by being present. Scary, but also enlivening, and despite her reservations, the energy of the crowd surged through her.

Liv smiled an apology at Daniel. "Sorry, lost in thought for a moment. Even on the first day the police were a constant presence no one could ignore, police helicopters creating whirling dust dervishes on the grounds. They squeezed me between Beata Lipman, who maybe you know hand-wrote the original *Charter* from notes taken at scores of meetings, and Ellen Khuzwayo, a social worker from Durban. Jaco arranged this and they took good care of me. Filled me in on all that happened. I'll admit I startled myself by feeling inspired by the courage and determination of the delegates."

Liv added, "Hardly a word appeared in the 'White' press about the meeting. For me, I can truly say, the Kliptown gathering endures as a significant catalyzing moment."

Daniel leaned forward in his chair and took both her hands in his grasp. "Thanks for sharing."

Liv gazed deeply into his eyes, "I trust you. We share more than you know."

In the afternoon, Daniel Molefe re-entered the study disguised as a respectful, middle-aged man, either as a member of the Church of Zion with a lapel badge to add the authentic touch or perhaps a lowly store clerk on an errand. Laundered too many times, his white shirt had faded to gray with a frayed collar under which he knotted a monotone tie. Patched at the elbows, his loose sports coat clearly came from a jumble sale or thrift store. The jacket hid his wide shoulders, whilst a thin, old, brown belt held up his nondescript gray trousers. Scuffed brown shoes two sizes too large gave him a Chaplinesque air. His beaten gray fedora sat on her desk.

"Good news?" He asked. Liv paused before remembering that Rosie's earlier call.

"No news, only something personal." Careful to choose her words, so as not to embarrass him, she added, "Maybe we need to be more careful about your presence here? Such as answering the phone . . ."

Daniel shrugged, then nodded, his eyes suddenly serious. "Okay, you're probably right." Then the sparkle returned. "Must be something good for a lucky someone to get a smile like that from Liv Weisz? Any chance one of these days there will be a smile for me?"

"None of your business," Liv laughed. They teased one another often, like familiar siblings. Daniel was older by a few years and often joshed her as she imagined a brother would.

Several times over the months as they had worked together, they had come close to an embrace, a caress, and even a kiss, but nothing ever happened. Daniel was charismatic. His wife and children lived in Accra. He had married a Xhosa woman (a member of the Xhosa royal family as was Nelson Mandela). Sobukwe discouraged liaisons between members of his inner circle unless they were married. Even then he asked if these ties were fair to spouses and children. He may have been questioning himself.

"Ties cloud your judgment," Robert Sobukwe said. "Complications can cause pain for others, panic if you are arrested, interrogated, tortured, even killed. We all need to be sharp and alert, single-minded as to our objective." He added that he struggled often with the question of whether activists should even be married. "But married or not, we need to move ahead, one small step at a time. We must keep focused on the next step and the one after."

Also, the reality of the vice squad loomed. Police units

circled like vultures, intent on implementing the Immorality Act, banning sexual relations between people of different races. The squad's scavenging talons and tearing beaks seemed to reach into every bedroom.

Unstated, but understood, Sobukwe's prescriptive warning formed a barrier between Liv and Daniel.

Car tires crunched the gravel circle at the front of the house. Daniel picked up the hat and placed it at a jaunty angle on his head. Moving to him, Liv positioned it at a more subdued slant and nodded with approval. But the political activist she knew in London no longer existed in this disguised, deferential byproduct of the apartheid system.

"Your lift, I believe. You look perfect—a perfect disguise. Take care."

Daniel raised his hat as he left the room, and she waved her right hand a little hesitantly. "Please be careful." He went to attend a meeting with Sobukwe and other PAC leaders somewhere in Sophiatown. Sobukwe relied on Daniel. They all realized this, even though none of them knew each other's exact movements or whereabouts, except maybe Sobukwe and his two closest lieutenants. Secrecy made it safer for all if any one of the cadres was arrested.

At the door, Daniel flashed his shiny forged passbook. "My identity. Mustn't forget the 'open sesame' ticket."

Moses Moekena knocked. "Car here for Mr. Molefe."

Liv relied on Moses, a nephew of Abel, as Sobukwe relied on Daniel. Over the years three generations of Moses's family worked for three generations of her family. In recent years, she relied on complete loyalty from Moses. They all lived in danger; the situation made starker with the complicating factor of her house being deemed "safe" by the movement. Daniel Molefe and others, both Black and a few White, often occupied the guest rooms.

"You do good work for us Africans, Miss Liv. But as a father, a man who has known you since your baby days, I say to you now, be careful."

Moses uttered this comment—his only observation—after Robert Sobukwe had stayed one night for the first time about a year ago and Moses served him and Molefe breakfast. Liv deemed it an honor to have Sobukwe in her house. The previous year, 1959, he had won election as the first President of the Pan-African Congress. Energetic, intensely intelligent, and a visionary, Robert Sobukwe was an easy man to like and follow. She could listen to his articulation of his thoughts for as long as he wanted to speak.

Liv, at her desk, mused; What strange path brings me to this juncture? My home now used as a "safe" house because less than a handful of people know my political affiliation. It is well situated close to Johannesburg, Pretoria, and the highways to the East Rand townships.

Even when Marion guessed at something odd in her mother's behavior, she never asked, covering her curiosity by preoccupying herself with friends and their doings. Liv admonished her own friends and family against ever "dropping in," except for Jaco. Dearest Jaco, her mentor, was her lifeguard in these choppy waters. But even he respected Liv's privacy.

Marion, living in a dorm at the university, always alerted her mother when she would be home, especially on weekends, though the visits became less and less frequent. She wouldn't even be home for Easter break but was embarking on a ten-day archeological trip with a group of students led by their professor to Israel, Greece, and Rome. Moses understood when the back-porch light shone, day or night, he must not come into the house or let in anyone else. This precaution protected him as much as her comrades and herself.

Now, here was Rosie, someone who seemed to want to break through the thick walls Liv had erected to preserve everyone's safety. Liv searched for ulterior motives behind every question Rosie asked, questions, she assumed, anyone would pose to show polite interest in a new friend's life.

After five years of living on the edge, Liv was becoming aggravated with the struggle that left her emotions withered. Comrades praised her, people admired her, others envied her, but at times she felt her life to be as dried out as the old sole of a leather shoe. In her lowest moments of discontent, she suspected she was in a prison, constricted by her beliefs, values, and moral integrity.

You need faith to live like this, like a monastic, an ascetic, in a devout order. What the hell am I doing to myself?

In her university years in Cape Town in the early 1940s—the war years—Liv's faith was cemented in the ideology of human rights. She wrote her senior thesis on Emmeline Pankhurst and the Suffragette Movement in Britain. But once she met Jaco and learned of the PAC struggle, there was no other way to live in South Africa. Or was there? These questions pestered her like flies.

Something is missing in my life. The touch of another person, loving and being loved. The very intimacy Sobukwe spoke of. Intimacy I know firsthand from a time long past. I feel desiccated and filled with loss. Yet, elated too, buoyed on my belief in our activism, our cause. I am such a contradictory person, presenting as a stoic by tamping my emotions and yet knowing I'm fully emotional. How can anyone know me if I hardly know myself? How can I trust others if I don't trust myself? Do I let Rosie in? My dawning response—Why the hell not? I want to be close to someone from "outside" the cause. And with Rosie, a sense of excitement and the inevitable seem to intertwine. Can Rosie be trusted?

But now her life hurtled in directions she couldn't control.

All those brooding thoughts about being alone, as well as about the struggle, turning now into a reality for which she was hopefully prepared.

This is what I want, yes? What we've worked toward.

"Further action to challenge the government. We must take advantage of the eyes of the world being on South Africa now," Sobukwe added. "After the Macmillan visit, the Mandela leadership of the African National Congress (ANC) also plans mass action. We must preempt them. We must act before the inevitability of even more restrictive government regulations are placed on 'the natives.'"

Scared and thrilled to participate in this historic moment, Liv did not question him. If he sensed this to be the decisive moment, let it be It was not for her to argue with his gut instinct. Earlier in their acquaintance, she had questioned him tentatively about the majority of Black people not seeing themselves as Africanists.

"Yes, you are correct," he explained with customary patience. "But everyone knows this. For many people, Mandela's ANC is like a religion, a church. Their parents and grandparents belonged to the ANC. A certain difficulty to change people's allegiance in such a short time to PAC ideas, Africanist ideas. Our task is to educate the masses and undo centuries of the settlers' brainwashing that has ingrained the concepts of White supremacy and Black inferiority. I'm waging psychological warfare."

"I'm an Africanist, too," Liv had countered boldly, "and this is my country. I am a daughter of the same soil as you, many in my family born here. I have the red dust of Ramoutsi in my blood, the blue ocean at Plett, and the green Knysna forests. The lion's roar in Kruger elicits the same atavistic response in me as in you. I recognize the hadida and the loerie as African birds as you do.

The drums every Sunday at Zoo Lake echo my heartbeat, my African heartbeat."

Sobukwe stared at her after her impassioned outburst. He asked, in his gentle way, "Your country, yes, my sister, but never your land. Who took your land from you?"

No rejoinder came to Liv's mind. No one won an argument with the Prof.

"If you are Black, you are oppressed." Sobukwe continued, "If you are White, you are an oppressor. Even if you support our cause, it is an intellectual stance. Until you give up the privileges of the wealth you enjoy and join the workers, you are an oppressor. Until you are prepared to go to jail for your beliefs, you are an oppressor. If you are part of the problem, how can you be part of the solution?"

Sobukwe's observations bothered Liv.

Am I prepared to go to jail for my beliefs? How do I even begin to answer that question? How will I know until I'm faced with that reality? Maybe, by then, I'll have no choice. All the lines crossed over. The choiceless choice. Was there such a phenomenon? My questions and doubts and fears, my eternal skepticism about my motives and the motives of others, would thankfully cease. I could relinquish the burden of responsibility I carry to right the wrongs of White South Africans. Will my mind ever release me from these questions faithfully clinging to my very core?

"But can't you use my 'privilege' and family wealth to further your cause?" Liv asked by way of an answer.

Many weeks later, Sobukwe, after Jaco Malan and Daniel Molefe convinced him of the depth of her conviction, responded. "Sometimes the lines blur. Issues are not so simple. You are correct. We can put your money to good use. In a way it is ours; after all your family built it on the backs of oppressed workers, especially in the mines that your family as shareholders 'own.' Your position in society will protect you for a while and therefore, us. We can make good use of your house."

Liv nodded, pleased; it's the least I can do for the struggle. When I renovated *Loeriebos* according to my vision for the house, for this garden, for the fields of wild grasses—a safe house was one use I'd never imagined.

Again, she wondered where her love of the red soil, of all of South Africa's land, arose. Certainly, Aunt Sally and her mother loved gardening. Her mother's pride had been her rose garden, as well as every spring the colorful bank of sweet-pea flowers she tended and that provided a profusion of perfume permeating onto the front *stoep*, porch, of their house. But it was Papa Helmut who nurtured her love of South Africa and its varied landscapes.

On her regular evening walk with the dogs through the grass fields. She remembered the stories Papa had told her about his arrival in South Africa, his marriage to Gittel, living in Ramoutsi and then Lichtenburg. She filled in lost details from her imagination, old photographs, and what Aunt Sally vaguely remembered from her very early childhood. To these she added what he had left unsaid when she was a child herself. These were the stories—in outline—she told her daughter, Marion, when she was around twelve years old and wanted to know the family history for a school project.

1890s
HELMUT AND GITTEL

Ramoutsi

Helmut had felt immediately at home in the *bushveld*, untouched scrubby grasses and low bushes, when he had arrived in Ramoutsi in 1891. His dream in his Lithuanian home attained an immediate reality. He breathed only warm air and opened his shoulders in the sunshine. He never donned a coat and soon exchanged his black frock coat for the clothes of the ranchers, many of them of British origin. He wore twill pants, open-necked cotton shirt, and rough-leather *veldskoen,* homemade leather shoes.

Helmut loved to be out at first light saying his prayers as the red disc of the sun crept over the horizon, etching the stark branches of the acacias in an almost unnatural brightness. He also enjoyed the quiet of dusk when the same red sun sank in front of his *pondok*, a crudely built hut, to below the line of the trees beyond the small stream in the distance. He quickly learned the names of the birds and could identify their call, such as the liquid sound of the wood doves and the jarring call of the ground hornbills. He even believed his primitive mud-and-daub abode, white-washed many years before he occupied it, held simple charm, uncluttered and unpretentious, so different from the cheek-by-jowl cottages at home. He anticipated that Gittel, his new bride, would enjoy living in Ramoutsi.

One evening, before he left Ramoutsi to meet his bride, as Abel was sweeping the store, Helmut had engaged him in conversation. Abel, not used to talking so freely to a White man, demurred at first. But he became more forthcoming when Helmut seemed genuinely interested.

"I was born in 1868. My family name is Moekena."

Helmut did the calculation. Abel was two years older than he.

Abel told him he was raised listening to the stories told around the campfire of his family's *kraal*, a collection of huts belonging to one extended family that included a fenced area made of thorn bushes to protect the livestock. Tales told of how the Brits and the Boers on their horses and with their guns destroyed the pastoral way of life of his father and all his ancestors stretching back before time. His father and the tribal elders thought of the White men as supernatural, not of the dried-blood red, black-and-brown African earth.

Drawing himself upright like a warrior, Abel leaned on his broom as if it were a spear. He continued, "My people are Bantu, coming from the brown-colored earth. Bantu do not know where the White man comes from or what white earth he belongs to."

Helmut shrugged. He didn't know how to tell Abel of snow-covered Riga, a place so far removed from Ramoutsi it could be on another planet.

Abel said, "I know the White man makes hills of white sand in Egoli, shining golden in the sunlight, golden hills from the rocks in which the gold is buried, where the Bantu have helped to dig it out of the ground. Sometimes, this worries me that the White man will turn all the earth white, pale, and sickly like himself."

Abel glanced quizzically at Helmut, but he did not voice further thoughts. He had observed Helmut, who read old books at night. Abel figured Helmut and other White men probably would know of the Badimo who lived below. The earth gods who made the ancestors, the great-grandfathers, the fathers, and men like himself who would make sons in their turn. This was the desire of the Badimo, who warned of the end of the world if the generational chain of the people were broken. This is what he had wanted to tell Helmut if he asked of his family. But he didn't know how to explain about the Badimo in the white man's language. Abel heeded the injunction of the Badimo to have children, so he added quietly, "I work for you, Baas Helmut, to make *lobolo*. Lobolo means payment to the bride's family for their daughter. I work to pay for Kelihiwe, my wife."

Helmut too was silent but pleased he had broken through Abel's reserve. What am I going to have to pay for my bride?

In June 1894, the congregation gathered in Germiston at the newly built shul, the third synagogue built on the Witwatersrand. The interior shone even in the diffused light from the stained-glass windows—the pride of the members. The dominant feature was the Ark (containing the Torah) curtained, situated center back of the *bimah*. Helmut and Gittel stood on the dais close to the Ark.

"Do you, Helmut Weisz, take Gittel Feinstein to be your lawfully wedded wife, to love, to honor, and to cherish?"

"Yes."

"Do you, Gittel Feinstein, take Helmut Weisz, to be your lawfully wedded husband, to love, to honor, and to cherish?"

"I do."

Gittel glanced shyly at the upright bearded man next to her, but Helmut concentrated on the rabbi and his words.

"Behold, you are consecrated to one another with these rings, according to the laws of Moses and Israel." The rabbi motioned to the *chassen*, the cantor, who placed a box at Helmut's feet. Helmut stepped heavily with one foot on the box. The congregation sighed relief at the sound of glass crushing and shouted their congratulations and good luck wishes.

"*Mazel tov!*"

Helmut beamed at his bride, his Gittel, brought from Lithuania four years after he had left, brought to this shul in Germiston to be his bride. His Gittel with her soft, brown eyes staring so questioningly into his own.

Helmut and Gittel led the procession out from under the *chuppah*, four thin poles holding a cloth roof. They walked down an aisle through pews filled with men and boys. Then, they glanced up at the women seated in a balcony, behind a wrought iron grating, segregating them from the men.

The guests, mainly a contingent from Johannesburg thirty miles away, were present at the invitation of the Beinash brothers, Mendel and Reuben, Helmut's cousins, whose business acumen resounded in the areas around Johannesburg. Even Sammy Markus sent his apologies and a handsome gift of a stinkwood grandfather clock. Everyone smiled, murmuring mazel tovs, speaking of the grace, the bearing of the groom, and the quiet radiance of the bride.

They were all Litvaks—*landsleite*—settlers from Lithuania or Latvia, enjoying a communal, happy celebration. Later Reuben, full-bearded and almost as tall as Helmut but portly, affectionately put his arm around his young cousin's shoulder as they watched the traditional dancing.

"Jews in America and elsewhere call us a Litvak colony, and they're correct. But we made the right choice to come to Africa. What do you say, Helmut?"

"Yes, Reuben, yes, this is where we belong."

Helmut replied inattentively, trying to see Gittel among the women at the far side of the hall. Reuben laughed at his distraction.

The morning after the wedding, Gittel insisted Helmut buy her a straw bonnet with a cluster of bright artificial fruits in the front and shaded by a large egret feather.

"Everything about me is new," Gittel told Helmut. "A new bride, new husband, new country, new hat." Gittel's face clouded over.

"What is it? What, Gittel?" he asked.

In a soft, hesitant voice she asked, "Will you want to do what we did last night every night?" She toyed with the mirror in her hand—a wedding gift from her mother. Helmut thought, if only their Muters had attended the wedding, they would have eased Gittel's qualms. Shaking his head, Helmut walked away: his Gittel, so innocent, she knew nothing of these things between man and wife.

After the excitement of the wedding, after the fumbling con-summation of the marriage in the double bed in Natie Feinstein's guest bedroom, Helmut and Gittel rode in a covered horse coach two hundred miles to Lichtenburg, a small farming *dorp* in the Western Transvaal. They rested in this town a while before con-tinuing another two hundred miles into the bush to Ramoutsi in remote Bechuanaland. Cousin Reuben and his older brother, Mendel, the family patriarch, lived in Lichtenburg. Helmut ran the store in Ramoutsi.

Helmut's prospects appeared bright. His generous cousins had promised him a future in which he would be a partner in their businesses: concession stores. The previous year, Gustav, one of his brothers, had joined them in Africa. Their litany became, "To make money, to save money, to buy a business in Johannesburg." Those words justified everything.

Helmut had traveled on the dusty, rutted road so often, the scenery was more familiar to him than any of his memories of the Latvian-Lithuanian landscape around their village in eastern Europe. He cast warm, amused glances at Gittel as she exclaimed at each new sight. He saw the Transvaal veld, the wide-open grasslands, anew through her eyes.

The horizon stretched away to low ridges all around them and so did the plains of grasses.

Occasionally they saw a small herd of game moving away from the approaching vehicle. The animals paused at a safe distance and watched the progress of the wagon.

"Wildebeest and impala," Helmut instructed her, proud of his knowledge of the different species.

Gittel exclaimed in Yiddish, "The sky is a huge dome. And look at the clouds, so white, moving so slowly and steadily like ships' sails on the sea."

When they arrived at Lichtenburg, Helmut happily showed off the family's large trading store in the diamond fields. He saw from Gittel's pride that she remembered the details in his letters of how the cousins built the store in Lichtenburg. It was obvious she reveled in her new family's success, thrilled by BEINASH BROTHERS GENERAL DEALERS, the hand-painted sign on a wooden board proclaiming the family name to the world. Helmut's brother, Gustav, worked in the store.

As Helmut had written to Gittel back in Riga, the world

was in Lichtenburg. Men arrived in droves from far away valleys and villages, towns and farms, from England, Wales, Scotland, Australia, Canada, Europe, from Kimberley and from Cape Town. As people rushed to Johannesburg in 1886 for the gold and Kimberley for the diamonds, twenty years before, so now they flocked in their thousands to Lichtenburg for the newly discovered diamond pipe, everyone hoping for another Kimberley, another Big Hole.

On the day the diggings were officially proclaimed in 1888, thousands of men raced across the dusty veld to stake their claim in the parched earth, a claim they prayed covered the rich diamond pipe said to lie, like the gold reefs of Egoli, hundreds of feet below them.

The Beinash brothers were self-satisfied about gaining the concession to trade with the population at the diggings. The business thrived beyond their expectations. Year by year they sold their merchandise, as much as they could handle, to the miners, their Black laborers, and then the women.

After they rested, Helmut and Gittel climbed onto an open wagon transporting goods and departed for Ramoutsi. They brought with them the grandfather clock safely strapped to the wagon.

Helmut let his mind wander as the wagon jolted them slowly over the veld. He remembered another journey, from Riga to Cape Town. Particularly he recalled his conversation with other Eastern European Jews waiting to board ocean liners.

Helmut had awaited his passage to South Africa at the Jews Temporary Shelter in the East End, the hub of British Jewry. He had recognized some of his fellow travelers from Riga. Many others were accommodated by Jewish institutions such as the Jewish Board of Guardians assisting transmigrants, predominantly those headed to North America. At the shelter, he met Jews from many different "home" countries, and Helmut realized the vastness of the outflux from Europe. Not only Jews from Latvia and Lithuania chased dreams in new countries but thousands from Eastern Europe and beyond did as well.

Often the Polish Jews spoke to Helmut in Yiddish, their common language.

"Why Africa, Helmut? Why not America? There're only Black people in Africa and wild animals. It's the dark continent. America welcomes refugees, people like us. They've built a giant statue in New York harbor, a statue to liberty. Come to America. Come with us."

Helmut shook his head and answered fervently.

"South Africa is the Promised Land. That's what my cousins say and all the others, too. There's gold there, sunshine, and freedom, too. A man there from Riga, Sammy Markus, has become rich, beyond any dreaming of it. I have faith in South Africa."

And I know nothing of America, he told himself.

But the more people he met, the more obvious it became that most people entrusted their futures to America. Only people like himself—*Litvaks*—Jews from Lithuania and Latvia and clusters from other Eastern European shtetls, those who knew Jews already there, pursued lives in Africa.

Gittel had asked him a question, Helmut jerked himself back to her presence on the wagon. She repeated her question, "How big is this land?" She scanned the land to the horizon.

He answered her in Yiddish, "All this land, uncultivated, miles and miles of open veld, scattered with bushes and small trees." He switched to English and waved one arm in a wide arc. "Called the bushveld."

"The bushveld," Gittel repeated stumbling over the unfamiliar sounds of the words. She wanted to show Helmut she understood and that she would try to learn English.

As their journey progressed, Gittel expressed alarm. "It's so hot and dusty and the flies sting worse than wasps."

"Tsetse flies," Helmut called them. "They kill the cattle."

"Helmut, is Ramoutsi also so dry, no grass, these flies?"

Helmut nodded happily.

"Yes, it's different from anything you've ever known. Once you get used to the dust, you'll love it, you'll see."

Gittel was not reassured, and he sensed it, but his obvious comfort in his surroundings silenced her.

At dusk they arrived at the store and the mud house behind it. Ramoutsi consisted of the store, its outbuildings, a rudimentary courthouse, a sketchy schoolhouse, barracks for the British officials, and a small hotel and bar. The British flag hung still in the dusty air outside the courthouse. A man servant of about Helmut's age greeted them and helped carry their bags.

"Gittel, this is Abel. I wrote to you about him."

Helmut had written that he liked him, and Gittel held out her hand in greeting.

"Hello, Abel."

Abel shuffled his bare feet in the dust and looked away. In an irritated tone, Helmut scolded her in Yiddish. "Whites do not shake hands with Blacks. He's your servant, Gittel."

Gittel drew back her hand in haste, but Abel shyly smiled at her. He and Helmut carried the bags and spoke incessantly in English. Gittel was puzzled. Abel was Helmut's servant, but they spoke together like friends.

The day after he arrived back in Ramoutsi, Helmut proudly reopened the store with great ceremony and did not notice Gittel's mounting dismay. Many Black people gathered around the store, sitting on the sandy earth outside their home. Glare from the sunlight burned Gittel's half-closed eyes. Films of fine sand were everywhere. Even as Abel wiped the furniture and swept the floor, the sand dust covered it again.

Helmut observed that over the ensuing days, Gittel was becoming accustomed to Black people, but it took her longer to accommodate to the dust and dryness. Hard work did not bother her. She was raised in an old blacksmith's hut and always shared in the household drudgery. Daily she told Helmut despairingly, "It's the strangeness of the Black people and their faces, language, and customs. And the dust, the flies, and the heat." After about six weeks she added to her litany, "But mostly it's because I'm pregnant."

Helmut expected many things but not that revelation. He shouted his shock at Gittel. "Well, what do you expect? We sleep together, you're a healthy woman, healthy like a breeding cow. Of course, you're going to be pregnant."

He barked at her for the first time and saw her fear. Helmut did not want to acknowledge that the news frightened him as well. He liked Gittel as she was now, a coltish, lithe young woman and his sole companion. She was pregnant, soon to be a mother and he a father. He was not ready.

He shook his head. How would they cope with a family in Ramoutsi?

"But Helmut, so soon, so soon. I hardly know you. There's no one here. We're so far from everything, everyone."

"Okay, sshh, don't cry. It's not so bad. Women have babies here every day. The Batswana are good midwives and there's a nurse at the mission hospital. Sshh, there now, you'll be fine. The baby will be fine."

Reassured by the thought of the Irish nurse at the mission hospital, they put aside their apprehensions.

As Helmut predicted, once Gittel became accustomed to the dryness and the dust, she did not find Ramoutsi unpleasant. The store was near a large settlement of Batswana people. The British colonial district officer and an assistant officer lorded over the small outcrop of rough buildings. The White ranchers and their families called regularly at the store. Gittel, a lively, open person, quickly became on first-name terms with most of the other White women. She acquired languages easily and could converse in simple English.

Helmut reluctantly complied to the unwritten law which forbade him anything more than the most formal of social contact with *goyim*. Except with Mrs. Fitzroy, the British woman so kind to him on the liner from England four years ago. Observing Gittel's interaction with these British women, he asked her to adhere to the stricture as well, although she could still be friendly, he said "…but distant. We have an excuse. These are their customers and neighbors."

In the store, Gittel chatted amiably to anyone who spoke to her, including the ranchers' wives and many Batswana women, as her head pounded with the litany—to make money and move to Johannesburg—anywhere away from this dusty isolation.

Helmut acknowledged to himself that he had broken that stricture, hadn't he? Mrs. Fitzroy, the English lady, a goy, had certainly hugely impacted him aboard the ocean liner. She fascinated him.

Like the other Jewish immigrants, his daily challenge had

been to obtain kosher food. He subsisted on his mother's bread and cheese. Early in the voyage, this matronly English lady with deep blue eyes smiled at him, and he accepted her offerings of fresh fruit from the first-class dining salon. Daily then, when their steps crossed on the decks as they both took their walks, they stopped to greet one another, and then walked in amiable silence.

What did Mrs. Fitzroy see? Helmut knew how he must appear to her. A tall, shy, earnest young man with burning dark eyes, shiny clothes, long curly hair, and strange mannerisms. When she attempted to speak to him, Helmut hoped she perceived him as an eager student. He was encouraged that she began to teach him the rudiments of the English language.

She spoke to Helmut often, who stood almost uncomprehendingly as she spoke, but he seemed to enjoy the sounds of the words. Once though, she spoke so softly that Helmut understood she was articulating her thoughts for herself, "I often undertake this sea passage to family in England and family in Cape Town. On those voyages back from England, I've introduced other wide-eyed young men leaving Eastern Europe to the niceties of the English language and English manners. I'm worried that with the restless Boers threatening war in the North, the future for the fledgling country and immigrants remained uncertain. Gold. The curse that caused this upheaval was the discovery of gold. The Boers want gold to finance their Republic, and Queen Victoria's government want to fill the coffers for the Empire and glory."

Deeply grateful for her sustenance and companionship, Helmut appreciated the gracious English lady and her foreign, elegant etiquette. Cautioned to be wary of goyim and not to seek friends among these non-Jews, nonetheless he ignored the warnings since Mrs. Fitzroy enthralled him. No woman he knew dressed like her with such colorful fabrics and elaborate dresses.

His fascination was almost childlike. The other British travelers entranced him, too. His avid eyes absorbed their stylized behavior. Most impressive were the ship's officers with their starched white uniforms and languid elegance.

By the time the ship neared Cape Town, his face and hands were tanned, and his body relaxed. He knew he was on the right path for himself and his family, fortunate to join his cousins in the promise of such a shining land.

Early one morning as the mist burned off the sea, a glimpse of Table Mountain on the horizon surprised him. His heart beat faster with joy. A gray-green mountain rose out of the sea, with a mountaintop almost flat, as if a giant had hand-packed it that way. The voyagers crowded the decks and cheered as they watched, Table Mountain loom closer and closer. A universal gasp of amazement rose when a thick, white mist appeared from behind the mountain and covered the upper reaches.

"It's called the tablecloth," said Mrs. Fitzroy standing at the railing beside Helmut. "Gives me a thrill every time I see it again. Well, goodbye Helmut," they shook hands. "Maybe we'll meet again someday!"

Helmut nodded, he had the same esoteric feeling, a mystical shiver—*maybe we'll meet again someday*—as when he understood a great truth from the *Talmud*, books of Jewish law. But then, he stood on the deck in the balmy sunshine, and the great mountain, the sentinel of the southern tip of Africa, rewarded him by displaying its magnificence.

Pensively, Helmut's thoughts returned to the village and the people he had left behind. Aside from Gittel, his betrothed, and his siblings, he doubted if he would ever see any of them again, including his parents. But he did not dwell long on the past, for ahead of him stretched his whole life, a great endeavor.

Helmut clutched his mother's parting gift, the small black, enameled box deep in his coat pocket. The ship berthed and he saw the familiar figure of his cousin Mendel Beinash standing among the throng of people at the water's edge.

Now, he stood in the store, watching Gittel and realizing that she had overcome her shyness and fright at living among Black people. She appeared to find the Black women friendly and enjoyed serving them, bargaining over the prices of bolts of brightly colored cloth they loved. They wrapped long swathes of cloth around their bodies, draping it over one shoulder. It was obvious that Gittel preferred the naturally dyed cloth they created, but Helmut appreciated that she understood their fascination with the array of colors and designs on the cloth in the store.

He tolerated these interactions and sometimes even looked on with amusement at the giggling women; Gittel trying to make herself understood in her half-Yiddish, half-English, while the Black women spoke to her in half-English, half-SiSwana. Curious about the women and their daily lives, Gittel tried to ask questions and show interest in their families. But the language barrier proved too great for complicated dialogue, and she feared crossing the line of social contact Helmut set.

Helmut knew her uncertainty of her status with Abel. She knew nothing of servants. "I don't know how to be a madam." He insisted she keep her distance from Abel.

"The Blacks don't count here, Gittel, at least not in a social sense. They're heathens, pagans. They're just like the goyim peasants in the Pale. How many did you know there? How many were your friends there?"

Accepting Helmut's stance, Gittel saw the impossibility of befriending Abel. But she remained curious about him. Abel came with the bungalow and the store. That was the way of Africa—servitude for Black people. Abel received his meager one-pound-a-month wages, his food, and his hut near the bungalow.

During her pregnancy Gittel craved fresh vegetables in her diet. Hesitantly she asked, "Helmut, can I have Abel dig a vegetable garden?"

Knowing the effort was folly, nonetheless Helmut agreed to Gittel's request and released Abel from his duties in the store, ordering him to help Gittel prepare the ground for a vegetable garden.

"I don't want to discourage you, Gittel, but there's not enough rain here for growing vegetables."

After Abel broke the ground near a copse of syringa trees, he dug a trench from the spring at the base of the hill behind the Weisz bungalow. They worked together when the time came for fertilizing and planting. There was ample manure around the store for fertilizing the soil. In the early morning quiet, before the heat made it cumbersome for manual labor, Gittel's questions were answered. She relayed Abel's information to Helmut.

Helmut smiled condescendingly; he knew most of this already. But Gittel was so eager to share her news, he didn't stop her.

"He told me that aside from the Irish missionaries who fifteen years ago taught him the basics of reading, writing and calculating, no White person has asked him anything about himself. I like Abel, Helmut. He's warm and friendly, and when we spoke, I think he knew I saw him as a person and not a servant. Once, in the store I overheard him tell one of the Irish sisters, that other Whites observe him the same way they looked at their horses and dogs. This can't be right, can it?"

Helmut shrugged, "Nothing we can do to change it, Gittel. Remember we are here to run the store. Nothing else."

Gittel tried to describe to Helmut how she loved the rhythm of cultivation: gloved hands in the fertile soil around the spring, the appearance of the first green shoots, and the satisfaction of producing fresh food for the table. "This is a way for me to develop a shared connection with the land and the people. The garden is my little patch of green Eden surrounded by the dry and dusty bushveld. In Genesis, didn't God tell Adam and Eve to tend the Garden?"

Helmut nodded pleased that Gittel had found something fulfilling to do. She tended her garden, and while producing nurturing food, she nurtured herself by growing the food. He loved the open veld and grasses, but she understood rootedness in planting beans, peas, eggplant, okra, peppers, tomatoes and, at Abel's insistence, *mealies*, maize, the staple food of southern Africa.

Soon fresh vegetables appeared on the table, and Helmut appreciated the caliber of woman he had married. Gittel sewed colorful curtains and white-washed the rooms of their crudely built pondok. She persuaded Helmut to let her employ Nandi, an older Batswana woman, help in the house, so that she could help in the store.

In his daily prayers, Helmut thanked Leah, his mother, for the long-ago betrothal settlement. He still prayed three times a day draped in one of his father's ornate rabbi's prayer shawl, the *tallis*. At first, he worried how he and Gittel would adapt to living together, for although their betrothal extended for four years, they were strangers, he in Ramoutsi, she in Riga. As he became more accustomed to her presence, he worried that behind her mostly happy self, at times she was detached and withdrawn. He also knew she feared his temper and hated him for shouting at her. At those times, Helmut hated himself, too.

One night in the summer of 1896 when it was breathlessly

hot and close, Abel conveyed the Irish nursing sister in the Cape cart over the rutted track to the store. They arrived to hear Bernard Weisz crying lustily into the African bushveld. A terrified but outwardly calm Helmut had assisted Nandi, a midwife, at the birth.

To Helmut's relief after Bernard's arrival, the rhythm of life in his small household in Ramoutsi continued as before. Bernard, a blessing to both his parents, cemented the still tenuous bond between them, a bond that grew stronger as their previous moments of strangeness and unfamiliarity faded after Bernard's birth. When Bernard was twenty months old, Gittel told Helmut she was pregnant again.

This time Gittel's labor began early and continued for many hours. Helmut transported her to the mission station. Sally, named for the Irish nurse whose skill saved Gittel's life during the complicated delivery, joined the family. As Helmut helped the Sister change the sweat-soaked, blood-stained sheets on the bed where Gittel lay exhausted, she said, "Problematic birth, grave danger for mother and baby. You almost lost your wife. No more children. *You must heed my warning!* Next time she may well die."

Helmut looked at his pale wife, huge eyes staring at him in fright. He was frightened, too. At one point in the last hour Sister Sally came to tell him that she did not think Gittel would survive. He prayed then, fingering the little black box with the finely wrought, gold *Magen Dovid*, star of David, his mother had given him when he left Riga, always in his pocket.

How would he cope with this new life and Bernard's life without Gittel? The sour taste of fear in his mouth rose again as he stared at the passive body of his wife. When the sister left them alone, he knelt beside the bed and held Gittel's limp hand in one of his own.

"Anything," he said, tears falling on their clasped hands, "I'll do anything, only don't die, don't leave me." Gittel smiled, a little whimsical smile, and fell into an exhausted sleep.

Shortly after Sally's birth, Helmut received the news that the cousins wanted to sell the Ramoutsi store. They needed Helmut in the Lichtenburg store, which was now an unmanageable size for three to handle. They accepted an excellent offer for the Ramoutsi store.

Helmut and Gittel were overjoyed. Such news helped to lessen Helmut's constant worry about Gittel, who was peaked and patently in a deep depression and nervous exhaustion following Sally's birth. She dragged herself through each day. Soon she would have the company of Fanny and Zelda, her cousins-in law, and Bernard could play with his cousins. They would hire a maid to help in the house and to help Gittel. However, Gittel was adamant only Helmut and herself would tend the baby.

Since Sally's birth, Helmut sensed that something was amiss with Gittel, but he had no idea of the extent of her terror. Gittel lived in dread, something which had never happened to her before. But she was afraid to tell Helmut that her mind which she relied on to show her how to look on the bright side, had plunged into dark depths from which she struggled to emerge. When, finally, she shared the reality of these dark moods, she registered the scared look on Helmut's face mirroring her own.

Outside the sun still shone, Abel and Nandi's conversational lilt comforted her, and people shuffled in the store on the wooden floorboards in bare feet. She cooked Helmut his meals. "No one hears my screams in the terrifying silence of my mind." She told him in a dull, flat voice. Helmut recoiled from these revelations.

They knew she must never have another pregnancy. But lately, he was angry when she twisted away from him in the night.

The impending move also excited Abel Moekena. Some of his kinfolks were in Egoli, working on the mines.

Once having made up his mind, Abel practiced circumspection while asking Helmut. He didn't want to risk a refusal. He waited until the cool of the evening as Helmut locked the store. Helmut's temper in the afternoon heat was well-known and a source of some amusement to his customers. Abel often bore the brunt of Helmut's temper, but Helmut always apologized in a gruff, tight voice afterward. Abel waited until he sensed Helmut to be approachable.

"Baas Helmut, will you need a houseboy, a store boy in Lichtenburg?"

Helmut glanced at the earnest man shuffling nervously in front of him. Only last night he had said to Gittel how much he relied on Abel and how much he was going to miss him. A small shadow crossed his mind. Had Gittel put Abel up to this? Helmut nodded at Abel, encouraging him to continue.

"I would like to come with the baas, the missus, the baby and Bernard . . . if you need such a boy?"

"What about your wife, Abel?"

"She wants to come, too. She has family in Lichtenburg."

"Good, then yes, I'd like you to come with us. Bernard will be lost without you. The store there is four times the size of this one. There'll be more money for you there, too."

Abel smiled in relief. "Thank you, thank you, Baas Helmut. Now I can pay the *lobola*. We will have money for new clothes for Kelihiwe and me, and for some of the furniture such as what

Baas Helmut's has in his house. Someday Baas Helmut, I dream of seeing Egoli. Lichtenburg is much closer than Ramoutsi."

"We do, too, and all our family, Abel. One day we dream of owning giant stores in Johannesburg."

"That day my baas, for sure will come, because you take Abel with you."

And a pact of sorts solidified between Helmut and Abel.

His agreement to Abel's request pleased Helmut. He found Abel willing and responsible. Helmut liked having familiar things about him, and he had grown accustomed to Abel's quiet ways. Abel, no longer simply a Black cipher and part of his property, was a person, an individual, despite what he said to Gittel. Helmut longed to talk to Abel about how strange he found it that he, an immigrant, could own land, a house, and a shop while Abel, a native Batswanan, was dispossessed of the land that now belonged to the British government.

Deep in thought about the impending move, Helmut walked the short distance to the bungalow. He heard Bernard's piping voice over Sally's fretful crying. Pleased as he was with the decision the brothers made, unexpectedly he found leaving Ramoutsi difficult. He valued the quiet, sensory clarity of the bushveld, the myriad variety of birds, the visible cycle of the changing seasons, and the soft laughter and gentleness of the Batswana people.

He would miss the thorn bushes, yellow-billed ground hornbills, black dung beetles, and huge herds of cattle raising vast dust clouds as the drovers moved them through Ramoutsi on seasonal migrations. These were his memories. He doubted if he would come back to Ramoutsi. Unlike Abel for whom it would always be home, his life here was only an interlude.

Helmut kicked impatiently at a stone in the dust. He would not mind forgetting his frequent bouts of impotent outrage at being closeted daily in the corrugated iron sweathouse of the store. The monotony of serving faceless Black people who always made the same few purchases caused Helmut to kick the stone again.

Later that night when they were both in bed, Helmut stretched to embrace Gittel. He wanted to hold her, to let her feel safe in his arms. He wanted to tell her that he understood her tiredness. He wanted to talk of his feelings of leaving Ramoutsi.

Gittel, too, longed for Helmut to hold her, to calm her fears, to tell her that everything was settling out positively. But when Helmut's long form moved toward her, her body grew rigid.

"No, Helmut, not that. Didn't you hear the Irish Sister?"

Helmut, hearing the panic in Gittel's shrill cry, turned aside. He wanted to hold her to him in warmth and sympathy. He felt lonely and sad. Sometime later in the night he heard Sally whimper, and Gittel slowly, heavily, moved from the bed to her crib.

A fretful baby, Sally took a long time to nurse and then seemed always hungry. She would not sleep for any length of time and when awake, fretted and niggled, content only when wrapped firmly onto Nandi's back.

Helmut failed to find a way to approach Gittel. He knew she aligned her own depression and lassitude with connection to Sally's unhappy disposition, but she found no exit out of the mire of nervousness and irritability into which she sank. He contemplated her wistfully as she passed. Gradually he spent more and more time at the store. At night he sat in the dim light of an oil lamp paging through the Talmud, striving to remember the interpretations and commentary he was taught in the freezing, cheerless, old stone cheder, the school built next to the icy stream in their village near Riga, a lifetime ago.

1898
HELMUT AND GITTEL

In their pondok home in Ramoutsi, Gittel packed their few possessions into her ship's trunk. Cousin Reuben was to escort her and the children, while Helmut and Abel managed the transfer of the store to the new owner. A transport drover moved them to Lichtenburg on his ox wagon.

On the journey, they camped for two nights and Gittel hardly slept because Sally needed to nurse so often. They arrived at Gustav's house and Gittel allowed Fanny, her cousin-in-law, to lead her to a cool room with a bed, clean, soft bed linen, a pitcher of clear water, and a shady tree growing at the window.

Helmut and his family settled quickly into life in Lichtenburg. He worked long hours in the store situated at the diggings. He berated himself. How was I so blind? Ramoutsi is clearly not a place for a new bride, not a place to bear two children. Whereas here, in the mainstream, hundreds of people are in the shop every day with daily stimulation. Gittel told Helmut, "Lichtenberg provides me with a sense of belonging to a family again."

In 1898, the outbreak of hostilities between the Boers and the British, the Second Boer War, ramped up. In Ramoutsi, they received only scatterings of news. They knew from Cousin Mendel's letters that several Johannesburg financiers and industrialists, among them some Jews including Sammy Markus, risked earning the displeasure of the leaders of the Transvaal Republic (to whom they paid taxes). They knew suspicion existed that there were Jews helping Cecil John Rhodes, the British imperialist financier in his ill-fated raid on the Transvaal Boer Republic. Mendel was mainly concerned about the Jews, settled now in Johannesburg, but he was also concerned with other *uitlanders,* foreigners, such as the hated British now that the Republic was at war with Britain.

He wrote,

"I'm pleased that hundreds of young South African Jews from eastern Europe's shtetls are fighting alongside the Boers in guerilla commandos."

Lately the main topic of conversation in the store centered around the war between the generals of the Boer Republics and the government of the British Empire. The commandant of the local Lichtenburg commando came to the store to requisition horses and ask Cousin Mendel to order certain goods the men would need in the field.

"Mijnheer Beinash, we will need supplies for living in the veld—flour, sugar, blankets, bandages, so on. Can you get them for us? Also, I'm asking you not to sell anything to the British if they come around with request for supplies."

For the Beinash and Weisz cousins, this latter statement posed a predicament. Their sentiments were that they sold goods to the Boers while they controlled the region, but they'd sell to the British if they gained the upper hand. Perhaps the Boer leader didn't need to know they had decided not to take sides in the war. "Yes, Commandant, we can do what you ask."

As the cousins kept themselves socially apart from the locals, never to be drawn into partisan arguments, their position was easily accomplished. If they lived under threat to their lives, maybe they would shift their position. But the dorp was not in danger. Skirmishes raged in the mountains and valleys and on the veld itself. The Boers with embryonic guerilla strategies had hamstrung the mighty British army in the veld.

The cousins heard that Johannesburg was now under military rule and sandbagged, awaiting a British assault. Commerce had ceased and even the mines were shuttered. Thousands of Black miners returned to their kraals. Thousands of White immigrants, including about ten thousand Jews of the twelve thousand living there closed their homes and businesses and fled to the safety of coastal towns. The Lichtenburg family also learned that many of the Jewish settlers returned to Europe for the duration of the war, visiting their families for the first time in a decade.

The only sign of the struggle for the Lichtenburg Jews was an occasional troop of Boer commandos in the town trotting through on their ponies. They were tough-looking bearded men with bandoliers slung across their bodies, Mauser rifles shoved deep into saddle holsters, and wide-brimmed, leather hats perched firmly on their heads. Bernard and his cousins chased after the horses in wild excitement, whooping and shrieking in their dust.

One Friday afternoon the troop commander, General Venter, entered the store. For months newspapers hailed him as a Boer hero after the many daring escapades he and his men had adeptly executed against the regiments of the British Army. The four cousins hastened to greet him. With pleasantries exchanged, Venter leaned on a counter. "One of my men, among my best soldiers, is a Jew—Moishe Lieberman. He practices the Sabbath ceremonies alone on Friday nights. Is it possible one of you can ride with me to the camp and invite Veld-Kornett Lieberman to your Sabbath dinner?"

General Venter told Helmut who rode with him to the camp, "Lieberman is an excellent horseman and marksman, and brave, so brave. Recently he single-handedly captured seven British soldiers trying to sneak in a water cart to the besieged town of Kimberley. He hates British imperialism as much as we do. That's why he volunteered to fight with us. He says British imperialism, like the imperialism of the Russian czars that his people suffer under, need both to be destroyed. The men admire Lieberman. Even General Louis Botha calls him our Jewish lucky charm."

Moishe Lieberman returned with Helmut, overcome by the kindness of the invitation. Short and powerfully built, he projected a strong yet almost silent presence. He shared that he was born and raised near Memel. But they did not speak much on the ride. Helmut asked him, "Please hold your stories to share with all the family at dinner."

Husbands and wives, the Beinash and Weiszes, sat entranced as Lieberman described the daily life of a Boer soldier. "I believe about two hundred and fifty Jews fight in the Boer Army. I've met several of them on the occasions that different troops unite for a specific battle.

"At Spioenkop, for example, one of the bloodiest battles so far in this war, they almost captured me. My horse was shot from under me. From the ground, I saw a British soldier with a bead on General Venter. A certain shot. I'd run out of bullets, but I put my rifle to my shoulder and yelled at the British soldier to drop his gun or I'd kill him. He dropped his weapon. The General called for me to mount behind him and we rode through the British troops surrounding us. We reached safety behind our lines. The General thanked me for saving his life. When I told him, I had no bullets in the rifle, he laughed, clapped me on the shoulder, and said he was recommending me for a medal for bravery. I did receive a medal and a letter from President Kruger who invited me to his home in Pretoria. And, yes, our troops prevailed eventually at Spioenkop but with huge losses of life on both sides. I believe we broke the spirit of the British Army in that battle."

Helmut and Gittel had moved into a small house on the same street as the other family members. Gittel liked the wide veranda around the house, shaded and cool on even the hottest days. She maintained the vegetable garden, her pride, at the back of the house. She told Helmut how much she enjoyed taking Sally for walks in the perambulator handed down from the cousins. They strolled along wide pavements with water running in deep furrows at the side of the streets.

Sally settled at last. The doctor reassured Helmut and Gittel that there was nothing to be concerned about. Gittel's milk lacked elements Sally needed to grow because Gittel was so rundown herself. He wanted Sally weaned. Gittel felt guilt and sorrow that she could not suckle her baby and that Sally thrived on a diet of cow's milk. A plump, gurgling baby, she resembled Gittel but both children carried Helmut's dark eyes.

One of their favorite games was to lie with Gittel on her and Helmut's bed and play peeking games in her silver hand mirror. On weekends, when Bernard played outdoors with his cousins, Helmut often saw how Gittel rocked Sally to sleep over her shoulder and then watched their image in the mirror.

"My heart aches with love for this little girl who looks like me," she told him. Once asleep, Sally's small head rested on her breast. Her own face was restored to its youthful glow. "Look, Helmut, if I hold the mirror just so, I can encompass all three of us. Please Helmut, I want to send both Muters a photograph of their grandchildren."

Helmut agreed they could sit in a town studio for a family photograph. Happily, Gittel sent copies home to Riga. One she displayed in a gilt frame in their living room.

Gittel acknowledged to Helmut that the move was a positive step. "I'm happier now with my Lichtenburg home and contented children than at any other time since I've been in Africa."

"You look more attractive now since you've been here," said Helmut. Her face had tanned from the African sun, matured with the experiences of living in Ramoutsi while bearing two children. Gittel was desirable again, but the nurse's warning about her not becoming pregnant weighed on both.

Although the Beinash and Weisz families were the only Jews in the town, Gittel considered herself less strange here among other Whites, even if they were Boers. She sensed they accepted her. She told Helmut, "It's because we are White and because they, too, are people of the Bible."

Gittel conceded to Helmut, "You assessed the situation correctly: Blacks do not count, not in our White world, not in our social circles."

At least Innocence, her maid, treated Gittel with the same diffidence Helmut saw in the maids of their cousins-in-law. Living now among other Whites, Gittel admitted to Helmut that he was correct on that score, too. "I can't befriend a Black person in Lichtenburg any more than I could have a peasant in the Pale."

Helmut slept in a makeshift bed in the baby's room. All he had wanted was to hold Gittel, not to enter her. Now he no longer tried to hold Gittel at night when he most needed the physical closeness of her warm body.

The situation burned a hole in the fabric of their marriage, the tension a palpable, breathing presence. Gittel dreaded Helmut being in the house. He shouted at Bernard, spoke curtly to her, and harangued the servants. For the only time since she married him, Helmut stopped his daily prayer rituals.

The weather continued hot and sultry. The summer rains were late and the air pregnant with moisture and humidity, oppressing humans and animals alike. Gittel left the doors and windows of the house open. She tolerated the insects for the open windows allowed some small relief from the stifling heat.

Late one evening, Helmut entered the house. The store remained open until sunset in December because of the days approaching Christmas. News had filtered to them of fighting in the hills to the west of the dorp. The small town clenched in an atmosphere of tension and panicked anticipation. Gittel's heart raced with foreboding. She prostrated herself from the sweltering heat and a trying day with Sally, who was beginning to toddle. Helmut signaled danger signs with an aggressive walk and aggrieved countenance. This time she knew he was drunk. She had suspected his drinking on previous occasions, but this time she smelled the cheap liquor.

In silence Gittel served Helmut supper. He pulled a bottle from his jacket pocket drinking blatantly, challenging her. He drank out of the bottle like a laborer, like the miners she saw drinking on street corners near the huge, tented camp.

Despite the heat, Gittel felt a coldness in her guts, which crept with icy fingers to clasp her heart. As soon as feasible, she left the room and locked herself in their bedroom. Afraid for the children's safety, she hurriedly carried Bernard to her bed and moved Sally, cot and all, to her room. She locked the door again. Silence reigned once more in the house. The crickets outside obliterated any other sound. Only the screech of a night bird penetrated the darkness. Then, inevitably Gittel heard Helmut's footsteps creaking on the wooden floorboards.

"Gittel, open the door. I want to talk." Helmut's voice was loud, his speech slurred.

"Go to sleep, Helmut, you've had too much to drink. We'll talk in the morning."

"Gittel, I'm asking you nicely to open this door."

"Go away Helmut you're drunk! I'm not opening the door."

"Gittel, I'm warning you now, you open this door."

There was a loud thump as Helmut kicked the door. Bernard whimpered in his sleep.

"Gittel I'm coming in, I'll break down the door, so help me. You let me in now. You are my wife!"

Helmut rushed at the door. He hit at the door with his shoulder, the hinges loosened and the door burst open. Helmut fell into the room with a roar of rage. He picked himself up from the floor, crossed to Gittel, and pulled the sheet from her. She clutched her nightshift tightly around herself. Helmut tore off his clothes. Gittel had only witnessed a naked man one other time, and her eyes rooted on Helmut's swollen, engorged penis standing menacingly out of a bush of hair. Her panic immobilized her.

With one movement Helmut ripped her nightshift apart. Gittel gasped and still couldn't believe what was happening. Not Helmut, not Helmut! The words throbbed in her brain. He fell onto her, his erect penis tearing into her dry, tight, innermost self. "Helmut no, no, the children. Bernard!"

At last, she moved, trying to twist herself out from under

him. But Helmut did not hear. He held her more tightly and drove himself more deeply into her. The more she struggled the more he rooted and rutted at her, heaving himself with great tearing jabs.

"Papa, Papa. You're killing Mama! Leave her! Leave her!"

Gittel opened her eyes to see Helmut's look of rage and fear and to see Bernard pushing at Helmut with all the power of his little body. Helmut pulled himself out of her, the last of his semen pumping onto her nakedness and smearing Bernard who had landed on top of her with the force of his own blows. Helmut had passed out on the floor next to the bed, but not before he had been violently sick. He lay in his own vomit.

Gittel and Bernard cried quietly. Her first concern was for Bernard. Once he was asleep again, stepping over the unconscious Helmut, she stumbled to the bathroom. Heaving great rasping breaths, she felt the nausea, but nothing rose from her stomach. Shocked, shivering, gasping for breath, she stretched out a hand to steady herself, forgetting the shelf under the wall mirror. Her movement dislodged bottles and brushes. The sound of glass breaking penetrated her consciousness. Careful not to stand on the broken glass, she moved back to the bedroom where the stench of Helmut's vomit overpowered her. She moved the children back to their rooms and, lay down on the cot in Sally's room. But she didn't sleep.

In the dawn light she returned to the bathroom. Her ornate silver mirror lay shattered among the shards of glass. She picked it up. Her hideously distorted visage in the cracked surface did not frighten her, reflecting the broken self she felt inside.

Sadly, accidently, she dropped the mirror to the floor.

The weather broke with a series of violent thunderstorms. In the cooler days that followed, Helmut and Gittel reached a quiet understanding. Helmut, ashamed and contrite, treated Gittel as if she were a porcelain doll. They both told Bernard he experienced a bad dream. A month passed peacefully.

Two weeks later Helmut reluctantly had to leave an increasingly depressed Gittel for several days, joining Cousin Mendel to assess another store in remote Mahalapye. Barney Weisz, a distant cousin, owned the store and had decided to join in the war. He asked his cousins to lease it while he was away.

Helmut explained to Gittel the facts behind Barney's decision to enroll.

"Barney feels differently from Mendel, Reuben, Gustav, and me. He agrees that as Jews, we should be neutral in the war. But he says South Africa is our country, too, and we should do what we can in the war effort. He's gone to join the Jewish Ambulance Corp—neutral. I don't know if he's right to join in the war or if we are right to stay neutral. Caught in the middle again. Our people, always caught in the middle, the Boers, the British. I don't care who wins the war as long as we can live our lives. I wish I could feel as strongly as Barney about this being our country, but I keep thinking of the Black people. It was their country before the Boers came north."

"What does Barney say to that?" Gittel asked thoughtfully.

"He says South Africa belongs to all the people. We're all going to have to learn to live together here."

A week before Helmut left with Cousin Mendel, Gittel told him she was pregnant, and the thought obsessed her that she carried the possibility her own death in her changing body. "I do not want another baby and I do not want to die."

Helmut watched as the Black despair returned to Gittel. "The voices in my head pin me to the darkness," she added.

Helmut tried but he could not tug her from her darkness. He hoped once she became accustomed to another pregnancy, the clouds would leave her. But instead, she became obsessed by the physical act of sex.

The voices asked Gittel, who then asked Helmut, "Who does Barney stick his thing into?" She heard the voices: How can he live alone in a broken-down pondok in Mahalapye? Perhaps he consorts with the goyim and Black woman and breeds a pack of half-breeds? Maybe I should have married Barney. Perhaps his thing cannot become hard and swollen like Helmut's, like all the men I see. Perhaps if he attacks me like that again he will loosen this baby, make it pop out like a pea from a pod.

Helmut was shocked. She spoke like an insane person. "Gittel, please, while I'm away, don't do anything dangerous to yourself, the unborn baby, or our children. It's only a few days, a week at the longest. When I'm back, we can talk to the doctor."

Days later, when a message from the doctor reached Helmut of Gittel's worsening plight, he rode uncaringly back from Mahalapye, through land where he knew skirmishes took place. He thought only of his desperate wife, of his disoriented children.

Gittel had died before he arrived. The doctor only shook his head sadly. The bloodied knitting needle and the tiny, bloodied fetus bore testimony to Gittel's despair.

Helmut's pain was beyond tolerance. His rape led to Gittel's death, knowledge he shared with no one. Only Bernard regarded him with what he thought were knowing eyes.

They buried Gittel in a section of the Lichtenburg Cemetery set aside at the request of the Beinash brothers. A rabbi came from Johannesburg to sanctify the ground.

"Baas Helmut, can I come to the burial of the madam?"

On the morning of the funeral Abel had stood before a deeply sorrowing Helmut, twisting an old brown fedora of Helmut's in his hands. Helmut nodded agreement, he said, "The difficult part will be to persuade the rabbi. Traditionally non-Jews are not permitted at a burial."

Helmut asked the rabbi, "Rabbi, Abel has been a faithful servant for many years. He wants to come to pay his respects to Gittel?"

The rabbi looked from the tall, sorrowing Helmut to the intent dark face of the equally solemn Abel. He was certain the Lord understood about servants. He answered Helmut, "Let him come, for has Isaiah not said, 'Behold, my servant shall be exalted and lifted up, and shall be very high.'"

Abel watched the proceedings at the grave with interest, listening intently to the mourner's prayers.

"*Yit-ga-dal ve-yit-ka-dash she-mei ra-ba be-al-ma di ve-ra chi-re-u-tei , ve-yan-lich ral-chu-tei . . .*"

The coffin was lowered gently into the dark red Transvaal soil. Helmet, his face tear-streaked, spaded the first earth over the coffin with care and love, aware of the finality of the thud as the clods of earth hit the wooden planks, the sound echoing in the still air.

Near the end of the proceedings, Helmut, on an impulse, surprised Abel by thrusting the spade into his hands muttering softly, "Say a prayer for her and for me."

Helmut, prompted by the rabbi's words, remembered more words from Isaiah. "Yet he bore the sins of many and made intercession for the transgressors." Perhaps Abel would say some words to the Lord that may be heeded.

Abel, extremely conscious of his singularity among these alien people from far over the sea, carefully shoveled the soil into the grave. He remembered Gittel's many kindnesses to him.

"Although her ancestors are not of Yourself, Modimo," he importuned silently, "she chose to come here to be one with our land. She may look pale and sickly on the outside, but her soul is of the earth, is earth-colored like my own. Take her to you, Ancient Ones, Badimo. For unless you do, her soul will wander forever."

While Abel performed his part in the ancient Jewish burial ritual, Helmut's fingers searched in the large pocket of his new frock coat to grasp at the tiny black box he had brought from Riga. A generational gift: his mother's grief was with him as if she were already aware of this twist in his life.

Bernard will do better, Mama, Helmut promised, I will see that Bernard will do better. Helmut sought across the grave for Bernard's solemn, childish face as he held tightly onto Fanny's hand. Their eyes met. Again, Helmut felt Bernard's knowing look burning into his soul.

"Ashes to ashes, dust to dust."

Helmut mourned Gittel's death quietly, but everyone noted he was a changed man. Once again, he became intensely and fanatically religious, poring over the Talmud and the Torah, praying three times a day, and visiting the nearest rabbi in Krugersdorp whenever he could. He cared for Bernard and Sally with patience and perseverance that astounded his family. Earning Helmut's gratitude, Abel agreed to leave the store to work in the house. He attended to all their household needs with concern and diligence.

Soon after the end of the Second Boer War, several more Weisz and Beinash brothers and cousins emigrated from Lithuania and Latvia to South Africa. They scattered over the country but settled mainly in Johannesburg.

Over the years, even as the Beinash and Weisz businesses grew in the western Transvaal and Bechuanaland, hopes of another Kimberley shriveled and slowly died in the dust. Unlike the rich deposit at Kimberley, there were not enough diamonds of value in the Lichtenburg pipe to sustain all the hopes and dreams.

By then, the Witwatersrand gold fields proved even more substantial and widespread than anyone imagined. Johannesburg grew rapidly. Perhaps now was the time for the extended family to move to Egoli, City of Gold.

Only once did Helmut's old temper and anger resurface. A White girl, the daughter of one of the local Boer farmers away fighting, had been found raped and murdered. An old miner found her body on the bank of a stream under the willows. The perpetrators were either a group of renegade Red Coat British soldiers or renegade guerilla Boers. The old man alerted other nearby White men. Mendel and Helmut came from the store to the scene. Helmut gently covered the girl's body with an old blanket.

"Filthy, rutting bastards! Men are filthy, disgusting animals!"

Mendel could not stand to hear the vehement anguish in Helmut's voice. He wondered from where this anguish arose.

In a rare display of solidarity with the Lichtenburg community, Helmut joined the hunt for the rapists. They were never found.

His own defilement of Gittel's body filled Helmut's nightmares; that coupled with what he had seen when he was seven years old. Then, sheltered with his family in a barn on a kindly Christian neighbor's land, they prayed for safety while the pogrom raged around them. Helmut watched in horror from a grimy window in the loft, as the soldiers in their white uniforms trimmed in red, rode on huge black horses trampling fleeing Jews. The riders swung their swords cutting through limbs, severing heads.

"Come, Helmut, come here!" Leah, his mother, covered his ears with her hands after she clutched him close to her so he could not see. But he had already seen too much. The screams of women and girls were carried on the odor of the blood-infused air . . . pillage and rape and burning houses. Helmut suffered pogrom nightmares his entire life.

1960
LIV

. . . on my stomach worming my way through a narrow tunnel, one of a network of tiny arteries deep under the earth, using my elbows as levers to inch forward, I'm clad in a boiler suit, rubber boots, and a miner's hardhat with a dull lamp that lights the area several feet ahead of me. The effort to maneuver my forward momentum is tortuous, my lungs gasping, harder and harder to breathe in the almost oxygen-starved fissure. Small jutting rocks hinder my progress. Red soil beneath me, on top of me, around me, the color of dried blood, dark-brown red. Surrounded by dried blood but with the smell of soil—damp and fecund. Places where roots take hold. The light on my hard hat flickers, fades. Within eye distance three wavering shapes . . . I will reach them this time, this time . . .

Liv woke abruptly. She twisted onto her back and breathed three deep breaths, then threw off the bedsheets, her body covered in sweat. That dream again. Dried red blood. In her dream, shadowy images carried intimations of a feeling that she couldn't grasp. The images remained as vague shapes in the semidark, almost like tiny wraiths. Almost in desperation, she grasped for more images, more sensations emanating from the dream, but her vivid dreams immediately vanished. Of late, upon waking from that recurring dream, she'd been plagued even more by questions and doubts hectoring her life. She wished she knew how to unclench her mind but didn't know if that was safe. Safety lay in mental preparedness. Doesn't everyone realize the world is a threatening place?

Liv sat and swung her feet to the floor. In the half-light of predawn, she padded to the bathroom still befuddled with sleep. She had met someone from London, an interesting woman.

She made me catch my breath. Why? Liv asked herself. As she brushed her teeth her mind cleared. Ah yes, blond and eager, Rosie, bounding up to me like a Labrador pup. Today she was to lunch with Rosie in Hillbrow.

Close to the appointed time, Liv's brisk stride slowed as the summer heat beat at her on the almost two-mile walk from the Wits University campus in Braamfontein to her lunch with Rosie in Hillbrow. She had excused herself earlier from the Gubbin's Library trustees' meeting at the university. Her Aunt Sally approved of Liv's philanthropy. Liv serving on nonprofit boards was good for the family's business reputation.

As she walked, Liv reminded herself not to share too much with Rosie until she knew more about her. A teenager when her mother gave her "the talk" about how to protect herself from fortune hunters and practice restraint, her mother had said, "Our family is well known. People talk. They wonder at our wealth, our mystique. Take care with whom you share too many family details." At the time the whole concept of her family and their prominent wealth shocked her. Years later, the tendrils of the awareness lingered.

Can I trust Rosie? Not only about money?

Slowing her pace, Liv paused, aware that paranoia spelled danger as well as futility. The realization jarred her. She walked in preoccupied unawareness of her surroundings to the border of Hillbrow and Braamfontein and now stood at the top of the hill in front of the notorious Fort Prison or The Fort—also known to the Black population as Number Four.

Two Black men dressed as laborers in soiled boiler suits passed her with their heads down. Instantly Liv recognized them both from a clandestine PAC meeting. She remembered them not as laborers but as trained, disciplined operatives and experienced community organizers. They did not acknowledge one another. Liv focused her gaze on the pavement. It was a bad omen to cross paths here. The moment passed and the organizers walked on at a steady pace. What Robert Sobukwe, the PAC President, said proved once again correct—eyes and ears were stationed everywhere.

He told her often, "You must assume secret police informants as well as protective PAC cadres are watching you." Liv reprimanded herself; she did not practice sufficient awareness. She began to walk again but a wall plaque netted her attention, placed outside the secured main gate of the prison to inform the public of the original building on the hill site.

This dreaded prison, built in the late 1880s, was used originally as a fort and manned by troops of the old Boer Republic. In the First Boer War, the earliest cannon shots were aimed at the British mining camp in the valley below where the miners lived and worked the initial gold-mining claims. The old prison, built inside The Fort in 1892, housed White, male, political prisoners.

Presently White male detainees—including Jaco, detained twice but never charged—were imprisoned in the Fort Prison itself and Black prisoners, the majority, imprisoned in the adjacent "awaiting trial" block. Female prisoner cells occupied a small wing.

The prison, built into the hill, situated most of the cells in floors below ground. The five-cornered shape, modeled on Jan van Riebeck's original, three-hundred-year-old fort in Cape Town, had each corner complete with a watchtower and armed guard. Perhaps the guards watched her even then as her uneasy glance swept over the towers? Earlier she had parked her car nearby, judging it a convenient spot closer to the restaurant but not too far from the university. From there she might efficiently fulfill three objectives in the minimum amount of time: attend the trustee meeting, have lunch with Rosie, and take her daily exercise.

They met on the first-floor patio of Café Wien. Rosie sat at a small table in the sunlight almost surrounded by colorful bougainvillea and ferns in enormous clay pots. Rosie waved a welcoming hand, greeting Liv with a warm smile. Liv only managed a muttered greeting. A current of emotions almost overwhelmed her.

What the hell is happening to me?

Constant traffic noise from Kotze Street buffeted the space. An acquaintance stopped at their table and greeted Liv, who introduced Rosie as a friend from England living in Hillbrow for a while.

When they were alone again, Rosie said, "When I saw your library, you mentioned you've collected books written by exiled Black writers?"

Liv nodded.

"I was wondering how do you get them into the country? The books, I mean?"

"Oh, nobody at customs seems to care, even the few plain-clothes security police they must have there. Customs regularly search my luggage at Jan Smuts when I return from overseas trips. They find the books. Probably they don't believe Black people can write anything worth reading or anything of danger to the state.

"I can't show them to anyone, I'm afraid. Most of the exiled writers are banned. That means their work, too. I want them in my collection, though; one day those first editions may be of great value to scholars and archivists." She scolded herself for giving more information than necessary. Liv switched the topic of conversation. "Now, what about you? What do you write?"

Blushing Rosie replied, "I don't like to talk about my work, you know. I prefer to let it talk for itself. Articles in various places, from gardening magazines to newspapers. I'm here mainly to cover Prime Minister Harold Macmillan's African tour of British Empire countries. As you probably know, South Africa is the final stop. Wind of change, and all that . . ."

New interest sparked in Liv's eyes as she looked at Rosie. Liv smiled again. "All right, then, tell me about your family."

Rosie waved a disparaging hand as if to brush off her family's presence. "Oh, there's nothing special about my family. My mother entertains. She's a society lady. My father died many years ago. I don't have siblings."

Liv nodded in sympathy. "Like me, an only child."

Rosie pitched her voice to an even tone and tempered her body language as if she hoped when she edged away, she would provoke Liv's inclination to follow her. Liv guessed Rosie may be flirting with her. Rosie continued. "Mother and I, we don't get along. We exist on different planets."

Liv acknowledged inwardly that Rosie, like herself, endured

a long journey away from family. Relationships with parents vexed them both.

"What did your father do?"

"It's pretty dull. In Russia he trained as a mining engineer and when he fled to England in the 1920s, he joined a financial house in London with international mining interests.

"Eventually he transferred to head up the South African mining operations, sort of a tour of duty for those on the upper rungs of the ladder. My mother hated it here—so provincial she said—but he liked it and so did I. We lived here for two years."

Rosie hesitated, then said, "I know you don't remember me, but we were together at Kingsplace, although you were several classes ahead of me. I noticed you at that time. In fact, I had a crush on you."

A shiver passed through Liv's body. "High school—too many repressed memories. Don't want to think about that time." Her decisive, stern tone stemmed any further conversation about those years.

Rosie dropped her gaze from Liv's face. Liv concentrated on her, noting her long eyelashes. Feelings of self-consciousness swept over Liv. Unbidden memories coalesced as in a kaleidoscope spinning into focus. She remembered Rosie now—vaguely—from those high school days, with her light blond hair and litheness. She spoke with an English accent their elocution teacher had praised as the Queen's English or BBC English; the refined bar aspired to by Kingsplace teachers. Liv and her best friend, Natalie, had fun trying to imitate Rosie's speech. But she didn't want to think of Natalie. Not now. Not ever.

Rosie sensed her consternation for she sought to reassure her. "The other girls didn't tease. Many of us had crushes on prefects— the older girls. Goes with the territory, as they say."

Again, their gaze joined. Disconcerted, Liv thought she glimpsed in Rosie's eyes a hint of an invitation, something sensual, a yearning. She knew to be careful of people who looked at her with yearning. Paul ... now where did he come from swirling into her consciousness. She knew to be careful of people who looked at her with yearning. Liv hoped she had learned that lesson years ago. Hearing of Rosie's adolescent crush warned her to tread with even more care.

"At the end of that time, we went back to London," Rosie continued. "Daddy died suddenly in his forties on a croquet court of all places. Keeled over. Heart attack."

"I'm so sorry." Liv leaned across the table to pat one of Rosie's hands, the comforting gesture of a relative. Rosie didn't draw her hand back, but Liv jerked her hand away to protect herself, almost as if she had touched a hot plate on a stove.

Rosie pretended to ignore the reaction. She shifted the conversation. "Tell me about yourself."

Liv almost didn't respond; she wanted to leave the table. She didn't want to be embroiled in this woman's life. Yet she steeled herself to sketch a polite reply. "I went to university, but after that I got caught up in the social whirl of the time. Back then I did not see it as an option for me to resist family and societal pressure to do what was expected of me. I was married too soon."

Liv hesitated. How much should I share? For sure, not something such as then I almost sabotaged my life.

A shadow crossed Rosie's eyes. Liv tried to read the glance and couldn't. They sat in silence. "I'm divorced now. Have been for several years. Our marriage lasted for a while. We have a daughter, Marion. Can't believe it. Time passes so quickly, but she started university last January."

Amid the silence, Liv gathered her composure. A church bell

somewhere down the hill rang the half hour. Sunlight still splashed on the tables even as the afternoon moved on. Her somber voice broke the silence. "Water under the bridge. So, to answer your question, that's my life. I'm not married now."

Except to the movement. Maybe that is a key to finding my answers . . . sublimation in a cause?

"And you?"

"Married? Me? No, I'm not the marrying sort."

"Then . . . at the Malans the night we met? The man with the umbrella . . ."

"Oh him." Rosie smiled a half-smile. "Ronnie. Ronnie Joffe. An acquaintance I made in a Hillbrow bookstore."

"Ronnie Joffe!" Alert, Liv sat upright in her chair and again tried to keep her face and voice neutral.

"When I mentioned Alan Paton to Ronnie that one time, we were both in the bookstore. He invited me, since I knew of his work, to hear Paton talk. I haven't seen him since that night."

Liv stopped short of responding, of telling Rosie that Ronnie had skipped the country. The information maybe a scoop for Rosie's newspapers, but could she trust her never to divulge her source? Was she even a journalist, as she said she was? Why place them both in danger?

Jaco had told Liv several days ago about Ronnie Joffe and Stan Goldstein, two of Braam Fischer's boys. He had said, "Communist Party. They're now in a 'safe' house in London. They managed to stay one step ahead of the Security Branch for a while."

Liv had another thought; no wonder Ronnie disappeared during the police raid. He knew the net was tightening. Maybe the police raid was about Ronnie, and Paton's presence an excuse?

And here's another foreigner who thinks she knows about South African politics. Liv heard Rosie as if from afar.

"I don't believe you've heard a word I've said."

Focusing her attention back onto Rosie, still irritated, Liv murmured, "Sorry. Something else on my mind. I apologize. I did lose track of what you said."

What had she been thinking? Free-associating . . . loopy . . . a momentary lapse . . . a rare occurrence. What in the world is happening? I must be more affected by Rosie than I know.

Sitting back, Rosie changed the subject. "Enough of me. Let's talk politics. Isn't that all you South Africans talk about anyway? MacMillan's speech to your Parliament last week on the 'Wind of Change' put the cat among the pigeons, don't you think?"

"Please, not politics," Liv sighed. She could not disguise her disparaging tone. "As you say, we talk too much about politics. But what you should know is that the political pool in South Africa is incestuously small. We keep bumping into one another."

Rosie moved her chair to ensure she sat more directly under the shade cast by the umbrella and tried to shift Liv's attention back onto her, teasing, "Don't want to mar my English complexion. Don't want to become a hearty, sunburned person like you striding about in the sun." Rosie added in a subdued voice. "By the way, thanks for removing that wine glass from behind my back that night. Hiding it . . . I was, obvious to anyone I suppose, paralyzed with fear."

"No problem." Liv nodded in a casual way as if her actions were an everyday occurrence.

How to verify Rosie's claims about being a British journalist traveling with MacMillan? Should be easy enough. A few questions here or there. Or a created persona to ambush me? Does this caution matter?

Over the past several years, Liv had shut the door on connections or relationships that didn't serve the struggle. But there was something different about Rosie floating into her life on a flimsy thread from their schoolgirl past.

After their lunch in Hillbrow, Liv and Rosie met several times, once at a showing by the Hillbrow Film Society of a new Ingmar Bergman film. Rosie explained, "I became a member as soon as I rented the flat. I love movies and movie houses. In London they are my hideaways."

They agreed to more dates: lunches, hikes around *Loeriebos*, movies, and occasional trips to the theater, but no classical music concerts. Liv was adamant. She had her reasons but would not elaborate. Liv acquiesced with a certain tone of resignation to all this activity after such a long drought. But she'd decided she'd join the game. Maybe this was a dangerous liaison. What did she want with Rosie? Was it only that adrenalin hit she craved?

When they whispered, heads close, at the movies, Liv experienced Rosie's presence as electricity but Rosie seemed relaxed and unperturbed. Once, as they left the bioscope, Rosie linked arms with her. "It is so good to have a friend I can talk to. Really talk to. I'm so pleased we met the night of Alan Paton's house meeting."

She thinks of me as a friend. How do I regard her?

Scared by the intensity of her responses to Rosie, often, when Liv was with her, she fought to retain her inner balance.

In early March, Rosie surprised Liv during a phone call. "I've an invitation to speak to a book club at a synagogue in Killarney next Wednesday night. Apparently, they belong to large group of affiliated book clubs. They say we can expect anywhere between one hundred and two hundred people. I'm a little nervous but quite excited. Do you think you'd like to come with me? I think you'll enjoy this."

Silence. Liv did not often think fast in the moment. She

gauged a measured, thoughtful response seeking to be impressive, honest, and generous, "Thanks, that's a kind offer. Yes, I'd enjoy being there with you. May I offer you the convenience of a ride? You may be nervous, and I know the area well indeed."

"Smashing! Thanks, I'll accept the ride. Most kind of you."

"Tell me when and where, and I'll be there."

Chauffeuring Rosie to the event, Liv learned the talk focused on women writers in the first half of the century and Rosie would read from some of her personal essays.

After the reading, the applause resounded in the room and admirers and autograph seekers surrounded Rosie. Liv remained on the periphery of the crowd, cognizant that Rosie split her attention between tracking Liv's movements and engaging with people. Some in the crowd recognized Liv. She noted the slight nods in her direction, the interested eyes following her. An elegant, older woman approached, a bridge friend of Liv's aunt. Liv wanted to leave, since the woman was a gossip snake, one to be feared.

Where the hell is Rosie?

But Liv conceded she was cornered. She gave perfunctory answers to the woman's prying questions.

Rosie joined her with a disarming smile, bathing Liv with open heart warmth. She asked, "Time to go?" Liv managed only a nod. She could not remember anyone—in private or in public—smiling at her accompanied with such a look. Maybe one person but that was so long ago.

Liv saw the positive energy pulsating through Rosie. Liv wanted to tell her: You look so attractive tonight. I heard several people say so. I have never seen you look so beautiful, so alive.

Yet she said nothing for that would be crossing a line. Instead, she spoke in a tone of controlled, casual firmness. "Thank you for letting me come with you tonight. You read like a dream."

Impulsively and unexpectedly even to herself, she said, "Your voice is like satin. I've loved your voice ever since we met."

Liv dared not meet Rosie's glance, overcome at the love she heard ringing behind her own words. Surely Rosie must be aware of it? Liv teared up.

Dammit, what's going to happen next?

Rosie murmured, "Thanks, I've never thought of this before, but since meeting you, well, I want to look my best when I'm with you. You're always so elegant, so, well, just right. You inspire me. And . . . I think your voice is lovely, too. So vibrant. Shining energy. In a room, for me, it's as if you are spotlighted."

This response surprised Liv. She tried to speak but swallowed and felt tears on her cheeks. They drove to Hillbrow in silence.

When Liv parked the car outside of Rosie's building. Rosie leaned across to the driver's seat and with one hand on Liv's chin, as if in slow motion, swiveled and tilted her face toward her. Tenderly, ever so deliberately, only closing her eyes when she saw Liv close her own, Rosie kissed Liv on her mouth. Liv tensed at first, but her lips parted and eagerly she kissed Rosie back. More than that, she leaned into the moment closing the space between them. When they separated, they stared at one another in amazement. Need became desire.

"I'm sorry, I didn't mean . . . I don't know what came over me," Rosie said.

Nonplussed, Liv said, "Forgive me, Rosie. This is not me. I don't kiss women like this. Lost my head for a moment."

A young policeman in uniform knocked on the ajar car window. "Shame on you people! *Hierdie is 'n publiek plek.* Don't you have a room, a home?"

They backed away from one another, shocked. The policeman

stood at the front of the car recording the number plate in his little black book. He strolled to the driver's side.

"Damn! I'm always so careful," Liv muttered under her breath.

"Your license, *asseblief*," he ordered, his voice quavering. He was young, tentative, and inexperienced.

Liv rolled the dice. She spoke in the most neutral and mildly authoritative tone she could muster. "Under what law, what regulation, do you want to see my license? I'm not breaking any traffic law and I'm legally parked. There is no law against two people saying goodbye in their car."

He hesitated. Maybe the Jag intimidated him or maybe she did, a little. Liv said to Rosie, "Maybe he knew *'n moffie* and *'n poofter*." Rosie looked uncomprehendingly at her. "Slang terms for homosexual men. Maybe we'll garner some sympathy." For whatever reason, Liv watched him relent.

Looking sheepish but brusque he told Liv, "Okay, lady. No trouble this time but be more careful."

He spoke English with a pronounced Afrikaans accent. To their great relief, they saw him rip out the page with the recorded number plate. Moving to open the passenger door, Rosie heard a click. Liv locked it by remote control. "Sit tight. Let me take you to the rear entrance of the building. There are too many people here."

Rosie gasped at the knot of onlookers—Black and White—on the pavement outside the car. "Heavens!"

Liv rejoined the flow of traffic. She stopped the car at the back entrance to the building. After a gentle kiss on the cheek, Rosie spoke in a low voice, almost a whisper. "Don't let this bother you. I'm not upset. Not one bit. About the policeman, I mean. As for us? When I am with you, I feel something so . . . so loving. You make me want to give you things. Not material things but good things like happiness and blessings. I want to find whatever it is you hold of the highest value and place it in your heart. You seem so sad sometimes. I want to make you happy. And I want to see you again soon." This time she did open the car door. "Phone me soon? Please."

"I'll try. Believe me, I'll try. But the next few days, weeks are difficult. I can't say more." Liv sounded desperate. "Don't phone me, it may not be . . . safe anymore."

On the drive home, Liv's mind skated with thought after thought sliding around at the momentous events of the past hour—the rapturous kiss, the encounter with the young policeman, and Rosie's plea to meet her again. Much as the thought excited and bewildered her, her inability to commit to a tryst highlighted part of the other struggle, too. On a small scale she realized the personal sacrifices Sobukwe spoke of. Never had she paused to reflect deeply on how much he must want to be with his wife, Veronica, and their four children instead of being God knows where in some rural township trying to reach people with his Africanist vision.

As she drove into the garage at *Loeriebos*, in a sad, almost inaudible voice she whispered, "I've tried to find something like this for such a long time. Why now? Why a woman?"

Entering *Loeriebos*, Liv hoped Daniel remained unaware of the heightened physical state surely written over her face and body. But from his absence she assumed he must already be in the usual guest room he occupied. There wasn't a light under any door, but he left a note for her at the foot of the stairs,

It is time to launch the campaign. On Monday, Sobukwe himself will march from his home in Mofolo to Orlando Pol Stn. I'm helping in Shville and other East Rand townships. Two members of the leadership leaving the country in case things go wrong. They can run the show from outside. It's good to feel the launch moving forward.

Liv's mind tumbled as she read Molefe's words, as if by one of those waves surprising her when body surfing in certain conditions on Robberg Beach. She felt tossed around like a piece of clothing in a washing machine, surfacing, gasping for breath, dizzy, and a tad nauseous.

With the campaign launch imminent, the apogee moment the leadership anticipated with such hope had arrived. Sobukwe was now in impending danger, with Daniel stepping into the cauldron of police reactivity. For her, another line would be crossed.

I'll be on the frontline, just as I always wanted, just as I always feared.

Liv paused for a long moment at Daniel's bedroom door, her body seething with desire. By Monday, Daniel may be dead. Deliberate in her movements, she pushed the door open and entered the dark room. She noted wryly that she was willingly about to embark on another journey.

HELMUT AND SALLY
1904-1913

Yeoville

Their journey began from Lichtenburg. Almost two weeks of road travel, one hundred and fifty miles from Lichtenburg in the western Transvaal to Johannesburg, Egoli, City of Gold. They trekked in almost a straight-line east, with a few jogs southeast, traveling with several open-transport wagons pulled by oxen and piled high with furniture and other household items. The slow procession of ox wagons and people seemed barely to shift across the landscape. Being August, hot, dry, and dusty weather prevailed during the day; spring rains would not come for another month. Dust devils rose high in the clear Highveld air. Although the nights were still chilly, they slept on the open veld.

The travelers were soon lulled into the rhythm of the creaking wagons, interspersed by the whip cracks of the drovers, the sudden excitement of seeing antelope of various kinds moving in small herds in the tall grasses, and viewing multitudes of many varieties of birds in areas with water. The occasional farmhouses in the distance rendered some excitement, until they saw skeletal hunks burned by the British Army in retreat, razed nearly to the ground. The war left scars on the Boer nation lasting for generations.

At night, the magnificence of the African night sky revealed stars that seemed close enough to touch.

Helmut and his two children, Bernard and Sally, Gustav and his two sons, and Wilhelm, a younger brother, the most recent arrival in Lichtenburg, and his three children were on the move. Three brothers and seven motherless children.

After Gittel died, Fanny and Zelda, wives of Gustav and Wilhelm respectively, died a few years before the move, from a virus sweeping through Lichtenburg's mining camp, killing thousands.

Help awaited in Johannesburg. The Beinash brothers, Mendel and Reuben, had left Lichtenburg six months earlier and procured a house in Yeoville for the entire Weisz clan. They leased a warehouse for the family general store with a large stable. Helmut wrote to his mother enclosing a large amount of cash in the letter, asking her to arrange transport for two of his younger sisters, spinsters, Rae and Trudi, to travel to Johannesburg as soon as they could, to take charge of the household.

Abel and Kelihiwe (still childless), and other servants, several from the Moekena clan, constituted the remainder of the party.

As they neared Egoli, the brothers and children spent a night in the one hotel in Ventersdorp and the following night in Krugersdorp, the only larger dorp on their way. Everyone bathed and scrubbed and dressed in clean clothes. The next day, when they passed the hand-painted signpost to Krugersdorp, they knew they were nearing Johannesburg.

On the road they now encountered closed carriages pulled by horses, more wagons piled with goods, and the occasional modern marvel, a Benz motorcar. Gasps of amazement followed the noisy vehicle. The children no longer roamed alongside the wagons and tried to keep clean and tidy.

Then, they were in the outskirts of Johannesburg, streets with tall buildings—two or three stories high—rising like mirages. Traffic and people, Black, White, and Indian, jostling one another on paved streets with wide sidewalks and large drainage gutters to catch the rainwater flowing into the drains and then into pipes under the town. Water was a precious commodity in Johannesburg, already the largest town in Africa not built at the coast or on a river.

After several hours, the procession found the way to Yeo Street in Yeoville. Cousins Reuben and Mendel waited at a large house. For once the seven Weisz children were subdued, almost stunned, by the buildings, people, deafening noise, and bustling movement. Silently they entered the large house set back from the street with empty rooms waiting to be filled by the family belongings to be unpacked the next day. They stared, awed, at the intricately designed pressed ceilings in some of the rooms.

Sally never forgot their arrival in Johannesburg. One of her most treasured photographs was the seven Weisz children, siblings, and cousins, sitting with legs draped over the side of the wagon, eyes wide with excitement and wonder, dressed in rough, country clothes out of place in the town. Hacked haircuts made them all seem exactly what the felt they were—country bumpkins. The other treasure was one taken in a studio in Lichtenburg, a formal image of her mother and father and two-year old Bernard standing next to their mother, while she, a sleeping baby, lay in her father's arms.

Rae and Trudi quickly established household order. Rae was the martinet. She spoke passable English but lapsed into Yiddish every other sentence. Trudi, a brave soldier, followed Rae's orders but not in the kitchen, her domain. She was the empathetic one, ministering to scraped knees and elbows and occasional colds and fevers. She learned English quickly.

Rae posted a handwritten schedule in every room with slots for bathing in the one bathroom for twelve people. The adults each bathed once a week late at night, the children each once a week in the late afternoon. Toilet facilities were an issue. The brothers commissioned an outhouse for the male members of the clan.

Twelve people sat at a long oak table for meals. At breakfast or dinner, Rae did not allow any of the children to leave the table until they cleaned their plates of food, even if the stricture prevented them from being on time for school. One of the children discovered a wooden ledge under the surface of the table, about a foot in from the table's edge. Many an unfinished meal of over-cooked *mealie pap*, a hot grits-like cereal, jungle oats, and over-cooked vegetables were stuffed on there. They acquired a stray dog, a handsome black-gray Great Dane, whom they named Kevel, a Yiddish word for dog. Once Rae and Trudi left the room, Kevel circled the table eating all the leftover food.

All twelve members of the Weisz clan attended Friday night sabbath services and services on Saturday mornings, and strictly observed Saturday Sabbath.

Abel ruled the household help. Under Trudi's tutelage, he became an adept cook. The family employed an assistant cook, who doubled as an assistant house cleaner to Kelihiwe, the house-keeper. Every day a washerwoman attended to the never-ending pile of laundry. A daily gardener kept the garden trimmed and planted. Under a giant fig tree in the backyard, Abel and Kelihiwe lived in a large room with an attached outhouse. Abel planted a stand of bamboo shoots along the back fence for more protection. No-one in the family knew where the assistant cook, the laundry woman, or the gardener went at night.

The family observed Pesach, Passover, in late summer and early fall, Rosh Hashanah, New Year, Yom Kippur, and the breaking of the fast in early spring every year. Family dinners included sixty people, as the Beinash cousins, their wives, and children often joined the celebrations.

Chopped herring, pickled herring, gefilte fish, chicken soup, matzo balls, kreplach and kneidlach, roasted turkey, all the trimmings, brisket, leg of lamb, a variety of kugels and bubka, challah or matzo, depending on the High Holiday, teiglach, sweet red kosher wine, and homemade lemonade involved weeks of preparation. Adults sat at main tables in dining rooms and children at smaller tables often in an annex. They partook in the pre-dining prayers and other rituals.

At Pesach, each year the next youngest child, always a boy, asked the four questions in Hebrew. "Why is this night different from other nights?" Each year, in descending order by age, a girl opened the door for the angel Elijah to enter.

Helmut, seated at the head of the table or Mendel Beinash, if they were at the nearby Beinash household, beamed with pride as they surveyed the array of family members.

They drank to one another's good health.

"L'chaim, Mendel."

"L'chaim, Helmut."

L'Chaim. To Life.

The long-ago dream in cold and dreary Riga, of a sunny, golden future in a city of gold manifested. But life would not be life without bitterness and sadness. At every celebration the deceased Weiszes and Beinashes were always remembered, along with family members in Eastern Europe.

In the early years in Yeoville, before their lives were consumed with friends, schoolwork, and sports, Bernard and Sally often sat on the kitchen steps where Abel whittled pieces of wood into spoons and forks, whistles, dolls, and small catapults. They asked him to tell them stories of their mother, their births, their first home in Ramoutsi, and of his village and his family. Bernard was still Abel's favorite. Helmut tried not to make it too obvious that Sally was his favorite. An avid reader, eager for life experiences, she was ready for any challenge, and the natural leader of the Weisz children, as she grew in the attractive Weisz mold, looking less and less like Gittel. Sally's favorite cousin was Micah, Wilhelm's son. She knew she wanted to have an impact on the world, and she wanted Micah to be with her.

Gustav's sons had aspirations, too. Maurice dreamed of flying an airplane and as soon as he was old enough, he took flying lessons in an old biplane at a rudimentary airfield near Johannesburg. When the First World War erupted, he left for England and joined the fledgling Royal Air Force. After the war he married and lived with his family in Sussex where he taught young men to fly.

His older brother, Jacob, as an adolescent excelled at school-work and in athletics. He was an interscholastic sprint champion. Chosen by the paternal Weisz brothers to be the only cousin to attend university he was destined to become an engineer. University was not even considered a path to adulthood for the Weisz girls.

From his childhood, Jacob had loved music and an older cousin, Wilhelm's daughter, Beatrice, was an accomplished pianist.

She played for him. Beatrice invited him to a performance of the Johannesburg Ballet Company (JBC) to hear an orchestra. Jacob was entranced with the dancers; and, thereafter, unwaveringly held to his secret aspiration of becoming a professional ballet dancer. He only shared his secret with Beatrice.

All the Weisz cousins abetted him in another secret. After dinner several nights a week, Jacob climbed out of a bedroom window and ran to a nearby ballet studio that Beatrice had found for him. Once the ballet teacher saw his talent and burning desire, she agreed with Beatrice that she would waive his fees. Jacob always left the house in his training shoes with his ballet shoes tucked in his vest. One night he was caught returning home in his sneakers and he told his father he had been out for a run, which was partially true. Gustav banned him from leaving the house alone at night. But Jacob still used the window to escape to his dream world.

A few years later, Beatrice and her father attended a JBC performance. A furious Wilhelm recognized his nephew in the corps-de-ballet. He and Gustav, in their most threatening demeanors, banned Jacob from ever attending anything to do with ballet. Jacob wondered why the older generation was so set against male ballet dancers.

As he was almost done with school, instead of enrolling in university, shocking everyone, Jacob ran away to London. Once there, he lied about his age, and because of his obvious talent and ambition was accepted into a prestigious London ballet school and then the ballet company. For many years, he danced on the London stage. Jacob never married and later lived and died in a proto-commune for artists of all kinds, in the southern French countryside. He taught dance at that retreat center.

Beatrice took many classes in music, speech, and drama. She

became a well-known speech and drama teacher in Johannesburg with her own studio. She read books aloud on South African Broadcast Corporation (SABC) programs. Later she recorded books for the blind.

The children were not the only Weisz success story. The business, Beinash and Weisz, prospered. Having established their general store, as Johannesburg's population grew, the family expanded business to include a large milling operation producing flour, mealie-meal, other milled products, and food staples for everyone. They bought a bankrupt milling business and over the years developed it into one of the largest milling company in South Africa.

On Sundays with the mill closed, while Helmut, Mendel, and Gustav worked on the weekly accounts, the children were permitted into the warehouses to clamber on the thirty-foot—sometimes higher—stacks of sacks filled with milled goods ready for delivery.

Once during a heated game of hide-and-seek, one of the children fell and lay trapped under the weight of a pile of filled sacks. Only his muffled cries saved him from suffocation, and the game banned in the warehouses.

None of the brothers remarried for several years after settling in Johannesburg. Gustav was the first to leave the household when he married a much younger woman, Gertrude. Not wanting to disrupt his children's schooling, he set up his new household in nearby Orange Grove. His children lived in the Yeoville house during the week and with their father and stepmother on weekends and school holidays. Soon, they welcomed baby Harry to the Weisz fold.

Wilhelm's marriage came next. He bought a small house in Yeoville near Helmut, Trudi, Rae, and the children. His three children moved with him. They continued to regard the Yeo Street house as their base and only used Wilhelm's "home" to sleep. Micah, one of Wilhelm's sons, and Sally were best friends for many years, stemming from their time in Lichtenburg.

Helmut, now in his early thirties, became the spokesperson for the businesses. He enjoyed the role, especially after the company helped him spread the word of Beinash and Weisz by providing him with one of the first Model T Ford motor vehicles produced in South Africa. An anglophile, Helmut loved to wear tailored clothes like the British gentlemen he met on his business duties. He and his brothers were tailored by Raphael Minthoff, Tailor of Fine Men's Wear, who operated his tailoring workshop in a large, open space on Eloff Street in the city center. The Minthoff family, also landsleit, had emigrated from East Poland.

One summer, ten-year-old Sally, patently bored, refused to play with the female cousins and moped around the house. Bernard, Micah, and the other older male Weisz cousins were away at a Young Pioneers for Palestine camp held in Potchefstroom. Helmut called her into his home office.

"How do you fancy an adventure, *meine meidel?*"

"Yes, Papa. Yes, anything."

"I've been loaned a house for a several weeks on the Indian Ocean coast at a place called Plettenberg Bay. There's no electricity but a water pump and outdoor lavatory. It's rough living, almost like camping with a roof over our heads. There are spiders and snakes, monkeys, and baboons. And the best fishing on South Africa's east coast, I'm told. I'm thinking of taking Abel to cook for us, to look after us."

Sally nodded in excitement. "Can I go fishing with you? How do we get there? Can we go in the Ford?"

Helmut laughed at her excitement. "Yes, you can come fishing with me. No, liebchen, not by motor. Too far. There are few roads suitable for a motorized machine. The only way is by train. It's a long journey. Cape Town by train, two nights and almost three days, another train to Knysna, one night. The train lines stop there. Then we take the foresters' train used mainly for hauling cut lumber.

"Plettenberg Bay is only a hamlet. Very few houses. One small general store, and a police station. In the mid-1800s, the Bay boasted a whaling station. There are small vegetable farms and sheep in the valleys behind the Bay. I went to the public library to learn all I could about the place. Come here. Let me show you on a map."

Sally and Helmut pored over the map on his desk. Helmut seemed as excited as Sally. Sally's heart beat a little faster. She threw her arms around Helmut's neck. "When do we leave?"

"Next week, Sally. Trudi will help you get ready."

The brothers, as well as Trudi and Rae, disapprovingly told Helmut to leave Sally with them in Yeoville. Helmut's eyes glinted angrily. "She's as tough as any boy. Fearless. And I like her company. She appreciates wild things and the wilderness. I want her to know all about this country."

Trudi cautioned him, "You are encouraging her to be a tomboy, Helmut. She's ten now. She needs to begin to act like a young woman. What is she going to wear there? Dresses? No, of course not. I suppose boy's pantaloons. That's all she wears anyway when not at school. And swimsuits that cover her legs and arms. She's always with the boys, climbing trees, building go- carts, playing cricket. She climbs that old fig tree in the backyard higher than anyone.

"No fear is not a good thing. She's growing up, Helmut. She

can't always pretend to be a boy. She's never held a doll in her life. Now you are taking her into the wilderness, for several weeks in the wild . . . and fishing!"

Helmut shrugged. Sally was his son and daughter. Bernard avoided him and when they were together, he stared at Helmut with hate-filled eyes. Together in unspoken agreement they shared as little personal contact as possible.

What's done is done, thought Helmut, misquoting Macbeth. It may possibly never be undone.

Several weeks earlier, Helmut had reunited with Mrs. Fitzroy at the British consulate's home on Parktown Ridge. The consul held a cocktail party for business leaders in Johannesburg. Astonished, Helmut recognized Mrs. Fitzroy immediately, for although she aged somewhat, her bearing was unmistakable. She shook his hand while they stood in the doorway of a grand entrance hall.

"You don't remember me?" He asked when she was free to mingle. "I'm the kid on the Union liner from London with whom you shared fruit and other food and taught me beginner's English. Maybe sixteen, seventeen years ago. I was seventeen and on my way from Riga to Cape Town. I so admired you then and I was thankful to you for befriending me."

Mrs. Fitzroy looking puzzled stared frankly at his trim frame, fine features, dark eyes, and hair, stylishly cut in the latest fashion, and his expensive, tailored, dark-blue suit. In a sudden flash of memory, she saw a gangly teenager, dressed in shiny, worn, dark clothes, with a too-large black hat on his head.

"Of course, I remember you, Herman . . . no Helmut! And look at you now. You speak English without any accent. Well done, young man."

Mrs. Fitzroy stood back to admire Helmut and then took

him by the elbow, "Let me introduce you to my husband. He's the consul here, now."

The consul, in dress uniform, had rows of medals on his chest. "Darling, meet Helmut, um . . ."

Helmut wondered if some of the medals were awarded during the recent Boer War, but he said nothing. "Weisz," Helmut answered. "Helmut Weisz, representing Beinash and Weisz, sir."

Helmut and the consul chatted for a while, then the consul moved on to other guests. Wine glass in hand, Helmut wandered about the large, paneled living room and paused at a wall festooned with photographs. He stared, transfixed at a photo of the consul, huge fishing rod in hand lifting an extremely large fish from a bank of rocks while white water frothed below him.

Mrs. Fitzroy appeared at his side again. "You're admiring Jack on one of the rock banks on Robberg—Meidebank—Plettenberg Bay. That's a musselcracker. Fed ten people, if not more. The embassy has a house there. When we were stationed in Cape Town, we used it quite often. Always an adventure. Jack is a fisherman above all else. Are you a fisherman?"

"I try, ma'am. I was hooked on fishing."

They both laughed. "When I lived in Lichtenburg several years ago, there were some good streams with lots of catfish and some bass, even trout, I was told, but I never caught one. Never fished in the ocean, though."

Mrs. Fitzroy winked at him. "Leave it to me, young man, I'll see what I can arrange. You have a wife I presume? Children?"

"Sadly, my wife died." Unexpectedly Helmut felt tears, and he swallowed. "I have two children, Bernard and Sally."

A man about Helmut's age approached him. He introduced himself. "Moishe Lieberman. You don't remember me, but I remember you, Helmut Weisz."

Helmut shook his hand. He remembered the name but couldn't place the man. "I was fighting with a Boer commando that rode through Lichtenburg. You rode to our camp with General Venter, I believe, you came to our encampment and invited me for Sabbath dinner. I was so grateful. You did look preoccupied at dinner, but you were the only one with whom I could have an exchange of ideas. You told me Moishe is your father's name."

Helmut's memories of his time in Lichtenburg were still hazy, clouded by Gittel's death, his guilt, and unconscionable behavior at that time.

They chatted about business and finding their way in a new city. Almost a graduate, Moishe was completing a medical degree in England but set on returning to practice in Johannesburg. Currently, he visited his family locally. Unexpectedly, Moishe asked Helmut if he would like to accompany him to Pretoria in February for the inauguration of Prime Minister Louis Botha. Botha was the acting Prime Minister since President Kruger's death earlier in 1904.

"General Botha sort of adopted me during the war. He said a Jew in his troops was a good luck charm. He's kind of a father to me. We were together when we captured Winston Churchill, a war correspondent and British nobility. Made all the newspapers. We exchanged Churchill for several of our soldier prisoners of war.

"None of my family want to attend. They never approved of my fighting for the Boers or fighting at all. What do you say?"

Helmut said, "Sounds like a good business opportunity. I look forward to the event." They exchanged contact information.

Helmut hummed a catchy tune as he drove to Yeoville in the darkening streets, some still lit with gas lamps. It had been a fortunate, promising evening.

Somehow Mrs. Fitzroy acquired the embassy house at

Plettenberg Bay for Helmut for several weeks in December. With the arrangement and dates agreed on, Mrs. Fitzroy conveyed details of his adventure. The house came with a cook who was also the housekeeper.

"Her name is Blossom. She's a treasure. She catches the milk wagon at The Crags early mornings whenever needed. Bertie Derbyshire, the milkman, owns a small dairy farm near Keurbooms. He'll give her a ride, but she'll stay on the premises till you leave. Bertie is your transport from The Crags as well. He'll be waiting for you at the train depot. Everything will be arranged, such as deliveries from Knysna with the supplies you need. We'll even make sure you have a local ghillie. Not safe to fish on Robberg alone, especially when you don't know the place. There's even an old Benz in the shed."

Overcome with gratitude at her kindness, Helmut sent her a splendid bowl of flowers.

After an exhausting train journey to Cape Town, a night in a hotel on the Sea Point seafront refreshed Helmut and Sally. The next day the train ride to Knysna offered new vistas: crossing mountain ranges outside of Cape Town to mile after mile of rolling veld grasses to old Cape Dutch farmhouses to their first glimpses of the Indian Ocean when they pulled into the station at Mossel Bay at dusk. By the following morning they were almost in Knysna and surrounded by forests of huge yellowwood, keurboom, stink-wood, and many other varieties of trees and vegetation.

Wearily, they found the siding where the much smaller for-esters' train awaited the handful of passengers from the Knysna train. Soon they chugged deep into the forests, snaking their way on the sides of ravines and across wooden bridges built over fast-flowing rivers and then, the end of the line, The Crags.

Sally didn't say a word on the train ride from Knysna, but Helmut read the wild excitement in her eyes and her enchantment at the overpowering atmosphere of the forests.

Plettenberg Bay fitted Sally as if she donned a pair of old shoes, giving her a feeling that she never experienced before, of belonging to a place. Over the following days, she felt wonderment and complete freedom and ease.

Blossom met them at *Milkwood*. She was a friendly, young woman in her twenties, with four children. Helmut and Sally liked her on sight. The morning after their arrival, Helmut and Sally walked around the spacious house with the many tall windows offering views over the Bay to the Indian Ocean beyond. A wide veranda stretched in front of the house. The garden sloped down the hillside.

"*Milkwood* belongs to the British Empire," Sally said, trying to explain the ownership to Blossom.

Helmut corrected her. "Embassy, not empire."

Sally shook her head unconvinced, "Same thing," she said.

She counted only eight other houses on the slope and none elsewhere in Plett. They drove to Lookout Beach and walked for miles on the flat, white sand to the mouth of the Keurbooms River. After swimming and dozing and swimming again in the clear, calm, blue water with fish visible beneath them, they sat under palm trees at Middle Beach. The beach formed the innermost arc of the curve of the Bay. They explored Beacon Island, a rocky outcrop on one end of Middle Beach, capped by a large, well-constructed building, now abandoned . . . an old whaling station.

Weathered, local fisherman casting on the Beacon Island rocks tried to answer Helmut's many questions about the whaling station and whaling ships, but he couldn't understand their patois.

They referred him to a retired ship's captain, Captain Stanley, living alone in a shack behind Middle Beach.

One afternoon, Helmut left Sally reading on the veranda under Blossom's watchful eyes, while he visited the captain. He returned with maps, charts, books, and a few captain's logs.

Sally asked, "Can I see?"

"Yes, of course, but no touching. I'll explain everything. Before we leave, I must return all of these. Intact."

Sally sensed her father's deep satisfaction at being in this scenic, peaceful place that she already loved.

Their favorite beach, Robberg Beach, was three miles of flat, white sand with the Indian Ocean on one side and towering golden sand dunes on the other. No houses or dwellings were in sight. Small wavelets formed frothy lace patterns on the sand. Rows of well-ordered waves crashed with foaming force before washing ashore.

Helmut cautioned Sally. "Not always as calm as this, liebchen. It's a summer sea now. Captain Stanley told me of ferocious winter storms all along the Eastern Cape. Hidden rocks and heavy fog banks. Many wrecks lie at the bottom of the ocean along this stretch of coast from Port Elizabeth to Cape Town. That's why there is a lighthouse at The Point on Robberg. To warn sailors of the rocks at The Point, as well as shallower waters in the Bay."

Sally found her first pansy shell on Robberg Beach, white with purple markings. Gleefully she picked up many others but this, her first, was her precious prize. Before the return journey to Johannesburg, she wrapped it carefully in tissue paper and brought it safely back to Yeoville. For many years it traveled with her . . . her lucky talisman.

Every step on Robberg Beach brought them closer to Robberg itself, which was a three-mile-long peninsula. The peninsula, a nature reserve, known only by its Afrikaans name, was never called by the translated name in English of Seal Mountain. The green and almost purple peninsula jutted three miles into the sea and rose to five hundred feet above the ocean and captured Sally's imagination. For her, Robberg became the pinnacle of the ocean and mountainous beauty of Plettenberg Bay. She would, if allowed, happily clamber on Robberg, exploring, every day. But strictly forbidden to climb Robberg alone, the singular order from her seldom-stern father made the peninsula more enticing.

For Helmut, Robberg meant fishing. The day after their arrival, an older man and his son rode to *Milkwood* on bicycles. Both men were darkly tanned. Speaking in heavily Afrikaans accented English, the man doffed his hat and greeted Helmut, introducing himself as Gerrit Myburgh and his son, probably in his late teens, Dawid. Gerrit was a local fishing expert, and Dawid trained in Knysna to join the police force.

"I am your ghillie, sir" said Gerrit.

Helmut grinned and held out his hand, "Call me Helmut. And this is my daughter, Sally."

Gerrit and Helmut set up a date for the next day for a fishing expedition. Gerrit provided all the gear, and Blossom packed a lunch and filled water canisters. The four of them in the Benz rattled over a rough path high on the hill behind the Bay and followed a rutted path onto Robberg.

"Only on foot from here, man. Only fishermen here. I hope the girl can manage?"

"Yes," replied Helmut. "She's fit and tough and sure-footed and not afraid of heights."

Sally easily kept up with the men. The group walked in single file, Sally between Gerrit and Helmut who brought up the rear.

After about forty minutes walking on a stony path, they

descended a steep, scarcely visible trail to a bank of rocks covered every so often by capricious swells breasting the outermost rocks.

"Meidebank," said Gerrit, unshouldering his haversack. "Good place to start. Next time we come here at dawn."

At the end of the day, exhausted but happy, Helmut and Sally presented Blossom with a sizable kabeljou, scales still glistening with color. Blossom exclaimed in delight, "Fried kabeljou tonight, curried kabeljou for many more nights."

When they returned to Johannesburg, Sally knew for the first time she was in love with a place. Helmut described their adventures to his brothers, and they agreed that as an investment to buy or build a house for the extended family somewhere near *Milkwood*. They reasoned that once transport became more readily available; Plettenberg Bay was sure to boom.

Helmut asked Mrs. Fitzroy for advice. He trusted her integrity and judgment and enjoyed sharing a cup of tea or a glass of wine with her.

"Coincidence, my dear Helmut. *Milkwood* is coming up for sale. The Embassy in Cape Town decided it's not used enough to warrant the expense of the upkeep."

After several weeks of negotiations, *Milkwood* belonged to the Weisz family. Helmut envisaged generations of the extended family, current and yet unborn, enjoying *Milkwood* and Plettenberg Bay, but none, over the years, as much as himself.

Several weeks later in February 1908, Helmut met Marierentia Magdalena Kruger, the youngest of the late President Kruger's sixteen children. Marie, as she was known, attended to her famous father, the late President of the Transvaal Boer Republic, when he died in Switzerland in 1905.

President Kruger achieved international fame as the Boer leader who, during two wars, held the might of the British Empire to a stalemate. Both sides desired the riches of the Witwatersrand gold mines. Kruger, himself an old man when the Second Boer War was fought between 1899-1902, relied on General Louis Botha, the man who invented guerilla warfare tactics and used them so successfully against the British Army.

Kruger's other claim to fame, a reputation that far outlasted his role as Boer hero, was his proclamation in 1898 of a wild animal preserve between the Sabie and Crocodile Rivers, stretching almost the entire length of the eastern border of the Republic and abutting Mozambique—thus, the birth of Kruger National Park. President Kruger wanted to preserve the wildlife from being hunted to extinction in the Lowveld.

In the United States, President Teddy Roosevelt soon followed Kruger's example and in 1901 signed legislation establishing several national parks.

As they drove the thirty-eight miles from Johannesburg to Pretoria, Moishe Lieberman shared this information with Helmut, as well as details on the battles in the two Boer wars.

"General Louis Botha is the temporary leader of the Republic. Tomorrow at the council hall—the Raadzaal—he will become prime minister and the lead negotiator with the British for the establishment of a unified South African government."

"You like him? Will you help with the negotiations?" Helmut asked Moishe.

"Yes, I like him, and I admire him. He's a fine man. An inspirational leader." Moishe laughed. "Obviously it helps that he likes me. He's mentored me, opened many doors. But no, I won't be at the negotiations. I've chosen medicine as my field."

Moishe asked Helmut, "Have you visited Kruger Park yet?"

"No," Helmut admitted. "Hardly knew it existed before you told me today."

"If you loved Plettenberg Bay, you'll love Kruger Park. Take your children."

When Helmut saw Marierentia Kruger, he fell instantly in love with the glowing woman in her early twenties. No other woman had attracted him as she did. He felt an ache when not near her and sublime joy when they were in the same place.

A decade earlier, his mother, together with Gittel's mother, had arranged their marriage. They were so young. Gittel, pretty and spirited enough, but theirs was a fraught relationship.

Dressed in the latest European fashion, her dark blond hair coiffed in the latest style, dazzling Marie in the Raadzaal was seated demurely at the side of her elderly and fading mother. Helmut poked his elbow into Moishe's side. "Who's that?"

"Marierentia Kruger, but everyone calls her Marie, Paul Kruger's youngest child."

"Introduce me after the ceremony." Helmut all but ordered Moishe.

Moishe appeared disconcerted, "She's attractive, Helmut, I'll grant you, like a bright bird among the dowdy crows around her wrapped in their black clothes and strict Calvinism. Sophisticated, too. She attended a Swiss finishing school. She speaks French, German, and English, as well as Afrikaans. But she's a Kruger, Boer royalty. You are an immigrant Jew. You'll bring the wrath of the entire Boer nation on your head. On all our heads. I'll introduce you. But I've warned you. Don't be tempted."

After the formal dinner, Moishe guided Helmut to Louis Botha's side. He introduced them, both men polite and gracious. Moishe used the opportunity to whisper in the ear of one of the new prime minister's aides. Obviously, they knew one another, probably fought together. The aide lead Helmut and Moishe to Marierentia, surrounded by a cloud of young men. Marie, behind a silken Chinese fan that revealed her startling blue eyes peered coquettishly at them but addressed only Helmut. His pulse raced. He swore he was in a Dickensian novel.

"I saw you staring at me all through the ceremony," said Marie, sotto voce. Then with candor that surprised him, she said, "I'm amazed your look didn't burn a flame through me, Mijnheer Weisz."

Helmut bent over her other hand, outstretched toward him. He lightly kissed her gloved wrist. "I must see you again."

In Afrikaans, she asked one of the ladies attending her to note Helmut's address, adding it was about a business offer.

Helmut felt as if he had drunk several glasses of champagne too quickly.

The next day on the drive back to Johannesburg, Moishe warned him again of the dangers of mingling with a Kruger. He proceeded to tell Helmut of the legend of the Kruger millions.

"The Kruger millions is a hoard of gold said to be buried somewhere near Kruger Park, possibly in the Blyde River Canyon, buried on the President's orders during the Second Boer War before he left for safety in Switzerland. Two million British pounds worth of gold and diamonds, a large part of the Boer Republic's Treasury. Buried to avoid the hoard being captured by British soldiers. So far, no treasure has been found. All types of treasure hunters scour the canyon and other likely places. No one knows who carried out the burial or where exactly the treasure lies. Some tried searching inside the park. One was trampled to death by an elephant, the other had a leg taken off by a lion.

"Probably only a rumor about the treasure, but rumors start somewhere with a kernel of truth. If you're involved with

Marierentia, they'll think you are after the treasure. Be careful, my friend."

They both laughed at the absurd idea. He, a Weisz, a Jewish treasure hunter? Blyde River Canyon and Kruger National Park were evocative names. Helmut surrendered to the pleasing prospect of other trips into the South African wilderness. Adrenalin rushed through his body at the thought of the danger he would inevitably find for himself if he pursued Marierentia Kruger.

Inevitably Helmut and Marie embarked on an affair. Their mutual attraction rendered into sexual passion even though they both knew and spoke of the dangers of their taboo liaison. Marie lived with several relatives in a house in Bezuidenhout Valley. For their trysts, Helmut rented a small flat in Hillbrow. Marie arrived on the tram; Helmut, for the first time in his life, neglected his business and family duties, told lies, and made excuses to his business partners, to be available when Marie could shake off her family.

"I can't imagine not having you in my arms," Helmut said, stroking Marie's lissome body after sating their sexual thirst.

"Enjoy what we have now, *skaat*, my sweetheart. You know this cannot last."

For several months they met secretly. For all her sophistication, Marie, scrupulously chaperoned by a variety of aunts, sisters, sisters-in-law, and her mother, understood there was little escape from her family bonds. Yet, she yielded to temptation every time they arranged to meet.

She loved Helmut, who was a gentle lover, urbane, cultured, and well-read. And he loved her.

Helmut acknowledged that possibly Marie's most precious gift to him, besides being a willing lover who gave herself to him without constraint, was her knowledge of contraception. He plied her with gifts: jewelry, expensive French perfume, silk scarves, and handkerchiefs. Marie thanked him profusely for every trinket but asked him to desist while placing his gifts in a drawer of the dresser in the furnished apartment. Sadly, she said, "I cannot use any of these beautiful gifts, *skaat*. At home they suspect I have a lover. I must be more careful than ever."

They met only on weekday afternoons. Saturday, Helmut fulfilled family obligations on the Sabbath; Sundays, Marie attended to her family obligations on the Sabbath. Occasionally, they met in the evening but never spent a night together. There would be hysterical family drama if Helmut didn't return to Yeoville each night. On those rare occasions they met for dinner at a fancy restaurant, Helmut then drove them to the flat in Hillbrow, and after they made love, he would drive Marie back to the city center, where she rode a cab to Bezuidenhout Valley.

Helmut noted the tension and misgivings about his recent behavior among his business partners, too. More than the others, his cousin Mendel raised his eyebrows every time Helmut left the mill offices for "an appointment." Mendel watched Helmut in services on Saturdays. Helmut, a famed Talmudic scholar and usually a leader when the congregation prayed together, seemed at once listless and restless, one leg bouncing up and down, as if he made every effort to stay in his seat and not walk out the door.

Sally chided him for not paying attention when she told him before dinner time of an escapade with the cousins or of something she learned in school. "Are you sick, Papa? You don't listen anymore. You look so tired. Maybe we need to go to *Milkwood* again, so you can rest?"

"Thank you for your concern, liebchen. I'm not sick. Matters at the office need my attention. Yes, we will go to *Milkwood* again, soon, I promise."

Yes, lovesick, like an adolescent, a fool. Moishe continued to warn him. "You are a Romeo in your thirties, and you are lying to Sally, to everyone."

Helmut knew shame and that the situation had to change.

Several months passed.

One afternoon, when Marie walked into the Hillbrow apartment, she was surprised to find Helmut still clothed and seated in a chair. Usually, he was naked and in bed.

He rose and with the utmost reverence kissed her on the forehead.

"Please, sit, Marie, we have to talk."

Marie sat on the edge of the bed. She unpinned her elegant hat sporting a prized egret feather and placed it on the bed. Helmut looked wan and apprehensive. Fear clutched her heart, thinking he or a family member was ill.

Helmut, on his knees before her, opened a small, red-velvet box with a large diamond ring. "Marieentia Magdalena Kruger, will you marry me?"

Marie gasped, her most longed for dream and her most horrible nightmare. She clutched at the pearls around her throat. "Helmut, I want to say yes, more than anything in the world, but you know it's impossible. You know that. We've spoken about it so often."

Helmut rose, crushed. He sat back in the chair and wept. Through his sobs, he said, "I know, I know, but I can't do this anymore. I want you by my side as my wife. I want you to meet my children, my brothers and sisters, and their children. I want you in my house, in my bed. I want to grow old with you."

Marie also crying, spoke hesitatingly. "We can't be married, *skaat*. My family would punish us both. We would both be pariahs and outcasts, the scandal too much to bear. I'm a Kruger, daughter of a Boer hero. I can never be a Jew. You can never be a Christian.

You said it before. We are like Romeo and Juliet. We belong in different tribes."

She brightened. "We could run away, live in Switzerland or somewhere else. But, here, never."

Horrified, Helmut stared at Marie. All these weeks he had plotted to marry her and bring her home while she was also thinking, but of running away, leaving everything here. Leave his children? His family? This golden country he loved. It was too high a price, even for Marie.

They made love, gently, sweetly, knowing it might be the last time.

Helmut returned to his office and shut the door. But seated in *his* chair behind *his* desk was a scowling Mendel.

"So, cousin, you remember you have work to do? You remember you are a partner in Beinash and Weisz?"

Helmut slumped into the client chair opposite Mendel and fought back tears. "I can't talk now, Mendel. Something has happened. I need time alone, time to think."

Mendel saw Helmut raw and open and pressed his advantage. He spoke in a soothing voice. "Tell me, tell me, as family, as your oldest cousin, tell me."

Helmut almost held back but then the dam burst, and he blurted his misalliance with Marie Kruger. The longer he spoke, the more outraged Mendel became. Sitting ramrod straight with growing self-righteous anger, he rebuffed Helmut.

"Are you mad, cousin! You want to bring a *sheiksa*—a non-Jewish woman—into our lives? And not just any *getuisem*—any nobody, someone not of our people—but President Paul Kruger's daughter! You've taken leave of your senses! If anyone hears of this, we will all be ruined, pilloried, and driven out of business, out of our lives here. All we've been through, all we have built, you want to throw it away on a sheiksa?

"The Boers only tolerate us Jews here because they think we are good for business. You'll bring down their wrath not only on your family's heads but the heads of all the Jews in South Africa for generations. You've defiled one of theirs, and she has defiled you. You can never do enough penance for this defilement, Helmut, so help me God."

Mendel held up a hand.

"No, don't speak, I'm not done yet. I need to tell you, I can't trust your judgment anymore, Helmut. We are finished. No more Beinash and Weisz. This I vow on my children's lives. *Never speak a word of this to anyone. Anyone, you hear me?* Your secret stops with me. Now get out, you traitor to Jews everywhere, to Judaism, to your God."

A broken man, Helmut rose and walked slowly out of the office.

He did not return to the offices. He heard Mendel set in motion the legal work to dissolve the company, citing irreconcilable differences. Mendel, as patriarch of the Beinash clan, forbade any of his family to contact any of the Weisz family.

Helmut told his brothers and sisters that he and Mendel had a fatal disagreement. But he would not discuss details. He promised to make amends to the entire Weisz family. Once all matters pertaining to the dissolution of Beinash and Weisz were settled, they would meet and discuss rebuilding a business for themselves.

Helmut informed the Yeoville household that he had not been feeling well lately. He and Cousin Mendel had a major disagreement, and Mendel did not want anything to do with the Weiszes. "We must respect Mendel's wishes. I need a break to reflect on all that happened. I'm arranging a visit to *Milkwood*, alone." All the children clamored to accompany him, but he said in a flat voice, "I need time alone and you must attend school as usual."

Before he left for Plett, Helmut arranged another tryst with Marie. Despondently, he saw an envelope addressed to him pinned to a pillow on the bed.

Darling Helmut,

It is with a heavy heart that I write to you. I accept, but truly, I have always known, that we can never live together as husband and wife. You have given me the greatest gift. Yourself. But I can't keep you in a drawer with my other gifts. We each have our lives to live.

Helmut did not know if he could bear to read the rest of the letter, but the final paragraph caught his attention. The words "married" and "pregnant" jumped at him. He read with disbelief.

I am to be married soon, to a wealthy Free State farmer, Hendrik Van Niekerk. I have known him for some time, but we've never slept together. No one knows yet but I am pregnant with your child. I wanted this so much. I hope the baby is a boy and we will call him Hendrik Helmut Paulus Kruger Van Niekerk. Please don't try to contact me. I couldn't bear it or the havoc that would descend on us. Please burn this letter. No one must ever know I carry your child.

Helmut beat his fist against the solid wooden door until he saw blood and became conscious of the pain from a broken finger. But the pain of losing Marie and never knowing his child, maybe another son, possibly carrying his name, he buried deep in his heart.

Time passed. The Weisz cousins attained adolescence. When she was twelve, Sally fell ill with scarlet fever and was isolated in an empty room in the Yeoville house. For three weeks she battled the fever and almost died. Despite the doctor's orders, every night Helmut half-slept in a chair by her bedside. He prayed ceaselessly. He begged God not to take Sally as punishment for his human weaknesses. He promised to do better. As the third week passed, Sally's fever broke. She spent another three weeks recuperating. The municipality sent a disinfecting team to the room Sally occupied and they burned or hauled away everything in the room, even the curtains.

The household slowly returned to its usual rhythms and routines.

The children, older now, and with Abel fully capable of running the household, Trudie moved in with her longtime friend and lover, Fritz Benjamin, an Austrian Jew, a well-known violinist and violin teacher. Rae married Moishe Lieberman, Helmut's best friend, who had wooed her for years while building a successful medical practice in Johannesburg. Helmut married Golda, a young widow whose first husband died of liver cancer. She brought into the marriage a four-year old daughter, Alice. Sally showed no interest in her much younger stepsister. Bernard remained estranged from his father and eager to leave the family nest as soon as he could.

Helmut had vowed to his mother decades earlier that he would establish all his siblings in a better life in Africa. One remained, the youngest brother, Leo, whom only Trudi remembered from her childhood growing up in Riga. She was seventeen when Leo was born. By then, all the other brothers were in Africa, and Rae worked in Memel.

In 1913, Leo tried to make a life for himself in London. World War I disrupted any plans Helmut had pondered concerning Leo. He told Sally and Trudi, "One day, *liebchens,* Leo will join us in Africa."

Sally anticipated this event with intense excitement . . . another uncle, much closer to her in age than any of the others, perhaps they would become friends.

1960
LIV

The previous night Liv desired Rosie with such intensity that she had sex with Daniel instead, because Daniel faced, within days now, the probability of his imminent death. Or so the logic of it had played out the previous night. He was her dear friend. Liv buried her head in the pillows. Her life was spinning out of control just like then, that other time.

Liv found a brief note from Daniel under her door.

"Have to leave now. NB mting today. We can talk
this evening."

Liv read the note with relief. By evening she'd try to attain some composure about her impulsive actions.

As the morning unwound, Liv found she could sideline her feeling of dread about how she seduced Daniel, for she would see him soon and speak to him but removing thoughts of Rosie proved impossible. The memory of those moments in the car and her emotional state the entire evening trapped her. They held far more significance than her inadvertent liaison with Daniel. There wasn't a possibility of ridding herself of the image of Rosie regarding her with such honesty as they kissed, almost as if she had found an answer. She had lingered, feeling the soft skin of Rosie's hand as she angled Liv's head to receive her kiss. This was a significant moment: the first time she kissed a woman with open-mouthed sensual intent. Indeed, as they kissed, Liv felt something in her soul rising. Maybe a truth.

Yet at this historic moment for the greater struggle—freedom and human rights—she did not know how to begin to explain her situation to Rosie. The situation gnawed. Because she lived with smoke and mirrors and because she kept disparate parts of her life separate—secret—she respected Rosie's privacy. Liv decided not to contact Rosie.

At dinner she concentrated—with almost embarrassed trepidation—on Daniel.

"Chicken, good. I'm ravenous." He spoke with his mouth full of roast chicken. "Discussion became heated today. All about propaganda. The Prof is adamant—Monday's march signals the onset of 'mass noncollaboration.'"

When would he broach the dilemma of the previous night? Should she? Instead, Liv responded in an interested tone. "So, the Prof is staying with his philosophy of passive resistance?"

Daniel shook his head. "Well actually, yes and no. He repeated today we don't hold to passive resistance as our only strategy. More and more it is evident that it is useless against such a violent government that even bans student marches. We believe violence may sometimes be necessary but will rule it out at this stage of our campaign because of the backlash it may create. So, we will stress nonviolence. Sobukwe says he will urge the township leaders to disperse if the police order them to do so. He's even planning to tell the police commissioner that we intend to launch our campaign on Monday."

"Tell the police commissioner!"

Daniel paused as if to say more but desisted. Liv, no longer able to sustain her patience, gripped his forearm. "Before you say anything else, we have to talk about last night."

Daniel leaned across the table and covered one of her hands with his own. He spoke with warmth. "Do we, truly? I think we both understand what happened. As you said, my note about the launch shocked you. You think I may die. We both knew something like last night might have happened . . . been building for weeks."

"Please try to understand," Liv pleaded. "Last night never happened. Never. Happened. I was overwrought; I acted on impulse."

"Do you regret it?"

"Yes . . . and no. You see," Liv leaned forward, a conspirator, "I'm confused. Midlife crisis or something. Don't always know what I'm doing."

She sat back, appalled at her revelation. Where did that come from?

"Poor Liv," Daniel patted her hand again. "You do hate being confused and afraid and having to trust me." He stared solemnly into her eyes. "You have my word. Last night never happened. I have a wife, children. The Prof will be outraged, thinking of betrayal by us. We don't want that. Not now, not ever. Our secret. Do I have your word?"

"Yes, oh yes."

They shook hands, declaring a solemn vow. Jubilant at this outcome. Liv relaxed in her chair. She knew her doubts and questions about her actions would not remain dormant for long.

How do I know I can trust Daniel's word?

"This is my last night here," Daniel continued after a lengthy pause, keeping his tone neutral. Liv focused on his words. "I'll be away until this is over. It's best if you stay at home this weekend and definitely on Monday. Jaco will come by and give you information."

Liv played a strange role in the drama. It was frustrating to be on the sidelines and because of her White skin not able to march alongside her comrades. In a solemn moment she hugged Daniel and wished him well. His body felt so solid, unmovable—so different from hugging Rosie—soft, melting.

"You truly may die!"

Daniel tried to mollify her anxiety. "It's a march. We're protesting about passbooks and we're trying to be arrested."

"I'm so grateful you trust me enough to have shared all of these details the last few days . . ." Her voice faltered.

"You are my sister, Liv, my family. In my family we share everything—*ubuntu*" he said.

"I can never be your sister now or you my brother. Incest . . ." Liv uttered her thoughts.

"So serious," Daniel tried to leaven Liv's mood. "Ubuntu—a term for the universal human family. If we think like you, we'd all be guilty of incest. You see what I'm saying."

Not trusting herself to speak, Liv nodded. She hugged him again.

Later, when she tried to quiet her mind and find oblivion in sleep, Rosie's face presented itself in her consciousness. The image prompted a smile. Daniel was a stalwart friend; Rosie was becoming a friend . . . but a lover?

1960
LIV

On Saturday morning around 10:00 a.m., a servant showed Liv into Jaco Malan's study. He sat reading the morning newspapers—English and Afrikaans—seeking any mention of the launch of the PAC Anti-Pass campaign.

"Liv?"

"Jaco!" Appreciative of finding him at home, she lassoed her arms around his neck, while kissing him on both cheeks. "Long time, no see?"

"Too much court work keeping me up too many nights." Jaco smiled. He said, emphasizing his insinuation with a raised eyebrow, "And you, Liv, are not often home, but gallivanting around town with our newest sensation, a young British journalist."

Liv reddened. Jaco's accurate, wicked barbs often caused pain. "Part of the cover," she mumbled, feeling disloyal to Rosie. "Daniel Molefe says it's important that the more things heat up, the more normal I keep my life."

Even mentioning Daniel caused her to blush.

Never mind, he'll think I'm reacting to Rosie.

"Normal?" Jaco raised an eyebrow. "Want some advice from your lawyer, co-conspirator, and friend?"

She nodded. Alarmed, she raised her eyebrows in a question.

"Mustn't worry. Nothing serious . . . yet. But don't implicate her. Draws attention in the wrong quarters and I don't mean the *lessie*—lesbian—underground, although be aware they may be watching, too."

Liv's hand covered her mouth. "Lessie?"

"What I mean is when Rosie visits Spiders, for instance, and someone watches and they link you and her, they can use it against you. If . . . if they ever pull you in, they have a way to break you."

Stiffening, she asked, "What is Spiders?"

Liv knew Jaco heard her fright, but he couldn't disguise astonishment at her question. His tone softened. "A women's only 'entertainment' club in Jeppe."

Her eyes widened. What else lay hidden from her? What worlds existed on her doorstep of which she knew nothing?

Jaco continued. "Seriously, there are eyes and ears everywhere. Hasn't the Prof told you often? If I know Rosie visited Spiders from my informants, you can bet the Security Branch knows, too. There are informants and informants informing on those informants. It's a snake pit. I'm not sure what 'cover' Molefe is talking about. If it's society woman or philanthropist, okay, but be careful, Liv, which lines you cross."

Speechless and vulnerable, she stared at him. Jaco's words shifted her from how she thought of herself, from one who sees others, into one whom others see in ways she never thought possible. A potential relationship with Rosie acquired further dimensions of danger—the unknown—whereas only moments before innocence and ignorance abetted her blindness.

"Anyway, you didn't come here," Jaco said, "so I can lecture you about your private life. What brings you to my home?'

"I was shopping nearby, so I dropped in. Also, Daniel told me you are to keep me informed. Anything I should know about? I'm worried about Daniel, Sobukwe, the others . . . even you."

Jaco smiled. "And yourself? Not worried about yourself?"

Uneasy now, Liv smiled back. "No, not me. Not yet."

Surely Jaco was aware during the past few days, with the launch of the protest campaign imminent, that her house had become a flurry of activity with Daniel in one of the guest bedrooms and people coming to meetings at her house. It wasn't her place to tell him. Different men and some women arrived late and left early, everyone imbued with a heightened intensity of anticipation and purpose. Other meetings took place in Soweto and in the East Rand townships. As far as they understood, no one watched *Loeriebos*.

Jaco added, "No information, yet. Don't bother to read the newspapers; there is nothing there. Someone phoned earlier to tell me *The Cape Times* has a small paragraph buried somewhere. Laurie Gandar at the *Mail* is meeting with his board of directors as we speak. Goddamnit, I'm in a foul mood this morning. Imagine the only respectable editor of the only respectable newspaper in this country having to go cap in hand to his board to ask for permission to cover this story."

He raised his hand. "Yes, I know there are legal implications, financial considerations, but this is big. Huge. What we have been waiting for. *Drum* will have a presence in the townships on Monday and hopefully the *Mail*. No one can predict what will happen. The Prof has already sent a statement to the police commissioner, a statement about the march. He's worried about a backlash if things become violent, like burning buildings, attacking policemen, and so forth."

"So, I'm right to worry?"

Jaco shrugged. "Do worries help anyone? I once read, 'Worries are like praying for what you don't want.' Let's wait until something happens that warrants us to worry."

The fact that Sobukwe worried rendered Liv more fearful.

"Here, take these with you." Jaco placed sheets of paper in her hands. "Molefe has already told you to stay put until we know the outcome of what happens on Monday. So, stay put. Sorry I must run. Busy day. Remember trust no one, not even Mr. Moekena."

"You? Can I trust you?" she asked in a faint voice, hoping Jaco joked in his remark about

Moses Moekena.

Jaco laughed. "Me, probably a safe bet. All I'm saying is keep your own counsel."

Still bantering, they left Jaco's house together.

"Two cars," said Jaco. "Liv, one must be for you! Be very careful where you drive, go slowly, let them know you know they are following you."

"Seriously?" said Liv. "Let the games begin then. Maybe I've had a tail for a while and didn't know it."

Jaco waved at the cars. Liv did the same.

As they exited the gates, the two cars pulled away from the shady pavement to shadow them both. Liv knew one had followed Jaco for weeks. She sighed. Life was getting more complicated and dangerous by the day.

Liv arrived home to a letter addressed in an unfamiliar hand. She slit the envelope, glanced at the signature, and her heart beat faster.

Dear Liv,

For several nights I've walked the Hillbrow streets trying
not to focus on what happened in the car but shutting
out that kiss proved impossible. Confession time. I owe
you this. As a writer I believe it my right to experience
everything that comes within my ambit. I decided to stay
here for a while and write about South Africa for publications in Britain. If my hunch about your secret life proves
correct, you portray a fascinating figure in the underground
political movement. Initially this seemed a convincing
rationale to continue to see you when the opportunity
presented itself.

Three nights ago, the night of the talk in Killarney, events
moved beyond gaining source material. Your eyes sparked
energy, heightened color touched your cheeks, and you
walked with hungry steps across the parking lot. Swept up
in your energy, I felt wet with desire for you. I struggled to
contain my response.

Then came the Kiss. Woman and woman, the kiss obsesses
me. Of course, I've kissed many girls and women, but my
feelings about this kiss differed: incandescent emotions
lighting me from the inside, a penumbra to your lumi-
nosity. Surely you must see the light you turn on in me ..
. soft, gentle, and so sensual. Coolheaded Liv facing down
the policeman, and protective Liv anticipating my discomfort among the onlookers. Concerned Liv driving me to
the rear of the building.

Do you want to control this liaison? You said I must not call, no, that it is not safe. Why? Hopefully you protect yourself by this injunction? But if I pursued you as part of a game only, why does your safety concern me? We barely know one another

Sapphic love? What do you know of this? I fall in love with women. My friends know. Maybe your closet political life, your secret life, operates much as does my Sapphic life—trysts, secrets, life in a shadow world.

What comes next? I will remain in Johannesburg for the present. I fall back on my favored position, wait and see, relieved finally to halt the incessant conversation in my head.

Yours truly,
Rosie

Enclosed was a Pan-Africanist PAC newspaper cutting. Glancing at the sheet, Liv read the words:

Newsbrief Embargoed. Not to be released until Saturday, 19 March 1960

On Friday, 18 March 1960, Robert Sobukwe, PAC leader, said at a press conference in Soweto that his organization was launching an Anti-Pass campaign. He said, "Circulars are printed and being distributed now to the members of the organization and on the 21 of March, on Monday, in obedience to a resolution we have taken, the members of the Pan Africanist Congress will surrender themselves at various police stations around the country.

"Sons and daughters of the Soil, remember Africa! Very soon now, we shall be launching. The step we take is historical, pregnant with untold possibilities. We must, therefore, appreciate our role. We must appreciate our responsibility. The African people have entrusted their whole future to us. And we have sworn that we are leading them, not to death, but to life abundant.

My instructions, therefore, are that our people must be taught now and continuously that in this campaign we are going to observe absolute nonviolence."

Liv clutched a hand to her throat. Did this call by Sobukwe signal the long-awaited moment, the African uprising?

Rosie's letter stunned her. In truth, doesn't receiving such a letter alter the recipient forever? She was loved. She was grateful and delighted. Someone she appreciated, appreciated her. Had she betrayed Rosie with her impulsive tryst with Daniel? Some questions elicited no answers and shouldn't even be asked. Would she behave the same way again given the same circumstances?

No answer except a plea: don't place yourself in that situation again.

Uneasy because of her ambivalence, Liv sat in a comfortable chair and reread both the letter and the cutting. Looking around, nothing had changed. The bright sunlight shone in a cloudless sky at the windows, the room familiar as always.

Shocked and curious, she remained seated and wondered how much of her secret life Rosie guessed.

A large part of the remnants of Saturday and all-day Sunday, she gardened and walked the dogs, but at the forefront of her mind Rosie's image remained, demanding attention. She wrote she was remaining in Johannesburg for a while. Only by exercising a strenuous effort of will, Liv succeeded somewhat in curtailing her fantasizing and worries about their relationship. She blocked thoughts of Daniel, easier to do so after their vow of silence. Nervously, she struggled to heed Jaco's words about worrying and to sideline her concerns until after Monday's march.

On Sunday afternoon, still at work in her garden, digging her hands into the rich brown-black Highveld loam, the thought that often arose came floating again. As a mother, should I be walking this dangerous activist path taking risks despite having a daughter who is still at such a vulnerable age . . . almost an adult but not ready yet for the leap into adulthood?

The warmth of the sun rippled, drowning her in waves of light and heat until she felt at the center of a Van Gogh painting. In the physical exercise, she found an outlet for many layers of apprehension and frustration, including the shock of Jaco knowing that Rosie visited Spiders. On edge, she questioned why Rosie risked a scandal. What if the British tabloids attained a whiff of that tidbit? And the police—did they know?

Everything in her own precarious situation screamed at her not to deepen a relationship with Rosie. But with compelling, almost fatalistic allure, the woman attracted her. Satiny and opulent, she unfolded like a rose opening in the soft morning light, delicate petals glistening with dewdrops.

Was she ready to plunge into new experiences, sexual experiences? Certainly, many years passed since her body yearned with warmth and passion for someone. Was a sexual experience worth risking everything? Wasn't that what she gambled with Daniel?

Plaguing Liv were some of Sobukwe's vague observations and beliefs, stating that Mandela, Tambo, Sisulu, and the other ANC leaders acted like puppets and that the White bloc of the ANC pulled their strings. No basis for her to judge the veracity of his claims beyond that he believed them to be accurate.

In her opinion, Sobukwe and the movement were not prepared. Sobukwe was a teacher, not nicknamed "the Prof" on a whim. However, in this instance he'd not even reached midterm in the education of his followers. The PAC, established only several years prior, lacked grassroots structure or clear-cut national leadership at different levels. The arrests of more than a thousand anti-apartheid leaders since 1955 and their ongoing trials sapped the energy of the people for mass resistance.

But Liv discerned what remained unsaid in Sobukwe's recent pronouncements: the leadership propagandized about nonviolence, but they hoped to goad the authorities into violence and provoke mass protest, rendering the country ungovernable. A dark premonition coalesced around this dangerous ploy. It might work, but it also gave the authorities an excuse for a crippling crackdown on all opposition in the country.

Liv had a strange thought; Rosie, Robert Sobukwe, and I are around the same age. But such different people, such different lives.

Sobukwe, like herself, was a person of action, and in this situation, their actions and decisions might look similar, both taking risky steps with high stakes. The march was a significant risk akin to entwining her aspirations with those of Rosie. Her gut clenched at the thought of this double bind. She and Rosie; do family patterns repeat themselves? What strange circumstances had aligned for her mother and Sally to become friends and lovers? Would she ever learn the real story?

1915-1919
SALLY AND MICAH

Johannesburg

Unlike the others, the cousins of Sally's generation shared a bond forged when they had lived together as children—close friends—in Lichtenburg and then Yeoville. Yet as they grew older, they slowly drifted in different directions. Sally missed Jacob, Maurice, and Beatrice, who being older were already forging their own lives. She was profoundly grateful Micah was still with her in Johannesburg. Of her stepcousins she carried a particular dislike for Harry, Gustav and Gertrude's only child. She had hated Harry ever since he was a baby.

From birth Gertrude threw a protective net of maternal love around Harry. "My only child, my son, Harry." This outpouring of Gertrude's motherly love onto Harry yielded unexpected results. He grew into a fat, flabby, supposedly complacent and passive adolescent. But his dark eyes glittered in his puffy face and the younger cousins told their parents of his lies and tortures. With no friends of his own, he preferred the company of his mother's friends. He loved to play at being an overgrown junior sheik among his harem of blowsy, pathetically girlish, flirtatious, older women. Uneasily Sally watched him. The women always touched him with sad gestures of tired coquetry. Gertrude encouraged Harry's morning visit to her bed well into his adolescence.

Observing Harry for many years, Sally witnessed how quickly he learned whom to flatter and when. He manipulated Gertrude's moods and emotions with barbed references to his father, brusque Gustav. He toyed with Gertrude as a cat plays with a mouse, honing his techniques of manipulation and ingratiation.

The more Gertrude and her friends fawned over him in response to his feigned attention, the more Harry despised women. And he hated his father for ignoring him, despising him, and for being obsessed with Weisz Corporation. He knew his father's Achilles' heel—his resentment of his older brother, Helmut. He'd act on his knowledge someday.

At family gatherings throughout her adolescence, Sally was acutely aware of Harry's intense, obsessive gaze on her as she moved among their relatives. When she and Micah were together, his gaze penetrated them both with hate-filled intensity.

Sally warned her brother Bernard before he left for Palestine. "I'm telling you again," she said. "I just know that boy is evil. He'll destroy this family. One way or another, he'll destroy this family."

"Oh, no, all he wants is your attention," said Bernard. "He's obsessively jealous of you and Micah. He wants to be like Micah, he wants you to be with him. Not Micah."

Sally was shaken, she replied. "I've never done anything to Harry to make him 'obsessively jealous.' Never interacted with him or even spoken to him."

"That's the problem," said Bernard. "The root of his obsession. People like him hate to be ignored."

At Bernard's engagement party, Harry had sidled to Sally in

the crowded dining room. Bernard and his fiancée were to leave for Palestine shortly after their imminent wedding. Harry pushed his flabby body hard against hers. Sally felt his sweaty hand under her skirt moving up her thigh while his eyes locked leeringly into hers, his contempt making her shiver. With difficulty she struggled away from him into the crush of people, but not before his hand reached her panties and a finger touched her sacred self.

"I know your lust for Micah. I see you."

"Leave me alone," Sally hissed. "Pervert! I'll tell my father about you."

"No, you won't," he sneered back at her with a leer. "No, you won't because I'll tell him about you and Micah."

Sally walked quickly away; she hadn't realized it was so obvious that she'd worshipped her cousin Micah ever since she was a girl in Lichtenburg. Two years older than her, he was the natural leader of the male Weisz cousins. They agreed on almost everything.

Several years earlier, thirteen-year-old Sally stopped Micah as they walked home from shul one Saturday morning. After her bout with scarlet fever when she had endless time to think, Sally had stood on a street corner, hands on hips, and with quiet but firm confidence confronted Micah.

"After I almost died, I don't believe in all this Jewish ritual and family rites."

Shocked and bewildered, Micah stared at her.

"I hate that I'm forced to sit upstairs with the women behind an iron grate while all the men and boys, even that creep Harry, sit with their fathers and uncles and cousins. And pray with them. Prayers like, thank God I wasn't born a woman—disgusting patrimony. I'm not allowed to pray. Only to say a prayer on Friday nights when the candles are lit. You had a bar mitzvah; all the boys do. But what about the girls?"

"But, Sal, we have five thousand years—"

"I'm not finished. *I don't believe in God!* There I said it. I said that word. And now we can see if I'll be struck dead."

Holding their breaths, they both waited. Minutes passed.

"I'm not sure what I believe," said Micah slowly. "My only certain belief is that Jews have a historic right to live in our own state in Palestine."

"Ok, I believe that, too. But that's history, not religion. I'm done with religion. I'm going to tell Papa that I will no longer sit at shul behind bars, as if being female is a crime. If I'm thrown out of the house, I hope you'll bring food to me."

Sally laughed. Micah laughed nervously.

"You're braver than I am, Sal."

After a major family upheaval and a long talk with the rabbi, Sally prevailed. She no longer accompanied the family to services. She supported the ideal of a Jewish state, a conviction of her own but mainly because Micah's passion burned with Zionistic zeal.

Amid great excitement within the Jewish community, they learned that Chaim Weitzmann, the Russian-born, British Zionist leader agreed to a lecture tour of South Africa.

At that time, Helmut (the same age as Weitzmann) proudly told Sally that almost a decade previously he'd been filled with the same first flush of Zionist fever such as she and Micah experienced now. But in his generation, the fervor rooted in establishing the Jewish community in South Africa. How pleasing that a younger generation was filled with the same fervor but this time to build a Jewish state in Palestine.

At Weitzmann's first lecture, most of the Weisz family sat in a hall in Johannesburg, listening attentively to the famous leader. All the family were well-known in the community. People watched them.

Chaim Weizmann proved himself a mesmerizing speaker. "I find myself in an unusual Jewish community scattered over a wide subcontinent in small groups but united in Zionist spirit."

Micah nodded, grinning happily at Sally. In passion, Micah surpassed them all. He burned to become a pioneer in Eretz Israel. Sally wanted to be anywhere Micah went. He was a wiry, nineteen-year-old. Sitting next to him, Sally felt the energy in his body.

Micah told her of the occasion two nights earlier when he had met Weitzmann at a private dinner for Zionist leaders given by the Weisz brothers . . . men only. Weitzmann, knowing a zealot when he saw one, shook Micah's hand warmly.

"So, when are you coming to Palestine, young man? We need pioneers of energy and vision."

"As soon as I can, Mr. Weiztmann."

With his hand still in Weitzmann's warm clasp, Micah glanced uneasily at his father, but Wilhelm's attention was elsewhere. Wilhelm wanted Micah to finish his education in South Africa before he left for Palestine.

His admonishment of Micah's request was harsh. "You go. You go on your own. Don't expect anything from me! You're too young, too headstrong. No education. Stay at the university. Finish your studies, then decide. You'll be worth more in Palestine with a degree. You can't build a country with bare hands! You need brains and an education. And think of your poor, dead mother. She would not want you to go. We need you here."

Helmut simply said to Sally the first time she asked, "Too rough; a frontier, fighting. Arab and Jews killing each other. Not for you. Any way you're only seventeen."

Sally and Micah's parental opposition strengthened their

bond. They knew that their convictions mirrored those of thousands of other South African Jewish families coming from Eastern Europe and the Russian Pale a generation ago.

Now, scanning the hall, Sally recognized many members of those families—men and women her father had worked with to build the Zionist movement in South Africa. Mendel Beinash, a leading Zionist and one of her elderly cousins, as well as one of her father's former business associates, despite the families being estranged, glanced at Sally and smiled from his seat on the platform.

Often with her father when he spoke business, she enjoyed being amid powerful men. Her father liked her presence alongside him. He always said it was a pity she was a girl because she had more business sense in her little finger than Bernard in his whole body. But he wouldn't let her into the business. That suggestion shocked him almost as much as her living in Palestine. She also recognized and waved to Jacob Minthof, Micah's new friend, standing toward the rear of the hall with his father Rafael Minthof, her father's tailor and tailor to all the Weisz men.

The audience sat back and bathed in Weitzmann's glow. His visit gave the community a sense of communion with the world body of Zionism. Being a Zionist for many of her peers was as fundamental as being Jewish.

The Weisz family, like other families descending from persecuted Eastern European Jews, heeded Theodor Herzl's 1895 cry to Jewish people everywhere, to band together and build a Jewish state. That call culminated in 1897 in the first Zionist Congress held in Basle, Switzerland.

Among the delegates from all over Europe and America, many Lithuanians attended, spreading the Zionistic message to every corner of the Pale. And thousands of Jews arriving in South Africa from Lithuania from 1902 onward brought with them not only generations of Jewish teaching and Talmudic consciousness but a rampant Zionism.

This was their legacy; Sally and Micah knew Weitzmann to be proud. Micah had told Sally he had overheard Weitzmann saying to Helmut, "All through this visit, at every dinner and every sermon, I can see how Zionism has grown here and how proud you all are of that progress."

When Weitzmann sat down after his address, Barney Beinash rose to speak of the early days of Zionism in the Transvaal. A tall man with a deep, sonorous voice, his audience listened intently as he described how Zionist societies sprung up in Johannesburg and in other Witwatersrand mining towns. This information was new to Sally and Micah, since young people were wont to immerse themselves in the historical details of Zionism rather than learn about its beginnings close to home.

This summation of their mission drew murmurs of agreement from the audience; Chaim Weitzmann nodded sagely. They applauded wholeheartedly for Weitzmann's rejoinder to Beinash's remarks. "Zionism is the only significant channel through which your isolated Jewish community on the tip of this 'dark' continent can be part of the mainstream affairs of world Jewry and be influential within that movement."

"I will become one of those leaders," Micah proclaimed to Sally after the meeting. She laughed gently at the serious intent on his face.

"I know you will," she replied, patting his arm, her face glowing with excitement. I hope I will too, she thought. Somehow, despite my father, I will.

After Weitzmann's visit, Micah became more convinced that his life was destined to be lived in Palestine. Yet he confessed to Sally that he had mixed feelings about his decision.

Recently their relationship deepened beyond the familial

warmth they shared. Micah, more of a brother to Sally than Bernard, and Sally were especially close the night after Micah's terrible fight with his parents when they learned of his disobedience as he insisted that he depart to Switzerland and Palestine. Although he and Sally expected an explosion, she was distraught at the outcome. Filled with anguish at the knowledge of his departure, she entered his room, as she had for years. But this time, she climbed onto the bed where he lay emotionally exhausted, begging him, "Let me get into bed with you. I'll warm you."

Micah nodded hesitantly. Without pausing, she shed her skirt and blouse and lay next to the hunched form of her cousin. She'd never been this close to a boy before. She leaned against him holding him tightly, feeling the tension in his cold body, the rigors passing through him. Then slowly, unexpectedly, as his body relaxed, her body grew hotter and hotter.

Suddenly he turned around to face her and she felt his penis, hard and demanding, pushing at her. She didn't know what she was doing, but she was ready for him; what followed seemed so natural, as if they'd practiced together. They kissed and stroked, and he entered her. She felt a sharp pain, then Micah's strong hard movements, and his cry of anguish or was it pleasure? He collapsed on top of her, saying her name, stroking her hair, murmuring indecipherably.

Surprised at such an anticlimax, Sally pondered on all that girl-talk at school and beyond of protecting one's virginity. Later he entered her again, and this time there was pleasure for them both. Sally left him then, nearly midnight, and her parents were waiting.

For two years her memory of what happened that night was her precious secret. She loved Micah. And now, after Bernard's engagement party, she knew Harry, hidden somewhere, watched them. She felt sullied, unclean. She experienced hatred then. She hated Harry even more strongly than before.

Micah did not leave for another year while he completed his degree in philosophy and politics. Sally completed a secretarial course and two years at language school learning French and Italian. As soon as Micah turned twenty-one, he begged Sally to accompany him to Palestine. During the two years since their first encounter, they made love several times, both feeling guilty and furtive at the taboo act. Obediently, once more, Sally asked Helmut if she could leave with Micah for Palestine.

"No, never! Out of the question! Don't ever bother asking me again!"

Helmut intuitively guessed the lure of Palestine involved her zealous cousin, Micah, rather than the Zionist dream itself. He embodied his role of family patriarch with great seriousness, not granting his permission to such an incestuous relationship.

One side of Micah thrilled at the perverse danger of where he and Sally were headed, while another part of him signaled caution. Plunging down the chasm of incestuous love in a family like their own was a long way to fall. Sally didn't think in such terms. She loved Micah and wanted to spend the rest of her life with him. Micah knew if he stayed in South Africa they would stumble on these evolving developments.

There was also the bond of his newborn friendship with Jacob Minthof.

"I'm trying to persuade Jacob to come with us to Palestine," Micah told Sally.

Jacob Minthof, at twenty, was a large man, an effect heightened by his shaggy beard. He and Micah had met at an annual reunion of the Landsleite Society. Later, Micah found himself alongside Jacob as one of the older men gave a speech. Fascinated at his own great need to share his thoughts with Jacob, they left the hall together and continued speaking as they walked to a local bar. Jacob was naive and ingenuous . . . a teddy bear.

"If it were not for the reunion," Micah told Sally, "I realize it was unlikely that we would have met, for our Weisz family lives in a world far removed from Jacob's 'ghetto' life of Doornfontein. But instantly, we were drawn to one another and often go to bars and cafes in Braamfontein and Hillbrow. You should join us."

Micah, the avid reader of Zionist literature, of Marxist literature, of modern political philosophy, shared his books with Jacob. Sally was often present at their café classes.

"I think I understand Marx, Micah, but this fellow, Nietzsche, he's too deep for me," said Jacob adding, "He has strange ideas. The Aryan superman. I can't agree with his ideas."

Sally and Micah tried to explain Nietzschean complexities to Jacob.

Sally could see that Micah found in Jacob a willing student content to be introduced to the theoretical underpinnings of his own sense of unease at what he saw happening around him in South Africa. For long hours she listened, as the two discussed theories applicable to changing not only the Jewish situation in Europe but their South African political reality. Ultimately Micah succeeded in persuading Jacob to accompany him to Palestine.

"We need you, your mind, Jacob. Together we can make changes happen. But by myself?" Micah smiled bemusedly as he thought of Jacob's constant self-deprecating comments about his own intelligence. "We can do it, Jacob," he assured his friend. "We belong in Palestine to do there whatever there is for us to do."

Sally wasn't jealous of the friendship, just envious of how much easier it was for men to take actions designed to change the world.

Currently, Micah, Jacob, and Bernard lived on the same kibbutz in Palestine. The finality with which Palestine was closed to Sally led her to explore other ways in which she could feel close to Micah, to his belief in Zionism. Reluctantly, because it was so removed from the reality of Palestine, she settled for a second-best option and began working at the Zionist Federation headquarters in Johannesburg.

In long letters she wrote to Micah, she shared how she fought her father to work at the Zionist Fed. Helmut, although he was closely involved in the Zionist movement himself, thought it a slight for his daughter to be a working woman, even if it was for a good cause. But she guessed he'd decided he'd bettered her in two battles and did not think he would win another so soon.

"I'm working in *hasbarah*, the division that provides ideological information about *aliyah* to persuade Diaspora Jews to settle permanently in Palestine," she wrote to Micah. "It's little compensation knowing that I can't come to Palestine yet. Maybe sometime soon, though. Let's both hold onto that dream."

The advent of Sally's working life caused immediate consternation in the family. Her dedication to the cause, which she often enunciated on public platforms, lead the family to believe she drew unprecedented attention on them as the first Weisz woman to work.

One of her tasks was to sort through the masses of stacked historical documents on the early period of the movement. Barney Beinash's speech at the Weitzmann meeting sparked her interest in this history. From the source material, she prepared a background report for the president as part of his annual address.

Sally sent Micah a copy of the report, knowing of his interest in the evolution of Zionism in South Africa. In Palestine, sitting on the small porch of his home on his Galilee kibbutz, Sally imagined Micah avidly reading from the report,

When Herzl died, the fervor for a Jewish state seemed to die with him, and Zionist movements around the world could only hold on grimly to what had been built so rapidly in so few years. In South Africa, the propaganda and fundraising for the state of Israel continued. The movement was handicapped by the great distance between South Africa and Europe, and South Africa and Palestine. But the Jewish National Fund collected a good deal of money for Israel, and a model farm was set up near Potchefstroom in the Transvaal to prepare young pioneers for life on Palestinian kibbutzim.

"It is interesting to note that the South African Zionist movement has been allowed to grow in South Africa, despite the fact that successive governments adhered to the doctrinaire state religion of Christianity. But Zionism was an aspect of Jewish life that evoked great public interest. President Paul Kruger, for instance, was sympathetic to Jewish causes, seeing Jews as the 'people of the Book,' the Bible, to which he and his followers paid faithful allegiance. General Louis Botha, the first prime minister of South Africa, opening a Jewish National Fund Bazaar in Johannesburg in 1910, aligned himself with Zionist causes saying he hoped for 'the creation of a great center which one should be able to look at as a Jewish home.' And the current South African cabinet in this year, 1923, made up almost entirely of Afrikaners, has declared unqualified support for Zionist aims. It is up to us to ensure that the state continues to view our efforts with sympathy."

When the president finished reading the report, he proposed a well-received vote of thanks to "Sally Weisz, a

daughter of our much-valued Weisz family, and a bright
star in our Zionist firmament, who prepared much of what
was in my report tonight."

A glow of pride reverberated in my family. So sad that I'm
alienated from them. How I wish you could have been
there that night.

Sally imagined Micah placing her letter and the report in one of his
pockets. She knew one of his interests lay in the continued commitment of South Africa's Jews to fundraising for the Israeli state.

What Sally couldn't imagine was Micah rising and leaning
on a wooden post watching the darkening night over the Galilee
valley. Or, that when he entered his tiny home on the kibbutz,
he climbed into bed with his wife, a fervent Zionist, a German-
Jewish girl, Gerda. None of his family in South Africa knew of his
recent marriage—and he knew of no way to tell them, especially
Sally. On the kibbutz, Bernard and Jacob were sworn to secrecy.

Helmut made the night of the Zionist annual general meeting
even more memorable for Sally. At her Yeoville home, he drew
her into his former study and pressed into her hand a small,
finely wrought ebony box. At his bidding, she opened it and saw
a delicate gold Magen Dovid. It was the most precious gift she'd
ever received. Clutching the box tightly in one hand, she flung her
arms around her father. He hugged her back.

"Thank you, thank you," she breathed.

His voice was gruff when he spoke; sorrowfully he wiped his
eyes with a large silk handkerchief. "Look after it. It is a family
heirloom, a gift from my mother to me, now a gift to you. Later a
gift for one of your children. You were a gift to your poor deceased
mother. Gittel would be so proud of you, my Sally. Not only

tonight. But for the way you are. So independent, so forthright. I watch how you struggle with the family. You'll be all right. You'll find your place. As soon as there is a suitable position for you in Weisz Corporation, we'll invite you in. I want you to use your talents for all the family."

They hugged as they shared the most significant moment they had enjoyed in years.

1920
SALLY AND LEO AND JANE

Yeoville

On the day cousin Leo arrived at Johannesburg station with his wife, Jane, his twenty-two-year-old niece, Sally, with many of the Weisz family were present to greet them. Leo, the youngest Weisz brother, at twenty-seven, was the only brother yet to set foot on African soil. Sally saw Leo's handsome face leaning out of the window and heard his voice. Eagerly, she had awaited his arrival.

Watching Leo greet Trudi, Sally remembered the stories Trudi had told her of Leo's childhood in Riga. Trudi was his constant companion since she had been seventeen, his primary caregiver.

Leo shouted to his wife. "Jane, Jane, there they are. That's them, all of them!"

Leo grabbed his wife's arm and pointed and waved and laughed. The train stopped and jerked once. His well-remembered sister, Trudi, jumped to him at the window, gesticulating and crying. The air was filled with a hubbub of voices: Yiddish and English cries of welcome below him, Afrikaans around him, a wash of African languages in the background.

Sally noted on Leo's face both bewilderment and gratitude as he saw the whole family, all his brothers, whom he never had met, present with unfamiliar spouses and smiling, restless children of differing ages, heights, builds, and sexes.

Through the train window, Sally saw Leo holding Jane in a hug of reassurance, then he hustled her along the narrow corridor to the carriage door, where willing hands helped her onto the platform.

Leo held himself with the distinctive Weisz bearing, an almost military, straight back and he had the family's dark good looks. Leo and Sally smiled at one other and acknowledged their immediate rapport. When Sally turned to Leo's shy wife, she didn't have the same instant sense of recognition, despite knowing that Jane, like herself, had wanted to live in Palestine.

She's a beauty in a soft gentle way, Sally thought. She carries an aura of needing protection. Jane dressed in fashionable European clothes, showed great taste and elegance. Sally felt dowdy next to her.

"A doe-eyed, gentle girl of twenty-three," Trudi whispered to Sally.

Jane, somewhat revived by all the excitement after a sooty, thirty-hour journey, smiled warily at Sally. Sally sensed in Jane someone she could talk to and trust—a friend.

Looking approvingly at the new arrivals, Helmut acknowledged his pride at fulfilling his promise to his mother all those years ago as he left their shtetl near Riga. All his siblings were in Africa. His one broken promise: Bernard, lost to him probably forever.

To the new arrivals, the second generation of family Weisz became a blur. Beyond their hovering faces, they saw the long platform and noted the Black porters wheeling pallets of luggage and Black vendors selling ice cream. Bright sunshine highlighted the scene.

By 1920, when Leo and Jane arrived, Helmut ran the head office of Weisz Corporation. His interests centered on the property market and finance with a passion for acquiring large properties in and around Johannesburg. Carefully he shepherded the family fortune on the burgeoning Johannesburg Stock Exchange and in other investments. Wealthy, slowly growing portlier, imposingly tall and forceful, he epitomized the patriarch.

Gustav, the second eldest brother, leaner than Helmut, also carried himself with an air of self-assurance. The family speculator, he nosed out deals in the marketplace, concocting schemes for investment and development. On principle, he clashed bitterly with Helmut over just about every business decision.

Wilhelm, the third younger brother, resembled Gustav. He administered the family's wholesale import business called Weisz Imports. Like the others, he was a shrewd businessman with his dream of a four-story building in the business district of the city located in the nerve center of his distribution network and the only store on the African continent stocked solely with imported delicacies.

Max, the fourth brother, ran a large hotel in Hillbrow in which Weisz Corporation acquired the controlling share. Leo, the youngest brother and a civil engineer, had been trapped in England and was now expected to join the corporation.

The sons in the following generation entered professions: doctors, lawyers, academics, engineers, and accountants. A minority ventured into the halls of Weisz Corporation. Several others journeyed to Palestine, to help settle the burgeoning Jewish state.

Daughters married into other Jewish families, their husbands aspiring to the same professions as the sons. They played bridge and tennis, ran households, held elaborate tea and dinner parties, volunteered in Jewish charities, shopped, and visited dressmakers and hairdressers.

The family ensconced Leo and Jane in the large house in Yeo Street, Yeoville. For Sally, who had never moved until then, the family bought a smaller house nearby. Leo and Jane remarked often that they were overwhelmed by the kindness and warmth of the family.

The more time Sally spent with Jane, the more enchanted she became with the hauntingly beautiful, decorous young woman. Even Jane's air of European gentility didn't daunt Sally for long. She often felt uneasy within the family ambit, so she guessed at and understood Jane's confusion. Family occasions could be overwhelming.

As the first female member of the family to enter the "firm," Sally knew the family speculated about her a good deal. Aware of the gossip, she and her father chose to ignore the pointed questions. Some of the aunts even asked Sally outright about her stated lack of interest in marriage.

"Like Jo, in *Little Women*" they said. But they were not too worried, for Sally made sure there were many eligible men around on suitable family occasions. In the Weisz offices, she worked diligently and with a flair that her father admired and shared with anyone who would listen.

One day, Wilhelm, one of her uncles and Micah's father, stopped by Sally's desk after attending a directors' meeting of Weisz Corporation. He sat heavily in a chair.

Sighing, he said, "I have news for you, Sally, news I don't know how to tell you."

Sally gasped, "Tell me! Tell me. It's Micah, right? He's hurt? Is he okay?"

"He's okay," Wilhelm sighed again. "But he asked me to tell you—all the family—that he's married."

Sally gasped again and covered her mouth with one hand.

"Yes, for several years now," Wilhelm said. "He apologizes for not telling you himself. Says he knows he's a coward. His wife's name is Gerda. She's a German Zionist pioneer. That's all I know." He leaned over the desk and patted her arm. "You're the first one in the family to know."

After Wilhelm left, Sally pushed aside the conversation and tried to concentrate on her work. But that night she sobbed for a long time while twisting and turning on her bed. In the morning, after a few fitful hours of sleep, she said aloud to her image in the bathroom mirror, "No more falling for men. This I promise to myself. My heart can be broken only once."

She vowed to make her shattered dream of life with Micah in Palestine fade, and to let Jane, already her constant companion, become a vivid figure in the foreground of her life. Despite her vow, she knew she would always carry her love for Micah, hidden somewhere in her heart. She was also aware that Jane was filling the void left by Micah, but she was happy to have her there.

In the following weeks, Sally spent even more time with Jane and Leo. Jane was her confidante, and they were becoming as close as sisters. Leo was amiable enough but in Sally's mind, a distant planet revolving around the star of Jane.

"A lovable rake," Leo's older sister, Trudi, said. "I pity his wife. He's always been a philanderer. As you know leopards never change their spots."

"By all accounts, an unreliable, lazy bastard," countered his oldest brother, Helmut. "But we'll sort him out. Hard work never harmed anyone."

Expectations for Leo in Weisz Corporation centered on his involvement in the heavy mining engineering company the brothers acquired recently from its bankrupt owner at a low price. Misgivings were among Leo's first responses to this new responsibility. Trained to build roads and bridges in open vistas and horizons, he knew nothing about heavy mining equipment.

If Helmut and the brothers were concerned at Leo's lack of enthusiasm for hard work, they concealed their concern. They trusted he would settle and forget the sophisticated pleasures of London.

As Helmut told him, "The Afrikaners fight each other in the Whites-only parliament and live by a stern Calvinist credo. The English-speakers run the gold mines and the heavy industry and play polo and grow roses and sweet peas and sip gin and tonic in their country clubs. Jews are left in peace to develop the commercial sector of the economy and grow as wealthy as we can, while importing our ethnicity into this foreign but wonderfully arable soil."

As the months passed, Sally's friendship with Jane held steadfast. During that time, Sally confidentially shared with Jane her fears about Harry and intimate details of her past relationship with Micah. Sally had told Jane weeks ago that Micah had married someone in Palestine. She shared she was grateful she no longer felt the sharp pain of Micah's loss, as she so enjoyed her camaraderie with Jane.

"I alone worry about the danger of Harry's obsessions, and I don't know what to do with that knowledge. Bernard is too far away in Palestine, and in family matters he's a self-righteous fool. Of our cousins I despair. They are kind and loyal enough but bovinely accepting of whatever the family elders tell them to do and be. My stepmother, Golda, chided me for being jealous when I tried to warn her about Harry. Jealous of what, I wonder? She only succeeded in alienating me further, making me feel even more strongly a stranger within my own family."

What she didn't tell Jane was how she was aware of Harry following her on the sidewalks near her home but never close enough for her to confront him. On several occasions she noticed clothes in her drawers not quite where she usually placed them, especially her underwear. But she told herself, she was being fanciful, she had misplaced them as she was always in a hurry to leave for work or to visit Jane and Leo.

Jane listened carefully to Sally and added some observations of her own. She too had noticed Harry's obsession with Sally. She also suggested that Sally's interactions with Trudi, the only family member with whom Sally felt an accord before Jane came, was neurotically preoccupied with what she saw as the dark realities of their lives. Trudi's views were stained by her relationship with Fritz, a well-known violin teacher—they lived together unmarried, a scandal, their relationship made even more difficult because he was not accepted by the family. And Sally, Jane surmised, protected herself by developing an inability to enjoy a physical dimension in relationships with any of the men she even vaguely liked. Sally knew that Jane's reading of these situations was somewhat accurate.

One night, seated at his dinner table, a weary Leo stared at Jane, and Sally, who had dropped by after her dinner. He pushed back his chair from the table, carefully folding his napkin. Pacing back and forth, he told them that over days, he had found out during work breaks at the factory, one of his workers, Tinus van Wyk, a zealous Communist, was sermonizing on Marxist ideology to the Black workers. His words and action provoked the vehement disgust of other White workers.

"Today, on the factory floor, van Wyk was beaten up by a group of unknown White men.

I asked my workers, 'What's happening? What's going on here?'

A burly young man, Henk van der Merwe, spoke insolently to me, amidst the nodded agreement of his companions. 'This van Wyk, he's a Commie, Boss. He wants to give them, those Black monkeys over there, a vote. He tells them to form a trade union, to demand their rights. He's putting dangerous ideas into their heads. We don't like it. All the Commies must be stopped!'

"I asked, 'Who were those men? The ones who beat him. The ones I saw running off?'

After a few moments of silence, an older man whom I know only as Oom Koos spoke. 'It's not your problem, Boss Weisz, don't worry about it. We know those men. Now Tinus knows them, too. It won't happen again.'"

Leo told them he drove van Wyk to the hospital. He added that the incident in all its ramifications shook him deeply. Looking at Sally directly, knowing she would tell her father of the fracas, he confided that he had found van Wyk to be singularly trustworthy. He had wanted to ask the board that van Wyk be allowed to manage the production side of the factory, a task he loathed. Now he accepted that was a worthless idea; none of the workers would heed van Wyk any longer.

"I feel more trapped than ever in the factory. I don't know how long I can live in this country."

To escape the gloom of the factory floor, Leo took Helmut's advice and moved around Johannesburg and the Witwatersrand goldfields introducing himself and the deep mining products of Weisz Metals. Sometimes Sally accompanied him now that she was in the executive offices at Weisz headquarters. They drove to small dorps where she previously, through her work at the Jewish Fed, had contact with the few families in the Jewish communities in these small towns. In the car they conversed at length about their own extended family.

Leo confided that he found no joy in the social life of Johannesburg as Jane and Sally did.

"The White community among whom I'm expected to move is so small compared to the anonymity afforded by the London masses. Here all Whites are divided into language, cultural, and religious groups, which makes the potential for social contact even more unlikely. The Jewish segment, so small in numbers and insular, as you know, is held together by a small-town intimacy, which I find stifling."

These sentiments sounded rhetorical to Sally, so she didn't respond. As well as being bored socially, Sally guessed Leo was bothered by other circumstances. Whenever she was with him in the surrounding towns, she saw Leo's eyes rove. Flirting was as natural to him as breathing air.

Ever the observer, Sally watched as discontented Leo eroded his relationship with Jane. The strains were evident before Jane tearfully told her, "It's a difficult period, Sal, because of his boredom and his inability to find stimulation and interest in his work. He finds most of the family boorish and dull. Trudi is the one family member whom he trusts. He's spending more and more of his time at her home, talking, listening to Fritz play his violin, eating meals with them. He told me last night he was disgusted to discover that Fritz was not acceptable to the family because his

Austrian wife won't give him a divorce. The family believes that he's forcing Trudi to live in sin."

Almost inevitably, Leo embarked on an affair. His liaison with Helena Anderson, the Scandinavian-born wife of a well-known mining magnate, became the talk not only of the Jewish community, but also of the town. The newspapers thrived on reporting the scandal. The corridors of the exclusive Rand Club (no Jews or Blacks allowed) buzzed with the scandal. The corridors of Johannesburg synagogues rocked as if a bomb exploded within their hallowed walls. The Weisz family closed rank and went proudly about their lives, fooling no one. Their brash unconcern confirmed their shame and embarrassment to all those who knew them.

After the affair became public knowledge, Jane and Sally treated Leo with the distance one accorded a leper. Sally was furious. She knew now that her instinct on first seeing Jane at the train station and that she needed protection was correct, but she would never have guessed from her own husband.

Sally began to hate Leo. Nothing like the hatred she felt for Harry, but a slow-burning hate for this man whom she suddenly saw as perfidious and hollow; Jane must be protected from him.

Leo saw the loss of respect on her face. "Damn you and damn Jane! You put me on a pedestal, you create an image of me for yourselves, and when I am what I am, you react as if I've broken that image, destroyed the pedestal. I never asked to be worshipped."

Leo did not come home that night, and Sally moved into their home to comfort Jane.

Weeks later the affair was over. Leo realized the extent of Jane's wounded demeanor, and deep anguish. Sally became their intermediary. Jane slept in the bedroom, Leo in the study, and

Sally in the guest bedroom. Leo told Sally, "I want to hold her safely and stroke away her anxiety and pain, but she gasps with fright if I move toward her. The irony is that Helena was a grave disappointment."

Narcissist. Why does he think I'm an ally? How blind men are, thought Sally.

"Leo, I don't care about your women. The less I have to say to you, the less I have to do with you, the better. But Jane insists I tell you that she's pregnant." Sally's voice was cold, dripping with antagonism. Before he even understood her words, he looked up in amazement at her tone.

Sally knew Jane's pregnancy would pave the way for Leo and Jane's reconciliation and for Sally to move out of their house. This knowledge already tore her apart, mainly because she had finally acknowledged to herself that she was in love with Jane.

"She was pregnant when she learned of your affair. She also wants me to tell you that besides everything else, she's frightened of your reaction to her pregnancy and terrified of miscarrying again."

"Ah, liebchen, don't be so angry at me. Pregnant. Afraid of me? My poor Jane. I'm deeply hurt that Jane kept this from me all these weeks. But I know how bewildered and afraid she must be. I'm sorry, liebchen. I apologize to both of you. Please now go and tell Jane I must see her."

"Please don't call me liebchen again, Leo. I find it demeaning."

She opened the door, where Jane stood pale, fragile, and holding a delicate white-lace handkerchief at her lips. Only Sally's willpower stopped her from gathering Jane into her arms. But Jane wasn't seeing her; she stared at Leo.

He approached her calmly and gently. "Cara mia." Leo hung his head contritely. "I'm sorry. I did wrong, but it's over, in the past. I want more than anything to hold you and feel our baby."

They both cried, and Leo moved back into the bedroom.

Sally had been shaken at the effect Leo's behavior had on Jane. She had borne the brunt of Jane's anguish, of her exhausting bouts of weeping, she heard her tales of Leo's London affairs. Jane also shared her reactions when in London, she miscarried fifteen months after they were married.

"So much pain, Sal, so much blood. And I wouldn't have relations with Leo for fear of becoming pregnant again. His behavior is partly my fault. One of his mistresses suggested a Harley Street doctor who helped me understand contraception. For a long while, things were good between us. But now he's bored again. I can't hold him. I'm not good enough for him."

"Shhh, dearest Jane, shh, not you, no. Leo is not good enough for you. He's the philanderer. He's the one, not you."

Sally helped heal the deep gashes of Jane's damaged self-esteem. If this was marriage, she didn't want it. She had another family secret to carry—she loved Jane. Even the feelings she had for Micah were as nothing compared to these emotions. It had happened gradually. She loved Jane with strong roots planted deep. Not like the sweeping emotions of love for Micah but a steady warm glow of love for Jane. Sally was jealous of Leo, and she was afraid to let matters take their own course. For the first time Sally understood the power within Harry, the knowledge that if she wasn't careful, she could destroy the family.

Leo recognized some of this depth of feeling, and he voiced his annoyance at Sally's constant presence in his home. "Be careful, Sally. Jane's becoming an obsession for you. She and I can never be alone."

But Jane defended Sally, saying she was always welcome to their home anytime because she had been good to her during "that time." Ironically, Leo's affair with Helena Anderson became the glue that bonded Sally and Jane.

Fate has a strange way of arranging lives. A month later, without telling anyone, Leo applied successfully for the civil engineering position on the design team of a joint project between the Portuguese and South African governments to build an irrigation scheme on the Zambezi River in northern Mozambique near Beira. His relief at relinquishing his post in Weisz Corporation was evident to all. The brothers, frustrated that Leo failed to take his allotted place in their sunny hierarchy, conceded that Weisz Metals was probably not the niche for him. Perhaps after his adventure in Beira, near where construction of the huge dam was already underway, he would return to Johannesburg and settle more easily.

The family agreed that pregnant Jane shouldn't be alone. Sally moved back into the Yeoville home on the day Leo took the train for Beira. Jane, six months pregnant, planned to join Leo as soon as the baby was old enough to travel. Leo welcomed the idea of change.

"Well, Sal, Jane and I can start over. Beira seems somehow more European than Johannesburg. Our family comes from the Baltic Sea. I always long to live by the ocean. At home, pines grow on rocky beaches. In Beira there are palm trees and sandy beaches. But it is the same sea, the same water, the same waves."

With Leo away, Sally and Jane easily fitted their lives together.

The family concern about Jane's welfare without Leo during her pregnancy abated. Confident of Sally's attentive care to succor her, Jane seemed happier than before and radiantly beautiful.

"Sally's so good for Jane," Sally overheard the aunts remarking, "Jane looks as contented and glowing as Sally. All Sally needed was someone to be her friend. Now that she's so close to Jane, and with Leo and Jane together, perhaps she sees the positive sides in marriage and not only the loss of freedom she says happens when a woman marries."

The family did not know the extent of Jane's childlike dependence on Sally or how Sally encouraged its growth. Jane needed to be held before she went to sleep. Sally moved into Jane and Leo's double bed to comfort Jane should she become frightened during the night.

"Ah . . . more . . . there. Just like that. Ah, that's so good. Feels so good. You've got hands of gold, Sal, healing fingers." Jane murmured as Sally gently massaged her pregnant body. She loved to stroke the fragile beauty of Jane's face, to feel the baby kick her hand from under the taut skin of Jane's abdomen. She loved the feel of the silky, blue-veined marbled heaviness of Jane's ever-growing breasts, to see the nipples spreading in amber triumph. Jane purred and sighed as Sally's hands moved over her. This was pure bliss for Sally.

Sally knew she led herself willfully into a situation where she would be hurt, damaged, and where the danger existed that she could damage Jane. They both knew about Jane's imminent departure after the baby came. Even the family was not as ignorant as Sally pretended. With a knowing glint in her dark eyes, Trudi said, "I'm so pleased you've found a friend of your own age Sally, but don't live too close to the flame. You can be burned. And remember I'm always here, I always care."

Leo's letters arrived regularly once a week, filled with his excitement at finally achieving success in his own right by utilizing his training and his skills and following his natural inclination. He described his colleagues, social life, and Beira in glowing terms,

Beira is a bustling seaside town with long stretches of white beaches, subtropical vegetation, plentiful seafood, and glorious sunshine.

He phoned Jane at regular intervals, both trying to cope with the difficulty of being natural and to say anything meaningful long distance with the line crackling and roaring and the operator counting the minutes.

The baby's birth came early one morning. Sally held Jane's hand until she was rolled into the delivery ward. Sally, the first nonmedical person to see Jane after the birth, reverentially entered the room. They stared at one another for a long time. Jane's eyes filled with tears at the enormity of feeling she saw in Sally.

Jane spoke in a soft tone of pure love. "She looks like Leo and she's perfect. Tiny fingers, all her toes, thick black hair, and she's also yours, Sal."

Sally couldn't help herself. She leaned over the bed and gently kissed away the tears in Jane's eyes. She found difficulty speaking. Tenderly she placed one hand over Jane's crossed on the bedclothes and passed to her the tiny black box with the gold Star of Dovid. Sally caressed Jane's hand. "A family heirloom. Keep it for your daughter. Give it to her when she has a baby one day."

Swallowing desperately on her tears, Sally tried to continue speaking. All the while she held Jane's hand curled around the box. "You've been marvelous Jane, wonderful, so brave."

Jane's exhausted dark eyes watched Sally's face intently. Disengaging her hand, she brought the black box to her lips. Her look of love conveyed her appreciation for the gift. Time passed before Sally spoke again. "Helmut's mother gave it to him when he left Riga, for his firstborn. But he didn't give it to Bernard, he gave it to me. Now it's yours. For your and Leo's child.

"I phoned Leo. He said to tell you that you're a clever girl, that he will be on the train today, that he loves you, that he would like, if you agree, to call the baby, Olivia. I like it. Sounds like a great lady. What do you think, Jane?"

"Olivia Weisz. Sounds as you say, somehow grand, different. Yes, I like it, too. Do you want to see her? Olivia?"

Jane rang the bell and the sister led Sally to the nursery. Through the glass divide she saw a tightly wrapped bundle capped by thick dark hair; she was not prepared for the hot rush of protective feeling engulfing her.

You're mine. More than his, more than his.

The words in her mind shocked her.

"Do you want to hold her?"

Sally became aware of the Sister's question. "Oh yes, please."

The Sister led her to the tiny cot and lifted Olivia, placing her in Sally's arms. Sally was still conscious of heightened emotions yet surprised by the enormity of her feeling for this tiny life. Olivia's face puckered and she yawned mightily.

Sally laughed and handed her back to the smiling Sister. "She's so perfect, so unmarked. It's all a miracle, isn't it?"

The Sister smiled, sharing Sally's exultation, "Yes, she's a lovely baby, and so lucky to have two mothers—Mrs. Weisz explained to me—and a father."

Eventually, three-month-old Olivia, a plump and gurgling baby, and her mother left for Beira. Sally would move permanently back into the large Yeoville house, her childhood home, with her current, smaller home rented out.

Both Jane and Sally cried a good deal in the weeks before Jane left. But always in the privacy of their bedroom they comforted one another. Jane became increasingly distraught.

"It's not so much the thought of leaving you, Sal, that upsets me, for I'm joining Leo. He's my husband, and it's the right thing to do. It's time Olivia knows her father. What truly upsets me is knowing how alone you will be. Why can't you come with me? Leave your job? Leave Weisz Corporation? Leave Johannesburg?"

Often, they discussed that possibility. But Sally laughed, albeit sadly, at the thought of Leo's reaction to a ménage à trois. "No," Sally firmly answered Jane. "You're married to Leo, not me. Your place is with Leo and Olivia, not with me."

"It's strange and sad and confusing." Jane shook her head. "I've never felt from Leo the love I feel from you. Somehow this whole arrangement has fallen apart. Our relationship has become too deep. Unnaturally deep."

Sally never knew if Jane ever assimilated all the implications of their relationship. Even when Jane said she loved her with all the fervor and commitment a person could muster, and they embraced with fires of desire burning between them, Sally didn't think Jane knew. But she would later. Once she was with Leo, she'd know the difference.

Sally would wait to see the future of this tangled web.

On the day of their departure, hugging Olivia, Sally thought her heart would break. Not aware of Jane in the room, she let tears roll down her cheeks.

1924
JANE, LEO, AND SALLY

Beira

Jane wrote to Sally that the train journey to Beira was uneventful and much more pleasant than the one she had endured from Cape Town four years previously. Olivia slept and suckled all the way. And then there was Leo at the station. She added,

I'd forgotten how handsome he is, how vibrant, how much I love him. And I see him now with Olivia, so gentle, so filled with wonder. Was there ever a man like Leo?

Sally's worst fears materialized: out of sight, out of mind. Was Jane that shallow?

Happily, Jane wrote that Leo had moved them into the small casa he rented for them in a block of similar houses built on the seafront with a view of the wide sweep of the bay. Jane's letter continued,

I marvel at the palm trees, the vivid color of the bougainvillea, the frangipani, the hibiscus. The air is hot and washed with salt. I've stepped into another world.

The tone of Jane's letters—emotionally distant but friendly and informative—helped Sally put perspective on her sense of loss. Through letters they made vague plans for Sally to visit in the future.

Sally immersed herself in a furious workload, and her influence at Weisz Corporation blossomed. She was appointed to the executive board, one of the first women in South African business circles to achieve that position.

Jane's letters kept arriving, and Sally realized Jane was settled after she saw a photo of her and Olivia, the baby a deep brown hue from sitting in her stroller during her mother's daily walks along the promenade. Jane also shared that she and Leo had reestablished their intimacy.

Sally carried the loss of Jane's constant presence in her life as a dull, aching pain somewhere in her abdomen. But somehow, she knew this was not the end of their story. She rationalized to herself, Leo will tire of Jane, I know he will. After that, I don't know what happens. Just bide my time.

Jane wrote to Sally that most of Leo's friends in Beira were Portuguese nationals, but all conversed in English.

I find it easy to interact with them, since most have European flair, and I've made friends with several. England, Europe, even Johannesburg seems far away in this piece of paradise. Olivia flourishes. Jane wrote to Sally in another letter,

I don't think I can be happier.

But weeks later, as Sally learned in a tear-stained, wrenching missive from Jane, her happiness had dissipated,

One afternoon, I paused at the top of the steps leading to

the garden of my friend Carolina's house to lift Olivia from her pram. The ladies had gathered for tea below. Vaguely I heard the conversation. They were gossiping about someone called Olivia and my Leo.

Oh Sal, the women's gossip was that Leo had had an affair with this woman. Feeling unsteady, I sat on the top step, holding Olivia, not knowing what to do.

Carolina came and sat next to me, supportive and caring. She asked if I had heard them talking of Leo and Olivia. She said I mustn't worry; it was an affair of lightning. Two beautiful people setting each other aflame. She told me this woman had left Beira many weeks ago with yet another lover. Apparently, she comes and goes, and works for the government. Then Carolina imparted the shocking news that Leo asked me to name the baby after her . . . this Olivia. Monstrous, monstrous.

Sal, I can't accept this revelation, which is a betrayal beyond my comprehension. Leo has sullied what we created together and named it for his infidelity, for another love. Surely, he must love this woman to have perversely asked me to do this for him? And after that horrible Anderson affair, after all his promises, I don't know what to do.

The letter ended. Too shocked at Leo's further infidelity, Sally did not respond. She did not know how to advise Jane. Two weeks passed until Sally received another letter from Jane, who wrote again of that fateful day,

I'll try and recreate the scene for you. When I returned home from Carolina's house a week ago, Leo greeted me. I couldn't look at him. No doubt he noted my stricken face for he said I looked shocked and forlorn. He added, "You know about Olivia Da Viera, then?"

I nodded again.

Baby Olivia began to whimper and I picked her up. Leo held out his arms for her, but I held her away. Oh Sal, I know that was bad of me. He is her father, but I couldn't help myself. Huge sobs shook my body. I asked him why he wanted to call our baby after that woman, his lover. I can bear anything but that. I insisted on one thing. *None of us, no one, ever, will call the baby Olivia again. From now on she is Liv.*

Leo begged forgiveness. But I cannot forgive him, ever, for this betrayal.

There is another terrible development.

Leo told me that around the time of his affair, Harry wrote to him that you and I were lovers. Leo said he couldn't grasp that his pregnant wife was having an affair with another woman. He told me he was mad with guilt, anger, and fear and crazed. That's the reason why he asked me to name the baby, Olivia.

Panic chased bewilderment from my mind. Harry? Affairs with women? Harry? Who was Harry? Then, I remembered Leo's awful nephew, your cousin whom I know you hate.

I told Leo Harry was evil poison. He must be punished. I said Harry was wrong about you and me. We love each other like sisters.

Sal, I'm sure I flushed with guilt as I remembered our physical closeness, especially on our last night. Please tell me what we felt and did then is not wrong? Please tell me you will not confront

Harry. I warned Leo never to tell you about Harry's letter . . . I said you would kill Harry; you hate him.

Leo stared at me for a while, then said quietly that some weeks ago, he wrote to you and Helmut and Gustav about what Harry told him. He reassured me that together you'll deal with him. This was shocking news; again, I felt cold fingers around my heart. I feared since you knew about Harry's letter to Leo, you'll try to destroy Harry.

I cannot forgive Leo for writing to you three about Harry's accusations.

Oh Sal, I'm so sorry about all of this.

What damage had Harry done? Sally held Jane's latest letter with dread and panic pounding her mind. What *had* Leo done? When she had received the earlier letter from Leo filled with Harry's allegations about her and Jane being lovers, she had brushed it off. The letter did not bother her as much as this most recent letter about Leo's further crassness of naming the baby after his lover. Also disturbing was how Jane decried and tried to deny she and Jane were lovers, the denial a wound in Sally's soul. She had lost the Jane she thought she knew. She had lost the Jane she loved and who she knew loved her back. But that matter could wait until they were together again.

The only urgent matter now involved Jane and Olivia . . . Liv. How could she support Jane and baby Liv?

Sally phoned Jane and over the long-distance line with crackling reception, told her she was making plans to come soon to Beira to bring Jane and Liv back to Yeoville.

Jane replied, "I can't hear you. The line is terrible. I'll call you back tomorrow."

On the same night Sally had called Jane in Beira, Harry

broke into the Yeoville home. Sally, hearing an intruder, confronted him in the kitchen. Fat and flabby Harry tried to rape her. She managed to grab a kitchen knife and plunge it deep into his body. Harry died hours later from injuries caused by the knife wounds. Although quickly released on bail, Sally had been held in custody for alleged homicide.

Nationwide headlines trumpeted the morbid details to an avidly interested public. Another Weisz family scandal.

Jane and Leo received incoherent and hysterical phone calls from various family members in Johannesburg. No one knew that Sally had reported Harry to the police on several occasions over the past months about waylaying her and threatening her with physical and sexual violence.

In the immediate aftermath of the tragedy, Jane made plans to travel to Johannesburg. She asked Carolina de Costa to look after the baby. Carolina agreed and made accommodations for Liv and her nanny. Leo would be away at the dam.

Sally was in Houghton, at her father's house, where most of the family mourned Harry's death by sitting shivah for a week. Jane hurried through the living room crowded with somber men and sad women dabbing at their eyes in movements filled with ritualistic significance. Truly, respectable, respected Jewish Johannesburg never coped with an event of this nature, a tragedy of this dimension, an aberration of Jewish family life with such horrendous implications.

Beneath the parading pomposity of their grief, the community did rally around the Weiszes, giving them a sense of belonging, of being able to share their bewilderment, their anguish, and being able to universalize their drama.

At the center of the storm, Sally sat upright in a hard chair in another shaded room. The family lawyers assured her that a plea of self-defense would be upheld in court, but what if it wasn't? She was free only because she paid the bail. Her father, stepmother, half-sister, uncles, aunts, cousins, and friends all assured her of their understanding and support. Even Gustav and Gertrude, whose son she killed, came to hug her and speak to her.

"An accident, a terrible accident," murmured Gertrude. Gustav maintained a steady grip on her hand. "All he wanted was to be your friend. He looked up to you, admired you."

In her sedated confusion, Sally didn't understand what Gertrude was saying, she waited for Jane and Micah.

When Jane came into the room alone, Sally smiled a small, wavering welcome, a nodding acknowledgment of Jane's presence. She held out her arms but did not rise from the chair. Jane rushed to her and held her closely and stroked her hair and found no words. Sally clung to Jane and spoke softly, slowly.

"If only I had gone to Palestine then . . . none of this . . . but then I wouldn't have known you or baby Olivia. Sorry, I mean Liv. It's only Micah now. I killed someone. Micah will come from Palestine; I know he will. You'll see. Then I can let go. I killed someone."

"But he tried to rape you, Sal. You acted in self-defense."

Jane sat by Sally and stroked the dark hair from her face, the dark eyes unfathomable pools now, dulled, her skin an ashen pallor. Sally spoke so softly Jane moved as close to her as she could.

"Only you know this. . . Not tried to . . . did. He did rape me. I killed him after. After. In cold blood. He wasn't expecting it. I heard someone in the kitchen, I went to check. It was Harry. He had a key. I received your letter that day about Leo naming our baby after his lover. I was only thinking of you and Olivia—Liv. I turned away, said something like, 'Oh, grow up Harry. When are you going to stop your stupid games?' You see, I didn't hate him anymore. I loved you, and I didn't hate him anymore."

Sally was aware that Jane flinched when Sally said she loved her.

"He tackled me from behind and threw me onto the table. He was on top of me before I could even think. I struggled but he was much stronger than me. When he was finished, he slid off the table and walked to the sink. I remembered the carving knife in the drawer under the table. He didn't even know I was behind him. I called his name, and he spun around. I pushed the knife as hard as I could into his stomach. I killed him, Jane. In cold blood. And I didn't hate him anymore. I loved you, and I didn't hate him anymore."

Jane noted that neither the tone of Sally's voice nor the dulled expression on her face changed as she recounted her terrifying truth. But Jane felt her heart squeeze as if clamped in a vise.

Jane stayed with Sally for several days both waiting for Micah. He would come, drawn to Sally by the power of her love for him, as surely as Jane had come.

Micah returned to Johannesburg with his wife. Sunburned and hardened by his kibbutz life, with his Old Testament beard, he made peace with his father, comforted his mother (who was quietly delighted to meet her daughter-in-law), and tried to speak to Sally.

Micah did not know if Sally perceived that he was married. Jane valued meeting Micah after all she'd heard of him from Sally. But the reality of Micah frightened her. He was stern, self-contained, and had little interest in Sally. Sally did not recognize him and remained unconvinced he was Micah.

On medical advice, Sally was committed to a sanatorium. Once, she almost died from an overdose of pills. But the staff found her in time. Slowly, she grew stronger. She did not remember much of the time after Harry's death. But she did remember that Jane came and Micah. But Micah and his wife and Palestine meant little to her now, she thought only of Jane, Liv, and Weisz Corporation. After some months, lawyers gathered depositions from her. The judge admitted her comments as evidence and the jury acquitted her.

The Weisz family mythology absorbed the tragedy. A fading air of mystery surrounded them that added to their stature and position in the community.

A year passed. Once more, Sally lived alone in the smaller Yeoville home. The "big house" stood empty. Before she started working again at Weisz Corporation, she made one trip to Beira. Entranced by fifteen-month-old Liv, Sally begged Jane to think of returning to Johannesburg when Leo's contract at the dam ended. Leo remained adamant about remaining in Beira. Jane and Sally guessed he was involved in another affair or possibly still with the Da Viera woman.

During the visit, Jane told Sally, "After I visited you in Jo'burg a year ago, I returned to Beira uncertain of the future. But everything is much clearer for me now. I became convinced that Leo's family need to know their newest member. And Liv needs a family, cousins, aunts, uncles, family love, and community, not two alienated parents. Most significantly, Sal, I accepted that I need you close to me, as much as I know you need me."

Sally's eyes moistened and she had hugged Jane as tightly as she dared without crushing her. Life's crossroads loomed.

After Sally returned to Johannesburg, surprising neither Sally nor Jane, Leo asked Jane for a divorce. He wanted to marry his Portuguese mistress, Olivia Da Viera, now pregnant with their child. Sally knew that both Jane and Leo acknowledged their marriage no longer held much meaning aside from convenience. Sally was proud of Jane for standing firm and striking a deal with Leo—she agreed to a divorce only if he gave her the ironclad right to return permanently with Liv to Johannesburg. Leo agreed.

Liv grew up in the Yeoville home—with two mothers. Her father visited twice in twenty years.

Before they moved back into the big house, Sally hired contractors to renovate the interior, gutting and redoing the kitchen and bathroom and adding two more bathrooms, each to adjoin one of the three bedrooms. Several walls were knocked down to provide more spacious living areas for privacy. The large dining room table was auctioned. While the builders renovated the house, Sally, Jane, and toddler Liv spent several healing weeks at *Milkwood* in Plettenberg Bay.

1940
JANE AND LIV

When Liv was five, Alfred, her mother's trusted manservant (son of Abel and Kelihiwe and uncle of Moses) had been her confidante, when she needed someone to talk to. Even more significant, he was the father of Nomzie, her best friend.

Alfred, an older man with noble bearing and a sculptured face, had lived in Abel's room behind the garage of their Yeoville home. Thick clusters of bamboo and an enormous fig tree grew outside his room. A favorite pastime of Liv's was to hide amidst the bamboo stalks as thick as her Papa Helmut's arm. Liv loathed the sticky, milk-white sap of the fig tree but relished sitting in the sun outside of Alfred's room eating overripe figs. Sometimes Alfred let her share his mealie pap, porridge laced with thick meat gravy. As Alfred told her stories of life in his Ramoutsi kraal, the delicious lumps of the mealie pap sank to her stomach

Alfred, the family cook, held a position of authority in the Weisz household. He treated Jane and Sally as if they were children in his care and openly resented Jane's presence in the kitchen.

Alfred had three wives and many children living at the Ramoutsi kraal. The youngest wife visited him once a year around Easter. Liv anticipated this event with great excitement. She was fascinated with Alfred's wife, a strange exotic figure who wore the tribal dress of her people—brightly colored cloth (predominantly blue) wrapped around her body, intricate beaded decorations around her neck and on her clothes, and the traditional scarf headdress wrapped in many intricate folds. The beads worked into patterns, holding symbolic meaning in tribal lore. During the days of the visit, she sat in the sun on the step outside of Alfred's room and crafted her beadwork, necklaces, bracelets, and other pieces.

Among her jewelry, Liv treasured the bracelet she had made for her, a traditional girl's bracelet of red-and-white beads in a well-ordered cubic design. Alfred explained that if she were a Tswana girl, it would be replaced when she was twelve.

Nomzie was Alfred's youngest child and his favorite. She and Liv, the same age, played contentedly together although Liv spoke no Tswana and Nomzie no English. They sung Christmas carols and Tswana lullabies to one another. Liv showed Nomzie her books and toys. Liv's dollhouse delighted both girls. One day Nomzie brought a tiny, clay figurine, a Black girl that Alfred molded and placed it on a dollhouse bed. They climbed the huge fig tree. They hid among the bamboo stalks frightening one another by disappearing. After a week together growing bolder, Nomzie stroked Liv's curly dark hair exclaiming at the strangeness of it, while Liv marveled at the feeling of the tight, knobby whorls on Nomzie's head.

"Why can't they live here with you, Alfred?"

"Our home is in Ramoutsi, the dry, sandy veld. All my people are there. Nomzie can go to the mission school there."

This answer did not satisfy Liv.

Liv asked Jane, "Why can't they live with Alfred here, Mom?"

"A whole family can't live in Alfred's room."

"Can't we build a bigger room?"

"Besides, all his people are in Ramoutsi; there are schools and villages. There's nothing here for children like Nomzie in Johannesburg."

"'Children like Nomzie'? Why, what's wrong with her? She's just like me. She can come to school with me."

Jane sighed. "There's nothing wrong with her, Liv, except she's Black—"

"And what am I?"

"You're White." Instantly her mother was impatient. "And that's that," she said in a firm voice.

Liv didn't understand the labeling, but from the tone of her mother's voice knew better than to ask more questions.

One night during one of Nomzie's Easter visits, young Liv woke and sat terrified in her bed. Alarm whistles and loud screams rent the air. In her child's nightgown, she rushed to the window overlooking the backyard. Alfred ran across the lawn to the kitchen door, banged on the door, and yelled, "Missus! Missus! Come quick! Come quick!"

Shocked, Liv saw Nomzie's mother vainly trying to rise off the cement floor but unable to move on the step of Alfred's room; her head was covered in blood, a tribal cloth scarcely wrapped around her body. Liv's gaze searched for Nomzie and as a policeman's flashlight lit the scene, she sighted her cowering in the bamboo. Liv screamed as the policeman's truncheon crunched onto Nomzie's skull.

By now, Jane had run to Liv in the bedroom and turned her—still screaming hysterically—away from the window and lead her out of the room, but not before Liv saw Sally, her dressing gown flapping around her pajama-clad legs, tackle the policeman and then swoop up Nomzie's crumpled body before handing her with care to Alfred. Only then did Sally turn and remonstrate with large gestures to the police.

The policemen left as eerily as they descended.

Liv, in Jane's bedroom, heard Aunt Sally at the end of the long hallway, explain to her mother, "Sporadic police raid, searching for illegal, unregistered, domestic workers."

Sally's voice faded as they moved to the kitchen.

"These barbarians used unnecessary force. I have their names. I'll report the incident to the police commissioner in the morning. His brother was at school with Bernard and me."

Despite her mother's stern injunction not to leave the room, Liv crept along the passageway and stopped near the kitchen, listening as her panic grew.

"But now we have a dead child and need to help Alfred and his family." Through the slightly ajar kitchen door, she saw her mother nod and wring her hands. Her mother murmured, "Liv mustn't see the body. She was watching from her bedroom window. I don't know how much she saw."

Her mother's slipper-covered steps shuffled to the door, and Liv scampered back to her mother's bedroom.

Liv didn't comprehend what she was hearing.

In the morning, she awoke in her mother's empty bed. She heard the rattling of teacups in the kitchen and with uncertainty, entered the kitchen. She rushed to her mother and clutched her hand.

"Where's Alfred? Can I see Nomzie?"

Jane knelt to Liv's height. She placed her hands onto Liv's shoulders.

"Darling, terrible things happened last night. Terrible. Papa Helmut has arranged for a Weisz van to take Alfred and his wife and Nomzie back to Ramoutsi."

"But I saw a policeman hit Nomzie over the head. She was bleeding a lot." In hysterics, Liv screamed.

"Sshh, the policemen are gone. Part of what you saw was a dream. Nomzie will be in Ramoutsi with her family."

"But she's dead. I heard Aunt Sally say she's dead. She's dead, like that little bird that fell out of the nest near the lawn."

"Yes, she's dead, like that little bird. Remember we placed it on cotton wool in a small box and dug a hole in the ground for the box."

Liv heard the cold tone of reason, the withdrawal she so dreaded, in her mother's voice.

"Nomzie will be sleeping in a box, too. A comfortable box. Safe in the ground."

"Not safe! The ants will eat her!" Liv screamed and slobbered over her mother's dressing gown, flailing her arms at her mother's body. "I want to see her!" Her voice pitched higher on the hysteria scale.

A hard slap across her face rendered abrupt silence. Her mother stood. "That's enough, Liv. Accidents happen. Nomzie is dead. You were dreaming. And I don't want to hear any more about this."

"You're lying. I can't trust you. It was not an accident."

Holding her stinging cheek, Liv ran to Lena, her nanny, and threw her arms around her waist. Jane left the room with her hand to her mouth. The maid stroked Liv's head until her sobs quieted.

No one mentioned Nomzie again. As far as the Weiszes knew, Alfred never returned to Johannesburg.

Years later, eighteen-year-old, Liv Weisz sat on her bed. Home from Cape Town University for the summer holidays, she'd rather be at Plettenberg Bay with her Papa Helmut than stuck in Johannesburg until after Hanukkah and the New Year.

Listlessly, Liv sat idly skimming through the box of old photographs of her parents and other family members. Disconsolate, she stood and ambled to the window. Raindrops silvered the glass and beyond them she could see the shrubs and lawn weighted down with water. A car passed the house, headlights isolating the slanting lines of rain in the gray gloom. Soon her mother would be home from her regular bridge afternoon. Aunt Sally was away overnight in Durban for meetings with her team from Weisz Corporation. Liv returned to the bed and packed away the photographs.

She paused at a picture of her parents on a beach promenade, herself an almost two-year-old, with curly hair trying to escape from her kneeling father and run to the photographer, Aunt Sally. The sun glinted steely gray off the sea, behind them tall palms waved fronds in the subtropical air. Beira. She had no memories of Beira. In the photo her father was striking and confident while her mother simpered in her usual lost way gazing adoringly at him. No wonder he almost drowned in her treacle love. *I would leave her, too, if I were married to her.*

She picked up another photo, one of Aunt Sally's favorites. All seven Weisz cousins, children's legs hanging over the side of a transport wagon. When she was a child, she loved Sally's stories of the cousins' arrival in Johannesburg, of life in the Yeoville house under the regimen of Aunt Rae, of Sally's boisterous cousins seemingly always in a pack inventing games and escapades. Being an only child, these tales fascinated Liv, who tried to imagine living in the original house with six cousins, three uncles, two aunts, and a huge great Dane. She didn't know where she would fit in.

Liv heard her mother's key in the front door lock and then her voice in the hallway talking to the cook. Guiltily she shoved the shoebox under her bed and hastily picked up a book she had let slip to the floor. Jane saw her intense concentration as she read in the little circle of light from her bedside lamp.

"Liv, still reading? You'll ruin your eyes reading all day."

Jane crossed to the window, her reflection bouncing bizarrely off the wet glass distorted in the small circle of light from the reading lamp. Her eyes loomed huge in her twisted face. Liv could not look at the reflection. Her mother closed the curtains with a flourish. It was unusually dark for a summer Saturday afternoon in Johannesburg. Liv sat up and ran a hand through her slightly curly hair and pushed a strand away from her face. Hearing her mother catch her breath, she looked questioningly at her.

"Oh, Liv, that was Leo's gesture. More than your nose or lips, your whole demeanor and your alert look of expectation are unmistakably your father's." Jane shook her head slightly. "How can you be so much like him when you haven't seen him for years?"

Papa Helmut often approvingly told her she was definitely a Weisz—a lively, dark-haired young woman.

Liv smiled at her mother and Jane relaxed. Neither felt like fighting. Liv did not want to cope with the recriminations her moods and attitude towards her mother brought into their home. Tonight, Abe Abelman was due later to show her mother how to use the new radiogram Papa Helmut gave them last week. Liv wanted to play records and listen to music on the radiogram.

"Mom, Mr. Abelman phoned. He said he'd be a little late. Why you bother with that furniture salesman I'll never know." Liv flounced off the bed. "If any of my friend's phone, tell them I'll meet them at the party." She disappeared into her bathroom.

Later, at the party a young man reached clumsily for Liv and caught at her dress as she backed away. The dress tore. Liv walked with him the few blocks to her house to change. They walked passed Feigel's Kosher Delicatessen, a favorite store for many of the Weisz family. He asked her, almost desperate to start a conversation, "What's your favorite food at the deli?"

"My favorite Feigel food? Sunday morning, early, freshly baked rye bread and pickled herring from the barrel."

It was a strain to talk to the awkward, gangling young man who swallowed his words. As they approached her home, she said, "Weiszes lived here since the early 1900s. Almost the only home my Aunt Sally knows."

Their Yeoville home, on Yeo Street, in the upmarket part of Yeoville, was comfortable, spacious, and set in a well-kept garden. But Liv was ashamed of it for it belonged to Papa Helmut. Liv struggled with torn emotions for Helmut Weisz, her beloved uncle whom she called Papa Helmut since she learned to speak. They shared a deep love, obvious to all the family. In so many ways, Helmut thought of her as Sally's child, his grandchild. Of all his younger relatives, he lavished love on her. Since cutting back on his Weisz business duties, Papa Helmut often invited Liv to *Milkwood*. She was as passionate about Plettenberg Bay as he and Aunt Sally. In this love, he appreciated and encouraged her. For that place of her heart, she thanked him. Relatives agreed he compensated for her no-good father, Leo, who abandoned his wife and child. But Liv didn't feel compensation from him, she felt genuine, grandfatherly love.

Yet, Papa Helmut never knew how she disliked staying in this home, ostentatiously named *Helgold* by her step-aunt Golda. Golda, a superficial, stupid woman who innocently with great feeling talked all about her wonderful Helmut taking in "poor, abandoned Jane and her child," succoring them with a roof and whatever else they needed to make up for his "ne'er do well" youngest brother who returned to London with a new wife and son. She said, "Leo feels himself too good for us and our ways in Johannesburg."

Aunt Sally dismissed Golda's sentiment on one occasion when young Liv tearfully confronted her. "Nonsense, this is not Helmut's charity. This is my childhood home and besides, I've earned this house many times over. I love sharing it with you and Jane."

Liv loved and admired her Aunt Sally, but confusedly, despised her mother for taking this charity, for not finding a job so that she could have some independence. Recently, fifteen-year-old Liv lost her temper one night at a family celebration when they discussed the family's annual charity giving to African causes. She told Papa Helmut and Golda and other family dinner guests what she thought of their charity and her particularly her mother's acceptance of it.

"It's not really charity, is it? You all, all the Weiszes, you've become wealthy only because the majority of people in this country, Black people, are kept subservient and do low-paid work. You make more and more money because they have no education, no property rights, little food, no hospitals, no doctors. No human rights at all, in their own country!

"Look around you, everything is 'Whites Only' All the sad stories you tell about the lives your parents and grandparents were and are forced to live in the Pale because they're Jews, 'No Jews Allowed' are being lived here. How can you live with yourselves? How can I live here . . . and . . .and do nothing to change all of this? Can't you see your "charity" is only giving back a pittance to people who earned your wealth for you?"

Silence in the room. Liv stared at her mother, Aunt Sally, and Papa Helmut.

Helmut revealed a hurt demeanor when Liv was particularly rude and provocative. This time he asked in anything but a quiet, calm voice, "Where are you learning all of this? In your fancy private school? And who pays for you to go there? Your no-goodnik father who left you with nothing? No! Aunt Sally pays! Weisz Corporation pays. Do you want to go to school somewhere else? Live somewhere other than your comfortable home? You have nothing except your poor, abandoned mother and your Johannesburg family. Count your blessings, child. You are one of the most fortunate girls in the city."

Seething at the rebuke, Liv left the room and the house, and started to walk home. Soon a car pulled alongside her, Aunt Sally.

"Get in Livvie, its dark, you can't walk on your own. We'll go home now."

In the car Liv flung herself into her aunt's arms. She sobbed, "I'm sorry for what I said. Papa Helmut is right. I live like all the Weiszs do and I know it's wrong. But I don't know how I can live here knowing I'm enjoying a privileged life while others suffer?"

"None of it is fair Liv, life is not fair. There are rich people and poor people everywhere. What we do with our privilege and wealth is what matters."

"I didn't hear all this at school, I heard it from my friend

Natalie's father. He's a lawyer, he works to try and make things better for Africans. I admire him. And, no, I don't want to go to another school . . ."

"Don't worry sweetheart, as long as I'm around, you'll have everything you want. Remember, I'm your other mother."

Liv had never known what this claim signified. But she smiled gratefully at her aunt.

After this incident Liv kept almost silent at family gatherings she was forced to attend. She spoke only in monosyllabic answers. She tried desperately to exonerate her father, and her mother's family from any responsibility to them. The London Goldmans had severed relationships with Jane when she divorced Leo and chose to make a life in Johannesburg rather than London.

Liv still blamed her mother. If she wasn't so malleable and accepting, maybe her father would not have wanted to run away. Leo wrote to Liv in a rare, recent letter she had not shown her mother,

"I felt myself drowning in this devotion. I wanted a relationship with a person, a human being who stood up to me, who would yell and shout and demand things of me. I could not survive Jane's claustrophobic adoration."

Lately, almost guiltily, Liv wondered whether her father's failure to stay with them had something to do with an inability on his part to face up to his responsibilities, to accept the day-by-day existence of family life. According to her mother, he was a restless and demanding man.

In her torn dress, Liv paused at the door. She motioned for the boy who walked with her to stay outside. Should she ring the doorbell first? Sally was away. Her mother didn't expect Liv until much later. She didn't want to frighten her. Perhaps she was with Mr. Abelman? Liv smiled at the thought, amused at fantasizing about her mother and Mr. Abelman. She placed her key silently into the lock and opened the door.

From the lounge came the sound of soft music on the radiogram. She moved quietly to sneak unseen across the open doorway. Involuntarily she glanced into the room. On the sofa, she saw two pale globes of Mr. Abelman's buttocks, moving rhythmically up and down, up and down over her mother. She couldn't stop herself. She gasped in shock and embarrassment. Mr. Abelman collapsed in a heap. Her mother's muffled cry of guilt haunted her. Liv fled to her bedroom in silent terror and locked her door. She did not know how to face her mother in the morning. How long the young man waited for her, she had no idea.

The next day, her mother's face was ravaged and her eyes red. After that first glance, Liv would not look at her.

"We must talk about last night, Liv. You're old enough to know about such things. I'm not a nun, you know. Why is it all right for your father to have his affairs and lady friends going back way before you were born, but me, a divorced woman must live like a saint?"

"Leave my father out of this. He has nothing to do with this."

"You're wrong. He has everything to do with this." Jane started crying again. "You're old enough, so listen to me now! How do I tell you of the depths of my despair, the dreadful damage when I finally knew the unsavory truth about your father, a man I trusted and loved? How do I tell you that your father asked that you be named after one of his mistresses? How do I make you see that needing Abe Abelman has nothing to do with us, mother and daughter?"

Liv sat upright, rigid with shock. Her mother's outburst pushed her over the brink of adolescence, sent her tumbling not quite ready for it, into adulthood.

"It's unfortunate that you had a shock last night, but you're not the only person in the world who matters. What about me and my feelings, and Mr. Abelman and his embarrassment?"

Liv tried hard to suppress a giggle as the vivid mental picture of Mr. Abelman's buttocks flashed across her mind. Men are so ridiculous naked. Now that her mother was defensive, Liv was losing interest in her moral justifications of her affair with Mr. Abelman, but she was intensely interested in the revelation of her father's infidelity.

I'm named for his mistress. Of course, Oliva, his wife's name. Promiscuous parents.

She tasted the phrase, savoring its flavor. She decided she liked it. The thought made her different . . . them different. Am I going to be promiscuous, too? Does promiscuity run in my blood? A femme fatale, a grand lady with a salon filled with the nation's most powerful men kneeling around the couch from which I elegantly dispense my favors.

Liv regarded her mother. She saw the desperation on her mother's face, desperation at wanting Liv to understand, to forgive her, to love her. Liv's incipient feeling of compassion for her mother evaporated.

She makes it too easy for me. She asks to be trampled.

"It's okay I guess," she said with ill-concealed contempt. "No one needs to apologize. Unfortunate as you say. Have you, I mean, have there been others, others like Mr. Abelman?"

Her mother nodded her head bowed. Liv could not see if she was crying. She twisted the knife deeper. "You mean here in this house with me in my room, asleep?" Her mother nodded again. "Where was Sally?"

"Only when she's away. She's so busy now that Helmut is retiring, and she's assuming more responsibility. With you away at university I get so lonely, sometimes."

Liv nodded.

"How did you find out about Daddy?"

Jane jumped unexpectedly to her feet and rushed from the kitchen table, sobbing. Liv realized she had pressed too hard. Aware of a certain amount of remorse did not lessen her feeling of triumph. She was emotionally stronger than her mother. She could hurt her mother, and her mother could not hurt her. This power excited her and reinforced the awareness she had of herself as the mistress of her own life. She would never allow herself to love someone as much as her mother had loved her father. The hurt of his rejection emotionally crippled her mother forever. No one would hurt her that way.

Suddenly sitting in the kitchen confined her. She felt uncertain and uncomfortable pursuing her mother. Closeted with her guilt over having deliberately sought to tear at her mother's emotions, she now found herself incapable of reaching out to mend the damage.

Liv left the house and walked quickly in the bright sunlight. A few cars drove slowly past her. The only other pedestrians were Black people. She recognized a group of friends of her old nanny, Lena, and waved to them.

Liv walked along a wide pavement lined with plane trees and intersected at long intervals by driveways. Most of the houses were creeper-covered with wire mesh or wooden picket fences on their street boundaries. Large trees shaded luxuriant gardens alive with color and intertwining foliage and groundcover.

As Liv walked, she heard the occasional thud of a tennis ball being hit or the splash of water in a swimming pool. The constant hum of insects foraging in gardens hovered on the edge of her consciousness. Liv wanted to sit and chose the trunk of a large plane tree for a backrest. She leaned back, closing her eyes and sucked at a stem of wild grass. She could not avoid her mother's face, strained with tiredness and hurt, floating into her consciousness.

It would be good to be away from her and back at university in mid-January. She loved Cape Town. They lived too closely to one another in Johannesburg. She wanted to be on her own, away from all this emotion and hurting. Just by being herself she must hurt her mom because she was a part of him—a constant reminder. Liv thought she missed her father. She last saw him when she was fifteen. He was divorced again. She never met her half-brother. No one spoke about him to her.

Liv hoped her father was safe in London. She worried about the news of the Nazi war machine, of Hitler's vows to invade Britain. She hoped the war would be over quickly, and that the European Jews her family were so concerned about would soon be saved.

1960
LIV

. . . I am on my stomach worming my way through a narrow tunnel—a tiny artery deep under the earth. Crawling forward, I use my elbows as levers, the aperture lit by my dull and wavering headlamp now brighter than before. Unaware of the stones pushing against my boiler suit or the fecund smell of damp earth, I see speckled in the dried-blood colored soil, pebbles of gold ore. The red soil passageway remains close around me, but I can't breathe easily, and I gasp occasionally for oxygen. The passageway is less frightening now and more familiar.

I drop into the low cavern below the aperture. Peering into the semidarkness, I approach the skeletons. I step over one skeleton and almost tread on another, much smaller one. A girl's face with a frozen smile shocks me. Immediate recognition dawns, although I hadn't seen this face for thirty-five years. Nomzie. I draw back in sorrow and pity. Kneeling beside Nomzie's skeleton I stroke her whorled black hair that has so fascinated me when we were both five years old. Tears furrow my cheeks; I rock back and forth on my heels.

"Oh, Nomzie, Nomzie, I'm so sorry, so sorry." Choking on heaving sobs, I sit for a long time, soothing the beautiful black forehead of my friend one last time. Then, I turn to climb back into the artery, worming my way back to the light.

6:00 a.m.

Liv awoke with a start, her cheeks wet with tears. Nomzie was an unmourned death in her heart. The memories tumbled around her like waves, although she dreaded reliving them.

"She's Black, you're White."

Nomzie spoke in a mature woman's voice; "You didn't understand the labeling back then, but you understand the blind racism now."

Liv pulled the pillows over her head, trying to block further memories, wraiths from her dream. She would honor Nomzie and not forget again. She mused, What will happen today to the children in the townships? All the Nomzies?

A little later, once fully awake, she moved in the kitchen, filaments of her dream clinging to her still as she carried her first cup of tea to the porch at the rear of the house, overlooking the swimming pool.

Why now, Nomzie? So long buried, why now? Why on this significant day, this day that Sobukwe and Daniel, others, lead the protest marches countrywide?

In her nightdress and favorite silk dressing gown, feet bare, hair brushed off her face, she believed herself to be as young and fresh as her twelve-year-old self once was. But truthfully, she was more like the garden presently—a young matron, mature but still in full bloom in the last phase of summer. Bougainvillea and granadilla vines cascaded over the white-washed walls. The arbor buzzed with bees around vines bearing heavy bunches of grapes ripening to perfection, their sweet scent suffusing the air even at this early hour. But the scent did not mask the distinctive, pleasing odor from one of Liv's favorite plants, a scent she forever associated with the Highveld: the blue-and-white, yesterday-to-day-tomorrow shrub with the botanical name *Brunfelsia calycina pauciflora*, planted in abundance around the porch. Successfully burying Nomzie again, Liv yearned to concentrate her musings on Rosie, but she suppressed that desire. Today was for today: Sobukwe, Molefe, and the protest march.

While she sat in the early morning peace, appreciating (as she did every morning) the tea table inlaid with the tesserae she found on Corfu, Robert Sobukwe in Soweto prepared for his walk to the Orlando Police Station to surrender and be arrested. Tantalizing to imagine what might unfold on this day.

Around the country in many townships, other PAC—Pan African Congress--leaders and rank-and-file members geared up for their protest marches. Somewhere on the East Rand, Daniel Molefe readied himself for his march to the local police station. Or so she imagined.

Back in the kitchen, Liv tuned the radio to the supposedly independent SABC—South African Broadcast Corporation—an insidious mouthpiece for the apartheid government. In the top ten minutes of the thirty-minute news broadcast and before the business and farming news and sports and weather reports, no mention was said of any action by the PAC. Turning the dial several degrees, she located the BBC but, likewise, found no news about any antigovernment action in South Africa. By now Moses had entered the kitchen and he reboiled the water for his tea.

"Boil fresh water, Moses; the tea tastes much better."

This she suggested often, but Moses always shook his head. "Miss Liv, same breakfast?"

This morning ritual seemed farcical in its normalcy. "Thank you, Moses, same breakfast."

The daily gardener, a younger relative of the Moekena clan, handed the *Rand Daily Mail* to Moses at the kitchen door. He carried it to Liv back again on the porch. Not expecting to find anything about the launch in the paper, a quick glance confirmed her expectations. Moses appeared with a tray: soft-boiled egg, whole-wheat toast, Robertson's British marmalade, and a fresh pot of tea.

Liv smiled her thanks. If Moses knew of anything unusual on this agreeable morning, he did not break with the inherent discretion and tact she valued among his most singular traits. After eating, she returned the tray to the kitchen and surprised him engaged on the extension phone in animated conversation in Tswana. He hung up when she entered and looked guilty, perhaps because she found him talking or because she held the tray. He began to explain about the phone call, but Liv stopped him. Days before, without explanation, she had asked him not to speak on the phone unless an absolute necessity.

"It's okay." She added, sotto voce, "I doubt they speak Tswana."

Already feeling that this had been a long day, Liv wandered upstairs to shower. As she dressed, she glanced in her appointment book. She must change her choice of clothes. Third Monday of the month. Of course, the Garden Club meets today. Boring as the meeting usually became, it presented a perfect excuse to leave *Loeriebos*. What possible objection might the Security Branch harbor toward the Witwatersrand Garden Club? What excuse would other members find for Liv if she were not present? This month's meeting was a review of the final plans for their Rand Easter Show exhibit in two weeks.

"Do you want a ticket for the opening of the show, Liv? Weisz Corporation has several family boxes this year since they have so many exhibits. Prime Minister Verwoerd will do the honors."

The chairlady handed out tickets.

My absurd life; the juxtaposition of township protest marches and family boxes at an agricultural/trade exposition. Maybe Sobukwe's judgment was correct when he said people like me being part of the problem disqualified them as part of the solution.

"Yes, I'll take one." Liv laughed and added with sarcasm, "Why the hell not hear him speak? After all, he is the prime minister."

And soon, maybe, if Sobukwe's gamble pays off, not for much longer.

"Only one?" The chairlady regarded her with curiosity.

"Okay, two, in case my daughter, Marion, wants to attend."

After the garden club meeting, Liv let herself into *Loeriebos* and found Moses twisting a dishcloth in his hands.

"The phone, ringing and ringing all morning," he said.

On cue, the phone rang, and she hurried to her study. "Hello, Liv Weisz."

"At last, I've been trying to reach you for hours."

"Rosie?"

Preparing for an emergency, Liv tried to reconcile the fact Rosie phoned when she asked her explicitly not to call.

"Yes, yes, it's me. What's going on? Do you know anything? Have you heard any news? A cleaner here told me thousands of men are marching at Katlehong Township. His son lives there. He asked to use my phone. He took a chance with me as a Brit that I'm a sympathizer. His son told him there are squadrons of fighter jets and helicopters flying over the East Rand townships. Oh God, they're not going to shoot the marchers from the air, I mean. Terrible, terrible to massacre the people."

"Rosie . . ."

What to say, what to share? Moved by Rosie's concern, Liv heard tears in her own voice. "Whoa, okay. Take a deep breath."

What did Rosie say about military aircraft? If she had heard right, that was a heinous thought. South Africa military aircraft shooting at South Africans engaged in a peaceful protest march. Instead, she stumbled through a reply.

"I have no news. You know more than I do. I've just returned from a wholly ridiculous, inane, and under the circumstances, inappropriate, garden club meeting I attend every month." She added, "It's what people like me are supposed to do."

She spoke into the long pause and reiterated her concern. "You're so upset. Do you want me to come over? It's truly not safe for us to talk on the phone."

"No, I'm okay, it's just I'm worried about . . . about you, about the marchers, about this country. About what's going to happen—"

"Okay, sit tight. I'm coming over."

"No, please don't, not now. Don't come now. It may not be safe to travel with mobs everywhere. I want to see you. I do, desperately."

The "desperately" shook Liv, aware of momentous feelings beating at her heart. She took several deep breaths and stopped herself. Don't say it. No endearments.

"Phone me later. We'll decide on a plan. Maybe later I'll

have some news. And don't worry about mobs on the street. The marchers, the clashes with the police will be in the townships."

She visualized Rosie nodding in relief. "Okay, thanks for listening. I'm sorry I'm so emotional but this is shocking, so sudden. But I feel better now that I've heard your voice." Her voice dropped almost to a whisper. "I'm so worried about you."

"I'm fine, okay? Now, you be careful, okay? We'll speak later."

Almost in slow motion, deep in thought, and with a gentle touch, she replaced the receiver, certain now that Rosie loved her.

Around 6:00 p.m., a serious and intense Jaco arrived at *Loeriebos*. On most visits he ambled with a rolling gait when he walked on the driveway, but now, as Liv watched from a study window, he almost ran to the house. Moving fast herself, she opened the door.

He pulled her into a hug and held *her* as if for support, something he never did. They separated. Dismayed, Liv sensed the turmoil in him. "That bad, huh? Come in, tell me everything you know."

"Whiskey?" Jaco asked, agitated, holding a hand over his heart. His family and many friends expressed concern about his weight and lack of exercise. Aware of a frisson of apprehension, Liv poured him a large tumbler of vintage MacCallan whiskey.

"Ice?"

He nodded and sank into a plush, upholstered leather club chair, a gift from Papa Helmut. Gulping at the whiskey, he swallowed, grimaced, and fell back into the depths of the chair. After a long moment, he smiled his characteristic crooked grin.

"Much better. Excellent Scotch."

"Please, please, tell me, tell me. What's going on?"

Jaco sipped the whiskey. "Good news or bad news first?"

"I don't care."

"Good news. As you know from the radio, the largest protests were here on the East Rand and in Cape Town but also a good showing in Pretoria and Durban. The Prof and PK and about one hundred and thirty others are under arrest and in jail at The Fort. Thousands have stayed away from work all over the country."

His jaw tightened. "Take a seat. Here's the bad news."

Liv moved to the chair behind her desk. Why do people always say 'take a seat' when there's bad news?

"This is what we know. I have this from my friend at the *Mail*."

Liv nodded.

"Benjy Pogrund came by as I was leaving, shocked and almost incoherent. It seems it wasn't until late morning the *Mail* received the go-ahead from their board to cover the story. Benjy and a photographer drove toward Vereeniging, where they received reports of thousands of marchers. On the road, they encountered a column of Saracens. They followed them to the edge of the crowd around the police station in Sharpeville. Some people in the crowd spoke to Benjy, complaining about the *dompas*, the derogatory name for the hated passbook ID document, their low wages, and their living conditions. At around 1:15 p.m., unheralded, he heard gunshots from the direction of the police station. Chaos. People ran toward their car screaming, 'Watch out, watch out! They'll shoot you!' The police were firing at the fleeing crowds. Injured and dead people everywhere. After about ten minutes of gunfire, there was total silence. Total bloody silence.

"A retreating mob surrounded Benjy's car, and they started throwing stones and rocks, shattering the windows and denting the car with *knobkerries*, Zulu fighting sticks, and other sticks. Benjy was terrified; he thought he was about to die, so they took off across the open veld until they found a road back to Joey's. On the way, they passed truckloads of troops heading for Sharpeville and Vereeniging.

"It took hours for the emergency services to arrive. The telephone lines were cut, and the police refused to provide radio contact. They told Benjy, *'Dit is nie onse werk te hulp hierdie kaffirs.'* In other words, they said it is not our work to help the injured. The *Mail* is receiving phone reports of hundreds of dead and wounded, all shot in the back. Ambulance crews are still transporting the wounded to the native hospital in Vereeniging in non-European only ambulances with African ambulance drivers. Since the police are not offering any assistance, you can imagine what a slow process this is.

"There were also a handful of protesters shot dead in Cape Town but nothing as high as the numbers at Sharpeville. As I was leaving, Benjy called to say the *Mail* has obtained some photos, probably taken by Ian Berry at *Drum*. They are graphic and horrifying. Bodies collapsed on the ground as far as the eye can see. Gandar doesn't know if they can publish them—not because they are illegal—but because they're too graphic. He's scared of provoking violent outbursts all over the country. The townships can erupt in flames." He gripped the arms of the leather chair and leaned forward, lowering his voice. "We're on the brink of something never before experienced in South Africa."

Listening, but inattentive, Liv heard Jaco's words in a vague way. Her prescience was now unfortunately validated. The plan to goad the police into a violent response backfired. The PAC envisaged mass arrests, whippings with sjamboks, beatings with batons, unleashed attack dogs, maybe even tear gas, but not people shot in the back as they fled in terror. The hairs on her arms stiffened.

"Numbers?"

"Nothing definite yet. You can imagine the chaos. As I said, they're still moving people to the hospital and bodies to the morgues."

"Children?"

"Yes, shot, some killed, likewise, no numbers yet."

All the children, like Nomzie, killed by the police. Liv tried to focus her thoughts.

"The others ... Daniel Molefe?"

Jaco looked stricken. "Prepare yourself for the worst. He was a leader in Sharpeville. Probably among those standing closest to the fence at the police station."

Closing her eyes, Liv held her head in her hands.

I know how that body feels, I know of the life in that body.

Jaco added awkwardly, "I'm sorry. I know you are fond of him."

Eyes filled with tears of confusion, pain, fear, and anger, Liv stared at him. "He is ... was ... is ... my brother ... ubuntu, you know? Any news at any time, tell me. I'll do anything to help him and the others. Can I go to Daniel? Can I see him?"

In a grim voice, Jaco said, "You know that's impossible. A White woman allowed into a 'native' hospital? Never. We don't even know if he's alive or not. I'll try my best to keep you informed about Daniel and everything else."

Jaco rose from the leather chair, kissed her on the forehead, squeezed her shoulder, and left in haste while she sat motionless at her desk. He said he needed to hurry to Marshall Square Police Station to facilitate the legal work for Sobukwe and many others, some of his clerks were already working there for hours. As he waved from the door, the phone rang.

"Liv?"

Liv could barely hear Rosie's low-pitched voice, shy and reticent, unlike the emotional interchange in the morning.

"Rosie, thank goodness you phoned. Are you okay?"

"Yes, thank you. But I've heard rumors about something terrible happening at Sharpeville."

Liv warned her in a gentle tone. "Not now. Not on the phone."

"Oh Liv, isn't that old hat? Everyone knows about the boycott and marches. All the flat workers were dismissed early; they're frightened of the police stopping them on the way back to the townships." Rosie's voice became livelier. "Is it okay if I come over? I need to be with you, to see you. I won't interfere with you if you're busy."

Liv hesitated, but besides her worry about Daniel and terror at how the people's anger over the Sharpeville Massacre might unleash itself around the country, no reason existed for Rosie not to come. Yet layers and layers of caution restrained her.

Rosie pleaded, "I have to see you."

Liv hated causing Rosie to beg or to gain a false impression about her own desire. She was tired of caution.

"Yes, of course. Come now before it gets too dark."

A little later, Liv appeared silhouetted at the open front door, dogs at her side. Rosie drove over the curving driveway, her headlights cutting through the darkening twilight shadows. Locking the car, she walked with deliberate steps to the house, aware again of the ubiquitous scent of eucalyptus.

When Rosie reached Liv, she embraced her, holding her—at last—as close as possible. Liv reveled in feeling the whole length of Rosie's body. Rosie murmured into Liv's ear, "Safe, alive. I stirred myself into a panic imagining terrible things happening to you."

Still intertwined, Liv exhibited the presence of mind to kick the front door shut. Already she had switched on the back-porch light and locked the kitchen door.

Once they broke their embrace, Liv ran her hands through Rosie's hair and their murmured endearments swept away any remnants of Liv's reservations, along with recent memories of her tryst with Daniel. Her affairs with other lovers, a dear one in particular, was so long ago now.

"Wild veld fire meeting wild veld fire," Liv whispered. "This is what I always imagined."

She covered Rosie's face and neck with impassioned kisses and fell to her knees, almost in supplication, certainly in gratitude. Liv butted her head into Rosie's abdomen, her arms clasped around Rosie's thighs.

Rosie's ardor and desire were no less overpowering. Liv felt her sink to her knees and seize Liv's face between her hands, her eyes closed while she kissed Liv's welcoming mouth.

They stayed clamped like limpets until one of the dogs began to whine, and they collapsed in a heap on the floor, laughing, legs and arms entangled. Liv felt Rosie's practiced hand on her right leg, while she shifted her position sideways to balance herself on the elbow of her left arm. One of her hands covered Liv's knee then moved over her thigh, fingers pulling at the elastic of Liv's panties. Liv moaned in pleasure as Rosie stroked her inner thigh. A wet tongue licked Liv's face; she sat up laughing.

"Look at us, grown women on the floor. Come, sweetheart, I have a bed. I have lots of beds."

Dazed, Rosie stared at Liv, who offered her a hand. They helped one another to their feet and climbed the thickly piled carpeted stairs to Liv's bedroom. She shut out the dogs in the passageway.

Not removing her eyes from Liv, Rosie unbuttoned Liv's blouse. Liv shrugged it off, exposing the small brown birthmark on her left shoulder. Liv unclasped her bra, while Rosie shook off her own clothes. Rosie's skin was milky pale, Liv's tan, except where her bikini had left lines on her lithe body. Gazing with appreciation, Rosie crossed to her.

"Oh my God, you're so beautiful."

Liv stared into Rosie's eyes and murmured, "So are you, my beautiful darling."

Leading Liv by one hand to the bed, Rosie stretched on her side and shifted to the far edge, supporting her head in a cupped hand, while with the other she patted the bed in invitation. Liv stood, comfortable in her nakedness, staring at Rosie's body in the soft lamplight.

Despite her outer calm, as Liv gazed at Rosie on the bed, her mind as well as her body burned with lust and desire. It was eons since she had felt this level of sexual urgency. Exhilarating—abandoning myself for the first time to another woman—like diving off a cliff, somehow trusting the water to be deep enough not to crush my skull, my neck vertebrae, and the life out of my body. This is a death-defying moment, death of everything I've previously known about sex, even the most satisfying sex with someone I truly loved. A truth moment.

Liv dived, sinking into the moment and the bed, finding the water deep enough. Rosie's flesh was soft and smooth unlike any man's she'd ever stroked. Rosie's breasts felt strange in her hands but also familiar. They kissed again—long exploratory kisses until they felt familiar, too. Liv had longed for soul-filled kisses and had only found them once before.

Later, exhausted, they fell asleep in one another's arms, settled with naked limbs entwined.

The following morning dawned in late summer perfection and as always, accompanied by outpourings from the animated avian chorus. Awakening first, Liv thought she still dreamed, albeit a lucid dream.

How much about my life is now changed? Surely not all is a dream?

Rosie's arm lay draped over her breasts and their legs were still intertwined on the French milled cotton sheets. Sighing, Liv remembered the pleasures of the previous night. Needing the bathroom, she disentangled herself with care. Rosie shifted and muttered but did not wake.

Moving back to the bed, Liv sat silent, watching Rosie sleep and then slowly awaken, smiling up at Liv, mouthing, "Good morning."

Through the window, from the garden, they heard discordant male voices. Alert now, Liv's body tensed; Moses Moekena argued with Jaco Malan.

"Sorry, sorry, Mr. Malan. I can't let you in. Back porch light is on. No one can go inside."

"This is ridiculous man," Jaco shouted. "I haven't got time for this. Wake her up for God's sake. The country is about to explode."

"Oh dear." Sitting, Liv ran a hand through her hair. "I don't believe this." She turned to Rosie. "Sorry darling, but I have to speak to Jaco." She set a playful kiss on Rosie's nose. "There'll be more and more and more of this. One day we'll be able to stay in bed all day if we want but not today."

Liv strode to the bathroom and returned wrapped in her bathrobe. She leaned out of the window. "You can open the door, Moses. Show Mr. Malan to the study. I'll be down in a moment."

"For God's sake," Jaco bellowed. "I know where your study is. And hurry up!"

Liv handed Rosie a spare bathrobe and stared at her in

appreciation. "Sleep longer if you want. It's very early. Shower or bathe. But please stay up here until Jaco leaves."

Rosie drawled, exaggerating her well-modulated British accent. "Reality already? I'll take a shower. I'll wait here for you. I know these are extraordinary times but nothing is as extraordinary for me as what happened here last night . . ."

Hesitating, Liv blew Rosie a kiss. "You know, don't you, how desperately I want to stay in bed with you?"

Rosie smiled. "Go now. We'll talk later."

Liv entered her study with a glowing aura of well-being, her eyes shining and the pink marks on her neck noticeable. She wondered if Jaco noted Rosie's car in the driveway. Waiting for his sarcastic comment and determined not to let anything he said squash her joie de vivre, Liv heard him mutter under his breath, "Sometimes a person's own business is private." Then he spoke in a normal tone. "I see I woke you. Sorry to burst in so early but I have a helluva day ahead. You said, 'any news, any time.' I won't be back this way again today. Probably not for weeks. We found Daniel. He's in Vereeniging Native Hospital under police guard. He's been placed under arrest. He's stable and conscious but has lost a lot of blood. He has serious leg injuries. He, too, was shot from behind. In a round-up through Sharpeville last night, the police arrested seventy-seven people."

"Thank God he's alive!"

"We have many PAC supporters working at the hospital. It's easy enough to get information. Somehow or other I'll keep you informed, but don't use the phone. Security Branch is on high alert and troops are mobilizing everywhere."

Jaco moved to the door. "By the way, read the *Mail.* There

are photos but not those photos I told you about. Maybe Gandar made the correct call, maybe not. We'll see."

He rushed away.

Opening the newspaper, Liv began to read the front-page article. The *Mail* reported sixty-nine people killed at Sharpeville, among them eight women and ten children. Of the one hundred and eighty injured, only thirty were shot in the front as they tried to run from the barrage of police bullets. The injured included thirty-one women and nineteen children.

Oh, my country! Oh, the children, the children!

Liv placed the newspaper on her desk to read later and ran a hand through her mussed hair. This gesture reminded her that Rosie was upstairs in her bed.

Moses entered the study with caution. "Same breakfast, Miss Liv?"

She may as well begin to prepare Moses about Rosie. Daniel is alive, even though the whole world seems upside down. Will it matter if I burn more of my caution in the fire sweeping the country?

"Same breakfast Moses, thank you, but for two. We'll eat on the veranda. My friend's name is Rosie."

"Yes, Miss Liv."

Liv asked him scores of times over the years to drop the "Miss" when she addressed her, but this he seemed incapable of processing. If she surprised him now as to the change of their habitual morning ritual, nothing showed on his face or in his eyes. This was the first time she shared breakfast with anyone, aside from Marion. They accommodated many overnight guests, more so in recent weeks, but she did not join them for breakfast or even wave goodbye in the morning.

"Rosie is staying here until we see which road the government takes." Liv added, "If they are reasonable and talk to all the leaders, then those in jail and those who are banned or under house arrest can avert disaster. But if they shoot more people and the townships become ungovernable and nobody returns to work, everything might be much worse."

Moses nodded in agreement. "Much worse." He asked, "So I make the bed in the first guest room?"

"Yes, I think so. The best sheets."

He left the room, trying to remember the unfamiliar name. "Miss Rosie . . . Miss Rosie."

1960
LIV AND ROSIE

On Tuesday morning, the day after Sharpeville, Liv drove Rosie to the Hillbrow flat to collect clothes and other items for what they agreed would be an almost two week-long stay. After that neither of them knew what would happen.

In the car, Liv glanced at Rosie. In the aftermath of the shocking events at Sharpeville, her happiness struck Liv as surreal. She had been here once before—flutters in her stomach, lurches of her heart, lightheadedness as if tipsy, and the illusion of walking on air. She concentrated on her driving while a song played on the car radio. Cole Porter's, "I Am in Love" enhanced her mood, the lyrics so fitting.

"You like this song?" Rosie asked.

"One of my favorites," Liv replied, "but it has so much more meaning for me now."

Rosie nodded, "Me, too."

Their affair might last a week, three weeks, a month, three

months; it did not matter. Rosie's fright over Liv's well-being the previous day struck her as compelling. She must not lose Rosie. The timing of this affair was bizarre. They'd never spoken of her involvement in the struggle. Her activism might pose a huge roadblock.

"I am so in love with you, Rosie Lann." Liv's voice echoed in the car. "Every time I think of you, I am so hot with love and desire, I am burning, feverish."

Rosie smiled and nodding agreement, reached across to the driver's seat for Liv's hand. They were both quiet.

Back at *Loeriebos*, Liv sensed Rosie's disappointment when she showed her to the guest room across the hallway from her own bedroom.

Liv said, "Let's ease Moses into this slowly. He's old school. He's known me almost all my life." She embraced Rosie and their kiss lingered in the bright afternoon sun lighting the room like a stage spotlight. Liv added, "Darling, we'll spend every night together. We're not going to waste another moment of our lives apart. I'll never forget how you looked at me last night, how you felt and how you touched me. Your smile takes my breath away."

While accepting Liv's rationale, Rosie emphasized, "We've nothing to be ashamed of."

Liv nodded. "I'm not ashamed, sweetheart, I'm simply aware of Moses's possible discomfort. Give me some time. I'm feeling my way here."

All week, they read the newspaper reports on the Sharpeville massacre and the political pundits' prognostications on the future. They listened to the radio news, broadcast in somber tones by the familiar voice of the newscaster. There was no new news, aside from patently propagandistic reassurances in parliament from Dr. Verwoerd.

Rosie phoned her mother in London and left a message with the housekeeper, relaying that she suffered no harm during the "unrest." Sally called and while she sounded calm, Liv heard her perturbation and turned up the volume on the phone so Rosie could hear.

" . . . to try to shore up support for the South African pound and the Johannesburg stock exchange, me and other executives from Weisz Corporation, along with a group of leading industrialists and bankers, plan to fly tomorrow night to London and then New York. As you probably know, international and local investors have stampeded out of the stock market."

Sally's voice became more animated. "Maybe you want to come and stay in our Yeoville house? I worry about you all alone on the farm in Rivonia."

"I'm fine. I have Moses and the dogs. Besides Marion will be back soon from her trip. She'll be here next week . . . you have a tremendously important challenge. Have a successful trip. Let me know when you're back."

"I will. And Liv, if you have spare cash, buy properties or shares in large properties. We'll never see these prices again."

"Thanks for the tip. I may do that . . . for Marion."

Rosie sat erect in her chair. Liv replaced the receiver.

"Your daughter is coming home? With me staying here?"

"No, you'll have to leave. It's okay. Only a week, then she's back to university. She knows I often have houseguests."

Looking solemn, Rosie moved to kneel in front of Liv who sat in a leather armchair. Folding her hands onto Liv's knees, her meaningful stare startled Liv.

"Sweetheart, I was hoping not to have to do this yet, but maybe it is as good a time as any, seeing as, according to your aunt, and this urgent trip to New York, the country is in danger of economic collapse. We may all have to make a lot of decisions damned fast."

Attentive, Liv watched the shadows crossing Rosie's blue eyes as Rosie chose her words with care. "This is all new to you . . . loving another woman. You are excited and in love and experimenting."

Liv bristled, but Rosie continued. "It is a brave, new world for you, but let me spell this out. From the 'normal' heterosexual viewpoint—your family, most of your friends—people like me are perverts, immoral, and disgusting. We struggle with these prejudices all the time. You have no idea of the periods of self-hatred and self-loathing I contend with. I meet someone and fall in love, and we build a cocoon around ourselves and everything seems exactly as it should be. Then the affair ends."

Liv opened her mouth to speak, but Rosie held up a hand. "Hear me out. I know this sounds preachy, and you probably intuitively realize most of this already, but I do want to have my say.

"I understand it is not easy to give up heterosexual privilege. I've seen this before. I've been with heterosexual women. This is a secret world. Women like me in relationships with other women are known in the heterosexual world as 'friends.' You've probably heard people say with a snigger, usually women with their hands covering their mouths, 'Yes, they are friends, you know. Companions.' Are you prepared for the scrutiny, the malicious gossip, and the stigma? Are you prepared to watch people you know whispering to one another and realize they are talking about you? Are you prepared for conspiratorial silence? Are you prepared to be a pariah?"

Rosie paused. Liv nodded in response, struck by the irony of how she was already a conspirator and a pariah in certain circles. "I understand. I've thought about this."

Rosie looked skeptical. "I want you to know the whole picture from the outset. I love you dearly, Liv. From the moment I saw you again, after so many years at Jaco and Pauline's that January night, I've loved you.

"This is my world." Rosie ignored Liv's hand raised to interrupt her. "When I first arrived in Jo'burg, through asking discreet questions, I found out that two women's clubs exist, the only places to find a partner for the night—Chick Venter's in downtown Johannesburg or Spiders in Jeppe. Both venues are near Hillbrow."

"I know where they are. I pieced it together after our first lunch. I guessed that's another reason you chose to stay in Hillbrow."

Once again Liv appreciated Sobukwe's prohibitive advice on relationships: no ties. How was she to live two, parallel, secret lives now?

Liv leaned down with her head close to Rosie's upturned face and they kissed for an intimate moment. When they separated, they stared into one another's eyes searching out the secrets of their souls. They spoke together in low, sincere voices.

Liv implored, "Don't break my heart."

Rosie responded, "I am yours anywhere on this planet. I belong to you."

"I hear what you're saying. We will have many challenges."

Rosie swallowed, nodded, and repeated. "Never be ashamed of who we are."

Shaken at the power of her emotion, Liv mumbled, "The last thing in the world I want to do is hurt you."

The two weeks with Rosie passed in a haze at *Loeriebos*. For Liv, it was a strange limbo after months of being in the flow of the nervous energy of the PAC plans for the protests. She had no contact with anyone from the movement; all the leaders had been jailed, with strikes by Black workers in every city and dorp in the country.

On Wednesday, the press reported the call of the older, former ANC—African National Congress—leader Chief Albert Luthuli for a Day of Mourning on the following Monday, March 28. Jaco sent a note by bicycle messenger explaining his absence and that his work overwhelmed him. Liv read on, eagerly hoping he added some inside information about either Daniel or Luthuli's stand. But all she read was,

"Do you know of the extent of the veritable flood of criticism and outrage from foreign governments on the massacre? It's pretty amazing."

To Liv's surprise, Moses adjusted without qualms to Rosie's presence. She was an unprecedented guest, quiet and undemanding. He never commented on the undisturbed bed in the guest bedroom. Each morning after breakfast, Liv and Rosie completed their errands, then read all the newspapers. Liv attended her usual round of charity meetings and lunches; Rosie visited with friends in Hillbrow.

On Saturday afternoon, the radio broadcast an urgent newsflash—the government was suspending the Pass Laws for a short period. Of course, Liv surmised, the government acted in panic. "My God, Sobukwe might just win this. He bet the house, and he may take the house."

Even news of the government's intention to introduce the Unlawful Organizations Bill before parliament the following

Monday, banning the ANC and the PAC, did not dampen Liv's excitement. She knew the PAC (and she supposed the ANC) anticipated this ban for weeks. How would Daniel react? Where was Jaco?

Almost on cue, Sally called to say she had returned the previous night. "We helped stave off the economic collapse of the country with assurances from bankers in America and financial institutions in London and Europe. Now we need to get the strikers back to work."

Only twice before had Liv heard that hostile tone in Sally's voice. Liv did not respond but knew the longer the strikers stayed away, the closer the PAC would be to victory. This was the moment the government's stranglehold on the country may be broken.

After she spoke to Sally, Liv sensed a change in Rosie's mood. Her curious, journalistic mind surfaced but Rosie kept her voice smooth as velvet, "I think, darling, this is a good time for you to tell me of your own involvement in all of this."

Liv explained about meeting Jaco at university twenty years earlier, their becoming friends, and his influence on her. How, through him, she met young, Black leaders from Fort Hare University, including Robert Sobukwe, and for one of the few times in her life, interacted with Black people on a basis other than master and servant. She told how she began to see her life and the lives of her family and all Whites and Blacks in South Africa in stark terms of oppressor and oppressed. She had joined the Congress of Democrats after her divorce—without her family knowing—and still influenced by Jaco, whom she trusted with her life. In June 1955, she attended the famous gathering, the Congress of the People, in Kliptown, Soweto.

She told Rosie, "After that meeting, Sobukwe mounted his internal campaign in the ANC. He stood against what he saw as the leadership's failure to abide by the principles of Africanism inherent in the Action Programme that he, together with Mandela, and the other young, Black leaders agreed to at Fort Hare only a few years earlier.

The following year in London—arranged by Jaco—I met Daniel Molefe and we struck an immediate understanding and liking. He's like a brother to me." Liv reddened as she uttered those words, pushing down on her guilt. "I offered my services to Sobukwe and his breakaway PAC, aligning myself with Sobukwe's conviction that only a vigorous Black nationalistic movement can succeed in countering the White nationalism of the apartheid leader, Hendrik Verwoerd and his cronies. After a long period of reflection, Sobukwe accepted my offer of support. *Loeriebos* became a 'safe' house and Daniel and other PAC members a constant presence."

Rosie's eyes widened as the story unfolded.

"But no guests now, except you, of course, and you're not a guest . . ."

Liv continued. "The leadership is in jail; others like Daniel are under arrest but hopefully recovering in a hospital. Some are in hiding and many have left the country for Mbabane, Maseru, London, or other European cities. I may be interrogated. In fact, it seems inevitable—"

"Interrogation?" Rosie sounded horrified.

Sitting back in her chair, Liv waved her hand. "Yes, that's what they do to political prisoners. They try to break us, so we inform on one another. For some even the thought of interrogation is too much, so they rat out sooner. And no one wants to reach the stage of torture. But don't worry too much. I'm a small fish in this swamp. So, there you have it."

Rosie sat in silence for a long while, and when she spoke, it was in a subdued voice. "I feel as though I've stepped from a warm bath into icy water. I have many questions but not yet, not now. I feel as if I've awakened from a dream. And, yes, I know what you mean. You mean you may be detained."

Liv thought, detention! If I'm interrogated, what are the possible implications for Rosie? Am I prepared to go to prison for my beliefs? Involve Rosie? Involve Marion? Sally, and my family? We're almost at that "choice-less choice" moment unless I skip the country. First time that's ever even been a possibility for me. I've lost so much already, and now there's even more to lose, particularly Marion. But not Rosie? Surely not Rosie? She says she is mine, anywhere on the planet. I love her, but can I trust her?

"Thanks for sharing." Rosie spoke into the silence. "I guessed a great deal of what's transpiring. I've wanted to hear it from you. It's easy for me to accept secret lives. That makes us the same but also different." Rosie shivered. "I'm cold now. I'm changing into warmer clothes. Give me time to think about this."

At breakfast on Sunday, the day she was to return to Hillbrow, Rosie began a faltering response. "You frightened me yesterday with all the talk of interrogation and detention. You don't like trusting anyone, but you have made yourself vulnerable to me. Why? Do you know?"

Mute, Liv shook her head.

Rosie continued. "If you ever unravel your motivation, let me know, okay? I don't like surprises."

Liv nodded. "Good to know that . . . about surprises."

"You see how I focus on us and love and not a word about politics. I realize how deeply you love your country, and like you, I want everyone to share in her bounty. Political actions I leave to you and your allies. And yet you must know I will support you in any way I can whenever you need me."

Amazed Liv shook her head. "Come here, wonderful creature."

Playful now, she offered Rosie a small piece of toast. Rosie opened her mouth and Liv placed it on her tongue. Rosie chewed, while they gazed at one another in silence.

Later, after Rosie drove away, when Liv retired to her study to write checks for her monthly accounts, she found an envelope on the desk with her name in Rosie's small, clear handwriting.

> Darling, here are the lyrics of one of our favorite
> Cole Porter songs, "I Am in Love."
> I adore you.
> Love, Rosie

Liv's heart warmed with appreciation. Rosie fulfilled every aspiration of love she had ever longed for. But something was still missing—only an echo, never an answer.

During the week Marion was home, Liv never broached the subject of Rosie, but one morning at breakfast Marion startled her.

"You've had a lover here, right?"

Liv taken aback, answered "How do you—?"

"Moses told me. He seems terribly shocked. He said you sleep together."

Memory flashed in Liv's mind's eye of Mr. Abelman's buttocks over her mother's body on the sofa. Of early school mornings, often seeing but not truly assimilating her mother and Sally in the same bed. She had an inkling of what Marion was trying to process now: an earthquake in her perception of her mother.

"He said your lover is a woman." Marion looked quizzically at Liv. Another memory flashed. Years earlier, Liv saw Marion's father look at her with that same expression. Every year that went by, Marion looked more and more like her father, so familiarly comfortable now that Liv never remembered their likeness until moments like this.

"You look more and more like your father, Marion, especially when you look at me that way. Yes, I had someone special staying here with me. Moses should not have said anything. He knows that. I'll have to speak to him."

"You're not going to make a mess of your life, are you?"

Liv hesitated. "I think I know what I'm doing, but now I'm not so sure."

"Am I going to meet her?"

"Maybe, maybe not."

Liv left the room abruptly. The cocoon she and Rosie had inhabited burst into fractured pieces of ephemeral emptiness. She saw clearly now the impossibility of introducing Rosie to Marion, to her family, and into the life she so carefully built since her divorce.

More secrets; she couldn't bear the shard of another secret in the mosaic of her life. Her life was too intertwined with her daughter, the Weisz family, with her friends, to say nothing about her activist comrades. She had lived with secrets for too long, secrets about Marion, cloak and dagger activism, her philanthropic persona. She scarcely knew who she was in the world. All she knew for certain was she had loved Paul, she loved Marion, Aunt Sally, Jaco, and she loved *Loeriebos*, *Milkwood*, and being rooted in South African soil. Much of the rest was mirrors and lies. Her love for Rosie filled a desperate need. And she was grateful for the opportunity to love Rosie, but as Rosie had asked, can it exist in her heterosexual life.

The next day, Liv phoned Rosie from a phone booth in the village shopping street. Rosie sounded startled to hear Liv's voice, and then her tears.

"Rosie, you're correct. What you said to me about how

difficult this relationship can be. I can't do this anymore. I love you but I can't do this." Liv stumbled through the words. "It's all too complicated. I'm not able to commit to anything with you. I live in secrets, and I can't deal with another secret now. Please believe me when I say I love you. But also, please don't try to contact me. You've given me a wonderful gift . . . yourself . . . but I can't give you myself. Please believe me when I say this has nothing to do with you and everything to do with me. I was swept away by your need of me. I wanted you in every meaning of that word, but I simply can't do this. My heart, Rosie, my essential heart, belongs to someone else, long ago in my past."

Liv's voice trailed off. Liv could not believe what she had revealed to Rosie. What a time for her long-ago love to re-surface like a ghost.

Frantically, Rosie said, "But Liv. Please don't do this . . . not like this on the phone. We can work out something . . . some arrangement. We must talk."

"Goodbye Rosie." Sobbing, Liv replaced the receiver on the phone hook. Someone knocked impatiently on the glass door of the phone booth.

The following day, March 30, before dawn, under emergency regulations promulgated in the declaration of a state of emergency around the country, Jaco Malan and eighteen hundred other people of all races were arrested and held in detention without trial. This event, although not unexpected, came as a shock. Liv anticipated her detention in the next round of arrests. Her demeanor serious, she called Marion to her bedroom. She explained about Jaco's arrest, and the implications for her.

"As for my role in the struggle . . ." Liv cautioned Marion. "Darling, they come for you in the wee hours of the morning when you are most disoriented. I'm waiting for this to happen. In my clothes closet is a canvas gym bag. The list of stuff in there is ..." Taking a small piece of paper from her nightstand drawer, she read, "Toiletries, sanitary towels, medications, and analgesics, several changes of underwear, writing paper and pen, and a couple of books. Although they may not let me read or write."

Marion paled. Seeing her distress, Liv hugged her. "If they have taken Jaco, darling, they can take me. Our family influence can only afford so much protection and then a line is crossed. These are extraordinary times. This is one of the consequences of my actions and decisions."

"It may not happen, but I want to prepare you. Hide this somewhere." Liv handed Marion a small piece of paper. "If they take me, phone this number and tell whoever answers my name. Only my name. Then phone Aunt Sally immediately. Here is her emergency number. She knows little about my political activity, about any of my life. But she's a canny person, she's probably guessed at some of it. The important thing is Sally must know I've been arrested and under what circumstances. She's my only confidante in the family."

"What about me? You've never told me anything about all of this. Don't you trust me?"

"I'm so sorry, darling. You're still so young, I wanted to protect you. There are many people involved. We must protect one another. Not a word to anyone, okay?"

Marion nodded, looking devastated and unhappy. "What happens if I'm not here when they come to take you ... away?"

"Moses will call you."

Liv's mind rioted with thoughts and emotions echoing the very state of the country itself, teetering on the verge of the abyss.

1942
LIV AND JOHN

On her stomach worming her way through a narrow tunnel—tiny artery deep under the earth. She'd been here before, crawling using her elbows to lever forward, the aperture dimly lit by her dull and wavering head lamp. She feels stones pushing against her boiler suit, smells the fecund odor of damp earth, sees the dried blood, red soil passageway so close around her. She cannot breathe but gasps for oxygen. All frightening and all familiar.

Through the widening opening she anticipates the cavern appearing. She'd not come this far before when she encountered Nomzie. Raising her body with care she crawls and then finds if she stoops low, she can kneel at the opening and peer into the semi darkness. The drop to the cavern floor about four feet. Hardly an abyss. Maneuvering her body into the drop, she half-falls, half lowers herself to the muddy surface. Relieved to stand, although stooped—her head touches the cavern roof—she stares into the semi-dark. Clearly, she distinguishes a shape on the muddy floor opposite her. Apprehensively she moves towards it; a skeleton, cemented into the sediment but with a recognizable human head. She draws back in horror at the wide-open blue eyes staring lifeless at her. She thinks she hears a voice, "You could've saved me. Someone could have saved me. I bled to death!" Muffling her scream, Liv turns to clamber back into the artery, to worm her way back to the light.

Twisting and turning in the bedsheets, Liv awoke from the nightmare. She heard herself muttering "Natalie ... Natalie ... Natalie." Why Natalie? Why now?

Slowly she returned to full consciousness. Predawn darkness loomed outside the window with diaphanous strands of the dream still clinging to her memory. She rolled herself in the top sheet to wick the sweat covering her body. It was the same recurring dream, but this time she brought back with her the presence of Natalie, her closest friend during their high school years.

Natalie was tall and lithe with long honey blond hair and shining blue eyes. Energetic, clever, popular, Liv attached her star to Natalie's after a group of girls surrounded Liv and shouted anti-Semitic slurs at her. One saying, "Hitler is right! Wealthy Jews, all Jews, are impure. You breed to destroy the purity of the White Christian race!"

Natalie raced to the group and pushed them aside. She stood alongside Liv, ashen and in tears, and placed an arm around her shoulders. Natalie shouted, "I'm not Jewish, I'm Christian, like all of you are supposed to be. Where are your Christian morals and values? Stop spreading conspiracies and nonsense. You are all from wealthy families otherwise you wouldn't be at this school. Liv is one of us."

The ringleader of the clash was expelled, and the others punished. This incident cemented Liv and Natalie's friendship. Liv clung to the belief, as long as I'm with Natalie, I'm not an outsider.

Then, in their final year, Natalie found a new boyfriend, Carter. Carter was forbidden fruit, older, a recent university engineering graduate, a glamorous attraction.

Liv said to Natalie, "Remember we swore we'd always tell one another the truth? Listen to me. Carter is too experienced for you. He'll lead you into all sorts of wild temptations. Remember you're a schoolgirl like me."

Natalie and Carter's car accident and death shocked the school community—students, parents, faculty. It even made the daily newspapers.

A storm, a wild Highveld thunderstorm robbed them of their future. The deserted country road after midnight was slick. The car spun out of control. Natalie, at seventeen, did not have a license, yet she persuaded Carter to let her drive or at least her body was found on the steering wheel side of the car, flung from the low-slung sports car when it slammed into a large rock at the roadside. Disobeying her parents, Natalie had snuck out the house after midnight, as she often did to meet Liv. But this time it was Carter with his Italian sports car. No one knew she wasn't at home until the police arrived in the early morning.

The postmortem showed Natalie and Carter had both been alive for several hours before they bled to death from their injuries. In the dawn hour, a driver in a van had passed the wreckage and reported the accident. Liv could never forget the capriciousness of that reality. They bled to death; they could have been saved.

At the funeral, Liv would not go near the grave. Instead, she stood towards the back of the large crowd of mourners, and remembered Natalie's laughter, the way they would laugh so hard that tears came, while others looked on in amazement.

She remembered the pranks they devised, some they even implemented. They were known as the rebels among their cabal of friends.

Liv and Natalie were co-captains of the school's swim team. Liv relived the elation of sharing cheering duties with Natalie, urging on their teammates. That final year of high school, their team won the provincial title for the first time in school history. Natalie, even more than Liv, was so proud. Such promise lay ahead for them both, a golden future. They had sworn to be friends forever. Liv felt Natalie's loss as if a part of herself was missing. She loved Natalie; they had sworn to share every particular of their lives—always. But Natalie betrayed her: her loyalty stolen by a fickle decision and a wild boyfriend with a sports car. Trust broken by illicit temptation. Liv realized that Natalie knew when she agreed to a joy ride with Carter, she was simply making the wrong choice; that is why she never told me.

Liv and their close-knit friends were inconsolable for weeks. Liv's despair shot through with anger hidden amid her sense of loss. She attended school at irregular intervals. Drunk at parties, she allowed herself to have sex with whomever asked her. Jane and Sally were distraught watching Liv fall apart.

After several weeks, she found the courage to visit Natalie's mother who begged her to "pull herself together," adding she now must live her life for Natalie, too.

Liv had trusted Natalie. Trust was not easily given. In some ways Liv found the broken pact harder to accept than Natalie's death. The shattered trust of Natalie's disloyalty and Liv's guilt at not trying harder to warn Natalie about Carter, heightened the reality that she was alive and Natalie dead. They had vowed to share everything.

In time, Liv settled, and studied hard and matriculated—for Natalie.

Did I fulfill my responsibility, then? I doubt I'll ever know the significance of accepting the responsibility of living my life for someone else. Thank goodness those memories are deeply buried. Mourning Natalie, mourning our loss of innocence, learning that actions have consequences, and mourning the finality of life-depriving death.

At seventeen, she had experienced and processed her losses, unlike that other time, that other death, Nomzie's death, so deeply buried she could only remember scant details or feelings.

But why now, Natalie?

Isaac Ivans' funeral was held at West Park Cemetery on a warm Sunday morning. A large crowd of mourners gathered, including not only the Ivans and Ivansky families but many of the Weisz family. Helmut and Isaac had been friends and active together in Zionist causes for many decades.

Isaac was buried in a plot reserved for those Jews who played significant roles in developing and sustaining the Jewish community and Jewish identity in South Africa. He was a leading voice of South African Jewry, and he even had General Jan Smuts' ear.

After the service, the crowd filed passed the grave and shook hands with a line-up of the Ivans family. Among the initial group of mourners was Helmut Weisz, who had traveled from Plettenberg Bay, accompanied by Sally, and Liv, who only agreed to be present because Helmut particularly wanted her with him.

When her turn came, Liv smiled enigmatically at Isaac's grandson, John, who had his head bowed. He glanced up into Liv's dark eyes filled with naughty liveliness. He held her hand tightly.

Liv murmured the age-old words, "I wish you a long life."

That evening, the first night of shivah, much to Helmut and Sally's surprise, Liv asked if she could accompany them. Helmut, in his chauffeured car, drove them. Jane was not feeling well and didn't accompany them—not an unusual occurrence.

"She's sensitive," Sally explained often to Liv.

Liv hated her mother's weaknesses but this time she surmised that maybe Mr. Abelman was coming to comfort her. She did not voice her thoughts but rather remembered John's strong grip while shaking her hand. She wondered from where the strength arose from such elegant, long fingers.

Helmut's teasing voice cut short her reverie. "Suddenly an interest in sitting shivah, *meine meidel*? My girl? Or could it be an interest in young Mr. Ivans, recently returned from Cambridge University?"

Liv blushed, pleased the interior of the car was dark.

Sally patted her hand and whispered, "Don't engage him in an argument. Not now."

"Whatever you say, Papa Helmut."

After the shivah prayers, John left off speaking to a group of people and sought for her. He held out his hand.

"John Ivans," he said, in an accent obviously cultivated at Cambridge.

"Liv Weisz," Liv said firmly, as they shook hands.

"Yes, of course," said John with a touch of sarcasm. "Weisz and Ivans. How unexpected. Who would have thought? I like you, Miss Weisz. I want to know you better. I'll phone you and we can set up a date." He saw the consternation on her face and turned back to face her. "Sorry for being so direct. I have a lot on my mind right now. Is it okay if I phone you?"

Liv nodded, for once at a loss for words.

On their first date, a week after the funeral, Liv asked about John's grandfather. "He worked a lot with my Uncle Helmut on Jewish charities and other philanthropies. Papa Helmut always spoke so highly of him."

"Yes, he was an amazing man," John replied slowly. "I've heard him described as a beloved visionary and philosopher. On the other hand, my father, Max, is a pragmatic businessman. Isaac and I share a bond greater than blood—our love of intellect, music, history, great literature, and philosophy. It was at Isaac's insistence that I was schooled and groomed for Cambridge in England.

"I was at our family home, *Duiwel's Hoogte*, near Cape Town when I received the call that he had died."

"Duiwel's Hoogte" murmured Liv, "Devil's Heights. Odd name for a family home?"

"Isaac bought it for a song in the 1920s," said John. "A two-hundred-year-old Huguenot farmstead in a valley in the Hottentot Holland range. Seemed remote then but with the new roads now, close enough to Cape Town. The house itself has been completely renovated but retains a lot of the old features. It's named after the most prominent peak in that area. After my first hike to the top of *Duiwel's Hoogte* with Zeidah Isaac—if I remember correctly, I was six years old— we really bonded. A bond that has and will last all my life."

"You like old things? Like old buildings?" asked Liv. "So, do I."

John nodded. "At first I was not sure I wanted to return to Johannesburg for the funeral. But, I guess, I'm still beholden to traditional Jewish burial rites. I knew it obligatory for an adult grandson to be at his grandfather's graveside, especially the oldest son of an oldest son. I remembered an image of a small, frightened boy of ten whose mother had recently died, wrapped in the protective tent of his grandfather's tallis, swaying to ancient prayers and words of mourning.

"The memory struck me now that Grandpa Ivans was dead. He used to say, 'You must be a bridge of knowledge to your children, Janeka. You must teach them of the past of their people, the persecution, the shtetels, the first pioneers to this land, and the traditions and practices of our people.'

"I told him, 'You belong to a time long gone, Zeidah Isaac. This war is changing the way the whole world thinks and operates. The bridge must go both ways, from the past to the present, but also from the present to the future.'"

John smiled at Liv and placed a hand lightly over one of hers. "Now I know I was there to meet you. If we were both not at the funeral, it's unlikely we would have met—"

"How so?" Liv pulled her hand away.

"I'm only in South Africa because of my father and his motor car plants, which are now designated strategic industries. The plants produce parts for tanks and other military equipment. Max said he needed me. So, I left Cambridge and my friends. And my music studies."

John shrugged. "We're planning to move some plants to Cape Town, and Durban. Close to the docks. Easier for transport to the war zones."

Liv and John chatted amiably. Inevitably the conversation turned to the war and the plight of European Jewry. They both had family and friends fighting the Nazis in North Africa and elsewhere, and they both had relatives in Eastern Europe and Palestine.

John said, "I remember a recent conversation with my father concerning the tragic plight of European Jewish refugees turned away from the United States, Britain, and other European countries, as well as Middle Eastern countries.

"Max said to me, 'Never forget. South Africa let in five thousand Jews. Not enough, but some. And Australia, too, has taken some thousands. Smuts' doing. But we, too, have been warned. If these Nazi-sympathizing apartheid Nationalists ever come to power, if they ever vote Smuts out of leadership, the Jews will be in danger here.'"

Liv listened thoughtfully.

"I told him, it's the Blacks they're after not the Jews. They fear the Blacks, their numbers, the fact that the land belongs to them. And they're frightened of losing their own sense of identity. They're only what they are unto themselves. You know what I mean? Nowhere else in the world does anyone speak Afrikaans. Nazi-sympathizers, yes, but do they have the will to impose their racial attitudes on a whole country?"

He asked Liv, "What do you think about being a Jew in South Africa?"

Liv answered, smilingly, "I think its late, and I have an early appointment tomorrow. Can we leave now?"

John paid the bill for their meals. She didn't share her thoughts, but after previous conversations with Papa Helmut, she had formed her position. As more and more news reached them of the tragic plight of their brethren in Europe, South African Jews were thankful for the foresight of their forebears, who took the plunge to leave the shtetels for this shining land. But she, like so many others, wondered whether that sheen was an illusion. If the Nationalists ever came to power, would they not be persecuted again like their antecedents because of their faith and being aliens? On the other hand, they worried how much longer the Black man would remain a sleeping giant in South Africa. And what would he do to the Jews when he awoke and found them waxing rich in his land?

As they walked out of the restaurant, John said rhetorically, "After the war, I don't have to stay in South Africa. I can live anywhere! The United States, Australia, Tahiti?"

Liv laughed at his whimsy.

John saw Liv back to the front door of her Yeoville home. She hoped he wasn't about to kiss her and was pleased when he did not. Being with John made her feel coy and virginal with a dreadful lack of self-confidence she thought she had overcome years ago. He was returning to Cape Town and had told her to be in touch when she was back at university in January. Maybe she would, maybe she wouldn't. He frightened her a little. He was a driven man, forceful and direct sometimes to the point of rudeness. Maybe that's why recently she had dreamed of Natalie. A prophetic warning not to be involved with someone older, with more life experience, someone who would put her in danger, as Carter did to Natalie. Metaphorically, he may bleed her to death.

He's too mature, too experienced for me, and too strange, she rationalized.

A year passed. Liv completed her legal studies in Cape Town. She had switched from liberal arts to a law degree. She did not contact John, nor had he pursued her.

Working now at Weisz Corporation, a junior lawyer in the legal office, her days were full. On her return to Johannesburg, she had found Micah Weisz, Sally's cousin and her second cousin, and his wife, Gerda, visiting from Palestine. They came for a short stay every several years to see Micah's parents and attend the inevitable family get-togethers. Travel was easy for them, even in wartime, as they had diplomatic passports, no children, and both traveled constantly on Zionist business.

Liv had become more tolerant of her family as she grew older. A strange sense of family loyalty interested her; observing how the family navigated crisscrossing currents of relationships flowing on waves of familial love, jealousy, suspicion, and one-upmanship.

Her close circle of friends she cultivated from outside the family. She avoided family gatherings whenever she could, but she couldn't avoid the lunches, teas, and dinners with Micah and his wife. Honored as a Palestinian pioneer carrying the Weisz family name to far-off Palestine, "Micah Weisz, the Palestinian zealot" was a celebrity in the family. On the kibbutz, Bernard, Sally's brother, (whom she'd never met) languished in Micah's shadow.

At a large family gathering to welcome him, Micah singled out Liv for conversation. She stared into the flinty dark eyes of a man about her height. Micah, approaching fifty, appeared no older than a man in his thirties, his body trim and sporting a deep Mediterranean tan.

"You watch them all with such an air of detachment. I want to know why?"

Liv laughed. "It's that obvious? There's no easy answer to why I feel detached, but I do. I'm happier now that I'm older to be a part of the Weisz family, but often I don't really feel as if I belong."

Micah nodded.

"Your cousin, Sally, felt the same way you do when she was nineteen. Looking at you now, I see a distinct resemblance."

"I live with Sally and I love her. And, my mother, of course, I love her, too, but we have a difficult relationship. You and Sally grew up together in the Yeo Street house. Were you close?"

Micah nodded. "Oh, do tell me about Sally. No one else will. They all clam up, mutter about a tragedy."

But Micah's eyes clouded, and his mouth set in a hard line. He shook his head. "Sorry, Liv, some things are best left undisturbed. Too much muddy water there. But if anyone can, your mother will be able to tell you the story. She knows Sally better than any of us. Ask her sometime."

As he glanced speculatively across the room to where Sally stood, he remembered the night, so many years ago, when she first crawled into his bed. He wondered if she remembered. She was always cordial to him but cold and distant.

Micah drifted away to speak to another relative. Liv vowed to ask her mother about Sally. Jane had kept that part of her life tightly locked away. Musing, leaning against a wall, Liv resumed her pose of detachment as she watched her family.

The Weisz family epitomized the ideal of *tzedakah*—ethical obligation. Not only in the community, where large sums of Weisz monies found their way into the accounts of various Jewish organizations and institutions and where large amounts of Weisz energies were expended on various boards of these same organizations and institutions but also within the family, too.

Liv vowed when she was a girl, she would never use the family money directly. No matter how many difficulties she encountered, she would study on scholarships and grants she earned. She did earn scholarships and grants, unaware that Sally, a major donor to the university in Cape Town, along with other Weisz Corporation donations, were instrumental in that process.

Thank God for my mind, she often said to herself, otherwise I would never have afforded university with their money, I would have become a hairdresser or a tea waitress at John Orr's, rather than allow the family to buy their way into heaven through me.

Only Helmut, while never overtly mentioning tzedakah, presumed on some sort of familial right, some familial authority over Liv. But he did so with a twinkle in his eye. The family knew he doted on her, the female image of his one failure—his brother Leo.

Not the only failure, of course, Helmut reminded himself. He had another child he never met, man or woman now, ten years younger than Sally. As Marierentia had requested, he had never sought her out or made inquiries about her farmer-husband, but he thought of her and his child often.

Best to leave it alone. My child is possibly living in the Orange Free State, the Afrikaner heartland, learning to hate Jews.

On a shining and clear but cold Highveld winter's dusk, Liv and Sally returned from work and entered the driveway of their Yeoville home.

Liv noted with slight dismay the presence of John's motorcar. She saw him through the window with curtains still undrawn, chatting to her mother. He rose from his chair as she and Sally stood in the doorway to the living room and half-smiled at her from under his scowling, dark eyebrows. He seemed almost shy, overcome at seeing her again. Liv composed herself and heard her cool, amiable responses to his welcome.

"Ah, Liv!" exclaimed her mother fluttering at the door. "I'm pleased you and Sally are home. John's been telling me about his father's retainer in Cape Town. Alpheus, right? Yes, well, Alpheus's family have been with the Ivans for years now. You know, the usual story. Alpheus's. Joined the ANC, whatever that is, and was arrested returning from a meeting night before last, after the curfew, you know. So, John did some hard talking on the telephone today."

She turned to John. "Why you didn't just let him sit in jail,

John, I don't know. Teach these natives a lesson. Now that the war is almost over, they're thinking freedom is coming."

John lifted a sardonic eyebrow in Liv's direction. "No, Mrs. Weisz. I don't think you'll ever know why I don't let someone like Alpheus sit in jail."

The disconsolation on Jane's face thrilled Liv. John's remark to her mother was the first real point of connection she felt with him. He understood about people like her mother; they were on the same side. Speaking pointedly to John, Sally changed the subject by commenting on the latest war news they heard on the car radio.

She told him, "We have cousins fighting in North Africa against Rommel and his troops. Some were captured at the battle of El Alamein. We have heard about a few, sadly two dead. We think others were captured and are now in prisoner-of-war camps in Italy."

John nodded. "My two best friends from Cambridge enlisted. They fought in Eastern Europe. I keep in touch with their families. So far, no news of either." He muttered almost to himself, "I won't accept 'missing in action—presumed dead.'"

Liv asked, "It's been a while, John. Where have you been?"

"Yes," he grinned crookedly, "I apologize. I've been mainly in Cape Town, totally pre-occupied with helping my father and his company switch some of the plants from car production to tanks. And then organizing their transport to North Africa. We are running smoothly now. And you?"

"Oh," Jane answered for her, "we're so proud of her. Completed her law degree with honors. She's working at corporation head-quarters now—"

"So, you're a lawyer?"

Liv steered John firmly by the elbow and walked him to the library.

Later that evening, Liv told her mother and Aunt Sally they had been "catching up." She anticipated the inevitable question with annoyance. "Yes, we have a date Saturday night."

As Liv lay in bed, she thought, if I encourage John, form a relationship with him, marry him, I'll be as wealthy as any in the Weisz family.

When she agreed to see John again, she did so more as a gesture of ascendancy over her mother than because she really wanted to be in John's company. Liv found John's style agreeable— how he dealt with waiters, managers, and officious petty officials who resented wealth in the young. Liv enjoyed the best seats, the finest restaurants, and good wines. She never declined John's gifts of French perfume, pure silk scarves, and leather-bound books.

He taught her about music, those lessons she enjoyed the most of all his gifts to her. He played the violin superbly, making her laugh and cry with Paganini, soar with Beethoven, marvel at Bach, and wonder at the genius of Mozart.

"How often I've cursed and blessed my mother for putting that instrument in my hand. She taught me my first, faltering fingering, and then, Fritz Benjamin was my teacher. Later I learned from among the world's best teachers in classes at my English public school and then at Cambridge. And during idyllic summer holidays in the mountains near Innsbruck at the home of Gustav Krinsky, prince of the violin. I was honored a place at the maestro's feet as a favor to my deceased mother, herself a former pupil of Maestro Krinsky.

"Oh Liv, those hours and hours of practice brought rage, frustration and moments of sheer joy known only to those of us who've scaled the peaks. The moments when the violin vibrates with the universal essence of pure sound. I could have had a career as a concert violinist. But deep within myself I know I don't have the ultimate dedication, the will, to subjugate myself and meld John Ivans the man into John Ivans the violinist."

When they made love, most often on the luxuriously piled carpet in his living room, the strains of Scriabin, Ravel, or Rachmaninoff drifted over their bodies. Lovemaking with John was satisfying enough. His body was hard and powerful—an accomplished mountaineer—and he was a careful lover, generous, waiting for her, which was more than she could say for the others before him. And she felt sated and satisfied. If she wondered at her lack of any heightened emotional response within herself, beyond a tenderness in the afterglow of their passion, she dismissed such expectations as the whimsy of poets.

One evening she agreed to John's request that they dine at his father's house. Liv noted the tension in his hands, his clenched jaw line, and the deep frown on his forehead. She didn't know what to expect. Max was well-known in the Jewish community, but unlike his father, not a national spokesman for the Jews in South Africa. He surprised her as an energetic man, candid, and friendly. He never remarried after his beloved Alice had died. Liv noted the concern and love with which he regarded John.

Liv noted, too, the richness of the furniture, the elegance and taste of the fittings in his home. There was warmth in this home. Above all, being with John suited her. She liked the way he compartmentalized his life. Within that framework, she would have freedom to live her own life and do what she wanted.

Liv wanted to travel and once the war was over, she envisaged many voyages to far away exotic places . . . places she read of, where others were inspired to write, paint, or create music, independent.

She wanted three or four children. Life could be wonderfully satisfying with John. If she didn't love him or if she felt a lack where she knew something positive should be, perhaps, in a way, that was good. It enabled her to view their relationship dispassionately not blindly.

She concluded life with John would be just right: suitable, practical, and civilized. Marrying John would be a most rational, a most important step in the right direction of her life, and she wouldn't be trapped in the treacle love her mother held for Leo.

Six months drifted by since Liv was surprised by the sight of John's car in the driveway—six steady and happy months. And then one night at a party, she met Paul Minfhof.

1943
PAUL, LIV, JOHN

Liv was aware of a person suddenly seated by her. In the cigarette and marijuana smoke-filled room, a young blond man had sat next to her on the floor. She was sprawled untidily on her cushion, her eyes half-closed but her body emanated tension.

He asked, "Hello, am I disturbing you?"

Liv opened her eyes in surprise. The man smiled disarmingly at her. Liv smiled in return. He had a stocky build with short, strong fingers, even features, and warmth in his unusual green-gray eyes.

She shook her head. "Hello, no! I'm expecting my boyfriend and for the first time in a long while, I'm hoping he won't show up."

Paul looked pointedly at her left hand. She smiled, amused.

"No, we're not engaged or anything. He's just a strange sort of guy with terrible moods. I'm Liv by the way. Liv Weisz."

She formally held out her hand to him. He took her hand, staring deeply into her dark eyes.

"Paul. Paul Minthof."

They discovered they were both in Cape Town during a timespan that overlapped, he working at the docks, she at the university. They both knew Bruce Harvey, their party host, through his poetry. Paul said he heard Bruce read his poetry one night and sought him out. They became friends. Liv said she tried to write poetry, but Bruce gently showed her that poetry was not her medium. "Amateurish stuff compared to his." She added, "My boyfriend is not interested in my university friends. Doesn't like impromptu gatherings like this, especially with marijuana and too much cheap alcohol."

Paul Minthof . . . his name was vaguely familiar. "I remember your name from somewhere. Have we met?"

Paul answered, "I remember your name, too. Yes, we met, years ago as children. Your name conjures up a blue swimming pool in a green lawn. We met at your Papa Helmut's home in Houghton.. My grandfather was the Weisz brothers' tailor. I knew even back then that I wanted to help people who needed help; not to make clothes for rich people."

Liv laughed out loud. "You made me so angry when you said that I pushed you into the swimming pool fully clothed and jumped in after you. Papa Helmut sternly reprimanded me, reminding me all Jews are connected."

They both lounged silently among the cushions, lost in memories. Liv changed the conversation, "So, Paul Minthof, do you live in Jo'burg now?"

"Not really, I go back and forth between Jo'burg and Cape Town. My sister Miriam lives in Cape Town and my sister Bluma and my grandparents in Johannesburg. After high school, I lodged with Miriam and her family while I worked on the docks. Most of the men I worked with were so-called colored, and from them I learned of the Dickensian conditions many of their wives and daughters endured in the garment factories in Cape Town. That's how I got involved in the trade union movement. I often joined some of the men and their womenfolk at secret trade union organizing meetings. Initially, I was interested in supporting my coworkers, but I became passionate about the work of trade union activists and asked if I could help as a volunteer. Soon after, I was offered a more permanent job as an organizer.

"I like talking to people and I'm a good listener. The stories I heard from the workers about their mistreatment, especially of abuse by some factory overseers, horrified me. So now I'm a part of the trade union movement.

"In fact, I'm in Johannesburg right now to meet one of the factory bosses, at his invitation. Boris Joffee. Do you know him?"

Liv shook her head. Paul lived in another world.

"I'm meeting him tomorrow for lunch. Maybe you and I can meet for a drink around six. I can tell you about the meeting."

Amazed at herself, Liv agreed. "But only for a quick drink. As a lawyer I'm interested in the trade union movement and the push for legal status for unions."

Suddenly, Liv's face flushed with embarrassment as she remembered her semi-commitment to John.

Why am I talking so freely to this handsome stranger whose eyes hold the inchoate longing of deep loneliness?

An imperious knock at the front door abruptly interrupted their conversation. The room fell silent. Their host, Bruce, moved to open the door. Framing the doorway was a powerfully built man who carried an aura of force and control.

"Is Liv here?" he demanded. "Liv Weisz? She said she would be here."

The brusqueness of his tone jarred Liv. She rose hastily and moved to the hallway, appealing placatingly to the stranger. "I'm here, John. I'm coming." Her soothing voice sounded like that of a mother who intent on avoiding a fracas spoke to a difficult child. For a moment she turned fleetingly to look down at Paul and smiled weakly, regretfully. Paul waved from the floor. He spoke softly. "Tomorrow evening, then?"

Liv half-nodded and waved back, even while inwardly acknowledging how difficult it would be to see Paul again. Then with a flourish, she swept her wrap around her shoulders and went to John.

The following evening, they met, as arranged, at a local bar in Hillbrow. Liv felt an adrenalin rush course through her body when she saw Paul. He was so handsome and so pleased to see her. There was a definite charged chemistry between them.

When they were seated at a small table with a bowl of peanuts in the center, they indulged in small talk as they waited for their drinks. Then Liv said, "I'm having dinner with John . . ." Disappointment crossed Paul's face.

Liv said, "So tell me about your meeting with Joffee. I'm interested."

But I'm more interested in you. All I want to do is touch you and be touched by you.

"Okay," said Paul with a grin. "Here's the short version. I told you I'm a good listener. Joffee agreed that I could make notes of our conversation when I explained they were for a report to my boss in Cape Town. Here they are—verbatim—with my commentary as well. You can read them and then ask me any questions if you'd like."

He handed Liv the note pages.

Boris Joffee is a businessman of ill repute because of his mistreatment of workers. He has garment factories mainly in Jo'burg but also Durban. He invited me to JHB for "a talk.' We met in the opulent setting of Joffee's downtown club and had a drink.

"How is your grandfather? A landsleit of mine, I believe?"

The Yiddish word sounded strange in the clipped English accent Joffee had acquired. We engaged in small talk until the main course—Beef Wellington— (I'd never heard the name before) was served. Despite my intentions to be as natural and unpretentious as I could, I made sure I used the correct cutlery from the array of silverware set in front of me. Ernest Oppenheimer and several other of the biggest names in the mining world were being seated at the table alongside ours, and I struggled hard to concentrate on Joffee's inanities. The he got down to business.

"Well, Paul, how is your organization of my workers coming along?"

His words jolted me back to reality. "Good. Better than we ever hoped. One more meeting and I think we'll have the votes for a trade union on your factory floor. Solly Sachs is coming for the meeting. We're hoping to join the Cape Garment Workers' Union."

"Yes, I know. Some of the workers have informed me of the meeting. They're not all with you, you know. They feel the union will discriminate against White and nonunion members. And all my workers know how my management feels about non-White unions. I agree with what your lot says: Not all of us in the industry have been fair to the workers, perhaps not even myself, but we know what's best for them. We don't want to spoil them. Give them too much, then our profits go. We have to cut back on workers and fire them. Tell me, Paul, have you ever asked them if they would rather have a job at a low wage than no job at all?"

I felt my anger rising but reined it in. "Tell me, Mr. Joffee, did anyone ask that question of your father and grandfather in the shtetel?"

Joffee sighed. "Paul, Paul, this isn't Europe, with its ideals of liberty, with the French revolutionary zeal for equality, fraternity, and freedom. This is Africa. Cruel, barbaric, splendid. We are Jews. We are meant to wander and survive wherever we find ourselves. At this moment in history here in Africa, we are on the right side for once, the winning side. After centuries of losing, we can win here in Africa and win big. If we do like them . . ." Joffee motioned with his chin around the room. "They don't exploit the unfortunate *schwartzes*, Black workers, themselves. They pay someone else to do it. Usually they use the *getuisem*, Afrikaner managers, who hate and fear natives, anyway. It's called survival of the fittest. This is a jungle . . . a golden jungle."

Joffee paused to sip his after-lunch brandy and offered me a long, tapered cigar. Obviously enjoying himself, he believed he was connecting with me. "Be smart. Come on the side of the winners. A clever, good-looking man like yourself. Presentable. What do you want with the schwartzes? It's not your fight. Would they fight for the Jews if the positions were reversed? No! Come on, man, be on the winning side. A man with your skills, your personality? Come join me in Signet Management merchandising and selling. We're opening new territory every day in Swaziland, Bechuanaland, and Natal. With this war mobilization, I've landed the largest clothing contract ever in this country for army uniforms. Forget about the workers. Come and build a dream with me.

"Already I employ three thousand workers across all our factories, and I'm opening two more this year. These are challenges, dreams, and achievements. Certainly, somebody must be at the bottom of the pile, only this time it's not me or my family. I'm building a future for generations of my children here in Africa. You can do the same for your family."

I smiled and said, "Thanks, but no thanks. I'm a worker, Mr. Joffee, I don't aim to be rich. My challenge lies in achieving some equality for all workers in this country. It's a dream, too. I don't know much of the French Revolution, but I do know of Moses's laws of loving one's neighbor, of Isaiah's prophecies on the brotherhood of man."

"It's a pity our dreams clash, Paul. I can tell you now, I don't like these trade unions and I don't intend to have one in my factories, even if it means calling in the police to break them apart. If you want a job with me and a start in the big time, you have one week to make up your mind. Otherwise, I will pay someone to deal with you, as I deal with the others'"

We shook hands. The chilling threat in Joffee's words stayed with me. I thought how horrifying it is that while hundreds of thousands, if not millions, of Jewish lives are under threat in Europe, Jews here make fortunes from the same war.

Liv sat in silence for a moment, then, handing him the pages, she said, "You're a good writer, Paul. I was almost sitting there at lunch with you." She leaned over the table and clasped his hands tightly in both of her own. Touching him registered for her like touching a hot plate on a stove. But she held on tightly, urgently, "Be careful, Paul, please be careful... Joffee sounds like a man not to be trifled with. He's warning you."

Slowly she disengaged her hands. Paul looked taken aback, too.

"I have to go now ..."

"Please, Liv, tell me where I can contact you when next I'm in Jo'burg?"

Paul's voice was thick with emotion. Liv, didn't hesitate, but took his pen lying on the table and scribbled her work phone number on a paper napkin. She fled the table, lest she say anything personally incriminating.

In the following weeks, every time the phone rang in her office, Liv's heart raced. Maybe it was Paul. A month later, Paul contacted Liv at work. She agreed to meet him at the same Hillbrow bar despite feeling guilty about John, who was away on business. Liv listened to Paul with rapt attention as he told her about his work in Cape Town. He was a captivating storyteller in addition to being a good writer.

Paul began, "Three weeks ago in Cape Town, I remembered Joffee's words as I walked into the large hall attached to a Methodist church, the only venue that supported our cause nearby to a large Signet factory employing hundreds of so-called Colored workers.

"A crowd gathered as more people streamed in. I maneuvered my way to the platform. Solly Sachs leaped to his feet. He was a small intense man, his dark eyes looming large behind steel-rimmed spectacles. Sachs was a central figure in the national trade union movement. I hugged him. A fearless fighter for the people, a believer in justice and equality for all, he introduced me to Bertha Soloman, also on the platform and not much older than myself.

"I knew her by reputation. She is Jewish and recently elected to the Cape Provincial Council. She has won press accolades for her persistence with matters pertaining to women's rights. The press promised her a bright future in politics. Sachs also introduced me to Wouter Bosman, our key organizer in the Cape. I shook hands with the tall, dark-hued man.

"Sachs complimented me on the size of the crowd and asked if I thought we had enough votes to form a union that night. I reminded him that we had to go carefully, since Joffee and others were threatening trouble. Moosa Moola, my coworker, a man of east-Asian Indian descent but born in South Africa, agreed with me. We both had organized the garment trade workers and tramped from factory to factory waiting outside gates to talk to people as they left work. I was conspicuous because of my White skin. At first the workers were suspicious and fearful of losing their jobs, but slowly we convinced them that their strength and security lay in their numbers and unity.

"The meeting started. Bertha Soloman spoke eloquently

on the special plight of women, who numbered many thousands among the garment workers. She pinpointed their double disability as women and exploited workers and talked about women being paid less than men for the same work. She encouraged all workers, not only women workers, to unite and fight since there was strength in unity.

"Moosa and I joined in the applause that rose to the ceiling of the long, narrow hall. The audience in hard seats shifted and changed their positions. When Solly Sachs rose to speak, palpable attention was evident in the silence. I listened carefully to him, too, not fully understanding the rolling cadences when he spoke Afrikaans but enjoying the way a skillful orator persuasively carries his audience. When Sachs sat down, there was no doubt which way a vote would proceed.

"We motioned to our stewards to prepare to hand out ballots. Carefully I began to tell the workers what was required of them in the voting process. Halfway through my presentation, the back doors of the hall burst open and a group of about twenty White men wielding chains, knobkerries, and sjamboks rushed the platform. They were dressed in grey shirts.

"Hurriedly, I pushed Bertha Solomon under the table and then Solly Sachs, who gesticulating wildly, had already lost his glasses in the mêlée. I grabbed a chair and prepared to defend myself, fending off one man and then saw out of the corner of my eye Moosa being hit over the back of his head with an iron pipe. With a cry of rage, I pushed two men out of my way and swung the chair at Moosa's assailant. I heard the satisfying thud as I hit the man who fell to his knees. Then I heard myself screaming as a burning pain seared me. A thick steel chain hit the back of my head and shoulders. Slumping to the floor on my knees, I clutched my left shoulder. Someone kicked me in the jaw and I fell, unconscious."

Liv gasped in consternation, her hand to her mouth. "Oh no! I thought there would be trouble."

Paul patted her other hand lying on the table. "It's okay. I'm all right now, mending well!"

"Go on," Liv said.

"Minutes later when consciousness returned, I heard sirens. Bertha helped me stand, and I leaned on her as we walked slowly to one of the ambulances. An attendant assisted me into the van. I wanted Moosa to come with us in the ambulance, but Bertha reminded me he was not White and couldn't be admitted. He was in her car and she would take him to her doctor. I insisted we all go to my brother-in-law who was also a doctor.

"Silently cursing the racism with which we all lived, I passed out again after giving Bertha the address. When I awoke, my brother-in- law said I had concussion, cuts, and a sprained shoulder. Feeling sleepy, I wanted to tell him that the Grey Shirts, a cadre of White supremacist racists of the National Party, did this to me and Moosa. I wanted to tell him they took vows to keep South Africa White and racially pure. They justified their actions with the slogan of *Swart Gevaar*—Black Danger. They believed in the danger to White identity being swamped in South Africa.

"I realized I was here to do what I had to do. The Grey Shirts made me see that truth clearer than ever. I'm trying to rid this country of its racist ideologues. The White man's rule can't last in this country. He's building too great a legacy of hate. And the Jews are danger. The Nationalists are going to win the next election, and they're all Nazis. First, they'll deal with the Blacks, and then they'll deal with the Jews."

Liv felt tears in her eyes. Paul experienced so much since she met him, while all she had to deal with was worry about upsetting John! She placed a hand tenderly on the livid scar on Paul's cheek. Unwaveringly their glances met. Paul lowered her hand to his mouth and fervently kissed her palm. Liv withdrew her hand and kissed her palm where his mouth had been.

"Let's get out of here," she said. "Suddenly I can't breathe properly."

Sexual desire rushed through her body. The smoke-filled atmosphere of the barroom was claustrophobic. She hardly knew Paul, and he had almost been killed. He had become so precious to her, so quickly.

He continued talking as they stood on the sidewalk. "We were so close to having enough votes to proceed with a union, but the Grey Shirts ended that effort. Who is behind them? I have my suspicions, but I'm not naming names. We'll have to start over with the garment workers. This incident traumatized me so much that I'm unable for the present to continue my trade union activities. The organization granted me a leave of absence to heal. That's why I'm here now. To sort out I where I go from here."

Paul placed his right arm around her shoulders, and they walked in silence.

How well we fit, Liv thought. Her mind raced. Paul lived his convictions. She rejoiced at the thought of his single-mindedness and idealism. Her heart, his heart, heart to heart. Something unnamable, but not unknowable jolted her, not just his good looks.

Now in the fresh night air, her head cleared and adrift on a wave of delicious anticipation, as if she had known Paul forever, she turned to him and studied his finely featured face, her dark head level with his.

"It's a funny thing," he laughed self-mockingly, "but I feel as if I've known you forever."

Liv smiled gratefully; she knew then that somehow, they belonged together.

"Yes, it's most strange you should say that. I've been thinking something like that, too."

They stopped in the middle of a moving stream of people and embraced for a long time. They shared a sweet kiss of welcome and promise of fulfillment, and they clung together, oblivious of the jostling crowds, unaware that half a block away another large crowd gathered to watch two White policemen manhandle a Black man, obviously drunk, sitting in the gutter, mournfully singing to himself.

The crowd flinched uneasily as one policeman brutally kicked the Black man in the stomach and the other policeman hit him a glancing blow on the head with his baton. Then they bundled him into the waiting police van. The group of mainly White onlookers dispersed sedately, continuing their previous conversations as if there had been no interruption.

"I've a studio flat a few blocks away," Paul muttered in a voice thick with emotion. "We'll go there?"

Liv nodded her acquiescence, her arm tightly coiled around Paul's waist, her head resting on his shoulder. They walked rapidly to the building and waited with growing impatience for the elevator.

Liv gazed in the mirror as they ascended. Her face was aglow with passion, suffused with shining desire, which almost made her a stranger to herself. She wondered at the lust in her eyes. John and their relationship suddenly slipped into her consciousness, yet her face reflected none of the sick apprehension she felt. His reality was as powerful as if he were standing with them in the lift.

John last night, Paul tonight. In a way I'm committing adultery. I'm promiscuous after all. She smiled faintly at herself. Paul caught her smile in the mirror and smiled back at her with such tenderness that she felt her stomach muscles tighten.

They were careful where they positioned themselves, as Paul's shoulder was not yet fully healed. They spent a restful time of stroking and exploring, and then he was in her. Afterward, Liv knew peace and a quantity and quality of loving in one lazy finger, which stroked the scabbed, beautiful face next to hers on the pillow. Her soul swelled with the enormity of loving Paul. She wondered at the immensity of the love she felt, if the love in one finger overwhelmed her.

Liv awoke early in the morning and turned to find Paul next to her. She panicked. Where was John? Then she remembered. She let her hand linger on Paul's muscled back. She looked around the room in the faint light. She noted the uncarpeted floor, the sparse desk laden with piles of books, and next to the bed on a small table a photograph of a wedding group. Paul as a boy stood in the middle of the group below the blond bride, obviously a sister.

"Liv," he said her name softly, tenderly, and reassuringly to himself. "Liv, Liv." He opened his arms. Liv held him closely, feeling her tingling excitement again. She surrendered herself to the pleasure of loving and being loved by Paul.

Later she tried languidly to leave the bed. "I must go. I'm giving a presentation this morning. I must change my clothes."

"You're right."

"Oh, Paul! It's not going to be easy. John's so volatile, so unpredictable. It's not that we're engaged or anything like that. It's just that we've been going out together for months, almost a year now. You know, steady, not with anyone else. I suppose that means some sort of commitment. But there's been no formal arrangement. We've just drifted into it. It has, sort of evolved. There are bound to be all sort of ructions. It's my fault, really. I allowed myself to just drift along, knowing deep down that it wasn't right for me. Now there's you. We've only known each other for hours. I don't know about all of this. I'm confused and afraid."

"What's his name?"

"John Ivans."

Liv felt Paul's shudder. He shook his head sadly.

"John Ivans, Max's son. He's a distant cousin. Too bad. Our families don't talk, you know. We Minthofs stayed on the wrong side of the tracks.

"I have two much older sisters. My father, Jacob, died before I was one . . . shot by Arabs in Palestine. My mother brought us to South Africa to my father's family. But she went back to Palestine after several years here, so my grandparents raised us. My grandparents were on their way to America from Europe to escape the pogroms but my grandfather, Raphael, was persuaded to come to South Africa."

As Liv pushed a strand of hair away from her forehead, Paul caught her wrist. She was surprised at the strength with which he held her.

"I don't know about him and you, Liv, but I know about us. I've been around some; I don't need hours or days. I know this is real and something special."

Liv watched Paul in bewilderment.

He continued. "It'll work out. It was meant to happen this way. You're frightened of him. Be honest with him. Only you know what you really want!"

Liv spoke softly. "I'll try and see him early this evening. I'll phone you after I've spoken to him."

"No, I'll be at your house by eight-thirty."

Looking at Paul, her heart ached with the pain of loving him so much. He was less of a stranger than John. She felt a stir of desire, a warm rush of sensation between her legs. She was finally, truly in love. The only doubt in her mind was her ability to successfully convince John.

Liv reached home. Sally had already left for work. Jane was still in her bedroom. Liv moved stealthily in and out of the house, conscious of a small bud of compassion for her mother. Perhaps her mother loved Leo, loves Sally, the same way I love Paul.

1943
JOHN, LIV, PAUL

"I'm sorry John, but it simply happened. We met and that was that."

After work, Liv met John in the upscale tearoom he liked to frequent. Without ceremony, she launched into the speech she'd rehearsed often that day.

Liv felt a squeeze of disquiet at the look of anguish and disbelief on John's face. His silence forced her to continue.

"I thought you and I were going to be all right together. I'd thought about it a great deal. But that was before Paul. I know you're shocked and hurt, but I'm doing the right thing. I know I am. For you, for me. I only hope you'll meet someone soon who'll mean to you what Paul means to me."

Speaking intently, John broke his silence, his voice rising to a snarl of anger. "Goddamnit Liv, you've only known him for less than a month!"

Liv refused to allow herself to be cowed. "It isn't a matter of time, John, it's a matter of recognition. We knew each other as soon as we met."

"As simple as that, hey?"

"Yes."

"You're sure it's not just a matter of sex? A physical thing? He's a good-looking bastard. That's all he's got over me. You know he's a distant cousin? Family never amounted to much. For God's sake, he's a trade unionist, Liv! The father was a terrorist in Palestine, the grandfather is a lowly tailor, his mother left the three children when they were babies and went back to Palestine. His father was killed there. This is the family you want to be with?"

"Oh John, please don't make this more difficult than it is. You and I are not committed to each other in any way. It could happen to you as easily as to me."

"Yeah, maybe," John agreed as ungraciously as he could, "but you can't marry the guy. You will struggle to find money to pay for things. You like good things, remember. You've never said no to anything I've offered you."

Liv cringed and turned away.

"What sort of a life will you have with a struggling trade unionist?"

"Stop it, John. It's no concern of yours what Paul and I will do and how we'll live."

John dropped his voice. There was a tone of chilling certainty in his words. "You'll never marry him you know, because you're going to marry me." He stalked off.

Several weeks later, Liv sat on her mother's bed one weekend morning and filled with her own joy told her she was to be married. Jane sat in bed and drew Liv close, hugging her tightly. "Such good news, sweetheart. You and John will be so happy."

Liv's feeling of goodwill evaporated. She drew away and said shortly, "Not to John, to Paul."

Aghast, Jane stared at her.

Liv knew what stirred in her mother's mind. "Well, I'd hoped . . . You see, Liv, love's all very well for a while, but without money, with nothing." She let her hands fall helplessly. "It's no good." Jane paused, threw up her hands, then spoke in a bitter tone, "You'll never listen. Invite your father, although I doubt he'll make the trip from London. Do whatever you want to do."

Jane started crying. Liv stiffened with cold affront. She tried once more. "Hey, come on there. I'm getting married. Your only daughter, your only child. You're supposed to be happy. I love Paul, truly love him. You said yourself that he's a wonderful person. Forget about John. We never loved each other. We would've ended up fighting and bitter."

Liv thought, like you, you old cow. Leo's the reason you rely so much on Sally. Why you often share a bed. I've seen you together. You love Sally like I love Paul. But you'll never admit it. You'd rather cry over your lost Leo, who probably never existed as a person for you but as an imaginative knight in shining armor.

As Liv knew she would, Sally applauded her announcement and said how pleased she was at the news. "Paul's perfect for you, and you for him. You can count on me for anything, Liv, anything. Remember that always. And don't worry about your mother, I'll speak to her. She'll come around. You'll see."

During the following weeks, Liv rushed to estate agents, the dress designer, caterers, and printers.

Wherever she went, all the news and talk of the town centered on the escalation of the war, of South African troops fighting in the North—the North African desert against Rommel and his troops. The Jews en bloc supported Prime Minister General Jan Smuts, both for his support of their Zionist causes but especially for allowing European Jewish refugees into South Africa a few months previously.

Liv, usually intently interested in political issues, had all thought of the war washed from her mind. At the end of the first week of her preoccupation with wedding arrangements, she realized with shock she was two weeks late with her period. She was never as much as a day late. People say if you miss two . . . she waited for another week. The doctor confirmed her fears.

The doctor smiled kindly at Liv, whom he had attended since she was a little girl, "You're around six or seven weeks pregnant."

He paused and lifted a questioning eyebrow. "What's so important about the date? You're getting married anyway, right?"

Liv smiled bleakly at him and shook her head. She wouldn't trust herself to speak.

She walked out of his rooms in a daze. She wandered blindly along Jeppe Street bumping into people, scarcely aware of where she was walking. Glum faces reflected her own dismay. The news from the European warfront was dismal. The Nazis advanced on all European and Russian borders and the Americans remained uncommitted. A cold wind of change blew through the streets of Johannesburg. Liv huddled into her sweater.

John's or Paul's? She and John had slept together on the night of Bruce Harvey's party and on several nights shortly before then. She made love with Paul three weeks later and on most subsequent nights.

Later she sat in her car, crying, hunched over the steering wheel while the African sun, now that she was out of the cold wind, beat down on her in the parked car.

Another month and she would have known and rejoiced that it was Paul's baby. Now, was it John's baby? Frightened, she felt trapped by this tiny being growing in her womb. A cold clammy hand of despair held her. This was the end of the world. Perhaps she should not have seen the doctor. Now that he knew, would she have to have the baby? He had promised her confidentiality. An abortion? Two girls she knew underwent abortions in Johannesburg. She could ask and find out who and where. But Liv knew that she would never have an abortion.

Slowly Liv assessed the computation of facts. If it's Paul's baby, everything would work out. They'd be blessed. But if it's John's and I marry Paul, the baby would be an awful reminder of how I compromised myself, my lack of character, my temptation, and of settling for a relationship with John, when I didn't love him. She could tell Paul next month after they were married, but then she'd be living with the knowledge of her deception their whole lives. If she told him now and if the doctor's right, he'll have to know it's John's baby. Can she ask Paul to be father to John's baby?

Liv started the car and moved through the traffic in the direction of Hillbrow. She knew Paul worked at the flat. He opened the door still dressed in his boxer shorts.

Pleased and surprised to see her, he became concerned as he noted her tear-stained face and pale cheeks. "Liv, what's wrong? Come in!"

Liv stood in the empty corridor in the stark sunlight staring at Paul as if she knew she would never see him again. Liv moved numbly through the doorway.

"Okay, now what's up? What's wrong?"

Liv rushed to Paul. Heart to heart. She clung to him.

"Darling, I'm sorry. I just suddenly had to see you and touch you. I'm all right now."

"You sure? You don't look too all right to me."

"Paul, hold me. Whatever happens, I love you. I love only you. Tell me you know that's true! Whatever happens I love only you!"

Paul intuited her panic. He regarded her seriously, holding her at arms' length away from him.

"Liv, you tell me now, what's wrong. No bullshit, either. I want the truth. Now what's happened?" His grip on her shoulder tightened and she winced in pain.

Liv rubbed her shoulders where Paul's hands gripped her. She had never seen him angry before. Liv breathed deeply. "Darling, I'm pregnant."

Paul stood still, shocked. He ran his fingers through his hair again. He sat down on the bed and apprehensively considered her. "Liv, I don't know what to say. A bit inconvenient, isn't it?"

Liv's mind and heart tensed. His eyes searched her face for guidance and reassurance. Before she could stop, she flung the words almost murderously at him. "I don't know whose baby it is. Either yours or John's. The doctor thinks because of the date that it's John's."

Paul rounded on her in fury. "You can't frighten me with that and punish me, stupid woman. I don't give a damn whose baby it is. You can't have a baby now. And that's all there is to it. It's inconvenient, there's a war on, and we've got no money. This is not the time to bring a baby into the world. We simply can't afford a baby now!"

Paul rose to his full height and towered over her with his fist clenched, his eyes hardened into a glaze of anger. Liv was frightened and hurt. She stared at Paul in a panic. She eyed him as if he was a stranger. Seeing her further panic, Paul tried to gather himself.

"Liv, I'm sorry. I shouldn't overreact like this. I need more time. Let's talk about this again tonight? Okay? You'll come here tonight?"

Liv bit her lip and nodded. She'd be calmer then, too. They embraced softly. Liv smiled at Paul through her tears. He walked with her to the lift.

Liv sat in her car even more agitated than before. Paul's spontaneous anger undid her. She loved Paul too much. No one should be able to hurt her like this. Even if he said he didn't give a damn whether the baby was his or John's, how did she know how he would react to the reality of living with John's child?

Liv covered her face with her hands, unaware the car rolled forward and down the steep slope of Nugget Hill, a one-way street up, other cars rushing to meet her, as the car careened out of control. Gathering momentum, the vehicle plunged crazily on the decline. Liv tried to grab the steering wheel and screamed in terror at the telephone pole festooned with newspaper placards looming ahead of her.

Liv regained consciousness to find herself in a hospital bed. Her aching body would not move. Plaster encased her right arm. Gingerly with her left hand she touched her face to feel a couple of pieces of sticky plaster. Slowly she remembered the telephone pole.

A nurse materialized at her bedside. "Now don't try to move, just lie quietly. You're fine, only a broken arm, shock, severe concussion."

Liv spoke so softly that the nurse bent over to hear her. "Am I bleeding? Down there?" Liv pointed with a shaking finger. The nurse looked puzzled. Liv's voice became stronger. "You know, menstruating?"

"Oh no! Why do you ask?"

Liv shook her head. So be it. Her eyes brimmed with tears.

"Your family's here. Your mother, fiancé, one, or two others. Shall I send then in?"

"Paul, only Paul."

Paul stood stiffly at the door. Liv smiled crookedly at him, awkwardly, because of the bandages and deep anguish in her being at the disaster she was about to set loose.

"Paul, my darling, I'm so sorry."

Paul knelt at her bedside, crying hot tears. "Liv, my fault. I should never have let you go, not like that, not after you coming to me like that. I'm a fool. I said I'd never let you down and I did."

Liv spoke quietly but with a chilling tone of finality in her voice. Unconscious of her gesture, her hand moved her hair off her face.

"Paul, it's over. Us. I'm sorry."

"What are you talking about?"

"My darling, my only love, I can't marry you."

Paul smiled tenderly at her and stroked her forehead. "You've had an accident. You must rest now. I'll come back later, and we'll speak then."

"My poor boy. You must be strong for me and us. And remember I love you, always."

She knew how vitally important it was to be present for Paul to understand but the morphine was too strong. Etched forever in Liv's mind was her anguish mirrored on his face as she floated away from him.

Liv refused to see Paul again. She agreed to visits from her mother and Sally but only for a brief time. Lying awake for hours, she stared at the ceiling, thinking of her situation. She rehearsed the forthcoming scenes over in her mind so often that when they came to pass, no one guessed that her loving self—the self only Paul knew—had withered and died.

Liv asked her mother to call John in Cape Town to come be with her.

John entered the room hesitantly, looking bewilderedly at her from behind an enormous bunch of white roses.

"Hello, John." She smiled shyly at him, noting with dismay his unprepossessing dark face and unruly hair.

"Thank you for the roses; they're beautiful. Please set them over there in the basin. The nurse will bring a vase later."

Nervously they stared at one another for a long moment; John crossed to the bed, leaned over, and kissed her forehead. Liv felt her stomach turn, but not an inkling of distress crossed her face. She had played this scene too often in her mind to falter now. She smiled sweetly at John and motioned to the chair next to her bed.

"Liv, I've been so anxious to speak to you ever since your mother called, but you had no phone."

John was tense. Liv noted the sweat stains around the armholes on his shirt. His tension gave her the confidence to continue. "I know. I cut myself off deliberately to give me time to think."

"Go on."

"I know now that you are correct. Paul has tremendous physical appeal for me. He's like a magnet. But marriage won't work. The accident made this clear. One can't live in that ferment of emotion and passion. I want to share something with you. When I awoke in this bed, I heard myself screaming your name. If we were still together none of this would have happened."

Did she overdo it? No. He stared intently at her with love and compassion, a dawning joy in his eyes.

The fool. My lies are exactly what he hoped to hear, what he wanted to hear. My words are murdering any future with Paul.

"So, if you'll forgive me, still have me, I want very much to marry you."

Liv bit her lip. She spoke the last words quietly, tears in her eyes betraying her.

"Liv, you make me so proud, happy. Only when you left me did I realize what you meant to me. I'll give anything, anything to get you back."

Gently, John placed his arms around Liv and lifted her from the pillow, kissing her tear-filled eyes. Liv found herself passionately kissing him back, imaging it was Paul. Would we never have met my love, my only love. I'm kissing you now, holding you.

"There's just one thing, John."

"Anything, anything."

"I want to be married as soon as possible. Now, this week, in the hospital, if possible."

John laughed. "Shouldn't be a problem. You just tell me when? Tomorrow, the day after, when?"

Liv laughed, too. What **fools** men are. What fools we all are.

"What about Paul, though?" John the victor could afford to be magnanimous, to show concern for the vanquished.

"I've already told him." She sensed John's triumph. She was his. He'd won again.

He patted her on the arm. "I'll go now . . . come back later. You look tired, drained. I'll spread the good news. Max will be delighted. Your mother, too."

He blew her a kiss.

The father of my child. Are you, John, the father of my child? Liv gambled with her future, Paul's future. But she couldn't really lose. John's child or Paul's didn't really matter now, not for her or John. Only for Paul. She couldn't bear to think of what she'd done to Paul. *I'll keep my part of the bargain. God help me but neither John nor Paul will ever know the truth of this baby's father.*

Unexpectedly, Paul's sister, Bluma, a woman in her forties, visited her in the hospital. She bore an uncanny resemblance to Paul. Observing her set face, Liv grew cold. She was sure Bluma read naked guilt on her face.

"I won't tell Paul I've seen you. He forbade me to come here. I don't want to lose contact with him, for his sake as well as mine. He's talking of going to Palestine, of joining the underground, the Irgun, like our father Jacob and our mother did, fighting the British, the Arabs, and fighting to establish a Jewish state. I'm encouraging him." She glanced at Liv. "The only thing for him now is to escape from here and be so far away that there's no possibility of seeing you. He'll either be killed there or find something to live for again." Once more she stared directly at Liv. "He's dead to everything here now.

"I'll keep in touch with you from time to time," she said and added her final words intoned in a voice of the driest irony. "Mazel tov! Enjoy your wedding."

The door closed with a click.

Liv's mind was in turmoil again. *If Paul dies in Palestine, does the blame fall on me? Haven't I sent him to his death?*

The possibility of Paul dying never occurred to her. Clearly, she hadn't thought through the ramifications of her actions. Liv believed herself cursed and damned. Tears rolled along her cheeks, and she grew still colder.

My God, what have I done?

John spared no expense in setting up a chuppa over Liv's hospital bed and persuading the rabbi to officiate at the hospital. The rabbi was reluctant to cooperate. He preferred the wedding take place in his new modern shul in the northern suburbs of Johannesburg where all the well-established Jewish families lived.

But John remained resolute and the generosity of his contribution to the shul's building fund overrode the rabbi's objections. Shaking his head in disappointment at not officiating over the magnificent spectacle of the Weisz and Ivans family members filling his pews, he agreed with an elated John. A few days later, he arrived meekly at the hospital with the chassen, the cantor. About ten guests crowded the comparatively large, private, hospital room.

After the ceremony, Liv aware of John's intense gaze, lowered her eyes as she returned his smile. He's not an ogre. He loves me. And I won't think of Paul. I'll forget Paul.

She smiled at Max and laughed at something he said to her. At the end of the religious ceremony, Max's emotions had overcome him, and he cried noisily into a large, white, silk handkerchief.

Jane, looking regal and still remarkably attractive in her much-desired gorgeous chiffon dress, basked in her triumph. Sally, formally stylish, was quietly pleased but not relaxed.

John's wedding gift for Liv was the original completed manuscript of his overture. Overwhelmed, silence was Liv's first reaction.

"I guess I started this piece when you met with me to tell me you'd taken up with that Minthof fellow. Never had I such surety of creativity. The notes melded into one another, the music surged and swelled around me as I penned in bars and phrases on my composition pages. My music lies here captured, refined, polished, and available on these, the completed pages of *The Liv Overture*.

John tapped the transcript.

"The composition sings of you, Liv. Phrases express your natural grace and poise, your moments of quiet repose. It captures your laughter and smile, the light you bring into any room. Your concern for others, your flashes of self-confidence, diffidence, enthusiasm, vulnerability, and captivating warmth. The music sings of your honesty and vitality. Most perceptively, I think, it captures some of your hidden self that shines and glitters among the reeds of your soul. It expresses my love for you."

Liv stared at him in disbelief. "I inspired you? How strange after what I'd done and said to you."

Embarrassed, John changed the subject. "When you're released from here, I'll ask Fritz to play it with me for you. Perhaps I'll try to find a few others, too. No one will know the composer. I've used a pseudonym, Isaac Hochstein."

Liv smiled. "Isaac Hochstein sounds imposing."

"I think so, too. Much more traditional than John Ivans. My grandfather's first name, my mother's maiden name."

Liv sighed. "You must tell me all about your family." She struggled to sound bright and interested. "I've so much to learn."

"We'll have plenty of time on our honeymoon."

Exhausted, Liv wished John would leave. The wedding service carried the harsh reality of her decision. She didn't love John and she'd bonded herself to live with him. Life stretched endlessly before her, loveless and cold. The commitment imposed by her vows began to oppress her.

Several weeks later in Beira, Liv shared news of her pregnancy with John. He grinned, remembering their honeymoon on the ship.

"Inevitable, not so? We went at it with enough enthusiasm. You pleased?"

"Oh yes." Liv felt herself reddening. "A bit sooner than I counted on, but I always wanted children. You?"

"Never thought about it before, but now that it's happening, it feels right. Do you want to have the baby in Johannesburg? We can have it anywhere you want."

"Oh yes, at home in Jo'burg. I'll feel more settled there, more comfortable with my Mom and Aunt Sally around. This war makes everything so uncertain."

"Okay, no need to rush home. If it's all right with you, I'll ask Max to keep his eyes open for a house. You can tell him the sort of thing you fancy. He can do the essential furnishing and so on. Save you the bother."

Liv nodded, overcome at how easy deception proved to be.

A month later, they returned to Johannesburg and moved into their newly decorated house on the same street as Max's own house. Despite her appearance of glowing health, Liv was deeply troubled. As the time drew nearer for their return home, she was constantly aware of images of Paul . . . his distinctive face and laughing eyes, his love for her shining in those eyes, his hands on her body, his voice caressing her with endearments only he ever used. Liv bore the loss of him as a deadweight. The baby moved in its cramped space, a constant reminder of the horror she had set in motion.

In the last weeks of Liv's pregnancy, Jane and Liv drew closer. Liv, heavy and burdened, could do little for herself and was content to sit and let her mother fuss and minister to her. In caring for Liv, Jane's memories of Sally's caring for her in the last weeks of her own pregnancy flowed into her mind. Try as she might, she could not bring the quality of loving to Liv that Sally had brought to her so many years earlier. Not surprised, Jane knew she loved Liv as a mother loved a daughter, but even then she and Sally loved one another passionately as any two lovers.

One morning when she and Liv sat in the garden under the shade of a giant spreading jacaranda, Liv casually asked her mother to tell her about the "tragedy" surrounding Sally in the distant past. Jane sighed, taken aback. The moment she had anticipated for years was now here. She thought for a while, then carefully chose her words.

"Sally had a cousin, Harry. Gertrude and Gustav's son. He was obsessively jealous of her. He died in a terrible accident that involved Sally as well. She lost her mind for a while."

Silence.

"That's it? No more details?"

"Yes, that's it."

Liv did not know what her mother had omitted, but it was evident she held deep layers of protectiveness for Sally.

"Maybe it's impossible for you to understand how I loved Sally then. How I love her now. A quiet and steady love, but then, it was distinctly different. I loved her more than I loved your father. She gave me more love than your father ever did. Without Sally, I would have been alone. You, too, Liv. You don't come close to me. You don't really love me. We've lived together but you abandoned me when you were quite young. Sally, back then, around the time you were born . . . such love only comes once in a lifetime."

Liv felt the baby move uncomfortably. Jane wasn't accusing her. She was her usual, self-referential self. Yet Liv acknowledged Jane was right.

Liv contemplated the nature of the love triangle that

enmeshed Sally, Jane, and Leo. Do patterns repeat themselves generation after generation?

She mused, Me, Paul, and John. Are we only a variation on the theme of Sally, Jane, and Leo?

Her cousin Micah was in town again. It surprised her that a man of his repute and energy paid so much attention to a dull, ineffectual woman as her mother. But she'd caught many a knowing glance between them as if they shared a special bond.

As the news from Europe worsened, Micah was in South Africa on behalf of the Jewish-Palestinian authorities. He was to persuade the Zionist Federation once more about petitioning the government on admitting even more Jewish refugees from the Nazi onslaught into South Africa. His piercing dark eyes burned with frenzied energy. He spoke to Max and Sally.

"They worry me, your other Jewish leaders here. I can talk, plead, exhort. They don't want to budge. They don't want to do anything that will allow the government to see the Jews in a negative light. I've told them there will be no Jews remaining in Europe if we leave them to be annihilated by Hitler. Some like yourselves do listen but not the majority. I fear for our people, Max, Sally, everywhere—Europe, Palestine, South Africa."

South African Jewish leaders accepted Micah's caution reluctantly. But they knew what awaited them. Conversations they had with Afrikaner business leaders worried them. Sally remembered a recent conversation.

"Jews like you are all right, Miss Weitz. Your family came here early. They grew up in the bush. The others come from Europe and live only in the cities. They don't know they're living in Africa. They can't talk Afrikaans or a native language. They use their overseas contacts to make money and take it out of the country.

Maybe Hitler's right. There's an international Zionist conspiracy to undermine the White man, to undermine Christianity. Jews are not loyal to South Africa. They know only of Palestine.

"We won't let our Afrikaner language, our Afrikaner identity, be overtaken by the dominance of English. Not on the *platteland* or in the towns where now there are so many more *utilanders*, foreigners. We're going to establish ourselves in the cities. We know they are the centers of economic and political power. Also, we must strengthen the will of the Afrikaners there, for they are assailed by assimilationist temptations in the British sphere of influence. But, more importantly, we need protect our White workers from losing their jobs to the never-ending sea of Black workers leaving the rural areas and swarming to the cities for industrial work."

"One doesn't have to be all that far-seeing," Sally told Max, "To worry for our family and descendants."

Liv knew she was in labor early one morning. John drove her to the Florence Nightingale Maternity Home. He chose to wait outside in the car.

Liv refused any chloroform. She wanted to be fully conscious at the birth. She immediately had to see this being who bore so much responsibility for the circumstances of the patterning of its life.

The pain was intense. The sister urged her to go with the spasms not to fight against them. And then satisfyingly, surprisingly, and triumphantly, the baby slid out of her body, yelling loudly in the delivery room.

"She's a girl," the doctor beamed at her. "She's big and healthy and beautiful."

Liv lay exhausted on the delivery table covered in sweat. She tried to hold out her arms.

"May I see her? Please let me see her?"

"In a moment. Just examining and cleaning her."

A bundle of white cloth was handed to her. Liv was too tired to hold the baby, but her heart thumped in anticipation. The sister placed her daughter on her breasts. The moment of truth arrived.

Paul's face stared at her ... the distinctive shape of Paul's face, the delicate arch of Paul's eyebrows, the curve of Paul's cheek, Paul's green-gray eyes. In her daughter she could see Paul and his sister and a long line of Minthof antecedents. Relief suffused Liv and then love. She stroked the down-soft cheek of her beautiful baby.

Now that I know whom you belong to, nothing matters anymore. Nothing, Marion. I'm calling you Marion.

Then panic overrode all her other feelings—they'll know now.

But they did not. They all agreed the baby looked like Liv but fair. She had John's curly hair. John was ecstatic about his little girl. Max thought the baby's delicacy of facial features was inherited from the fragile beauty of his deceased wife, his beloved Alice. Only Sally held the baby and then stared at Liv, questions in her eyes. Jane saw Sally in the baby and the fine features of most of the Weiszes. She kissed Liv and pressed into her hand a small ebony box. "I was given this when you were born, Liv."

Later when Liv opened it, she exclaimed her appreciation as she saw the delicate golden Magen Dovid, Star of David. She clenched the box tightly. Everything was settling in place better than she'd hoped. Except for Paul, except for Paul.

Several weeks later, much to Liv's consternation, Bluma, Paul's sister, phoned.

"Liv, you sound so surprised. I thought you might like to know that Paul's in a hospital in Jerusalem, a faulty hand grenade or something. He's out of danger, but badly burned, they say."

Liv felt Bluma's dismay through the silence on her end of the line.

"Liv, you still there? I wanted to let you know. Thought maybe you want to send a message, let bygones be bygones? By the way, congratulations on the birth of your baby. Come and see me some time and bring the baby."

Thrown off-balance by Bluma's call, Liv heard her words from a long way off. She'd been dreaming of Paul again in the long nights, sleeping in snatches between waking to tend to Marion. The previous night he had called from the top of a dune of shifting sand. She struggled to reach him, but the more she tried, the more the sand shifted and swayed around her. She couldn't bear the sound of his voice calling her name on the wind in a dead, hopeless monotone, "Liv, Liv, Liv."

After that dream, she cried as she fed Marion. Her tears dropped onto the tiny body snuffling and suckling at her breast. Paul's baby, whom he'll never know. Paul's baby. He needed her. She knew that now. She had heard his cries in the night. Heart to heart. Her mind raced, but there was no way she could find, no excuse to make, to leave John and Marion and flee to Paul.

Paul; badly burned, Bluma had said. Arabs and Jews fighting in Palestine. Liv heard scanty details from Helmut, and her father-in-law Max, Sally, and other older relatives still involved in Zionist causes. Her Uncle Wilhelm shared some content from the occasional letter from Micah. He was not fighting on the ground but in the halls of international diplomacy for a homeland for the displaced Jews of Europe, at least those who escaped Hitler's concentration camps.

Paul badly burned. Where? How? Not his face . . . his beautiful face. Every time she looked at Marion, she saw Paul as he had been, as she fervently hoped he remained.

1950
PAUL AND LIV

1948 was a momentous year for South Africa and Israel. At the United Nations, Israel was recognized as a Jewish state. In South Africa during the national elections (Whites only), the Afrikaner, apartheid National Party came to power. Finally, they could declare the victory denied them in the stalemated Boer Wars almost sixty years earlier. The new prime minister, Dr. Danie Malan, brought to Parliament a stringent series of apartheid laws to be enacted, aimed at entrenching political power in the hands of the White Afrikaner minority and permanently disenfranchising the Black population. The trenches were dug for the building of a draconian police state. Many Ossewabrandwag cadres previously serving sentences for treason in prisoner-of-war camps during World War II were entrenched in the new government.

John, Liv, and Marion lived in Johannesburg with occasional visits to *Duiwel's Hoogte* in Cape Town. Max had retired from their business to concentrate on his Zionist activities. As his business demands grew, John surrendered the violin and composing, hoping to return to both someday.

When Marion was at daycare most mornings in Johannesburg, Liv reconnected with some of her university friends including Jaco Malan. Budding interest swelled in her to be involved in resistance movements like the embryonic Black Sash.

In 1949, Paul published a book *In Search of Dying* not available in South Africa until 1950. Many people she knew praised the read. In Johannesburg, Liv bought one of the first copies on the bookshelves. Initially she was reluctant to open it, but she succumbed to her curiosity. The book had an evocative cover and intriguing title, but there wasn't a photo of the author. She read the blurb.

"The unique and sensitive story of Paul Minthof's struggle to overcome his challenges. Mr. Minthof's clear, honest appraisal of himself and his fellows is admirable. He writes of horrifying reality with precision and acceptance. This is a book of one man's triumph over personal adversity, universalized into a song of praise for the human spirit."

Liv was impressed. Paul really wrote all that?

"Inspirational!" "Profoundly Moving!" "A Triumph." "Sensitively Written." "I do not remember having read a personal account of challenges overcome which has moved me more."

She opened the book, turned to the title page, and gasped in shock.

FOR LIV.

Thousands of people read that dedication. No one had said anything to her. Liv felt uneasy, but the book gripped her from the opening sentence. She read of how Paul stayed in Palestine for the duration of World War II. In early 1946 he headed for war-torn London. Among the rubble and desolation, he had found a semblance of inner peace. He wrote that the ravages of his face seemed to belong in the ravaged city, both scarred almost beyond recognition.

She was horrified and saddened to learn how a defective hand grenade caused him such horrific injures. But one passage seared her to her core. She felt guilt and helplessness; she had made the wrong choice, and Paul was desperately injured. She would carry this added burden of guilt always. Paul wrote the following,

I decided not to open my eyes again. Perhaps I'd die. More than anything I wanted to die. For many days now I'd attuned my senses, willed my mind to encompass only death. But still I lived. And now that I was no longer drugged, now that the world beat around me, I knew I could never return to it. They knew that, too. Why else had they secured me to the bed so that I could not move, if they didn't know I wanted to kill myself?

Evangelists for life binding me to them again with bonds of the living; well, I wouldn't have it. It was my life to do with as I chose, and I chose death. There, then, in the Judean hills, I chose death. Fucking hand grenade. How could it fail to fully explode as I threw it and still leave me alive? Shit, after what I'd seen hand grenades do to people, how can I still be alive? For the longest time I would not believe it. I thought that indeed I was dead. Death became this floating perception of memories of life gone by. But no, damn it, I was alive.

One good thing, though. Perhaps I'd be so hideously ugly that no one would approach me. I was as ugly to look at as the ugliness I felt inside. I smelled the rotting stench of mortality around the ward. Relationships decayed into a stench of the foul corruption of the soul. My cry echoed so loudly in my head; I was surprised the ward didn't fall silent. Where are you? Where the hell are you? I need you! I need you.

When Liv reached the end three nights later, she placed the book in a desk drawer. She remembered how at the time of Paul's injury and hospital stay, she had dreamed she heard him calling her, but she could not leave Marion, John, Sally, her mother, or Johannesburg. She struggled to suspend those thoughts and feelings. Remorse and thoughts of what might have been threatened her emotional equilibrium. She knew for the sake of everyone who depended on her that she had to rise above that unlived life and keep her balance in the life she created.

The blurb told her that by day Paul had worked as a clerk for a bank far from any dealings with the public, and at night he wrote. Paul's psyche ran to deep emotions, high ideals, and sensitivity. Liv acknowledged that his writing caught and reflected the depths of his soul.

A year later in 1950, Liv read in the newspaper how Johannesburg quietly welcomed a newly famous son, Paul Minthof. South Africans, a deeply reverential people, respected Paul's need for privacy with his family. Recently, Papa Helmut, who kept tabs on his fellow elderly landsleite, told her Raphael, Paul's grandfather, had died and his grandmother, frail and ailing, wanted to see Paul.

John told her that his distant cousin Paul, "your old flame," was in Johannesburg. John had bumped into Bluma, Paul's sister at a business conference.

"She told me," John said offhandedly, "that it's a difficult time with him around. Hard to put his family at ease since the children run from his face. They all compensated by overreacting to him. They were uneasy about his newfound stature and fame. He just didn't belong anymore. Of course, his sisters Bluma and Miriam and brother-in-law Abraham continue to support him." John paused for a moment. "Fortunate for you that you chose me and not him."

Liv thought, Fortunate for you, you mean.

A week later, Liv, John, and Marion were at *Duiwel's Hoogte* for the winter school holidays. John, as he often did, was climbing on Table Mountain and had not returned the previous night. Liv was worried but not unduly so; John had spent the night on the mountain before. Early in the morning, she received the call she was waiting for—not from John but the Mountain Club Rescue Unit.

"We found Mr. Ivans. He's lucky to be alive. The internal bleeding needs monitoring. We're taking him to Groote Schuur Hospital."

As Liv entered John's private room, she paused. Pale and bruised, he had deep shadows of exhaustion etched on his face. Intravenous drips were attached to both arms. Liv sat at his bedside watching him in his drugged sleep. Earnestly, she examined his dark blunt face slightly plumper now than when she had first met him, his curly hair thinning. She allowed herself the long-denied luxury of examining her feelings toward him while she is in his presence. She shared her life with this man and although she knew he trusted a close intimacy with her, sadly, he knew little about her real self. She had kept that self away from him.

Yet she was anxious when he hadn't returned the previous night. Relief had overwhelmed her when they told her he was alive. She admitted to a warmth toward him. He cherished her beyond her expectations. Being Mrs. Ivans suited her. If there was a price to pay for everything, she might as well continue to enjoy it.

John opened his eyes. "I'm sorry, Liv. I was a fool. I should've listened to you. Should never have gone on the mountain so ill-prepared."

John had tears in his eyes. Whether tears of genuine concern for her or tears of self-pity, Liv didn't know. Sadly, for them, she acknowledged it was unimportant for her to know. Liv leaned over the bed and kissed him lightly on the forehead; he clung tightly to her hand.

"It's all right darling, everything's all right," she heard herself saying. She wondered at the murmuring tone of love in her voice. "As long as you're alive, everything's okay."

John slept again. Liv stayed a while longer, then left the room. Her thoughts wandered to her concern when John hadn't returned. Liv sighed. It wasn't love but somehow, they fitted now.

After leaving John's room, she donned her large sunglasses and stepped into the sunshine. Still early, she could lunch with Marion and then later they could play on the beach.

Suddenly, her heart seemed to stop and she froze. Then, without pausing to think, she ran after an upright blond man walking slowly toward the car park. She had recognized the way he walked.

"Paul! Paul!"

The man hesitated for a moment, then hurriedly walked on. Liv ran after him. "Paul! Paul!" She heard herself panting and laughing. She touched him on the shoulder, and he shuddered as if a bolt of electricity hit him.

Undoubtedly, it was Paul. Then abruptly, almost savagely, he faced her.

Liv recoiled in horror at the sight of his beautiful face— destroyed. She reached out to touch the changed features, feeling tears on her cheeks. He jerked his head away.

"Oh my God," she breathed the words.

They stared at one another, neither of them moving.

"There doesn't seem to be anything to say?"

Liv didn't hear Paul. She only knew she could not let him go. "Where're you staying, Paul? I have to see you, speak to you."

"No! No, Liv this hasn't happened. I cannot see you again."

Paul turned his back on her. She would remember his eyes filling with pain as he stood etched against the mountain and the clear blue sky. When he reached his car, she still stood, watching him.

Liv sat in her car for a long while. He had a right not to be disturbed if that was what he wanted. She had absolved herself of every claim to him. What was it she wanted from him? She did not see bitterness or loathing in his eyes. What she saw was longing and that inchoate loneliness, which so haunted her when they had first met.

The sexual charge was there between them. Despite his shat- tered face, he could have taken her to bed immediately. Heart to heart. She had never felt this raw lust, this desire for John. For sex, maybe, but never for John.

Liv drove slowly back to *Duiwel's Hoogte*. She knew Paul was correct in leaving the present untouched. But it would be easy to find out where he was staying. She greeted the staff and reassured them about John's well-being. She walked onto the patio and kissed Marion, all her actions conveying her usual calm, masking her turmoil, her writhing thoughts and emotions, and memories and lust.

"Can we eat now, Mummy?"

Liv pressed a hand to her forehead. "Yes, darling, of course. I'm sorry."

This time, Liv knew, she must do right by Paul, herself, and Marion while protecting both Marion and John. There must be a way to bring Paul and Marion together without doing any more damage to anyone.

The next morning, she attended to her chores and visited John at the hospital. But she couldn't get Paul out of her mind. His book had touched her deeply, but why had he dedicated his work to her? Again, she could hear Paul's voice, see the patient amusement in his eyes, and trace the curve of his mouth. But now he had the face of a stranger.

While she sat musing in the sunlight, Marion approached her. She held aloft a strongly colored painting of a starfish still dripping paint onto the flagstones of the patio. Somehow without imploding around her head all the edifices she so carefully created, Paul must be made aware of Marion.

Liv hugged her daughter closely. "You're more precious to me than all the starfish on all the beaches in the whole great, big, wide world."

"Oh, Mummy, you say such funny things."

Momentarily, Marion clung to her mother and then wriggled free.

That afternoon Liv stood outside the door, hesitating to ring the doorbell. She wiped her hands on her skirt. Taking a deep breath, she pressed the buzzer. The door opened, and Paul stared at her in amazement. He attempted to close the door in her face.

"No, wait, Paul, please. I must speak to you. It's very important."

Paul hesitated, then opened the door motioning for her to enter. "I suppose you know what you're doing?"

Liv nodded.

"Okay, what's all of this about then?"

Liv glanced around the room. There was a typewriter on the table with a small pile of paper next to it. It was as sparse as his room in Hillbrow all those years ago. She gazed at his face to imprint its image over the passage of time.

"Your book is beautiful, Paul."

He accepted her praise with a slight movement of his head.

"I don't know why you dedicated it to me, though, but I'm pleased and proud."

And guilt-ridden that you called to me then and I couldn't be with you.

They chatted amicably but politely like distant acquaintances. Liv said, "I thought you were in Johannesburg . . ."

"The materialism of Johannesburg disturbed me," answered Paul. "After London, the soulless city center with no night life depressed me. As a contrast, an old friend from trade union days invited me to Alexandria township to a *shebeen*, a sort of pub . . . with a lively vibe."

Liv said, "I know what a *shebeen* is, Paul, and I know that in the shantytowns people live amid desperate poverty and lack of services. I volunteer once a week at a Black Sash crèche in Alex."

"Well, anyway," said Paul, "I came to Cape Town mainly because of the promise held by a famous plastic surgeon's reputed skill."

"And . . ."

"Well, the surgeon was noncommittal at first. He took some

skin samples and told me to return in a week. In the interim, I explored the city. I was shocked to see the apartheid master race had razed District Six to rubble. I used to hang out there with Moosa. Wonderful community; filled with life and music and camaraderie. Now, they've all been forcefully moved to a sterile, windswept location, called New Horizons situated miles from Cape Town. The people there see unwelcome new horizons. It feels desperate here in South Africa with all these apartheid government changes.

"Miriam told me there were signs that Whites were waking up to what's happening, to the juggernaut advance of the racist policies of the apartheid government. Take the Torch Commando, ex-servicemen who've banded together on a massive scale.

Liv interjected, "Then there's my group, the Black Sash. I joined them because I admire their bravery. Last week we picketed parliament wearing black sashes to signify the demise of constitutional rights in South Africa."

Paul continued almost as if he didn't hear her. "I did return to the hospital for another round of tests. The surgeon grafted a small sample of my skin taken previously from my left thigh onto a tiny area below my hairline. Told me yet again to return in a week.

"That time he spoke quietly and slowly to me. He said, that despite the fact that the graft took very well and grafting procedures will be routine, in his opinion further such surgery was inadvisable. The technology does not yet exist to provide the basic framework to reconstruct my face. If, however, I decide to go ahead with more grafting, he can change the shape of my mouth, perhaps lower my left eyebrow, but he added that he hardly thought the overall effect will be worth the trauma.

"I said I would think about more surgery. This news stunned

me. I realized I had counted on him to restore me to some resemblance of my former self."

Paul stared intently at Liv. "I don't know for how much longer I can live with this ogre face."

Liv swallowed her words. Sympathy was not enough in this stark situation. She said nothing but couldn't stop the tears rolling down her cheeks.

Paul stood and towered over her. Changing the subject, he asked angrily, "What the hell do you want, Liv?"

She spoke softly. "It's time for truth, I guess."

Paul responded, "Truth? What truth? The truth is staring at you."

Liv forgot the text she had drilled herself to remember. Instead, she heard the forbidden words rushing from her. "I told you then I loved you, Paul, and I'd always love you. It's true. I love you now, more than before. Nothing changes that. Not even being married to John. I love you."

Paul sat again and leaned forward in his chair, gesturing imploringly to her. "Liv, please stop."

Liv choked on her next words, swallowing desperately. She began again. "I know now that you've always known that. I know you love me because I hear you at night. I hear you speaking to me. Then that time in Jerusalem, when you were injured, you wrote in your book that you called to me. I heard you. I wanted to come to you. I would have, but Marion was so tiny. I was nursing her, so many other things that I didn't, couldn't . . . I failed you, then, too."

Silence. Liv hesitated. She lifted her eyes to Paul, but he was turned away. "You see the truth is . . ."

Paul was on his feet again, then he knelt in front of her and held her hands in his.

"Liv, Liv, Liv. The past, all the past, no longer exists. You really don't have to explain, say anything." Paul shook his head, barely restraining himself.

Liv saw the old longing in his eyes. Suddenly she knew what to do, and her uncertainty and hesitancy fell away. It was easy, so easy. She stood up and led Paul to the bedroom, standing close to him. She started to unbutton his shirt.

"No, Liv, you're married."

"Darling Paul, it's all right. I want this more than anything."

They made love gently, almost solemnly. Afterward, as they lay entwined on the bed, Liv spoke softly. "I'm not going to tell you the truth. I'll bring the truth to you tomorrow."

Liv dressed Marion with special care. She told her they were visiting an old friend, someone who hadn't seen her yet and who would be most surprised when he did see her. However, she explained it was their special, special secret. Marion nodded, her eyes steadily watching her mother's face. She loved secrets. She was used to keeping her mother's secrets.

Sensing her mother's anxiety, she became strangely excited, too. Liv told her that, while she stayed to talk to this man, Amina, her nanny, would take her to the swings in the park next to the sea. She knew that park. Liv had brought her there before when they visited an old aunt.

Liv rang Paul's doorbell, aware again of her wildly beating heart. Marion stood trustingly at her side. Liv waited, terrified of the enormity of the risk she was taking.

Paul opened the door, a smile of welcome in his eyes. Liv noticed he hardly moved his lips when he smiled.

"Hello Paul, I've brought someone to meet you. Say hello to Paul, Marion."

Marion stared silently at the man with the strange face. She clutched one of her mother's hands. The man stared at her as if he had never seen a child before. He dropped to his knees in front of her and gazed into her face.

"No, it can't be, it can't be, it can't," he breathed the words like an incantation.

"Aren't you going to invite us in? I've told Marion how one can watch the ocean from your window and the ships to and from England and Europe."

"Yes, of course. Come in."

His eyes never left Marion as she walked tentatively ahead of them into the room. And then Paul turned to look at Liv. It was impossible for Liv to read his expression.

"She's very beautiful."

Paul spoke so softly, Liv strained to make sense of the words. She shivered, tightly trembling with tension and excitement.

"Marion, come here so Paul can see you properly."

Marion forgot her shyness in her excitement of seeing the wide expanse of the Atlantic. She moved to stand in front of Paul, who perched nervously on the edge of a chair. He stared at her for a long moment and then stretched out a hand to stroke her dark blond hair laying over her shoulders in a silken sheen. Marion stood still, gazing intently back at Paul and his face.

"Don't be frightened." He spoke softly and reassuringly.

"I'm not frightened. You're like my father."

Liv was filled with pride at Marion's response to Paul. She placed her arm over Marion's shoulders, hugging her. "Come on. Paul and I will put you into the lift. Amina is waiting for you."

"You stay here. I'll take her." Paul held Marion's hand, and Liv waved to them both, sinking back into a chair.

The door opened, and she looked apprehensively at Paul. Sitting opposite her, he clasped her cold hands in both of his own.

"Thank you for bringing her to me. I can't say more. I don't know what to say."

Silence.

"It's a shock, dammit." His voice rose alarmingly, and his hands shook. "Go! Please go and leave me alone. I need time to think and process this earthquake."

As she brushed passed him, he pulled her close and hugged her—heart to heart—as if to imprint permanently the memory of her body on his. When he released her and turned away, she left hurriedly, uncertain and aware of momentous portents around her, but unable to comprehend the prophecy.

Strangely, Marion never mentioned the incident, not even when John asked, "And what's my favorite girl been doing?"

Liv held her breath, anticipating the storm. But Marion remained silent about her visit to Paul. She chattered about horses on the beach splashing through the waves. She asked if she could learn to ride.

John nodded. "Good idea!"

Safely, Liv and John moved to neutral ground and spoke of familiar domestic matters and national politics, a shared interest.

"Did you read the paper today? Did you see that Div's going along with the government again? The United Party is no opposition to the government. Div thinks that by supporting the government, he can win back the votes the United Party lost in the election."

"We need a new opposition party."

John nodded his head, so Liv continued. "The other news is that Helen Suzman beat Joyce Waring in the nomination contest in Houghton. She'll be standing for us in Houghton in the next election. I'm pleased to be able to vote for her. It will be a pleasure to vote for an intelligent woman for a change. I'm sick of those gray-suited men who all look the same."

Sporadically, sometimes years apart, the letters came. Paul addressed them to Sally. Sally without comment, aside from a raised eyebrow, understood to hand them, at Paul's request, unopened, to Liv when they were alone. Liv never responded to the letters. Paul had returned to London, to continue building a life for himself. His doctor said new research might lead to protocols to help reform his face. He was dating someone, then someone else. The letters stopped coming.

In 1952, Jane Weisz succumbed to breast cancer when Marion turned ten. During the final weeks before Jane's death, Sally and Liv had spent many hours at her hospital bedside. At that time, Liv told Sally the truth about Marion's parentage.

"Paul's her father, not John. No one else knows. Swear you won't tell anyone!"

Sally said, "Of course I won't tell. I guessed as much from when Marion was born but never said a word to anyone."

"Swear!" Liv repeated urgently. Sally looked at her, perhaps surprised at Liv's intensity. She said softly but earnestly, clasping Liv's hand across the bed, both their hands resting on Jane who lay under the hospital blanket, "I solemnly swear."

Jane, in a morphine-induced state and barely conscious, must have heard some of the conversation because a small smile appeared fleetingly on her lips. They heard the rasped word, "Goodbye."

Jane died that night. Liv mourned her loss with the love she never felt when her mother lived, regretful now that she never fulfilled her role in the mother-daughter bond Jane wanted so badly. After Jane's death, Liv often surprised herself with sudden bursts of jagged sobs. This phase lasted for weeks. John insisted she see a psychologist, but she never did.

Sally was bereft after Jane's death, but she mourned her deep loss alone. She would not talk about Jane to anyone, including Liv. Her coping mechanism was to work even harder at Weisz Corporation.

Soon after, Liv and John divorced. He confessed his infidelity to Liv and wanted to marry his mistress, a younger woman, who truly loved him with a love he had never felt from Liv. Liv received a large divorce settlement. She did not realize the tension she had lived with until she experienced great relief at John's absence. At last, she lived her life free of guilt for having deviously married him.

John continued to be a conscientious father to Marion until two years later. In an old Ivans family album, he found a photograph of Paul as a young man. Immediately he saw the connection and was outraged that Liv had duped him so blatantly.

Liv defended herself quietly. "I never deceived you, John. I believed the doctor. He said you were Marion's father. I truly believed you were her father."

They agreed that for Marion's sake and to avoid a public scandal, they would keep Marion's paternity secret.

John cut himself off from all contact with Liv and Marion. Along with his second wife, he moved permanently to *Duiwel's Hoogte*, and when Max died, he established his corporate headquarters in Cape Town.

Marion was now in a weekly boarder at Kingsplace, Liv's old, suburban high school, when Liv decided to tackle a daunting project. She bought a dilapidated farm called *Loeriebos* in Rivonia on the outskirts of greater Johannesburg. She embarked on rebuilding the derelict farmhouse and crumbling tobacco sheds into her home. After the renovations and her move, she learned to understand *Loeriebos'* moods in different lights.

Marion loved her weekends home at *Loeriebos*, a break from boarding school, usually with two or three friends in tow, always including her best friend, Betty, whose family lived on a farm far from school. *Loeriebos* was adjacent to a riding school, and Marion loved to ride whenever she was home. Marion matriculated to Witwatersrand University in 1959, where she lived as a full-time boarder in the Sunnyside dorm.

After Helmut's second wife, Golda, died, and as he was nearing eighty-five and ailing, the family settled Helmut in the Jewish Old Age home in Johannesburg, where he lived in the Weisz wing among several other members of the family. After his stroke, when he could barely speak, he tried desperately to tell Liv and Sally about his child with Marierentia Van Niekerk.

But they could not make sense of his slurred words.

Several months later, he died with his secrets and left a large portion of his Weisz Corporation shares to Sally but nothing to his estranged son, Bernard. He had set up trust funds for Bernard's two children and for Liv, who he always considered his grandchild and Sally's child.

Sally became the chief executive and chairman of Weisz Corporation. She achieved fame as the first woman in South Africa to hold that position. Weisz Corporation with international connections in England, the United States, and countries in Europe required she travel frequently to London, and the company owned a flat in Green Park. If she ever saw Paul, she never told Liv, and Liv never asked.

Micah Weisz rose in the ranks of the Israeli government. A favorite of Israel's first president Chaim Weitzmann, he always accompanied Weitzmann on diplomatic trips internationally. When Weitzmann died, Micah retired to the kibbutz he had helped establish in the 1920s. He and his wife, Gerda, never had children, but his cousin Bernard and Bernard's children, and their growing families living on the kibbutz cemented the Weisz presence in Israel.

All the Weisz family in South Africa, through successive generations, continued to enjoy Plettenberg Bay and their family home, *Milkwood*.

1960
LIV

Liv awoke early as she did most mornings. But it was only on relatively recent mornings, after she cut off contact with Rosie that she did not awaken with feelings of guilt. She had loved Rosie, Rosie had loved her, and she had killed that love.

Little point in brooding about it now, I am a sullied soul, I hurt people, especially those I love the most, something is so twisted in me. Maybe, after all, I am only meant to be faithful to causes. And no cause is greater now than staying faithful to Jaco, Daniel, and human rights.

It's Saturday, Jubilee Day, dawning brightly. The past three weeks has been a surreal and frightening time for every South African, as the country backed away slowly from the chasm of anarchy. Liv tried to imagine early morning scenes around the awakening city and environs.

In Soweto and the East Rand townships, people proceeded with their lives, not believing how close the government tottered on the point of collapse. They couldn't imagine that they possessed any political power while armored troop carriers patrolled the streets and police stations fortified with sandbags and barbed wire bustled with more police personnel than they had witnessed before. The police had always acted as an occupying force rather than protectors since the National Party came to power in 1948.

Johannesburg's city center breathed quietly on this morning, broken only by the "chop-chop" of several military helicopters, a continuous irritating noise from the southwest. Since the Sharpeville Massacre, the sound had formed a familiar feature of life on the Witwatersrand Highveld.

In the White-only suburbs, birds abounded—gray loeries, bokmakieries, carmine bee-eaters, long-billed sunbirds, crested barbets, hoopoes, crimson-breasted shrikes, butcher birds, wagtails, weaver birds, hummingbirds, and doves.

Even farther north in Rivonia—the peri-urban expanse of small holdings between the more exclusive Johannesburg suburbs and small Highveld dairy and vegetable farms serving the city— Liv stretched in bed and fell asleep again. The mourning doves cooing in the wisteria outside her bedroom window did not disturb her.

The eerie uncertainty of the past three weeks, when the country existed in a disquieting limbo, resonated in life at *Loeriebos*. The procession of arrivals and departures ended abruptly with the Sharpeville Massacre and subsequent crackdown. The fields around the house further isolated the inhabitants from outsiders. Liv sat on the bed as the reality of South Africa's current situation flooded back into her consciousness. She had not heard anything from anyone. With both the PAC and the ANC in disarray, the organizations were operating underground. Someone would come soon with information.

Brave Pauline, Jaco's wife, visited briefly and told Liv, "Sobukwe is using a prison cook at The Fort to convey instructions to his lieutenants. Jaco's imprisonment is a huge blow. We need his legal expertise as never before. But I think they will release him soon. He is too well-known internationally, and legal associations around the world are pressuring for his and the others' release."

Liv headed for the bathroom. She assumed Jaco and the Prof must know the PAC was banned yesterday. Maybe it would be her turn for detention soon? She didn't understand why they hadn't come for her yet. But what about Marion and the Weisz family? *Loeriebos*? Loose ends with Rosie? Should she choose exile?

If she left, where would she go? Liv lingered at the bathroom window with the wisteria in bloom, the eucalyptus trees beyond, the deep blue sky, and the spectacular golden sunlight. She shuddered. If she left, they may not let her back in. She belonged here. Maybe some part of her wanted to go to prison . . . to prove something . . . to show she truly was part of the struggle and the solution, loyal to Sobukwe and to PAC principles.

Had she peeked into that dark dilemma that dogged her for years? Did she want to go to prison? Flustered, Liv knew she was trapped. She missed Rosie and acknowledged she had cut off their contact in the cruelest way.

At around half past one in the afternoon, Liv arrived in the Jaguar at the Rand Easter Show members' parking ground. Dressed in a summer frock, she also wore the straw hat and large dark sunglasses made fashionable by Jacqueline Kennedy and Audrey Hepburn.

She walked through service roads packed with White-only pedestrians. Rand Show visitors were eager to enjoy various ethnic foods and fun fair rides. People visited many exhibition halls, viewing the latest machinery, scientific breakthroughs, and manufactured goods from different nations. In the South African Pavilion, the mining and industrial sectors mounted fascinating models of their latest innovations attesting to South Africa being the world leader in deep-mining technology and other industries. Weisz Corporation was named as a leader in South African industry.

Outside the exhibit hall, South African Defense Force Sabre and Impala jets, Saracens, and other armored vehicles drew much attention. Children climbed over and explored the equipment under the watchful eyes of armed soldiers. A larger uniformed police presence patrolled the grounds than in previous years.

Liv muttered to herself, "It's the plainclothes goons we have to worry about."

Entering the main arena through the Members Only tunnel, many people greeted her. One of the Witwatersrand Agricultural Society members, a middle-aged man sporting a large official nametag with a purple ribbon—*David Pratt*—shook Liv's hand.

"Don't forget to see my trout exhibits," Pratt called after her as he continued toward the area where his reserved seat situated him as one of the platform party.

Ushered to a Weisz family box, Liv saw Marion sitting with several aunts and uncles as well as younger cousins. Liv sat next to her daughter, "This is a pleasant surprise; didn't know you were coming."

"Last minute. An invitation from Aunt Sally. Easy for me and a short walk from my campus dorm. It's good to see so many family members. We haven't connected for a while."

Sally, unmistakably the family matriarch, told Liv, "I'm taking a break from all-day meetings with other key industrialists and government finance officials. I'll leave after the prime minister's speech."

David Pratt, seated on the speakers' platform to the right, waved to the Weisz box. They sat in the box on his left. Nodding in his direction, Liv and some of the others waved back. Liv whispered to Marion, "That's David Pratt. You may be interested to know he wanted to become part of our family, to marry one of our cousins years ago but she refused him. He's a little odd. Early fifties, a gentleman farmer, and socialite. He loves Monte Carlo, St. Tropez, Biarritz, and all the hot spots. He lives on a beautiful estate on the Hartebeespoort Dam with his family and has three children. He has interests in several Weisz agricultural ventures around the country. Sally says he's a good businessman, but she would never trust him with a blank check."

Marion smiled. "Interesting stuff, but right now, I'm not particularly interested. Although it might be fun to have had family on Hartebeespoort Dam. Waterskiing, you know. Climbing in the Magaliesberg."

A fanfare of trumpets announced the prime minister's arrival, and shortly thereafter, Dr. Verwoerd stepped onto the platform and walked to his seat. He wore a light-gray suit with a South African flag pin on one lapel and a curled yellow rosebud on the other. He shook hands with the platform party, waved to the packed arena, and occupied his seat.

Colonel G. M. Harrison, chairman of the Witwatersrand Agricultural Society, formally opened the 1960 Rand Easter Show and introduced the prime minister. Verwoerd stepped up to the microphone and made a speech celebrating the achievements and contributions of all South Africans to the fifty years of growth and development of the country. He made no reference to the events of the past three weeks. Liv tried to relax her stiffened spine as she listened to Verwoerd, while experiencing unease and foreboding. Never this close to him, his presence filled her with horror. He was the very heart and mind of the apartheid beast.

"Mephistopheles," Liv hissed under her breath. Only Marion caught her word and she shook her head in warning.

Unexpectedly, in her peripheral vision, Liv saw movement on the platform. David Pratt approached Verwoerd seated in the front row. No one moved to stop him; he belonged on the platform. His lips moved as he called, "Dr. Verwoerd," and pulled an automatic pistol from his jacket pocket. He fired two shots directly into Verwoerd's face.

Pandemonium ensued.

At the sound of the shots, Liv leaped to her feet and pulled Marion with her. Everyone first stared with shocked attention at the scene unfolding on the platform, and then they exited the main arena among the throng. The crowds in the showgrounds did not know what transpired and continued to mill around the exhibit halls. Within thirty minutes of the incident, the SABC cancelled all regular programming and broadcast somber music, interspersed with frequent updates on the shooting and the prime minister's condition.

"If old Hendrik survives," as they surged with the crowd Liv posed the rhetorical question to Marion, "can he ever run the country again?" She shook her head in disbelief. "How can anyone who looks so avuncular with his silvered hair, rosy cheeks, and cheerful demeanor harbor such race hatred? Almost as if he were a Biblical prophet and leader, the chosen one destined to solidify the White Afrikaner Herrenvolk's eternal domination of millions of Black Africans on this southernmost tip of Mother Afrika."

"Beats me, too," replied Marion in a somber voice.

"I want you to come home with me, Marion. I don't want either of us to be alone tonight."

Marion nodded, "Me neither. I don't want you to be alone tonight."

Back at *Loeriebos,* they settled on the veranda and listened to the transistor radio, along with the entire country and much of the world.

Later, the police gave an account of the assassination attempt as a broadcast and then published the information in the *Rand Daily Mail* and every other South African newspaper,

"On 9 April 1960, Dr. Verwoerd opened the Union Exposition on the Witwatersrand to mark the jubilee of the Union of South Africa. Having made his opening speech, he took his seat. A man stepped up near the front row of seats in which the prime minister was sitting. A shot was fired at point-blank range into Dr. Verwoerd's right cheek from a .22 automatic pistol. A second shot was fired into his right ear. Colonel G.M. Harrison, president of the Witwatersrand Agricultural Society, had leaped up and knocked the pistol from the gunman's hand. After the pistol fell to the floor, Colonel Harrison, with the help of Major (Carl) Richter (the prime minister's personal bodyguard), civilians, and another policeman, overpowered the gunman and hustled him to the showgrounds police station. The detainee, David Pratt, was soon thereafter hurried to Marshall Square police station."

"You know, darling," Liv shattered their silence, while sighing with resignation, "there is no good outcome to this. David Pratt doesn't have a political bone in his body. I swear he acted alone and I can't even begin to speculate on why he did this. The timing is so strange. After the three weeks we've all been through with the Security Forces on high alert . . ." Shaking her head, Liv said, "If the PM dies, watch out. We will become a police state overnight."

By dinner, the only news broadcast continued to report Dr. Verwoerd's arrival, still conscious, at a Pretoria hospital some hours earlier. Specialists called in surgeons to remove the bullets.

Later, that night a loud banging noise at the front door awoke them. Rolling over, Liv, through a sleep haze, glanced at the alarm clock: 2:00 a.m. Cold terror squeezed her heart. Awake, startled, she stared at Marion, eyes large with fright, now standing at her bedside.

"Marion, we don't have much time. I must let them in before they break down the door."

They clung together for a long moment. "Remember what I told you to do," Liv whispered.

"This can't be happening." Marion's voice quivered. "Remember always, we all love you, Mom. Aunt Sally will set this right."

"Stay here," Liv ordered. "Remember the phone calls." "Of course," Marion answered. "But I'm coming down with you."

Together in their dressing gowns, they descended the stairs. The dogs stood bleary-eyed in the hallway. Liv unlocked the front door.

"Olivia Weisz?" A uniformed police officer asked, as another policeman hovered behind him. Liv identified herself. "We are arresting you under the Emergency Regulations. No warrant needed. You have five minutes to dress and pack a few personal items. Strijdom. *Gaan met haar.*" He directed the young officer to go with her.

Under the watchful eyes of young Corporal Strijdom, whose singular feature were his acne-covered cheeks, they returned to Liv's bedroom. In the bathroom, Liv changed into slacks and her customary ivory silk shirt. In the bedroom, Marion fixed an implacable stare on the young policeman. He shifted from foot to foot. Liv emerged, holding her head high, not looking at Marion, who sealed her lips in a tight line trying not to cry out in anguish.

In the front hallway they shared a brief embrace but said nothing. Two policemen led Liv to a car where a third ran the engine in readiness for her departure.

1960
LIV

The Fort, Johannesburg
May

On the eighteenth day of her incarceration, April 27, panic fluttered in Liv's throat. By now Sally must have exerted her influence and should have been able to secure, if not her release, perhaps some concession about gaining access to her. During the recent crisis, Sally had stood strong at the epicenter. What did her being ignored mean? The terror Liv restrained for so many days of not knowing what occurred beyond her prison cell washed over her, like a freak Robberg wave. Maybe Marion never contacted her? Maybe the whole country somersaulted and collapsed into anarchy? What of Jaco? What has happened to Daniel?

For three weeks, Liv glimpsed the wardresses and occasionally a Black female prisoner on her knees scrubbing the old linoleum floor under a guard's watchful eyes. No one spoke to her. For three weeks, each morning as she awoke dreaming of the ghosts in her life, she vowed not to think of them again that day.

If she was going to survive this prison ordeal, she must be present to her situation.

Perhaps Sally, learning of her detention from Marion, wanted nothing more to do with her. Liv had plenty of time to think and relive memories while she walked the steps along the way to her prison cell. But memories, long buried, now became vivid to her.

The epic row with her mother as she was about to graduate from university. Eighteen years earlier, after her studies at UCT, she had emerged as a well-educated, left leaning, politically and socially aware adult. She and her classmates primed to carry forward the flag of liberalism and human rights. Back then, with determination, she tried to focus her mother's attention on the political direction of the country, the slow drift to a more oppressive regime, to help her foster some realization of South African reality.

The bitterness of their disagreement—the chasm that opened—led them both to agree never to discuss those issues again. One of her mother's outrageous justifications for the wealth generated by the conglomerate headed by Papa Helmut became almost a mantra for her.

"We give the natives jobs. What else do they want?"

They want a living wage, human rights in their own country, and a stake in the wealth they dig from arteries of golden ore deep in the earth.

Moral blindness. Liv clung to that phrase. Her mother was not a bad person and Liv supposed she loved her, but she was blind to South Africa's reality. Liv never forgot her mother's grim, hostile voice.

"We're White. We live here. We have to look after our own. Do you think for one moment 'they' would care what becomes of us?"

Liv grimaced, remembering her mother's coldness. At present, Liv imagined the worst-case scenario. Maybe Marion never called Sally. Maybe Sally doesn't know she's here? Liv's searing self-questioning several weeks earlier that maybe she wanted to go to prison to prove her commitment grew more and more urgent with each day.

On that morning of April 27, she felt sick and vomited into the cereal bowl containing sloppy oatmeal. Sweating in the chilly cell, her heart beat wildly. She was having a panic attack. In fury, she slammed and broke a wooden chair against the cell door, screaming, "Wardress! Wardress!" One of the women who sometimes directed her to her daily walk came running along the corridor.

"Put the chair down and back away," she said to Liv, her eyes staring from a six-inch grate in the heavy door. "What's wrong?"

Collapsing on the floor Liv tried, but failed, to stifle a burst of frenzied laughter at the Kafkaesque question.

"Come on Weisz, you're hysterical. Sistog, pull yourself together or I'll have to get the prison doctor. Maybe you need a shot to calm you?"

Leaping at the door, Liv tried to grab the woman's hands but of course the opening proved too small.

"No! No shots."

Shots scared her. She would be tranquilized into a vegetative state with no control over her body. She imagined a prison doctor similar to one from a Nazi concentration camp eager to conduct experiments. She made a strenuous effort to control her behavior.

"I'm okay; just lost it for a moment. Truly, I'm okay."

Later, at noon, as she chewed an almost unpalatable ham

sandwich, she bit on what felt like a piece of wax wrap. Annoyed, she used her tongue to isolate the plastic in her mouth and spat it into her hand. Hidden in the tiny twist, she found a scrap of paper. Untwisting the wax, she extracted the scrap and read, "JM is on your case. Petitions for your release." She almost stopped breathing. "Destroy this."

The bare cell held no plausible place to hide the note, so taking deep breaths she swallowed it with the remnants of the sandwich. Jaco Malan—JM—was out of prison and the PAC network was able to communicate with her. Her body felt weak, and she heaved in violent spasms as she lay on the cot. Later in the afternoon, she struggled at first to walk on the sand circuit in an inner courtyard for the half an hour exercise period. The cold late autumn wind revived her.

Every few days thereafter, an abbreviated note appeared somewhere in Liv's lunch packet.

"Your family is creating hell for the Cab."

"Suzman and RDM demand your release."

"ANC and PAC in disarray."

"Verwoerd survives unharmed."

"Be prepared. Your interrogation starts tomorrow."

Who scribbled the note? Can they be trusted? Affirmation of their veracity came in the corroborating form of her first interrogation in the wee hours of the morning on the following day.

During the night of May 4, several hours after Liv fell asleep, a wardress appeared at her cell and ordered her to dress. Sleepy, Liv followed a little behind her through many barred gates the wardress unlocked and with a clang locked behind them. They descended several floors in a lift to the bowels of The Fort. After the wardress left her at the door, alert and on guard, Liv entered the interrogation room alone.

A middle-aged man, well dressed in a dark suit and tie, motioned for her to sit opposite him at a wooden table. He smiled and she noted his understated good looks, long, but well-cut, hair, kind eyes crinkling in the corners, and a dimple on one cheek that indented when he smiled.

"I'm Kevin Steyn, and he's Hennie Van Niekerk."

In a corner, half-hidden by shadows, slouched a middle-aged, scowling White man with brush-cut hair, sunken cheekbones, and the dark, burning eyes of a fanatic; he glared with menace and intense hatred at Liv.

Liv stared back at him. His eyes, something about his eyes, remind me of someone. He has Weisz features. But why such hatred towards me? She mentally shook herself. Me, being fanciful. Stop this. Concentrate on the good cop.

Liv glanced quickly around the room. Windowless—about twice the size of her cell and lit by a naked light bulb hanging low over the table—crackled with danger. A closer look revealed the white washed walls, unpainted in years, and a linoleum floor with crevices in many places. Clinging antennae of claustrophobia threatened to close her throat. Damp, dank, and cold, the smell of musty air permeated the space, despite the one small Capel heater that made little difference to the room's temperature.

Unnerved by Van Niekerk's stare, she concentrated on the first man who had introduced himself as Kevin Steyn. He surprised her with his well-educated, English-speaking accent. Good cop, bad cop. Over the years how many people suffered interrogation in this room arranged like the set of a mediocre American crime movie? Jaco had warned her to prepare for this set-up.

"We have a few questions for you," Steyn began. "You can help us and yourself by giving complete answers."

He paused, but Liv made no comment. Jaco rehearsed with her a "just in case" scenario weeks ago. Cooperate and give truthful answers to all the questions because the Special Branch knew the answers and would use lies as traps.

"Tell me how you know Robert Sobukwe."

Giving a full account of the history of her involvement with Sobukwe, Liv concluded, "I don't know him well. We have spoken several times, especially in the last months. I admire him and his vision for a nonracial South Africa."

"Where did you meet? At your house—at *Loeriebos*?"

"Yes, there, but also occasionally at public meetings."

"And Daniel Molefe? What do you know about Molefe?"

In detail, Liv explained how she had met Daniel in London several years before and how he and some of the other PAC members stayed at her house when they attended meetings on the Witwatersrand.

"Sometimes they held meetings at my house, but most often I wasn't present." Aware of her provocation, she reminded Steyn, "The PAC was not banned at the time, and its members were free to stay anywhere, even in my house, even if it is a so-called 'White area,' as long as it did not become their permanent abode."

Steyn chided Liv in his soft-spoken manner. "I know the law. What is your relationship with Daniel Molefe?"

Liv's danger meter screamed.

The other man strode to where she sat at the table and lifted a hand as if to strike her. "*Hoekom swart mense? Kaffirs? Hoekom?*"

Liv recoiled in fright as he asked her, "Why Black people? Kaffirs? Why?"

The "good" cop spoke, annoyed. *"Laat los Van Niekerk! Let it go. Sit stil man of uit die kamer gaan! Listen to me!"*

Van Niekerk muttered as he returned to his chair in the corner. Steyn shuffled some papers on the table, gathering his composure.

For the moment, Liv accepted the validity of Steyn's surprise at Van Niekerk's outburst, not knowing if it was a staged scene when Steyn ordered Van Niekerk to sit still or leave the room.

"Have you ever had sexual relations with Daniel Molefe?"

The question startled her and she shook her head without hesitation. A solemn vow is forever. "No."

So, they trotted out the tired, old saw of White women desiring the sexual prowess of Black men.

"Are you sure?"

"Yes, I'm sure."

"What if I told you Molefe said he had sexual relations with you several times?"

Steyn's voice, filled with sudden intensity, alerted her. Several times! They don't know. Even under torture, Daniel—given his innate steadfastness—would never lie about her and never implicate her. A solemn vow is forever. She harbored no doubts as to his loyalty.

"No, I did not have sexual relations with Daniel. He is a brother to me. I don't practice incest."

In that moment, she regretted the remark as unskilled and unnecessary. From his corner, Van Niekerk's increasing outrage was palpable and Liv's ire rose; she cautioned herself to be careful. But Steyn did not comment; he stayed with his script.

"David Pratt? What can you tell us about David Pratt?"

Liv shared her few interactions with David Pratt.

"Is Pratt a member of the PAC? Is he close to Sobukwe?"

"I don't know the answer to the first question. I doubt if he and Sobukwe ever met."

"Do you know this for a fact?"

Liv shook her head. "My guess arises from my understanding of both men."

Steyn repeated the questions several times—Sobukwe, *Loeriebos*, Molefe, Pratt—and each time Liv tried to replicate her original answers. In the end, Steyn called for the wardress and she escorted Liv back to her cell.

Exhausted, Liv fell into a troubled sleep. She awoke after several hours to the silence of the predawn prison. She was dreaming of Sobukwe, Molefe, her parents, and the Kliptown Congress, where speaker after speaker thundered the question at her: "Why? Why you? Why?"

Liv lay curled in a fetal position on the narrow cot, half-awake in a semi-deluded state and tried to answer them, feeling like a Kafka character on trial.

"I have a pervasive sense of justice. I cannot live my privileged life without working toward sharing the wealth of the country. I have a moral compass. True north for me is the Freedom Charter. At university I learned about the Nietzschean "will to power" that the apartheid ideologues embody. I hate that millions of my fellow South Africans are not treated as people in their own land. I hate that they suffer in my name as a White "European," a settler. I hate that two of my cousins and an uncle died fighting in North African deserts against Nazi racism and Hitler's herrenvolk, only to see that same ugly racist beast rise to power in my beloved country. I hate that my aunt and other industry titans pay their workers such meager wages. In many ways they abet the apartheid government's talons of oppression."

Liv stared at one of her accusers on the stage. "Yes, Papa Helmut, you and Aunt Sally! Yes, I'm conflicted about our family's wealth. Our family's fortune rests on the backs of thousands of underpaid miners and laborers. As is written in the Freedom Charter, 'South Africa belongs to all who live in it, Black and White, and no government can justly claim authority unless it is based on the will of all the people.'"

Liv heard mocking laughter echoing in her cell. She tried again. "Maybe part of my motivation, too, stated in simple terms, is I crave danger and adrenalin. Perhaps I need this secret life that teeters on a precipice and need to be part of something so much larger than myself."

Now fully awake, she discerned the plain truth revealed in her hallucinatory defense—truths she would never utter. Yet answers to the questions at the deepest level evaded her.

Why me? Why this path? Look where I am now. At least in some measure I wanted to go to prison, but I didn't know I would go mad.

Over the next three days, they enacted the interrogation scenario five more times—the same room, the same two men, the same questions, the same answers. The daily prison routine monotonously ticked like a mechanical clock around them, but each day she became edgier, waiting every moment for the wardress to summon her again for another interrogation session. Her sense of reality blurred because of the hysterical compulsion she had developed that someone else was experiencing the repeated interrogations and occupying her prison cell.

She approached a breaking point. Constant nausea, shortness of breath, troubled sleep, loss of appetite and a foreboding horror of being tortured convinced Liv she stood at the threshold of something terrifying. She tried to balance her soul on the razor's edge of madness. For the first time, Liv accepted her sole offensive strategy might be to begin a hunger strike.

On the fourth day, as she entered the interrogation room, she noted a telling change: Steyn was not present. Van Niekerk, the lone interrogator, spoke to her in broken English in his guttural Afrikaans accent.

"*Today jou vriend Steyn is not here. We are alleen.*"

Alone, with fanatical Van Niekerk.

Foreboding silence soaked the air as Liv sat in her familiar seat. Van Niekerk glowered and stood with one hand on a pile of photographs as he threw them, one by one, across the table. His dark eyes glistened with hate.

Those eyes. I recognize those eyes. But whose are they?

"We know who was at your house, when they were there, how long they stayed, who they came with, and who they left with."

As Liv glanced at the photos, a sudden deep terror she never experienced before pierced her body. Warm vomit clawed at her throat, and she swallowed in desperation, almost choking on the acid. Some of the faces in the photos she identified; the others were strangers. Feeling faint, she grasped the table.

"How . . . how did you get these?"

"You're a clever woman, *nie so nie*? You know where these were taken?"

Yes, she did. The only vantage from which these photos emanated was a window in Moses Moekena's living quarters at *Loeriebos*. Moses whom, like Daniel, she relied on never to betray her. Not Moses, who knew her since babyhood and to whom she entrusted her life and the lives of her comrades? Moses had warned her after Sobukwe's first visit surfaced.

"Be careful," he had said.

He had tried to warn her. Jaco's half-joking remark about not trusting even Moses swam into her mind. Her self-control, like a cord in her brain, snapped. Lunging at Van Niekerk, she screamed, "What did you do to him? What did you do to the old man, so he let you take these photographs for over a year?"

Relishing his chance, Van Niekerk swung his hand across Liv's face with full force and the blow sent her crashing to the floor. She shivered in fear and pain, too frightened to attempt to stand. Instinct allowed her to use her hand to break her fall thereby injuring her left wrist. Also, a sensation like an electric shock shot through her left ankle.

Van Niekerk stood at her side and with a jeering smile kicked her in the ribs. Liv screamed in agony.

"You attacked me, *jou teef*. You bitch! Now I have you! What do you think we did? We took two of Moekena's sons into custody and threatened to kill them. We sent photos every so often to show him how they were doing in prison. They are not pretty pictures."

He spat at Liv, half-conscious, as she lay on the floor.

"You rich, English-speaker, Jewish bitch. *Jou rich Engelse, Jood bitch.* Playing games. This is war, lady. *Kaffir sussie.* You are a Kaffir sister. You are the enemy. My name is Hendrik Helmut Paulus Kruger Van Niekerk, Helmut to you. You should know me. Now you'll never forget me. I'll teach you."

Liv, in terrible pain, was past the point of making sense of his words. Van Niekerk placed his hands under her armpits and dragged her like a ragdoll across the floor to the next room. Losing control of her bladder, the sensation of warm liquid ran down her legs. The acrid smell of urine and the intense pain in her wrist, ankle, and ribs caused her to faint. She was vaguely aware that in one jerk, he had torn the gold Magen Dovid from her neck. She almost gagged at the sudden pain.

When Liv regained consciousness, she lay naked on a cold steel surface—a mortuary slab—in the innermost chamber at the heart of The Fort. Torture. Frantic, she tried to summon the will-power to defy her torturer, this sadistic madman, and to deny him the satisfaction of knowing her terror. Futile effort because even she smelled terror. Straps were tied across her shoulders, waist, and wrists; her knees were buckled to the table. While she lay unconscious, Van Niekerk had attached electrodes to her nipples, fingers, and toes.

"I have some more photos for you," Van Niekerk hissed, his lips close to her right ear.

Liv fought her instincts and forced her eyes closed.

"Open your eyes, *meisiekind*, girl, or I'll open them for you!"

Defiant, Liv opened her eyes and almost spat at his face so close to her own. But she desisted, frightened that the vomit she forced down hovered near eruption. Van Niekerk's dark eyes gleamed. The photos swam before her and she fought not to focus on them because she knew what they captured: Rosie—pictures of Rosie—stepping from her car in the driveway at *Loeriebos*, Rosie at the swimming pool, Rosie with the dogs.

"My friend," Liv croaked. "Since Sharpeville, she stayed with me for a few weeks. Haven't seen her since."

"*Sistog, lessie hoer.* You lessie whore. You pervert. You can do better than such a lie. You ever have a man inside you? You ever have one of these inside you, you disgusting cunt? Do you and 'your friend' play with one of these?"

He lifted a battery-driven sheep prod before Liv's eyes. "Do you know where your girlfriend is cavorting while you are locked away in prison? Do you? Answer me, bitch!"

"Noooooooo." As Liv whispered, gold and white spots danced before her eyes.

Screaming in anguish, Liv exploded in a shower of red-hot madness.

With a triumphant cry, Van Niekerk twisted the prod into her vagina and activated the electrodes on her body. "Now we have you—broken!"

Unconscious, Liv did not hear his words or the commotion in the abutting room.

Hours later, Liv awoke in the night with dim light around her bed and everything white . . . the ceiling, walls, and the blankets covering her. She tried, but failed to lift her head, yet she could move it sideways on the pillow. She had drips in both arms and a plaster cast on her left wrist. Apprehensively, she shifted her right foot and encountered a bandage on her left ankle. A thick sanitary pad slathered in a soothing gel lodged between her legs. A curtained screen surrounded the bed and the form of a nurse in a white uniform swam before her. The nurse had applied a film of healing ointment around her neck where the Magen Dovid had been brutally torn from her. Gingerly, afraid of disturbing the drip, she touched the place where it had been.

"So, you are awake, you poor thing," the nurse whispered, observing Liv's staring but unfocused eyes. "Here's another shot. Morphine. Helps with the pain. You are in shock and you need to rest. Doctor's orders."

Liv floated in peace in vast, inner spaciousness, yet at the edge of her consciousness, there was a teasing awareness that Rosie may be consorting with a covert lover—a man? Liv succumbed to morphine confusion.

Days later Kevin Steyn came to her bedside. He stood next to her bed. Embarrassed and uncomfortable, he bent closer to her and in a quiet voice informed her that he received daily reports on her medical condition.

"I am pleased you are healing but you are not eating or drinking. We can't allow a hunger strike, so we are force-feeding you through the drips. There are three other women here whom we are also force-feeding.

"You're also not talking or interacting with your nurses. We know you went through a shocking experience. Shocking. It was never supposed to happen. We're a Christian people; we never torture women."

Liar. But Liv did not have the strength to challenge him. You torture Black women, but they are not women to you, not even people.

Too tired to reengage with the world of racial hatred and torment, Liv wanted to die.

"We discharged Van Niekerk from the force. He was sent to Sterkfontein for mental evaluation. Many of us suspected all along of him being a psychopath, so we've been careful not to leave him alone with prisoners. You know, he insisted he be part of your interrogation. He's obsessed with you. The fact that he's a grandson of Paul Kruger carries some weight with senior officers. Officially, I objected several times to working with him. He forged my signature on an interrogation order so he could be alone with you. Someone heard you screaming and came storming into the torture room—not a moment too soon. We believe another round of shockwaves probably would have killed you. If it is of any comfort, there'll be no more interrogation for you. Try your best to recover your strength."

Why? Only for Marion, a voice in her head told her.

Licking her dry lips, her voice weak, Liv asked, "Where . . . where am I? Does my daughter know about this? May I see her?"

"You are still in The Fort, in the prison infirmary, but we have doctors and specialists attending from Jo'burg General which, as you know, is nearby down the Hill. I wish you well." He ignored her second question. Kevin Steyn disappeared behind the screen.

Over days, Liv reentered the world. Her sprained ankle healed well under the careful daily ministrations of a physiotherapist. After two weeks, the cast on her wrist was replaced with a smaller elasticized bandage. She suffered two broken ribs, but the attending orthopedic surgeon reassured her, within a month, she would be pain-free. On his first examination of the vaginal lacerations, the gynecologist who came once a week to examine her, shook his head and muttered under his breath. Gentle and sensitive, he administered a local anesthetic and stitches.

Whenever medical personnel attended Liv, a wardress accompanied them and she did not permit communication beyond medical information and instructions. All the visiting medical staff signed confidentiality documents forbidding them from talking to anyone about their prisoner-patients.

The other women in the ward communicated in soft voices and Liv listened but did not speak. After so many weeks of silence, broken by the interrogation sessions, the idea of speaking frightened her. The women did not introduce themselves.

From their conversations, Liv learned they numbered among twenty-two White women held in The Fort from around the country. Only two in the group underwent solitary confinement.

All, like her, were denied habeas corpus. The women sent a joint petition to the Minister of Justice in early May, among other demands, petitioning to be tried and to be able to defend themselves against any charges. Seven of their husbands endured imprisonment as well and together they left nineteen parentless children. They began a hunger strike around May 12 for eight days before the prison authorities started force-feeding them.

Events did not seem to cohere. Knowing there were other female detainees in the prison somehow changed her solitary confinement experience. Frustration and bitterness now colored the alternating boredom and terror she remembered and more recently, panic around losing her sanity.

Eventually, Liv was weaned off morphine and the fog in her mind dissipated. Thankfully so far, she had managed to block any memories of the interrogation sessions, at least when she was awake, beyond the strands continuing to obsess her—Moses' betrayal of her and her betrayal of Rosie's love for her.

Brooding on Moses brought welcome tears to her eyes; they signaled a crack in the numbing cement in which she had cast her soul. Compassion arose for the old man and his dilemma; she promised herself to find Moses Moekena wherever he lived at present and apologize for the impossible situation into which she had without any intent placed him. Liv prayed his two sons would survive their prison ordeal.

On May 27, almost three weeks after her first interrogation, walking on her own and almost pain-free, Liv left the ward. She shared a cell with an older, silent woman, and she welcomed the quiet companionship. Silence made it easier to hold onto the pieces of her fragmented self.

On May 28, a wardress surprised her. "Weisz, you've been

given visiting rights. You can have one visitor the day after tomorrow. Please give me a name and phone number."

"Marion Weisz." In a dull voice but without hesitation, Liv recited her daughter's phone number.

"And Weisz, wash your hair in the shower. You look a fright."

The visitor's room—a cubicle in a short corridor of similar spaces—allowed some midmorning light through a small, barred window. Each cubicle contained a small wooden table and two chairs placed opposite one another. The wardress led Liv to a chair.

"No touching, no passing of notes or any other contact. I'll be here, inside the room with you."

"No privacy?"

"No privacy," confirmed the wardress.

Footsteps echoed in the corridor and another wardress opened the door for Marion to enter. Liv's eyes focused on the table. Marion gasped when she saw her mother. Liv's hair was disheveled and lifeless, the prison clothes hung on her, and she sunk into herself with her shoulders rounded and her demeanor one of sullen defeat.

As Marion slid into the chair opposite her, Liv lifted her face and stared at her as if at a ghost. Marion's eyes filled with tears, yet she managed a smile of reassurance and struggled to find the appropriate words. Marion spoke in as quiet a voice as possible, desperate to convey all the love she felt.

"Mom, what have they done to you?" Tears fell down her face.

Liv stretched her right hand, trying to grip Marion's hand. "Tell Jaco and Sally I'm all right."

Marion nodded speechless. Liv couldn't stand the reality of this encounter.

"I love you, darling," she said, as she pushed back the chair and with her head still down, charged passed the wardress and barged through the cluster of wardresses at the door, leaving a hubbub of consternation behind her.

"Mom!" Marion's desperate cry followed her down the corridor.

Once back in her cell, Liv curled on the cot and her body heaved with spasms. She cried, sobbing, the sobs arising from deep within her abdomen. Her cellmate sat beside her, stroking her back, patting her, and speaking for the first time.

"There, there, have a good cry. Let it all out. Let out all the poison. This is good. This is good."

Two days later, the doctor monitoring Liv visited her and aware of the wardress listening at attention, Liv asked him, "What happened to my visitor the other day? I abandoned her."

Liv needed to convey the depth of her remorse and contrition. She needed to be out of prison. The following day she pleaded in a measured tone, wanting to reassure the doctor and wardress and make them understand she was not a danger to anyone. She spoke, "Something snapped in my brain in the visitor's room. But I'm okay now. The visit woke me up. I'm okay." The doctor nodded, his eyes showing empathy.

Almost a week after Marion's visit on May 31, Union Day, 154 detainees at prisons around the country obtained releases "as a gesture of goodwill."

On that day, when a wardress escorted Liv back from the showers, she found her civilian clothes on the cot in the cell. The wardress informed Liv of her release, but, in her state of stoic, day-by-day nihilism, Liv gave no credence to the information. She obeyed instructions and like an automaton, donned her clothes. They felt three sizes too large, and she did not know the person to whom they belonged. The ivory-colored silk blouse felt unde-servedly luxurious against her skin.

Liv's cellmate had already vacated the cell. Following the wardress through the warren of passages and barred doors to the elevator, Liv joined the queue of women shuffling forward at the front desk, their set faces blank. Finally, she reached the desk, signed the release form, and heard her release was "conditional," her status "house arrest."

A wardress read the list of conditions: "Olivia Weisz is restricted to the magisterial district of Johannesburg. She must not go out between seven in the evening and seven in the morning, unless with the magistrate's permission. She must report in the morning, daily, to the local police station. She must not attend gatherings or communicate with the press or anyone else who was detained or with anyone who is or has been a member of a banned organization except if that person is her personal lawyer or doctor. She must not engage in any political activities and not divulge any information about the places of her detention. She may interact with one person at a time at her abode. Family members and servants are deemed part of her household and brief communi-cations restricted by the above conditions are permitted. These conditions to be reviewed when the state of emergency ends."

The uniformed policeman behind the desk pushed a tele-phone toward her. "You can make one phone call, Miss Weisz."

"I want to call my lawyer, but he was detained in March for a few weeks."

"Under the Emergency Regulations?"

"Yes."

"Technically the conditions of your house arrest do not apply until you are at your home. If he is your personal lawyer, you may speak with him but only according to the conditions. So, go ahead, phone him." The man's face broke into a quiet smile. Liv gathered from the general conversation around her that today marked Union Day, a public holiday. She hoped to find Jaco at home. Be home, she prayed as she dialed his number, be at home.

"Jaco Malan."

His voice sounded as if it belonged to a stranger. Swallowing several times before she spoke, Liv did not recognize her voice. "Jaco, it's me . . . Liv. They are releasing me. Can you come and get me?"

"Liv. Thank God. Wait outside the main entrance. I'll be there as soon as I can."

Thanking the policeman, Liv bent to lift her overnight, canvas bag. As she straightened, she recognized the wardress who had appeared at her side. Wardress—now Superintendent—de Ridder had admitted her to the prison almost eight weeks earlier.

"Miss Weisz, come with me for a moment."

Liv's cautious heart that had begun to unfurl one petal of hope, slammed shut. What now?

The superintendent opened the door to her office and gestured her inside. She walked to her desk and pointed to a small packet covered in brown paper and tied with string. "Here, Miss Weisz, this packet is for you. Every day since your fourth day inside, a blond woman about your age brought a sealed envelope for you. She handed it to the wardress on duty and left. I instructed all the wardresses to bring me the envelopes. I never gave any to the interrogators. I considered them your personal property and kept them—unopened—for you."

The packet sat on the desk, an unexploded bomb.

"It's okay. Put the packet in your bag. And Miss Weisz, I'm sorry, truly, for what happened to you. Good luck . . . outside."

In her hurry to leave, Liv forgot to ask the wardress about the missing Magen Dovid.

1960
LIV

Loeriebos
June

Outside The Fort, Jaco's white Mercedes drew up at the curb. He skirted around the car to the passenger side, and they shared a quick embrace on the pavement. Once in the car, Liv leaned into the plush leather seat, thankful for Jaco's awareness of her mental fragility. The bright, African sunlight glazing the sky deep blue flooded her senses, and she covered her dazed eyes with her hands. Jaco remarked in a gentle voice how he remembered several years ago the unreliable nature of his sensory perceptions the first time he was released from prison. He patted her on the thigh for encouragement with one hand, while with the other he steered the car into the line of traffic, thin because of the public holiday. Liv cringed at the physical contact.

"So, old friend, I see they tried but they did not quite succeed in destroying you?"

Hearing his direct question, Liv understood it demanded a direct answer, but she did not feel capable of responding so soon. The brilliant sunlight forced her to scrunch her eyes; the PAC precautionary detention directions she received months ago did not suggest packing sunglasses.

"My mind is destroyed. Not all here. Part of it will be forever in my cell. I'm aware I am mad. I don't know what happens next. I prayed to die. I thought I was dead . . . but here I am."

Jaco glanced at her face and trembling lips and chin but said nothing.

They arrived on Catherine Street and several blocks along, Jaco turned left into a side street so as not to drive by Rosie's building in the next block.

"Remember, I've been through this. It takes time. You will never be quite the same, but you will recover." He managed a cheerful tone. "So where to? *Loeriebos*, Sally's house, or home with me and Pauline?"

Shivering, she responded in a halting reply, "Of course, you don't know yet. I'm under house arrest. In case they check on me, better be *Loeriebos*."

"House arrest? You poor thing. They are determined to do their damnedest. But don't fret. You can talk to me; I'm your lawyer. We have a privileged relationship, even though we are among the latest ex-detainees."

"What did they do to you this time?" Liv's voice reverberated in her ears.

"Nothing except empty threats. I was in Pretoria Central for two weeks but not in solitary. No interrogation. They probably detained me and hundreds of others, only for intimidatory purposes. All released fairly quickly. No house arrests. Probably they bowed to outside pressure. But there are still thousands of people detained under the Emergency Regulations."

"Daniel?" Liv could hardly bear to utter his name, afraid of what she might learn.

Jaco glanced at her questioning eyes.

"The truth; please, tell me the truth."

"Daniel was also in Pretoria Central but in High Security. I found out only after I was free. When imprisoned, he had not fully recovered from his Sharpeville wounds. He'll always have a gimpy right leg. Are you sure you can handle all the details? It's pretty gory."

Nodding for him to continue, Liv did not share her dismay or apprehension at what he relayed. She owed it to Daniel to know.

"They interrogated and subsequently tortured him. They built up to the helicopter. He suffered severe head injuries. He's lucky to be alive. He escaped."

However hard she tried, nothing stopped her imagination from detailing Daniel's plight during the dreaded helicopter torture. A sack covering his head, upended and held by the legs while his torturers stood on a table or chair and swung him like a pendulum, battering his head on the floor through each swing.

"Escaped?"

"Yes. Rosie played a part in his escape. He's in a hospital in Mbabane. False identity documents. He has another name now. Doing quite well, I believe, but his recovery will take a while."

"Rosie helped Daniel . . .?" Liv spoke distractedly. She didn't think she was hearing properly.

Jaco glanced at her and patted her knee. "Long story but not for now. She was brave. She stepped up when we needed her. You do know she has left South Africa? Back in England now. Your aunt has contact details, I believe."

Liv was too discombobulated to press for more details. She didn't know whether to be relieved or distraught that Rosie had left. Had she chased her away?

"Mbabane? Swaziland? Rosie?

Liv shook her head in disbelief. She sat silent for several minutes, then uttered, "Thank God, Daniel is alive. Sobukwe?"

"He was tried in early May along with eighteen other PAC leaders. All sentenced to three years imprisonment for 'inciting others to support a campaign for the repeal of the Pass Laws.' We believe he's on Robben Island, but we have no confirmation yet."

Liv's sustained silence was unusual. Jaco turned to her in concern. He spoke in the same gentle tone. "And you . . . rough interrogation?"

Liv nodded.

"Torture?"

Liv's reticence answered for her, and they paused for a long moment. "Can't say. House arrest orders. Can't say what happened in there and don't want to talk about it, even with you."

"So yes, torture," he said, sliding into advocate mode. "This is another step toward totalitarian brutality, the brand name of the apartheid regime. This is why you're in shock, so nonresponsive, and why you distrust communication. It will take you a while—if ever—to talk about your incarceration. This is a form of madness. Poor Liv, you need all our support, love, and patience. You shouldn't be alone at *Loeriebos*."

Yes, you are correct, I shouldn't be alone. Rosie should be with me. Marion should be with me.

"Marion, maybe Sally—"

"Not Marion . . ." Jaco hesitated. "It's her midyear exams. Marion told me you ran away from her at the prison."

"She told you?" Liv's shock echoed in her hurt voice. She felt ashamed and betrayed.

"Not because she was feeling sorry for herself. Her concern was all for you. After seeing you, she was desperate that we try even harder to procure your release. I told her we had done all we could. Sally has done everything possible for you.

"Marion asked me if I knew what they did to you. She cried when she said she had trouble recognizing you. After a while, she calmed down and asked me what more we could do.

"None of us knew. Since Sobukwe was convicted and sent from The Fort, there is no line of communication from there. I told her you might have been interrogated and undertaken a hunger strike. By your actions, it sounds as if you lost your ability to reason, to keep perspective on reality. It happens to some prisoners; they go mad. Most recover when they come out." Jaco shook his head sadly, "Others, never."

He squeezed Liv's hand. "Marion had to hear me say there was little more we could do for you. There are still thousands of detainees being held without trial in jails all around the country. The Justice Department is overwhelmed. There were no more stones for us to turn. Your family, especially Sally, are beside themselves with worry."

"They are?"

"You are a lucky woman to have such a stalwart family."

The Weisz family closed ranks in exigent circumstances. Had she misjudged them for all these years?

After a tense pause, Jaco shifted the conversation. "Let me prepare you. There are changes at *Loeriebos*. Moses Moekena disappeared after you were arrested. He is not to be found. Sally and some of the other family tried to find him, but so far none of his family has seen him in Ramoutsi . . . or so they say."

Clasping and unclasping her fingers, Liv did not comment as she thought of martyred Moses and his sons sacrificed on the apartheid anvil.

Jaco continued in his clipped, advocate's manner as if

addressing a jury. "Your family by-and-large are deeply concerned about you. Your detention changed them. They have climbed a steep learning curve on the realities of South African politics and the limits of position and wealth to impact ideological force. Sally used every avenue, every ounce of influence to have you released. No one can do more than what she tried."

"And John ... Anyone heard from John?"

Jaco shook his head sadly. "Not that I know."

Liv stared ahead. John couldn't be bothered to ask after her well-being? John was a deep wound of sadness in her. She felt sorrow and shame that she had so little trust in people, especially for Sally and Marion. I'm the untrustworthy and skeptical one. I wasn't thinking about them and what my incarceration meant to them.

"We will phone Sally and Marion as soon as we are at the house. Sally employed a married couple for you to replace Moses—Martha and David Tshwane. They used to work for friends of hers who are immigrating to England. Martha's a cook and housekeeper. David drives, does odd jobs, a gardener. They take exemplary care of the property. I think you'll like them."

"The dogs?" Liv asked hesitantly, fearing the worst.

"Edith and Marcel are safely in Yeoville with Sally. Been there for months, ever since your detention."

The dogs, safe and cared for was the first good news on the ride home. She said nothing and continued to stare ahead, anticipating that the conversation must shift to Rosie eventually. Her mortification terrified her. She needed time to accustom herself to this person who now inhabited her—a person capable of mad thoughts and deeds. Liv closed her eyes to secure her silence and opened them when she recognized the familiar sound of tires on the gravel driveway.

Loeriebos glittered in the winter sunshine. Liv murmured, "I'd forgotten how beautiful it all is."

"Welcome home." Jaco stared at her with serious intent. "Listen to me now. Give yourself time. Give yourself time to rest, eat, walk, sleep, whatever you need to do to regain your strength. Sleep is most important in regaining your equilibrium. Sleep all day and night for as long as you like. But make sure you sleep. You are returning from Hell . . . a long journey. Let us all fuss around you and help. We love you. We want you whole again."

Despite Liv's protestations, Jaco stayed until Sally would arrive. Meanwhile, Liv climbed the stairs to her bedroom, showered, changed into clean clothes, met the servants, and found them likeable and unobtrusive.

Martha apologized for her inability to produce lunch for them. "Nothing to cook with, Miss Liv."

Jaco spoke on the phone again and Sally soon arrived with the dogs and supplies. Edith and Marcel bounded across the driveway and almost knocked Liv to the ground in their enthusiasm and joy, both at seeing her and at returning to familiar environs. Burying her face in their fur, she tried to mask her emotions. If the tears came at this reunion, they might never end. Sally and Jaco watched in sympathy but did not move to interrupt.

Sally spoke first. "Welcome home, dearest. The entire family will help you in any way we can. We'll do anything to help restore you from your ordeal."

Liv stared at her in pleased surprise. She'd hoped Sally would react this way. Liv crossed the space between them on the driveway and they clung together.

Liv hugged Jaco before he left while he patted her shoulder. She tried to express her gratitude but words eluded her and, in despair, she threw up her hands.

"There, there." Jaco's compassionate voice soothed her as if he comforted one of his daughters. "There, there. *Alles sal reg kom. Moenie worry nie.* Everything will be all right. Don't worry." He turned to Sally. "Phone me any time."

As Jaco's car disappeared on the driveway, Sally draped one of her arms around Liv's shoulders. Liv shrank inwardly from the unexpected physical contact but tried to relax.

"I'm staying with you until you are more yourself, my dear," she stated in a voice that never brooked any argument. "All arranged. I will take one of the guest bedrooms."

Sally, after her first glance, did not look in a direct way at Liv again, perhaps because she was appalled at her appearance. But she murmured with love, "I see you are exhausted." She kissed Liv on the forehead. "Go now to your bedroom, darling. Have a nap. We can talk later."

Grateful for her ministrations and company, Liv climbed the stairs to her bedroom for the second time within an hour. *Loeriebos* was so beautiful with the handpicked furniture, and the airy, spacious rooms.

Freedom. Liv floated between worlds, exhausted and hollow. Edith and Marcel shadowed her every move. They leapt onto the bed with her, assuming their familiar places, one on either side. Appreciative of their company, Liv fell into sleep.

The next morning, when she awoke in the dawn light, Liv yawned and stretched, enjoying the luxurious width of the double bed. Patting the space next to her, she searched for Rosie's warm body but caressed Marcel instead. The desperate present flooded her mind. No Rosie, no heart. Shattered mind and life.

Locating her dressing gown and slippers, Liv padded downstairs to make a cup of tea. Sixteen hours was a long time to sleep. With caution, she unlocked the French doors to the veranda and was surprised by two Black security guards drowsing at the patio table. They saluted smartly when they heard her, and Liv noted the Weisz Corporation badge on their uniforms.

"We are here to look after the house and to protect you now. We have been here for two months. There are three of us." When he recognized her, the taller one spoke with great respect in his voice. "We go off duty at seven o'clock. Return at six o'clock in the afternoon. No worries for you. Any trouble, we take care of it. Soon you will hear the company van from the hostel. It will bring us back this afternoon."

Nonplussed by their presence, Liv conceded defeat with a slight smile. Sally won this round. For years Sally had nagged to let her deploy night watchmen from the corporation's security force at *Loeriebos*. The dogs sniffed at the men. She, like everyone else, including these watchmen—were but one small pawn on the national political chessboard. Never again, she had vowed in prison, would she take her privilege as a right. *Loeriebos* did not belong to her, it belonged to the land, to Mother Afrika. These watchmen wanted to try and help her. Sobukwe taught her that eyes and ears were significant.

Liv smiled at the men, grateful now for their presence, and they saluted again. As they walked away, she heard them greeting their third companion.

She walked to the arbor. The grape, granadilla, and bougain-villea vines had shed their leaves months ago. Stepping out of her slippers, Liv relished the feel of the crisp, frost-wet grass under her feet. Smiling again, she raised her face to the golden fire lighting the cirrus clouds above the eucalyptus trees in the east. At least at this moment, she felt vitally alive.

The water in the pool sparkled aqua in the early morning light and mist wisped off the surface, the air temperature cooler than the water. A covey of finches swept and wheeled overhead, settling nearby in a bare-branched hedge as if to greet the eastern sun and Liv.

Surveying her domain, much as Adam and Eve must have done, awakening each morning to the fresh wonder of Eden outside their bower, Liv knew this Eden to be rotten at the core, saturated with the stench of the fetid suffering of the sons and daughters of the land. The acrid smell, like sulfur, lingered in her nostrils, like the commercial chemical cleaner they used in prison. She left the arbor and returned to the veranda.

Sally stood in the kitchen doorway, dressed in a business suit with the hint of a pearl necklace and small pearl earrings, stylish and elegant. Her graying hair bushed behind her ears in a kind of page-boy haircut. Sally joined her and kissed her on the cheek.

"I'm pleased to see you look more rested, my dear. I've spoken to Marion. She'll call you this afternoon. She has an exam this morning. She'll be home on the weekend, and she is very concerned. I told her you are strong and you're going to be okay."

"Thanks . . . and thanks for the night watchmen."

"You met them? Good chaps. I feel better knowing they are here each night. Not always the same three, but they are the regulars. These are extraordinary times; they call for extraordinary measures."

"Do you have time for a cup of tea?"

Sally assented and followed Liv into the kitchen.

"I'm flying to Kimberly this morning—business meeting. But back tonight. We can talk then."

"Thank you for all you tried to do on my behalf."

"Thank Jaco. He's a good chap. Top-class legal brain. I knew that from hearsay but never appreciated it. Among the best we have in this country. And thank Rosie."

Liv almost jumped with shock at the mention of Rosie's name. Sally continued. "I've seen quite a bit of Rosie. Been in touch on a regular basis. I haven't heard from her for a while. She mentioned she was thinking of returning to London. Don't know when, though. I have her contact information there. Don't know if you could have a stauncher or more loyal friend. She will do anything for you. Anything. Lovely gal."

Liv nodded, mute. All those weeks before her imprisonment, she had hidden their relationship and now Sally and the others knew Rosie, maybe even knew of their "friendship." Yet, they held Rosie in high esteem.

"How do you know Rosie?"

Sally glanced worriedly at Liv. "Marion phoned me immediately after you were arrested. She said you told her to. A day later, Rosie phoned me. She read of your arrest. Poor girl, so upset and in shock, your arrest was headlined in all the papers. She wanted details, so we met the next day. We hit it off. Been in touch every now and then, since."

Liv nodded. "I'm pleased you like her. She's a wonderful . . . a special person." Liv started to cry and dabbed at her eyes with a table napkin. Sally's concern added to her discomfit. "I'm sorry, I'm not myself yet. I forget things and that's okay, I think, because there is so much about the last two months I want to forget."

"Take all the time you want, Livvie. Anything you want or need you only need to ask."

After breakfast, Martha insisted she accompany Liv to the family doctor for a check-up. "Miss Sally said I must not leave you alone anywhere. I'll wait in the car." David, her husband drove.

The doctor assured Liv of the stability of her vital signs. She added, "You've lost twenty pounds. You know what you need to eat to reach a healthy weight again. Internally you're healing well, as are your wrist and ribs, but I am worried about your mental state. You show symptoms of shock. If sleep, exercise, and a healthy diet don't return you to a more normal state, we'll consult a psychologist.

The days rolled around one another like a skein of string. Two weeks later, Liv had regained some weight. She rested whenever she was tired and walked the fields, sometimes with the dogs and sometimes with Sally or Marion. The movement of her outer life melded with the cycle of the days and the winter season—later sunrises, earlier sunsets, cold mornings, and warm sunshine at midday. She checked in early every morning at the local police station per her house arrest conditions. She was driven there and to the shops and Sally helped her write the checks for her bills. As her mental focus grew stronger, talking guardedly she returned phone calls from concerned family and friends, knowing the telephone harbored a tapping device to a recording station somewhere in the underworld of the secret police. She established household routines with Martha and David and read the *Rand Daily Mail* again.

Jaco visited every several days to check on her and Liv welcomed his visits. No one mentioned Rosie's name, but Liv's longing to speak to her was a constant nudge. Appalled at how she dishonored and hurt Rosie when she so abruptly ended their contact and feeling such deep remorse, Liv avoided the question of whether the hope even existed for them to overcome her actions and build a friendship.

On the eleventh day of her release, Liv drove alone to the nearby shopping center. Outside the grocery store, she recognized two women she knew from charity boards they all had served on. Liv lifted a hand in greeting but the women hurried passed, ignoring her.

She shrugged. It would take time, as Jaco said, to learn the parameters of her life after prison. Liv appreciated how scary it must be for those women to have someone from their own circle, not only in prison but in solitary confinement.

When Liv drove into the gas station to refuel the car, three of the Black attendants rushed to her. The attendants knew her well and over the years, they had always appeared friendly, but with masks of indifference in place.

One of the men spoke in a soft voice, undetectable to his White overseer. "You are one of us now. You go to prison so we can be free. You are our sister. We know you."

Later as she walked on the pavement from the dry cleaners with Sally's business outfits draped over her arm, three Black women dressed in domestic servants' uniforms strolled toward her. On any other day, they would avoid Liv's glance but today one of the women met Liv's fleeting look and smiled at her as she said to her companions, nodding at Liv, "*Thandiwe.*"

Thandiwe—beloved by all. They exchanged smiles. Their eyes read the apartheid darkness; their ears heard the messages in the wind. Being seen—recognized—signified a great deal.

Later that evening, after dinner, as Liv and Sally sat in the library sipping brandy before a leaping fire, Liv thanked her for her support. Confident of her ability to cope on her own with the servants' help, she suggested that it might be timely for Sally to return to her Yeoville home. They agreed but only on a trial basis. "You only have to phone, and I'll be back here with you."

They sat in reflection until Sally interjected into the silence. "There is something I have to say."

Liv's heart beat faster.

"There is someone we know who loves you with all her being—Rosie—and you love her. The first night you were home you had a nightmare. I rushed to your room but didn't wake you. You were screaming Rosie's name with such pain and anguish and thrashing about in the bed, it broke my heart. I don't know what happened between you. For both your sakes, make it right."

"Has she spoken to you since my release?" Liv asked, the blood draining from her face. "No, not a word for almost four weeks now. Maybe she's returned to London."

Liv lowered her eyes.

"I'll support you in whatever decision you make." Sally perceived Liv's distress and tried to end the conversation about Rosie. "But," she echoed her previous advice, "try to make this right."

"She told you about us . . . about living here?"

"It's all right Liv, don't fret. I loved your mother like that, fiercely and intently and passionately. We worked out a way to be together. No regrets. You don't have to explain anything. I understand. Love is love. We loved each other and we loved you."

Liv stared at Sally and then the tears came. She crossed to Sally and hugged her. On her knees, she said, "Thank you for sharing. Growing up I didn't understand any of it. Of course, now I do."

Listening to Sally, Liv marveled at how far her mother must have traveled to love Sally and live so openly with her.

Liv questioned Sally. "You've never asked why I was arrested or about my involvement with the freedom movement, the PAC, or my clandestine political actions."

Sally paused before she answered. "Of course, I'm interested but we'll have plenty of time for that. I suspect one revelation for tonight is enough for you to process. Over the past several years,

I did suspect that you were involved somehow. For now, maybe you'll like to know how pleased I am that a Weisz woman stood up for freedom and human rights in our country. That a Weisz family member used her wealth and status for the common good. That a member of the Weisz family rose and is counted among the brave."

Liv kissed her aunt good night and left the room with a warm glow around her heart.

The next day after her aunt had left, Liv sat at the yellowwood desk in her office. She lifted a photograph of Rosie into her hands, kissed the image with fervor, and held the frame over her heart.

I can't make it right, I can't. I have lost you; I have lost my Rosie. There are many reasons I can't, there is no split between personal and political. After my imprisonment, the personal is political, perhaps it always was, but I never acknowledged that fact.

Edith whined and cocked her head. Liv read her thoughts; Let's go for a walk in the bright afternoon sunshine, please?

"Yes, you are right to ask. It does no good to sit here with a hole in my heart on such a gorgeous afternoon."

On her way to the door, Liv whistled for Marcel. A sudden and compulsive urge stopped her at the bottom of the stairs, and she remounted them to the bedroom. From a shelf in the walk-in closet, she hoisted the canvas gym bag she had carried to prison, opened it, and removed the packet of letters, placing them in the pocket of her light jacket. She returned to the entrance hall. Alongside the front door, Liv unhooked two leashes off the hat-and-coat rack, prepared in the event they ran into a snake, honey badger, porcupine, or any other such creature with which they shared *Loeriebos*.

The fields lay fallow. The natural grasses of the Highveld had reclaimed the earth with abandon, a haven for birds like the weaverbirds who built their Gaudi-like colony nests in bushes in the fields. In autumn and winter, the tasseled, tawny-brown and pink-tinged feathery crowns waved as the grass undulated into wind-driven oceanic swells. Liv and the dogs made a path through the grasses. She imagined herself as a ship cresting the waves.

Liv settled into her favorite lookout, a small outcrop of light-gray rock. She faced north, sheltered by an ancient gnarled *suikerbos*, a sugar bush protea, with roots wrapped around rocks like blood vessels spreading throughout a body, covering each crack and crevice between the rocks. Her large sun hat shaded the packet of letters. Raising the packet to her nose, Liv dreaded smelling the odor of the chemical cleaners used on the linoleum and prison walls. The lavender potpourri she placed in the canvas bag ten days earlier had almost removed the prison smell.

Carefully, she untied the string Superintendent De Ridder used to secure the package. Forty-two envelopes lay in her lap, each one dated, numbered, and unopened. Only one date was missing from the sequence—May 4—the day her interrogation began. The final envelope was dated May 25, handed over the day after Marion's prison visit. With sweaty fingers and fascinated reluctance, Liv opened the first envelope. The dogs lay panting at her feet, ears cocked for every sound, nostrils inhaling streams of scents indecipherable to her.

13 April

My darling, it has taken your family three days to find you. Thank goodness your aunt phoned me with the news of your whereabouts. You are in The Fort less than a mile from my flat. Jaco Malan is out of prison, released yesterday. He and your aunt demand your release and are so considerate, making sure I know how they are trying to help you. Helen Suzman pursues your cause in Parliament and demands you (and all the others arrested under the Emergency Regulations) be tried or released. The opposition and international press are following your detention.

My darling, be brave. You have no idea the loss I feel without you. For twenty nights, you brought me to the full flowering of my name. I am your open rose.

14 April

Liv, my darling, darling, Jaco says you are not allowed to write, says you will not receive these notes, especially if I write any political news. Or any news. But it is my only avenue to feel contact with you. So, every day I walk the short distance to The Fort and hand an envelope with your name to the wardress who unlocks and opens the heavy, wooden door embossed with iron studs. So medieval. And I will continue to write every day until you are released, hoping somehow, they allow you to read these letters. Be strong, my darling. One day you will walk out of prison into my arms. I miss you so.

Liv began to skim through the envelopes.

18 April

Darling, Jaco says he cannot find out why you are being detained or for how long! He thinks you may be a pawn in a power struggle in the cabinet. Be strong. So many still in prison, but you are among the most well-known. I am desperate enough that I will take any reckless action if it helps you.

24 April

I found your note with the Browning love poem stashed
in the back of my journal. It's my most precious possession
and always with me. I have read it so often the paper is
starting to break along the folds you made, and the ink
runs from my tears. Your hands wrote the words, your
mind created this note, and you touched the page. When
I hold it in my hands, I am holding a part of you. You are
the most enlivening person I know, so polished, brave, and
selfless. Sometimes, when I think I may lose you forever
to the awful prison, I go mad with despair. I am coming to
love this country but I hate, hate, hate this government.

28 April

Darling Liv, Time apart and distance apart make no
difference to our love. . . .

15 May

Darling Liv, These are the darkening days of winter, and
they draw a comforting cloak of secrecy over my nightly
musings (and wanderings) when I can't sleep. Some nights
from the rooftop of my building, I watch the deep-black
sky lit by diamond-hard shards of stars. I long for the dawn
of our love to unfold again with the crystalline, crisp, blue
sheen of a Highveld winter day, when the sun etches in
gold the bare branches of the trees. How we will enjoy our
winter walks through the tawny, white gold (and sometimes pink-tinged) grasses of the fields around *Loeriebos*.
How I will love to see your eyes shine with liveliness and
light as you stride slightly ahead of me naming bushes,
birds, grasses, and scents. I see your silhouette against the

sun—a goddess with a dark-haired halo, lustrous skin aglow, your very being bursting with life and energy. You are at the center of my soul. I am enwrapped by you, and in you, even as I embrace you whole. Images of you are with me always; I revel in the truth we share. I touch the intangible essence of you. So precious. A soul-jewel warmed forever in the palm of my hand.

24 May
My darling, all I want is to search your eyes again for our soul-truth love.

I cannot accept the words you uttered in your phone call shortly before your arrest. Oh, the stress you must have been experiencing.

25 May
Dearest Liv. My heart breaks because of what they have done to you and made you become. You are hurt and broken, too. Your aunt told me what your daughter saw. I love you even more because you are so shattered. If you hate me now and cannot bear to be with me, I understand. I will not write again. My letters may be adding to your anguish. I know with certainty the time will come when we will be together. If I can only hold you in my arms, I know I can be a salve to your soul. I will wait for you, darling Liv.

Twice Liv read the letters, unable to comprehend such a love existed and, even more incomprehensible, for her. If Superintendent De Ridder had relinquished these letters to the interrogators and Hennie Van Niekerk had read them . . . Liv shuddered, thinking of the certain fated outcome—her death at his hands.

Rosie was so clever with words, so attuned to feelings and motivations, so sophisticated a thinker. Liv loved her for many reasons, among them because she lived as a true innocent in an evil world. It never occurred to Rosie that these letters, this unbelievable testament of love might harm her.

Darling Rosie, your letters explode any hope I may have, even in my subconscious, of trying to approach you. You shame me into the deepest sorrow that we ever met and I embroiled you in my life. You are simply too good, too pure, too loving for someone like me.

Standing with numb thighs from sitting so long on the rocks, Liv tried to whistle for the dogs but her mouth was dry. She trusted the dogs enough to follow her She admired the sky filled with the red glory of the sun setting behind the far-off Magaliesberg. The air cooled rapidly and she shivered, despite zipping her jacket. This outcrop lay about forty minutes from the house and she did not want to be out alone with darkness descending quickly. When the dogs found her, she leashed them and they hurried home.

That night she wrote a letter to Rosie. Sally provided her Rosie's address in London.

26 June, 1960

Dearest Rosie,

This afternoon I sat on my favorite koppie amid the grasses of *Loeriebos*, a place where you and I sat several times and watched the sunset. There, only now, almost a month after my release from detention, did I read your letters.

Your love and concern on every page affect me deeply.
I will keep this packet and these letters until I die. If
I received them in prison, things may have turned out
differently for us or maybe not. We'll never know.

A sympathetic wardress kept them for me and gave them
to me as a neatly wrapped package on my release. I knew
the packet was from you because she described the woman
who brought them.

Rosie, dearest, please know that during our brief time
together before my detention, I loved you without any
doubts. I entered our relationship with no qualms, only
gratitude and appreciation. I truly loved you and wanted
you in every sense of the word.

But things changed.

After you left *Loeriebos*, when Marion returned from
Europe, she questioned me about you. I realized then that
the time we lived (oh so briefly) together at *Loeriebos* was a
sublime moment outside of real time for me—and unsus-
tainable in the complex entirety of my life.

My shame still overwhelms me at the abrupt way I spoke
to you from a call box as I ended our contact. I panicked
then.

I panicked once before, many years ago, with almost
disastrous consequences for three people, two I love beyond
words. I'm a flawed person, Rosie. You and I never spoke

of our past relationships and that is a good thing. But I realized in prison that my heart belongs to only one person and has for decades.

Sex with you was an indescribable, wonderful surprise. You have taught me so much about my own body. But I belong to another, whether I ever see him again or not. When we began our relationship that rainy night in January at Alan Paton's talk, I willingly embarked on our liaison. By then for years, I was married only to the struggle and felt so dried up in every way. You opened me to new longings, new desires, new experiences. You may know of a name for someone who can love men and women, someone like me. I do not.

And I do not regret any of it.

Sally said you and she are now acquainted. She understood everything about us, although I never uttered a word to her while we were together. Strange as it may seem, she loved my mother as you loved me. They lived together for years, sharing a house and sometimes a bed, and sharing me. But my mother loved her ex-husband, my father, who abandoned us when I was two. Still, my mother and Sally found a companionship that worked for them. Sadly, I cannot contemplate such an arrangement for us.

Sally said you have returned to London. I hope, one day, when the horrors of the apartheid government abate, and my house arrest is voided and I can travel again, we can meet in England.

Part of me is always with you,
Love always, Liv

The following day, Saturday morning, Liv awoke with an unequivocal conviction gripping her. For the restoration of her health and mental balance, she needed to return to Plett for several weeks.

When Jaco arrived at Liv's home for one of his now twice-weekly visits, he held her at arm's length after they greeted one another and said, "Still thin, but much more like the old Liv. Your eyes are coming alive again."

Sipping tea Martha served on a tray, they sat by the swimming pool and talked pleasantries. Then Liv asked in an even-toned voice, "Please tell me now that I'm ready to hear about how Rosie helped Daniel escape."

Jaco gathered his thoughts, much as he does in a courtroom, Liv suspected.

"We met at the Zoo, probably around the date they started interrogating you. I took my girls as cover and told the Special Branch cops who tailed me that I was taking my girls for a treat. Rosie took two buses from Hillbrow. I'm ninety-nine percent sure, I wasn't followed.

"I told her that the PAC leadership wanted to ask a favor of her. We had information on Daniel Molefe that verified his torture and severe injuries in prison in Pretoria, injuries added to those he sustained at Sharpeville. We also knew Daniel was due to be released the following Monday from Pretoria prison hospital and transferred to Robben Island. We didn't believe he'd survive the road trip to Cape Town."

Liv's eyes widened. She had a suspicion of what was coming.

"We asked Rosie to drive Daniel across the border to Swaziland. I told her the Prof wanted him out of the country. Sobukwe had smuggled instructions from The Fort.

"I explained the risks. As far as we knew, the SB was not watching her. Since you were taken in, she had aroused no suspicion. There appeared to be no concern about her whereabouts or movements."

Liv said, "You didn't explain the risks, Jaco, you minimized them."

Jaco looked down at the grass, "Well, yes, maybe a little. But she wasn't alone, you know. She had a driver with her to the rendezvous point. After the transfer of a sedated Daniel, who was safely strapped into the back of a van, a Swazi doctor accompanied her across the border. She has a British passport, which added to her value for us."

Seething with emotions because of all the danger into which they placed innocent Rosie, Liv nodded for him to continue.

"I gave her a manila envelope with all the information and instructions and told her that if she agreed, she must memorize them, destroy them, and bring only the AA map from the packet. I told her I knew this was a colossal request.

"After a while she said, 'This is what Liv would do for anyone, let alone for someone as close to her as Daniel. I can't believe I'm agreeing to this, but I will do anything for Liv.'

"Fortunately, everything worked like clockwork. She left Johannesburg early Monday morning and was back at her flat by early afternoon Tuesday."

Liv sat back quietly, still roiling with emotions. But she knew

Jaco did not appreciate drama, so she kept her voice in an even tone. "Thanks for telling me. I can't decide if I'm more furious at you for the danger you put her in or so proud of Rosie for undertaking this operation. It's going to take some time for me to process all of this."

Jaco nodded sympathetically. "Of course, you understand, not a word of this to anyone. Not Sally and not Rosie. The SB have a black eye for having let Daniel escape. If word of this reaches anyone—and you know there are informants everywhere—you are at the top of the danger list for being thrown back in prison, then me, then the people who helped Daniel. Rosie is safe in England, and she gave her word not to speak of this. She understands the danger she can cause for us."

Liv nodded. "Not a word. Thanks for telling me." After a pensive silence, Liv said, "I have something to ask of you. I need to be at Plett for a while. It can be beautiful this time of year. The air crisp and clear with Robberg shining in the winter light. Darkness falls early, but seeing I must be at home by seven, that's not a problem. Maybe two weeks or three?" Pleading, she grasped his arm in earnest. "Can you talk to the Johannesburg magistrate? There's a small police station in Plett; I've known the man in charge, Sergeant Dawid Joubert, all my life. He's the son of one of Papa Helmut's fishing buddies. If need be, I can report to the magistrate in Knysna. I *know* several weeks at Plett will help me recover."

Jaco paused for a moment. "You'll be awfully lonely."

"It's what I need . . . quiet time to reconnect with myself."

Jaco nodded, thought for a moment, and grinned his familiar boyish half-smile. "Good idea, I'll see what I can do."

By the following weekend, he had obtained a magisterial permit for Liv to leave the police jurisdiction while still under the same house arrest conditions of the Johannesburg district. She must report every morning to the Plettenberg Bay Police station and return in the last week of July.

Over the next several days, Liv read and reread Rosie's letters until she almost memorized them. Every time she read them her conviction grew stronger not to contaminate Rosie again. With the letters never too far from her reach, Liv vowed to ensure they remained with her until her last breath. She packed them in the gym bag she had taken to The Fort. She felt around the bag for the precious black box with the family heirloom, the golden Magen Dovid. She found the box but not the heirloom. The horror of the torture room returned; Hennie Van Niekerk had torn it off her neck. He had probably pawned it by now. But she had the box, which would have to suffice.

1960
LIV

On the morning Liv left for Plettenberg Bay, she felt more at peace with herself than at any time since her detention.

While being driven to Jan Smuts Airport for her flight to Port Elizabeth, they detoured from the main road. David, Liv's driver, parked the Jag in the almost empty lot at the entrance to the Rivonia Police Station. Liv's breath vaporized as she hurried from the car into the front office, the desk constable's acknowledgment of her presence almost imperceptible as he continued to work on a large ledger while he slid a thin register titled, "House Arrest Daily Record 1960" across the counter. Quickly, Liv located the most recently filled entry line, wrote the date July 5, 1960, below it in the correct column, entered the time, and printed and signed her name.

The house arrest order rankled her. Half-smiling at the policeman, she reminded herself it was not his fault and hastened away.

He called goodbye after her. "*Totsiens, Mejuffrou Weisz.*"

On the plane, Liv settled into her seat and exhaled. But the peacefulness of the early morning had vanished. Tense and on edge, she closed her eyes, not believing she was headed for Plett. Surprising her, nightmare images arose of her incarceration; Hennie Van Niekerk's menacing leer as he snarled, "Pervert! Whore!"; the wardress's grim demeanor; the other inmates nightmare screams of fear, despair, and the names of loved ones; and Marion staring at her in The Fort's visiting room, her look of horror mingled with love as she whispered, "What have they done to you?"

Somehow, Liv managed to shut off that stream of consciousness and for the moment suspend her fears of re-arrest, so recently brought to a full boil by Jaco. She succumbed to the smooth ride at thirty thousand feet and dozed. At Port Elizabeth, she clambered into a Weisz Corporation tiny six-seater for the short flight to Plettenberg Bay. Less than an hour later, they began their descent to Plett's rudimentary sand strip: a bush runway in a cleared field. A moment before they landed, a mirage below them appeared, Robberg Peninsula on the right of the plane while they circled for the landing. Always mythic, Robberg transfixed Liv. At times, in detention, she despaired, not knowing if she would gaze at the promontory again. Silently, she met the moment with triumph in her heart.

I made it; I survived.

At the last instant, a White horse galloped onto the landing strip. Swearing under his breath, the pilot lifted the small plane, circled to his left, and prepared his approach once more. Someone chased the horse from the strip. Bumping and snorting like an animal itself, the plane came to a sudden halt.

The pilot turned to Liv. "Sorry about the landing. In a couple of years, they say there'll be a new runway here and a municipal airport building with at least some radio contact. All we have now is that old windsock."

"Can't be a more beautiful site for an airport anywhere in the world. Not with Robberg lying in front of you like a sleeping leviathan."

A Colored man in a faded-blue boiler suit trundled up the steps to the plane, and the pilot helped Liv disembark.

"I need to refuel," he said.

"Thanks for the flight."

Walking toward the small Quonset hut providing travelers with shelter from the weather but no other amenities, Liv's eyes remained fixed on Robberg, basking undisturbed and clad in an array of green, shaded vegetation.

"Welcome home." Bert Hall, the town official who administered the airport, greeted her warmly.

She returned his smile. Retrieving the car keys from his desk, Bert appeared shocked at Liv's appearance. "Our Liv, come back to us. We're very happy you are here."

Liv inquired as to news of his family, in particular his son, who had been her best friend growing up. "Four grandchildren now. Keeps us all busy."

The pilot entered the hut to sign the logbook. "See you in a few weeks, Miss Weisz. I have already radioed HQ that you arrived safely."

At the doorway, he grinned and made a thumbs-up sign. "Have a lovely holiday!" he shouted, as he always did, and disappeared into the plane.

Tired from the day's tension and travel, Liv retired early to the master bedroom at *Milkwood* and lay awake in the large bed. As a child and before air service—with Papa Helmut or Aunt Sally and Jane driving—the journey loomed for her as a three-to-four-day adventure from the Highveld to the Eastern Cape. They drove over sand roads and on mountain passes with switchbacks dangerous to traverse. Even now, no train tracks, aside from those for the foresters' train, ran through the forests and gaping ravines. Thankfully, Plett remained a remote haven in 1960.

In the morning, seated in the warm kitchen and drinking steaming mugs of tea, Liv stared with appreciation at the winter garden sloping on the hillside where shy Knysna loeries called and responded "kwok-kwok-kwok" in the red berry bushes. The telephone jangled in the country stillness, but Liv did not want to talk to anyone from her Johannesburg life. A knock on the door and a key turning in the kitchen door lock was followed by Blossom's dark-brown, weathered face peering around the door. Wisps of gray hair escaped from under her *doek*, a colorful head scarf.

"*Ahi*, Missie Liv, you are here. You are home." She grinned toothless.

Feeling a rush of affection sweep over her like a low tide wave on Robberg Beach, Liv leaped to her feet to hug the bent-over figure. But the gesture would have embarrassed the old woman so she shook her hand instead. Blossom bobbed a subtle curtsy. Gesturing for her to pour a cup of tea for herself, Liv anticipated her demurral. They fell into the familiar banter.

"Ten past nine. I know your knock at the kitchen door. The railway bus came on time?"

Blossom nodded, still staring at Liv as if she could scarcely believe she sat in the room. "Still stops at The Crags?"

"Missie Liv?"

"Yes?"

"I say this only one time. Your Aunt Sally told me you were in trouble. I pray for you every night. Now I see that you suffer. There are bad, bad people in Johannesburg. But now I cook all your favorite foods. Put some flesh on those bones." Blossom shook her head. "*Ahi*, so sorry. So sorry. May Jesus—"

Rising again, interrupting the old woman, Liv clasped one of Blossom's hands in both of her own. "I'll be okay. Some Plett air, some walks on Robberg Beach, some food from my nana." Tears arose at the corners of Blossom's rheumy eyes.

"Don't cry, don't cry. I've cried enough for us both."

Half an hour later, showered and carrying Blossom's shopping list, Liv drove through the one-street village center. The sun shone from an unclouded sky as she passed The Formosa Café, The Village Bookstore, and Melville's Butchery and Grocery.

Headed to the police station for her daily check-in, Liv surrendered to a compulsion to walk on the beach. As she drove down the hill and around a bend, the vast expanse of the bay stretched before her, shimmering in sunlight. Her response to the panoramic view was visceral. Parking in the almost deserted small lot in front of the landmark Beacon Isle Hotel, a converted whaling station from the previous century, she traversed the rickety, wooden footbridge over the tidal stream, the mouth of the Piesang River. Stepping onto the beach, Liv removed her sandals and rolled her pants to knee height.

The surf crashed in large waves on the golden-white beach sand and formed frothy lace patterns. Walking in and out of the water, Liv found herself among schools of minnows while seagulls cruised the air currents, sandpipers scurried around the curling wavelets, and periwinkles buried themselves in hidden holes until the next flowing tide. Four riders astride their horses cantered near her in the opposite direction. A few families sat under beach umbrellas. In July, the cold water discouraged swimming but winter school holidays and idling on the beach remained linked.

Suddenly Rosie's presence appeared. Liv intended to introduce her to Plett at the first opportunity, but that long-held daydream never manifested. Liv interacted silently and intently with Rosie as she meandered at the water's edge, showering loose beach sand into clear water with perfunctory kicks.

A shell appeared, floating in the shallows. Liv stooped, caught it, and shook sand off in the water. The delicate purple-and-white shell in Liv's hand evoked a warm feeling, which loosened, somewhat, the iron grasp clamped on her emotions. Sighing, content in this moment, Liv allowed herself to daydream about Rosie.

After a steady hour of walking, at the far end of the beach with the powerful presence of Robberg protectively behind her, Liv clambered to the top of a sun-warmed rock banked with barnacles and oysters, gazed over the length of beach she traversed, and raised her face to the sun. Leaning toward the oysters, she used car keys to pry several off the rock. She imagined how she would offer one to Rosie and watch as Rosie lifted the half shell to her lips, draining the juices with delicate sips and tilting her head as she swallowed the flesh.

Sobs engulfed Liv—body-jerking spasms. For once she did not exercise restraint. There weren't any witnesses or wardresses here, only the roar of the surf as successive waves washed over the sand. Her severance from Rosie continued to gouge a chasm through her heart. Several deep breaths helped calm her.

Unbidden, more visions of Rosie appeared: delicate, pale complexion; pink, rose-colored cheeks prone to blushing so easily;

the almost white, downy hair on her arms; the dark, honey-gold bush between her legs; her taste there like the liquor of an oyster; and the trusting way she opened her mouth when kissing.

In an abrupt movement, Liv stood on the rock. These unendurable memories became too much to continue. Walking with slower steps to the car, Liv tried to stay in the present, awake to the natural beauty around her, pushing down on her guilt and anguish.

On the road about a mile up the hill from the beach, Liv swung over to park the car at a small cement building covered with a tin roof. A wooden door stood partly open, flanked by windows on either side protected by wire mesh burglar proofing. Granadilla vines grew on the low wire fence in front of the building. *Plettenberg Baai Polisie Stasie.* The weathered, wooden sign hanging above the door was older than Liv. Turning to face a westerly direction, from the veranda she gazed into the distance at six folds of purple mountains stacked one behind the other: the Tsitsikamma and beyond them, the Outeniqua. Reluctant to leave the view, she pushed open the police station door.

"Olivia Weisz. How good to see you!"

Dawid Joubert's familiar, guttural Afrikaans accent overlaid his English words, but he spoke with Cape softness, not like Hennie Van Niekerk's harsh bray. Seeing her, his smile of delight warmed her. He lumbered to his feet, rounded the desk, and swept Liv in a bear hug. In the standard khaki shirt and shorts police uniform with long khaki socks covering his bulging calf muscles, he stood about six feet tall. A large beer belly, blond hair bleached by the sun and twinkling blue eyes complemented Dawid's loud voice. On his father Gerrit's retirement, he was the presence of law and order in the district.

"Our little Liv, all grown up and involved in politics in that

Sodom and Gomorrah called Johannesburg. I told you to stay here. You are a true strandloper. You belong to Plett. Forget all this PAC, ANC, Sobukwe, and Mandela nonsense."

He introduced her to his younger assistant. "Meet Johan. Sergeant Johan Rousseau."

Rousseau's implacable face stared at her as they shook hands.

"I've known her since she stood knee high to a tickey. Only three years old but scrambling all over Robberg with her dear old Uncle Helmut and old Gerrit, both deceased now, and our ghillies. Not scared of anything. Never tired, never a nuisance. We love her here."

Turning back to Liv, he scolded, his voice earnest but good-humored. "No use being mixed up in all the political nonsense. Because of your house arrest, my good fortune is I get to see you every day now, except Wednesday, Saturday, and Sunday." He laughed. "Wednesday is fishing duty on Robberg. Saturday is house duty under the wife's supervision, and of course, Sunday is church. I'm a deacon now. Dutch Reformed Church in Plett, Piesang Valley. We compete with the Anglicans and Methodists."

Dawid's heartwarming welcome gratified Liv. Now that he (like others in the village) had accepted her as she was before her detention, maybe she could regain the self-worth she had lost in prison.

"I admired the purple color of the Tsitsikamma this morning. It's only in the winter you can see them this clearly. I do love this place."

"Well," Dawid chuckled "you enjoy this beautiful day. Johan will be here tomorrow, and we'll plan for check-ins on the weekends."

"Thanks for the welcome. And thanks for making this ritual of daily house arrest so easy for me."

He touched his hand to his forehead and said, "You'll always be a lady in my eyes."

When Liv returned to *Milkwood*, she ate a light lunch and decided to read for a few hours before venturing onto the stone-flagged veranda that ran the length of the front of the house. In the summer months, it offered refuge from the heat, but now in July, the deep shade chilled. A sharp southeast wind blew across the bay from the direction of Robberg. Wanting to breathe fresh air, she donned a thick sweater, settled on a chaise, and pulled a rug to her hips.

Unexpected again, unpleasant recollections surfaced of when Jaco drove her home from The Fort after her precipitate release on the last day of May. Panic waxed but soon after waned.

She craved catharsis. She did not need a counselor to empha-size that, but house arrest conditions forbade her from telling anyone of her experiences since her arrest and incarceration in April. She hated and feared paper trails.

I am safe at *Milkwood*. Still, I am a truth-seeker, and my intuition compels me to try to commit my experiences to paper. Maybe then the images will cease to be so chilling, so alive in my head. My truth, the true north of my moral compass, obviously includes others who may be at risk. In the current political climate, I trust no one to read it, now or ever. Not my beloved Rosie, Marion, or Aunt Sally. Maybe Paul.

She stopped momentarily, finger to her lips. Paul. She had believed her memories of Paul were long buried somewhere in her soul. She shrugged. Liv found a writing pad and pen in the study and moved from the veranda to a wooden bench in the garden, the only spot sheltered from the wind and remaining in the afternoon sunlight.

She lowered herself to the grass, back against the bench seat, knees bent to provide support for the pad. After a few minutes, she assumed her favored position, lying on the grass on her abdomen from where she could see the ants and tiny, many-hued mesembryanthemum. Beyond them, the dark loam bed of last summer's sunflower stalks loomed surprisingly large from the ground-level perspective. The words started to flow.

Two days later, in the evening, Liv finished writing of her experiences in The Fort. She stood on the veranda and stretched her arms to the sky. What a release; her mind felt like a boil lanced.

Later, after eating the supper Blossom left for her, she sat before a toasty fire in the living room. She did not feel tired. The writing energized her. Reflections and thoughts had demanded to be placed on paper. She added a concluding paragraph.

My Notes: Postscript
These, my written memories of those months, are stowed safely in the canvas gym bag along with Rosie's letters to me during my detention. I did not write to reminisce but to try to induce the catharsis these notes thankfully provided and to tell the truth of my incarceration—of how these circumstances warped my mind and to bear witness to evil, so no one can say they "did not know." If anyone ever writes about me, they may feel at liberty to omit or change facts. But in bearing witness to my experiences—in the name of truth—know I cannot lie to myself!

Yet even now, after completing those notes, the deep unhappiness she tried to conceal shrouded her. She had lost Rosie forever. Possibly, she might never see her again. Rosie must be anguished, too, at what transpired and like her, bereft at such loss. The catastrophe of her own making oppressed her.

Steadfast, Liv jammed the notes into her canvas gym bag in a dark corner at the back of the large wardrobe in Papa Helmut's bedroom.

1960
LIV

Two people stood in the shadows of the Quonset hut doorway at the Plettenberg Bay airstrip, one was Sally. Sally had surprised Liv the previous night with a phone call to tell of her arrival for a week to ten-day visit to see how Liv fared.

Over the next several days, they revisited their favorite places, walked the beaches, drove into the Tsitsikamma Forest, and lunched at Storms River Mouth. There, at the Matjies River overhang, they examined the primitive cave art left by the early strandlopers, the indigenous people of South Africa, over one hundred thousand years earlier. Hiking back, they scanned the vastness of the bay, with the geophysical features of Robberg clearly delineated in the clear winter light.

The next morning, Liv glanced at the large, antique barometer on the living room wall. "The weather will hold today. Let's take some sandwiches and explore Robberg."

"Your spiritual home. I'd love to, but we need to go slowly.

These old bones are not as spry as they were when you were a girl, when even then you dragged me all over Robberg."

"In The Fort before the interrogation started, every afternoon in my head I walked around Robberg. One of my lifelines to sanity. I know every step of the path."

Sally said, "This is the first time you've mentioned any detail of your incarceration."

After parking the car on top of the promontory amid the green coastal scrub, they felt the heat-laden air heavy from the burnishing sun. Through the incessant hum of flies, they walked to the low stonewall edging the car lot and marveled at the vastness of the southern Indian Ocean.

Hoping she did not sound too portentous, Liv expounded. "Before us for thousands of miles is this blue-gray-green ocean and eventually the continent of Antarctica. That small spur of white beach on our left splits the ocean and leads to that jagged, black, rock formation known as The Island, frequented only by seabirds and the occasional fisherman."

Sally remonstrated gently. "I've been here before, Liv. Many times. Many years ago, admittedly, but you don't have to be my tour guide."

Grinning in an offhanded manner, Liv shrugged. "Okay, I'll be quiet."

Sally joined Liv across the almost empty parking lot to the bay side of Robberg. At once, they smelled a faint mustard scent from a local fynbos plant found along this part of the Eastern Cape coast. They saw several rows of the purple green Outeniqua Mountains in the far distance and closer in the Tsitsikamma Range.

They started their hike along a path covered with loose, rounded pebbles from an ancient riverbed, and lines of large, black ants. Far to their left, in the arc of Plettenberg Bay, the famed Beacon Isle Hotel lay half-hidden in the faint mist, like a fairy castle. Sally had told Liv many times of how Helmut had met retired Captain Stanley and learned the lore of Beacon Island.

The path edged along cliffs with four-hundred-foot drops. About twenty minutes into the hike, they paused at The Gap.

"I learned this last year in a science mag after the geologists were here. This is the mouth of an ancient riverbed. A geophysical feature formed when Plettenberg Bay was the apex of a huge valley, before tectonic shifts lifted subterranean plates and allowed the ocean to pour in from The Point at Robberg to Storms River Mouth thirty miles across the Bay." Liv pointed to an indent on the other arm of the bay across miles of ocean and barely discernable. "That's where we were the other day at the mouth of Matjies River when you pointed out Robberg."

On one of the giant boulders at The Gap, a brass plaque, rusted to a gray-green patina, marked the death of a South African Air Force pilot in the Sahara Desert during World War II. The simple words read, "He loved Robberg."

"Always stops me in my tracks," Liv said. She continued reading from the same plaque. "He died in the desert so far from the ocean he loved."

Liv thought, I don't want to die far from the ocean I love.

Once across The Gap, they scrambled along a slippery path to a large overhang where Liv paused at a rock shaped like a huge throne. "Ever since the age of twelve when I was allowed to wander alone on Robberg, I've sat at sunset on this throne. Let's sit a minute."

They squeezed together.

"Water?" Liv offered Sally the canteen.

"No, I'm okay. Thanks." Sally appeared stunned by the view,

experiencing the sense of oceanic quietude. "I've forgotten the beauty and spell of this place."

Sally waved a hand at the vastness of the sea and sky. "We're both lucky to have grown up with all this," Sally said. "Helmut brought you here more often than he brought me. When I was growing up, he and the brothers were growing the business."

"I know, and I am grateful," Liv said.

"Your mother loved Plett, too, although she was not brave enough to venture too far on Robberg. But we had fun here. Don't know if I ever told you this. One visit, we were the only people on Middle Beach. We took a chance and swam nude. We emerged like drowned rats." Sally dabbed at her eyes with a tissue. "I do miss Jane . . ."

Liv patted Sally's arm. After a while, Liv said, "From here on, we'll be lucky if we see anyone. It's out of season. Only a few ghillies about, and they'll be on the other side toward The Island."

After an arduous descent, they arrived at The Point, where they rested in the only shade available: the shadows cast by the small hut built by the Plettenberg Bay Angling Club.

Liv said, "Fishermen make the trek to The Point at dusk and sleep in the hut in order to fish before dawn's first light."

Sally rose slowly and clutched Liv's arm in excitement. "What a sight, what a view! I'd forgotten the grandeur of it."

"This is a wild place." Liv acknowledged the menace under the natural beauty.

They unpacked their snacks and drank water in judicious sips from canteens; there was no fresh water source on Robberg. Liv and Sally lay on their backs on the stone floor of the porch at the angler's hut and closed their eyes.

Sitting with a sudden movement, Liv faced Sally, who also sat. Liv said in an urgent, choking voice, "Thanks for bringing me back to life. The worst prison is the death of one's ability to love and trust. I lost those in The Fort. These past days you've begun to give them back to me. Begun to free me. You came here and wanted to be with me. I feel so defiled. I didn't believe anyone would want to be with me again."

Sally's voice sounded calm but the pulse in her throat beat faster. "I'm your other mother, darling. Nothing can end my love for you." She clutched Liv's arm, "Tell me what happened to you in there."

"I can't. I'm not supposed to speak of it to anyone. House arrest orders. Also, I don't want to implicate you or to think about it. It only revives the horror. In there, I'd permit myself to think once a day of you, Marion, Jaco, the family, and Rosie ..." Liv's voice dropped to a whisper, "... when they led me outside to exercise. Only all of you, *Loeriebos*, *Milkwood*, Plett, and my memories of Robberg kept me sane for a while. And alive, I suppose. For me, you are all conjoined with Robberg. If they detain me again, I won't be able to stand it. I will find a way to kill myself." She gripped Sally's shoulders.

Sally stared back, then lowered her eyes away from Liv's adamantine gaze. "Leave South Africa. Why wait for that to happen?"

"Not so easy. They revoked my passport. The only way I can leave is with an exit permit. An exit permit means exile: a one-way ticket out. I would have to find a country willing to give me asylum. They wouldn't let me back into South Africa. I don't know if I'm ready for that step, to leave the struggle. It means they win."

"No one wins or loses. This isn't a contest. It's life or death ... your life. You can move to Mbabane.

Her mind whirled again. "Mbabane?" Liv couldn't ask Sally

if she knew about Rosie saving Daniel. She had given her word to Jaco.

Sally continued. "I'm just thinking aloud. Mbabane is close, four hours from *Loeriebos*. You'll be across the border. You can fly from there to England, Europe, anywhere via Nairobi."

Aware of the grim set to Liv's face, Sally gently tried to change the subject. "Now is the time for you to tell me a little of what happened to you in there to make you go mad. I've read reports. I know what they do to political prisoners."

Despite her house arrest restrictions, she concluded Sally was owed an explanation. "None of this is ever repeated to anyone. But I'll share a little."

Sally said, "No one will hear anything from me, Liv. I don't get to run a huge corporation without being discreet."

"One of the interrogators . . . a mad bigot . . . had a vendetta against me because he thought I was a pervert and because, in his warped eyes, I am a wealthy Jew—an English-speaking traitor. He forged an interrogation order and kept me alone with him in the interrogation room. He showed me photographs, many photographs taken from Moses's flat at *Loeriebos*. Photos of all the PAC people who came to *Loeriebos*—"

"Moses!" Sally interjected.

Liv nodded. "Yes, Moses. Photos of you, too. Moses betrayed me because he had to. They held his sons in prison. They picked them up from where they were living in Soweto. They tortured them and showed him photos of what they were doing to his sons. No wonder Moses acted so strangely toward me at the end. Now he's disappeared."

Sally shook her head in disbelief.

"I was already going mad after almost a month in solitary. When the torturer showed me the photographs, I lost all control.

I tried to tear the photos from his hands. He hit me, and I fell. He kicked me in the ribs, and I passed out." Liv paused. "I can't . . . say more . . ."

Sally rose to her feet, doubled over, and heaved in nauseous spasms. Liv patted her back. They clung to one another for balance, both rigid. A chilled breeze blew off the ocean. After a while Sally whispered, "You could have been lost forever. He wanted to kill you."

"But he didn't, and I'm here, so we go forward. Don't know what happens next."

Seagulls wheeled overhead. Huge tumbling waves—frothy blue-green monsters—crashed over the rocks. High above, a jet liner's vapor trail etched white calligraphy in the blue sky. Towering over them, the lighthouse on the green edge of the cliff above The Point stood motionless like a timeless sentinel.

Sally said, "Don't worry about that now. There's much to talk about. Plans and decisions you need to make about staying in South Africa. We can talk later, but we had better go now before we stiffen up. We're only halfway, remember."

Finding a tissue in her shorts' pocket, Liv blew her nose. "Okay, let's go."

Feeling somber but also as if a crushing weight had lifted, Liv quickened her pace. Both had much to absorb. Liv thought again of what Rosie did, of how scared she must have been driving Daniel across the border.

They traversed an area of large, seaweed-strewn boulders when Sally tapped Liv's shoulder. Liv turned and Sally shivered. "There is no point in waiting for them to detain you again. You must leave South Africa. Jaco and I can make all the arrangements."

Liv nodded. "I'll think about it, but I can't leave now. I'm under house arrest. They'll never let me go. Besides too much history—family history, personal history for me here. Too many regrets, paths not taken. And I don't want to abandon Marion."

Sally used her soothing voice. "Marion will be fine. I'll see she's taken care of. She can join you wherever, whenever. Don't worry about details. We can arrange everything."

"I should have told you some of this weeks ago. But if they find out, they'll arrest me again. I never found the right time and truthfully, I didn't want to remember. I buried it all deeply inside."

In single file again, they did not talk. Liv's mind clicked through ideas and scenarios at a frantic rate.

How do I leave South Africa if it becomes inevitable? I will return, I'll come back. But only when an all-embracing democratic government enacts the Freedom Charter. Vivid scenarios of being in prison haunted her . . . caged, tortured, and abused.

They hiked back on the ocean side of Robberg with the path at sea level. The tide flowed higher and higher and this slowed them, forcing them to climb above rock pools rather than skirt around them at ebbing low tide.

Concerned, Liv reassured Sally, who noticeably lagged. "We don't have far to go. Another twenty to thirty minutes. No hurrying now."

She's my real mother. It's about time I said it out loud. She's willing to risk life and limb for me. I can't remember Mom ever setting foot on Robberg. But Aunt Sally came to stay with me, despite my restrictive house arrest, hiking on Robberg although she was uncertain about her ability on climbs like this. I can trust Aunt Sally with everything; she risks her life for me. Her blood . . . my blood . . . Weisz blood.

The path ascended to The Gap along the outermost edge of a cave, not even six inches from the lip of another precipitous drop. Like the large cave overhang they walked under, Liv knew strandlopers had left middens of shellfish remains, fossilized fish, and seabird bones toward the back of the deep overhang . . . their trash deposits.

Liv said, "Middens can be found in similar caves at several places in the nature park, left by the first human inhabitants in the Eastern Cape thousands of years earlier. They belong to archeologists now. I think I've evolved directly from strandlopers."

They rested briefly. "Such a feminine landscape," murmured Sally. "Left and right, all the soft curves of the coastline plunge into the ocean. What lucky people to emerge from their cave each morning and see all of this."

After resting again, they ascended to The Gap, retracing the path to the parking lot, and collapsed in the car.

"The entire hike was magnificent." Sally tried to mask her stiffness and discomfort. "An unforgettable adventure. Thank you for suggesting we visit Robberg again. I'm indebted to you for sharing it with me."

"I admire you. You are so brave and game," Liv said in a rush. "You're so precious to me. You are my real mother, you know. I love you dearly." Tears came to Liv's eyes.

Sally's eyes moistened, too. She squinted against the sunlight, silent and thoughtful. "It's not so bad, Livvie." Sally placed a hand on Liv's thigh. "And it could have been much worse. Broken bones or some other calamity. But this isn't only about me, is it?"

Swallowing hard, Liv tried to speak but the words stopped in her throat. As they drove out of Robberg Nature Reserve, Liv managed to eke out, "I have this feeling . . . I know in my gut . . . I'll never hike Robberg again."

"Of course, you will. You're overwrought."

Liv did not answer.

Tired from the hike and the emotional storm at The Point, they relaxed comfortably on the old couch in front of a roaring fire at *Milkwood*. A full moon shone through the uncurtained windows, soft moonlight illuminating the room. Sally murmured but Liv heard her.

"You have such a strong heart, strong legs, competent and elegant in a drawing room or in such a rocky wild place. This is you. Robberg is you. Who you are."

Liv sat alertly. "What do you mean, who I am?"

Sally sighed. "Don't know how to explain, something about the scale and the perspective of the landscape. Too tired now. Maybe in the morning I'll be more lucid. I'm going to bed."

Later as Liv dozed, waiting for sleep, she struggled to understand what Sally observed on Robberg.

"You become one with Robberg."

Such an observation needed time to gestate. Robberg doesn't belong to me; I belong to Robberg. My roots are deep in the salt and seaweed-covered rocks and tidal pools, fixed as they are in the littoral. Wherever I am on the planet, like a compass needle, I'll turn to Robberg, the true essence of my being.

When I can articulate these thoughts with more clarity, I'll share them with Sally. Today, she gave me a most wonderful gift—a key to unlock this conundrum.

1960
LIV

. . . on her stomach, worming her way through a narrow tunnel. The efforts to maneuver much easier now that she knows what to expect but still harder and harder to breathe in the almost oxygen-starved fissure. Within eyesight, three wavering shapes appear. She knows two of them, but will she reach the third this time? She is less apprehensive as she drops into the cavern, able to cope with what will be revealed.

Beyond the skeletons of Nomzie and Natalie, Liv distinguishes the third shape—an adult skeleton. She inches closer and kneels beside it.

Liv glances at the bones of Nomzie, cracked and almost the same color as the earth, stained dark-brown . . . almost red. Natalie's cracked bones are a grayish white. This older skeleton is even whiter and show small splinters. Suddenly she knows this skeleton, Leo, her long-lost father. With careful, gentle strokes, almost like light wind, she caresses and kisses her father's brow. She kneels beside him until the position

cramps her knees. Slowly she rises, reflective and with reverence, and
clambers into the passage, worming her way back to the light.

Liv awoke in the dark room at *Loeriebos* where she had returned
over a week earlier. The calm that suffused her dream cocooned
her in a sensation like silk. Instinctively, Liv understood the nightmares would not plague her again.

For all these years, I couldn't fight my anger at my losses;
Nomzie, my first friend, brutally murdered by the police; Natalie,
my best friend, tragically killed in an accident I may have prevented; and my deepest loss, my father abandoning my baby self
even before I truly knew him. Why them, why now? Perhaps they
crept out of my subconscious mind and now I can experience
completion about those lost lives and loves.

She experienced another epiphany. Maybe I channeled
that anger at those losses into the energy to fight the apartheid
regime. But completion doesn't change anything about human
rights injustices. Nothing changes that for me. I'll fight all my
life for the human rights of all the sons and daughters of South
Africa. For baby me, my father, Nomzie, and Natalie. They are lost
to me, but I'll help to bring a fuller life to all the children, their
children, and their children's children. A noble cause. Maybe like
Don Quixote, I'm tilting at windmills, but at least I'll be riding
this anger instead of it corroding me. My anger will give birth to
change. If my character possesses any redeeming traits, a sense of
responsibility and loyalty to a cause are foremost among them.

Liv lay her head back on the pillow, hoping for sleep to be
refreshed for her meeting with Helen Suzman in the morning.

Helen Suzman regarded Liv, seated opposite her, with a steady
gaze. She commented on how fit and relaxed she looked. Liv

told her she had returned, a week earlier from a winter break in Plettenberg Bay. Seated in the elegant lounge of Helen's Melville Road, Hyde Park home, Helen, five years older than Liv, frequented many of the same social circles, yet they knew one another more by reputation than acquaintance.

"Your Aunt Sally and I play bridge together. She asked me about an exit permit for you. I have spoken to the justice minister about your case. The government is clearly agitated about you. They seem to feel you played, and maybe are still playing, a more pivotal role in the PAC than they can prove."

They chitchatted for a while about family and other acquaintances.

Helen picked up a manila envelope from a well-polished, dark-wood coffee table, adorned with a large silver bowl filled with early spring white and pink roses. She handed Liv the envelope. "I hope you choose not to use it. I know how much you love South Africa, but I agree it is best to be prepared. An exit permit to Britain is a one-way ticket. There will be no return to South Africa until the government changes or this government has a change of heart. The Broederbond drives the government. Yes, the infamous secret cabal, a Band of Brothers, feels threatened by activists like you. They believe your sole purpose is to disband White supremacy, which they've sworn to protect. You'll make the Broeders smile if you choose to leave. You're a fly in their ointment."

"Thank you, Helen."

Holding the exit permit in her hand helped subdue Liv's ever-present fear of being caged in another prison cell at The Fort. Helen accompanied her to the door, and they shook hands.

"Good luck. I hope we meet again."

Several days later, a beautiful morning, Liv walked the dogs on the wild grass fields around *Loeriebos*. She sat on the outcrop of rocks where she had read Rosie's letters after her release from prison. The golden sunlight burnished the grasses. Liv wore a large, straw sun hat and dark sunglasses. Craning her head upward, she lost herself in the vast emptiness of the inverted bowl of clear blue sky. She relaxed back onto the rocks and dozed.

Over to her left, a dark smudge emerged in the distance above the ridges of the Magaliesberg. Moving closer and growing larger, it appeared as a solar eclipse blocking the sunlight. Half-awake and half-asleep, Liv was conscious enough to watch a daydream unfold, where she saw herself lying on the rocks. In the daydream, Liv removed the hat and glasses and squinted to see the shadow more clearly.

The figure hovered above her. A huge Black woman dressed in a colorful, dyed, traditional dress with an elaborate, cotton cloth headdress peered at Liv from her lofty position. In one hand she carried a sangoma's whisk, the sign of a traditional healer, while the other hand rested on her hip.

"Greetings, daughter of my soil!" Her thunderous voice roared and echoed over the sky and fields. "I am Afrika, mother of this great land and all her people."

Liv fell to her knees and bowed her head in awe, fright, and excitement. The towering figure flashed a vast smile, lighting the sky like a prolonged sheet of lightning during an electrical storm. She waved the whisk over Liv, and the grasses rippled and swayed as if a covey of a thousand finches swept low over the fields.

"Your African heart is part of the drumbeat of all our people, Liv Weisz. Your tears of suffering watered the land. There is no need for more.

"Leave this place. You'll have us with you beyond the seas. Your family and other ghosts will be with you, always, in your heart. You will return. You will commune again with the Mountain of Seals, Robberg, the place of the old people to whom you belong. Leave this place with my blessings."

Mother Afrika turned and lifted her large feet. Soaring lammergeyers with their six-foot wingspan glided on hidden updrafts of hot air currents, like a living crown around her head. From her kneeling position, Liv saw the enormous light-brown soles rise and fall as she strode into the distance toward the mountains. As her figure receded, the sunlight returned to the landscape and Liv rose, too.

Returning to the house, Liv wanted to share the vision with someone, but instinct stopped her. Her vision was gifted from Mother Afrika. The gift would enrich her, but to speak would dilute the power of magic.

Instead, Liv remembered the envelope with the exit permit. She had tossed it in a dismissive gesture to a drawer containing insurance policies and other legal documents, thinking she wouldn't need them for a while.

Marion, who had been spending a weekend with her, asked, "Mom? What won't you be needing?"

Grinning, feeling sheepish, Liv muttered, "I'm getting used to the idea of exile. It may be prudent, after all, to make more plans." Thoughtfully she had opened the drawer and drummed the envelope in one hand onto the open palm of the other.

Marion nodded, feeling sad. "If you go, I'm coming with you!"

When the doorbell rang, Liv opened the front door to find Kevin

Steyn, The Fort interrogator; she gasped and screamed Marion's name. Steyn removed his gray fedora as Marion rushed to her mother and clasped her arm.

"No one will take you away, Mom. They will have to kill me before I will let you go."

"Sorry to frighten you, Miss Weisz."

Steyn looked at Marion. "Ma'am." He turned back to Liv. "I'm here in person because we want to give you some information."

"I've come to warn you. We learned last night that Hennie Van Niekerk escaped from Sterkfontein Mental Hospital. We think he might be headed this way to you. His doctors say he continues to be obsessed with you. Please take this seriously. Don't walk anywhere alone, even in daylight, even with the dogs." The dogs moved behind Liv and Marion. "If you go out at night, make sure you have protection when you enter the house."

"I can't go out at night. I'm under house arrest." Liv's voice was dulled with shock.

Silent, Steyn glanced at her, and for a moment she thought it was in sympathy.

"We asked the local police station commander to post two constables on duty here around the clock for at least a week or until we find him. They should be arriving any time now."

"Thank you. I already have three watchmen here at night, but I'll be pleased to have the constables, too."

Hennie Van Niekerk frightened Liv—another forceful indication that she must leave her home, her motherland. Liv's warm and sunlit country was now an alien and dangerous place. Perhaps it always was, but now she saw the truth. She thanked Kevin Steyn for informing her in person.

He smiled. "We'll let you know when we find Van Niekerk. And we will find him."

Marion patted her mother's shoulder after she closed and locked the front door. Feeling how cold Liv was, she hugged her.

Liv broke the uncertain silence. "Sobering, isn't it? Where are you going?"

Marion turned to the stairs. "I'm going to pack a small suitcase for late summer in Europe. I want to be ready to leave at a moment's notice."

Casting a long look around the rooms, Liv sighed. Everything exactly how she wanted. "I'll come with you and do the same. I feel the inevitable moment coming closer."

"Mom, do me a favor?"

"Anything."

"Call Aunt Sally and tell her what's happening. I'll feel much safer if we have protection from Weisz Corp here in daylight, too. A psychopath on the loose—obsessed with you—is terrifying. Sounds like an Agatha Christie novel."

"Okay, good idea. And darling, please don't open the door to anyone, at least not until the watchmen arrive. I'll tell the staff. It's a siege, isn't it?"

1960
LIV

In the late afternoon, Jaco arrived, looking flustered when he saw the police activity on the driveway. Liv opened the front door for him before he rang the bell.

"Policemen and guards everywhere? What the hell is going on?"

Lowering her eyes, Liv let Marion speak. "Hennie Van Niekerk, the interrogator who almost killed Mom at The Fort, escaped yesterday from Sterkfontein. The police think he may be headed here or be somewhere around here already. They are confident they will find him."

"Oh, Christ." Jaco sank into an armchair in the lounge. "Is there no end to all of this?"

They sat in silence as Jaco assessed the information. "Be careful, Liv. No more spontaneous walks. And Marion, don't let her out of your sight. Go everywhere with her. I've been involved in cases with psychopaths. They are unpredictable and dangerous. Obviously, Van Niekerk wants to finish you off this time."

After a silent pause, Jaco brightened and shot a mischievous glance at Liv. He tried to lighten the mood. "Hey, by any chance do you have some of that incredible whiskey you served me once?"

Crossing the room to the liquor cabinet, Liv removed the bottle of MacCallan. "What brings you here?" Liv asked, as she poured the whiskey over ice cubes and handed him a glass.

"I have some important documents for you," he grinned and with enthusiasm added, "I've left them on your desk."

"So quickly?"

"Pulled a few strings."

Liv's will, leaving *Loeriebos* and all her belongings to Marion, went into the drawer with the exit permit.

The week passed without more surprises. Marion refused to return to the university until they caught the psychopath. Each day they felt safer, protected by the presence of the police and security guards. Each day, they expected to hear search parties had found Hennie Van Niekerk. The previous day, a large contingent of police had spread in line formation and combed the fields. They came across several places where someone might have been sleeping, but no signs pointed away from hobos and toward Van Niekerk.

On Tuesday morning, August 30, Jaco arrived, braking hard with a screech of tires on the gravel circle. Liv and Marion rushed to the front door. It was an unusual occurrence for Jaco to visit in the morning, even at midmorning. One look at his face, and Liv's heartbeat quickened.

"What is it, Jaco? What's the hurry?"

Jaco, sweating, although the air felt cool in the early spring morning, pushed his way into the hall.

"Hurry you two. Get dressed for a long plane ride. I'm driving you to the airport—now! You are leaving in a few hours for London. BOAC flight."

They stared at him in amazement.

"Hurry, hurry. No time. I'll explain in the car. Don't forget the exit permit, Liv. Marion, your passport."

In disbelief, Marion and Liv changed hurriedly into comfortable traveling clothes and carried the small bags they had packed the week before.

Seated in the back seat with Marion, Liv demanded, "Okay, Jaco, tell us now. What's going on?"

"Eyes and ears," said Jaco. "My own network verified by another. Last week Daniel Molefe turned up in London. The SB has a clandestine operation there working from the South African Embassy. He uses another name now, of course, but someone watching recognized him when he arrived at a PAC safe house in London.

"Back here, they've been working on the case of his escape for months. Still festers how we sprung him from one of their high security prison hospitals and spirited him across the border."

Liv gasped. Jaco looked quizzically at Liv. "They found one of Rosie's co-drivers to Mbabane and tortured him. Someone informed on him and, under extreme duress, he admitted to his involvement in Molefe's escape."

Jaco turned to Marion, who sat ashen in the back seat. "Your mom can explain later. He named Rosie, I'm afraid. I'm not clear about the rest. But because of your affair with Rosie, they believe you were involved. Strange because at the same time you were already in prison being interrogated." He shook his head. "They always believed you were more involved with the PAC than you were telling them. They followed Rosie's trail. A border clerk at

Oshoek recognized her passport photo, said he'd seen it on a British passport. He remembered she traveled with Dr. Dlamini. Fortunately, she left SA when she did. They can't touch her in Britain."

Stricken, Liv glanced at Marion. They held hands while Jaco spoke. "The net has drawn in, Liv. At this very moment, the SB is on their way to detain you. Your aunt is at Jan Smuts with two tickets to London on this afternoon's flight. She also has the British consul from Pretoria with her. No wonder she's the chief executive of your family's corporation. Amazingly competent. The consul will accept you as a political refugee into England. He will wait with you in the diplomats' private room in the international transit lounge and board the flight with you. The SB cannot follow you there."

They drove the rest of the way to the airport in silence. They found Sally pacing impatiently on the curb. She opened the Mercedes' door, kissed them, and passed the plane tickets to the consul waiting with her. No one said a word. Liv and Marion hugged Sally and Jaco.

Sally gave Liv a packet of British currency, "I'll be in London soon as I can to help you settle. Look for Paul at the airport."

Another warm rush of adrenalin coursed through Liv's body. *"Paul?"*

But there was no time to talk. The consul rushed them to the BOAC boarding line and hurried them through security, using the queue reserved for diplomats and privileged political personnel. The passport officer looked twice at Liv's exit permit.

"Hurry man," the consul ordered, his voice hardened by his concern. "We don't want to miss our flight."

The passport official smiled. "It's okay. I just haven't seen one of these before."

They reached the ground floor in the international transit lounge and found safety in the diplomatic personnel private room.

Speaking only when necessary, all three watched the hands of the large wall clock move slowly around the dial. At last, their flight was called. All three joined the crowd on the tarmac and boarded buses to the aircraft. Once again, the consul ushered them, to the front of the queue for the first-class cabin. He spoke to the chief petty officer and informed him of the slight possibility that, once airborne, the South African Air Force might order the BOAC plane to return to the airport. The consul shared this possibility with Liv and Marion, adding, "But that would be an extreme measure causing such an international outcry, I doubt they would go ahead, even if they think of it."

The consul stayed with them on the plane, departing prior to the arming of the plane's doors.

Airborne at last.

Sitting in the window seat, Liv watched the East Rand suburbs and golden mine dumps disappear beneath the plane's wings. Tears stung her eyes.

On a flight path for Nairobi, the plane took forty minutes to leave South African air space. They flew over the Lebomba Mountains, the border with Mozambique, and they relaxed for the first time in several tense hours. Liv ordered drinks. Mother and daughter reflected the sadness in one another's eyes.

"It's all right, darling." Liv reassured Marion. "A new beginning. We have our whole lives in front of us. You can come back any time but not me. I've chosen exile."

Marion could only nod and offer a wan smile. "Mom," she whispered, "who's Paul?"

Placing a finger over Marion's lips, Liv spoke in a quiet but firm voice. "Shh, long story. I'll tell you soon. It is in the past and nothing to be done about it." She added, "Thank you for coming with me. I know it's a wrench to leave your studies midyear, but I'd rather be here with you than waiting for Hennie Van Niekerk at *Loeriebos*." For further reassurance, she whispered, "Do you have any idea how much I love you?"

Marion smiled and gulped at her Coke. "And me you. He's my father, right?" She leaned back in the luxurious seat and closed her eyes.

"Yes," Liv answered slowly, "but as much a stranger to me now as to you. Right now, I can't explain. I'm feeling numb to the loss of home and country. But I have so much to be thankful for. And all I want and need right now sits here beside me. And you?"

"Relief and sadness. We'll be together. I won't have to worry about you going to prison again. We'll be safe. All things are possible now."

Liv settled back in the ample seat and closed her eyes. Where will I live? I love France, often thought of Cassis and Carcassone, but not London or anywhere in England where it is too damp and gray. I am of the sun and light. I like the picture of me living in a sunny villa in the south of France.

Liv sighed, I am content for the moment in this strange limbo of the airplane's cabin. In a finite way, I'm leaving behind all the markers that make me who I am.

When Nomzie died and my mother did not allow me to mourn, she tried to teach me a Black life is worth nothing. Even then, I knew it was not true. No one would or could explain to me how a girl my age could be bludgeoned to death because she was visiting her father. I came to understand I lived in a different reality. I became one who used the lens of an outsider. The incident alienated me from conventional viewpoints—acceptance of family values, peers' behavior and attitudes—and a refusal to wear White South Africans' racial blinkers.

For years, this knowledge was buried in me. Natalie's death, a loss I experienced fully, aided this sense of alienation. There is no one else I know who was asked to live her life for another. I had trusted Natalie but she let me down. I blocked the responsibility her mother tried to impose, but my decisions and actions at that time were for Natalie, too.

Growing up without a father and with two mothers, my guilt and shame and loss almost buried me. I couldn't be a good person if my father abandoned me.

I compromised these three people who lived on in my nightmares—Nomzie, Natalie, and Leo. I vowed I would fight for them and for all the children—for a better life—replete with the rights their humanity endowed upon them. I'd help them all claim their personhood.

I never believed that people trusted me because I never believed in myself. I never trusted people because I never trusted myself. After witnessing Paul's shocking injuries and leaving him a second time to be with John, and then divorcing John, those roles slowly fell away. The pupa of my real self, sitting here now, emerged from the cocoon, an activist participant in a terrible human tragedy perpetuated in my name as a White South African.

Now, I know who I am—an outsider in the eyes of the world but no longer in my own.

They arrived at Heathrow where a British homeland official met them and as arranged, on behalf of Her Majesty's government, granted Liv's request for political asylum. He escorted them through customs and passport control. In the VIP passenger lounge, through the window, Liv searched for a uniformed driver holding a placard with both their names.

Standing next to him was a balding man. Paul's face was almost restored fully, eyes shining with anticipation. Paul waved, and Liv's heart raced as she steered Marion by one of her elbows to her father.

Paul embraced them both in a reassuring hug.

"Welcome to England, Liv. Welcome, Marion."

The driver, a West Indian, drove them in the Bentley to the corporation's flat in Green Park. On the sidewalk outside the building, Liv stared at a nearby newsstand and pointed out the glaring headline.

"S.A. Apartheid Government Surprise: Ends Six-Month State of Emergency."

They read the headline aloud in the gray light of early morning on a busy London street on Wednesday, August 31, 1960.

Early that evening Liv received a phone call from Sally.

"Darling you left just in time. *Loeriebos* was burned, badly damaged, last night. The arsonist was found at the staircase, unrecognizable, burned to death. The police believe it was Van Niekerk. That psychopath really wanted to kill you."

2005
LIV

Carcassonne
December

Paul died a year ago, 2004, and with my loss still stinging, I lacked the will to sort his personal items into some order. His dresser in our bedroom and the small table on his side of the bed waited undisturbed for his return. The view from the bedroom window—the steep-sided valley he loved so—enticed me, as always. Our eighteenth-century house, built on lavender-covered slopes amid garden terraces I had designed, overflowed with blooms and scents in every season. Paul and a gardener had planted the terraces and tended the plants. Our home and garden were situated within the precinct of the ancient, fortified Cité de Carcassonne, which loomed over the more expansive lower city—the *ville basse*. Spectacular. But without Paul, the world seemed flat, empty, and dull.

On this first anniversary of his death, I pleaded with myself to stop playing Miss Haversham. I heard Paul chiding me about being mired in misery. We were so fortunate for over forty loving years together. But it is difficult. I miss him every day. I speak to him when I walk through the garden or the town and sometimes when I drive into the countryside.

Slowly, day by day, I began to sort his belongings. As a writer, Paul naturally kept all sorts of papers, clippings, drafts, and letters. I turned first to search for anything Paul might, in his casual manner, have set aside under some clothes or in an old box or container. Sorting through his desk drawers filled with manuscripts, notes, and research, I hoped to find paperwork his personal papers. I didn't want any of them to fall into the wrong hands and cause any controversy. Disposal of his clothes and personal effects I left to our housekeeper who called on several ladies from her church to help her. They could dispense with them as they pleased.

Paul kept all my letters somewhere, along with lists and brief messages. He entrusted me with them only near the end of the irrevocable progression of his illness.

"When I'm gone, look in the back of the bedroom wardrobe."

I wondered what I'd find. Many times, prior to coping with such a dreadful year of his illness and death, we sat with a tape recorder between us, a difficult task for Paul since he liked to be engaged with a project in the garden, around the house, or in the village. I asked him to talk about his memories. He humored me. We recorded many hours of his reminiscences.

Eventually he said in a firm tone but with a laugh, "Sweetheart, you can't drive forward if you are forever looking in the rearview mirror." The recording sessions ended.

I agreed with Paul.

But now I'm moving closer to the days when I will begin to share stories about my life and our families' lives as I promised my great-grandson, Adam, when he had asked on my eightieth birthday.

If I do look into the rearview mirror, the images stretch for miles: settling in Carcassonne in winter 1961 amid the acceptance and friendliness of the villagers; wandering the narrow, curving streets of the ancient walled city where the building facades conserve the medieval feel of tiny windows (festooned with flower boxes) and miniature balconies; the scale of the small, intimate, and inviting village; shopping daily at the farmers' market amid the warm embrace of vendors; entertaining Marion, and then annually, Marion and her family from America; and entertaining other curious and appreciative family and friends from South Africa, England, and elsewhere, including Sally who died twenty-two years ago.

Often, I had wanted to contact Rosie to hear her story about Daniel's escape, but I never did. We were not in touch at any time after my phone call from the telephone booth near *Loeriebos*. Rosie and our affair remained a precious and sweet but troubled and fading memory.

Not a French-speaker when we had settled there, I relied on Paul who spoke serviceable French. We made some friends, especially once Marcel and Edith arrived. Known then and until he died as the "l'Afrique du Sud couple on the hill with French poodles." If our succession of housekeepers gossiped about us, we never heard a whisper.

I missed *Loeriebos*, *Milkwood*, Plett, Robberg, and many other favorite places in South Africa. Paul knew how I ached to see them again.

Almost immediately after our arrival, I had plunged into local affairs and served on the village council. Most other members communicated with a range of English language competency and in that manner, we managed two-way communication. After a year, I spoke decent French but with an atrocious accent. Paul and I took French culinary classes together and delighted in the experiences, although at home Paul became "chief chef."

My passion for gardening survived transplanting my African roots to southern France, and we brought to life our wondrous and highly scented hillside garden. This project fulfilled me for a while. Many tourists stopped to gaze. I said to them, "Come in. Meander along the terraces."

Soon after, twice a year—spring and fall—the local tourist board featured our garden as one in a series of open-garden venues. They organized attendants to limit the crowds to thirty persons per session each day.

In 1961, once we settled safely in France, the besiegement in my final weeks at *Loeriebos* by the psychopath Hennie Van Niekerk began to intrigue Paul. His interest was further piqued when we were surprised by a visit from a woman who claimed to be Hennie Van Niekerk's great-niece.

We sat on the terrace drinking tea. Our visitor was approaching forty, a fading beauty, and spoke perfect English with a heavy Afrikaans accent. She introduced herself as Marie Schroeder.

"My husband, who is German, and I are visiting his family and traveling around Europe for a while. We live in South Africa on the family farm in the Orange Free State. I managed to find you both by nagging your publisher, Mr. Minthof."

Paul nodded, a little crossly, I thought.

"On the farm, there is a large cemetery where the Van Niekerks and their spouses and children are buried, going back one hundred years. My great-aunt Marierentia Magdalena Kruger Van Niekerk is buried there alongside her husband. She bore seven children and four survived. They are or will all be buried there. Hennie van Niekerk, the eldest, and one of her sons, was the 'black sheep' of the family. His name on the gravestone intrigued me: Hendrik Helmut Paulus Kruger Van Niekerk."

My heart beat faster.

"There is no other Helmut on the names on the gravestones. I did some research on Hennie. I found he had a troubled youth, cruel and unkind, especially to the little children and their pets. The family disowned him many times, but he always crawled back. He was called a psychopath in medical records. He was only allowed to join the police force because his grandfather was Paul Kruger.

"Family lore has it that on her deathbed, Marierentia confessed she had an affair before she was married, an affair with a Jew named Helmut. And she was pregnant when she married. She never divulged her lover's last name, but she insisted he was Hennie's father.

"You can imagine the consternation this caused in our conservative, strictly Calvinist family. When, he learned he had Jewish blood, the family says, his anti-Semitism became rampant. Self-hatred because of his blood, and hostility toward all the Weisz family, but mainly because he never knew his father. He joined a secret neo-Nazi group. The family never saw him again.

"The papers were full of the story of your house burning, Mrs. Minthof." Wrestling with my own secrets, I did not bother to correct her as to my marital status.

"Also, about your exile to escape being re-arrested. When I saw the name Weisz, it was easy to connect the dots. Weisz Corporation is so well-known in South Africa. Also, as you know, your founder, Helmut Weisz, is a legend in business and philanthropic circles. He must have been your great-uncle . . ."

I nodded.

"... and Hennie's father."

"I'm so sorry, Mrs. Minthof, that someone from our family, and in truth your very own illegitimate half-uncle, tried to burn you in your own home. I am ashamed."

Those eyes, those eyes, in the interrogation room, I knew I'd seen those eyes before—Helmut's eyes.

Marie Schroeder rummaged in her tote and brought out two manilla envelopes, one large and one small. Gravely she opened the large one and retrieved a thick, foolscap-sized, soft covered book. She proffered it to me, "Found at his flat, Hennie's scrapbook. It's filled with newspaper cuttings, photos and articles of you and your family going back decades. You will see he circled particularly Helmut Weisz and yourself. On some press clippings he wrote 'Hate' and 'Kill all Jews'. He was obsessively jealous of you, Mrs. Minthof.'"

Aghast, I felt Paul's hand on my shoulder. I needed several minutes before I spoke. In a flash of a memory, I heard my mother's voice, "He was obsessively jealous of her." But I couldn't recall the context of those words. Mrs. Schroeder was watching me with concern. I pushed away the scrapbook, "I don't want this! Ever. Please destroy it."

"Sorry to have scared you, Mevrou . . . but I think you may want this. . ."

She shook the smaller envelope and the contents fell into her hand. She opened her fist. On her palm lay a delicately wrought gold Magen Dovid and a chain.

She held it out gently toward me. "I believe this may be yours. It was handed to us with Hennie's remains. He was wearing it when he died."

Overcome, I gasped in amazement and gingerly accepted the

proffered six-pointed star in one hand, while dabbing at my eyes with a tissue in the other. Paul hadn't moved his comforting hand from my shoulder. Hennie's secret ghost, like one of mine—we were both abandoned by our fathers.

Wait till I tell Marion and Sally.

I said, "Thank you very much, Mrs. Schroeder, this is a family heirloom . . . and for seeking us out and sharing all of this. Hennie Van Niekerk was obviously a tortured human being, a self-hating Jew and a psychopath. You sharing these objects brings me some peace and closure. I certainly understand much more now of the horror that happened to me when I was detained last year."

The conversation turned to day trips around Provence. Marie Schroeder stayed for scarcely half an hour.

Later, in bed, Paul and I discussed the ramifications of Mrs. Schroder's visit. Finally, Paul said, "One of these days I'm going to start writing a detective series on solving psychopathic murders."

In those early years we traveled—with the dogs—like gypsies, in a converted Volkswagen minivan, roaming from Portugal to Greece, Scandinavia to Sicily.

During that time, I avidly followed news of South Africa by listening to the BBC shortwave radio and reading various London newspapers we picked up each day in the village. There was never any good news to share. Each day painted a bleaker and bleaker picture for my country, my motherland.

As the apartheid government regressed into a more repressive regime, Jaco Malan gained international celebrity as a defender of those activists brought to trial. Likewise, Helen Suzman achieved international stature for her impactful and solitary opposition in Parliament.

"But" I said to Paul, "most of those thousands arrested are

still voiceless—either incarcerated, under house arrest, banned, or exiled. As international boycotts, restrictions, and divestment campaigns develop, the apartheid government, embattled and defiant, has gained notoriety as a pariah state."

Soon after we settled in Carcassonne, both PAC leaders in exile and the ANC government-in-exile contacted me. Several high-ranking members of both congresses visited and extoled me for my contribution to the struggle.

After each visit, I felt restlessness in me. "I should be engaged again, doing something."

But during those first years, I did not participate in an overt way in the struggle. Our life entered a peaceful phase. Paul wrote, cooked, and gardened. I gardened (a little), engaged in local government issues, and entertained many guests, which included both family and friends.

Marion studied at London University. At that time, she visited often. Next, she completed a doctorate in international politics and economics at the Wharton School at University of Pennsylvania in Philadelphia. Her doctoral thesis was on South Africa's economy, past, present, and scenarios for the future. Later, she published the thesis as a book. I am so proud of her.

Marion married one of the junior lecturers in her department at UPenn. My son-in-law has been a full professor for many years. They have four children. We visited them occasionally in the ensuing years, although I was always in Philadelphia to help when their children were born. Marion and her family visit us in France once a year in the summer. We speak often on the phone. When all the children were in college, Marion became active in progressive movements, specifically as an advisor on economic policy.

Often, Paul and I acknowledged our gratitude for our deepening relationship.

"Loving you," I told Paul, "Is exciting, sometimes challenging. You are as headstrong, rebellious, and obstinate as ever, but also enriching. I appreciate your devotion and caring. And that you are so amorous. I love you."

"And you . . . you're perfect as you are," he told me often, enfolding me in a warm embrace. "Every day I am so thankful we are together. Every day with you is a gift. I love you, too."

He knew his introverted need for privacy when he was writing irked me. In everything but his writing life, Paul was content to walk in my shadow.

Inevitable change came to our idyll. The ANC government-in-exile nominated me for the post of Deputy General Secretary for sub-Saharan Africa in the United Nations affiliate International Education Initiative for Refugee Students. Once my appointment was approved, the education program became mine. I organized teams to raise funds to establish schools and universities and provide scholarships for refugee children in sub-Saharan Africa.

Twice-yearly meetings of the international body and monthly meetings of the subcommittee I chaired, all in Geneva, necessitated purchasing a studio apartment in the city. We almost always traveled together except when Paul wrote on a deadline, or the dogs were ill. My fundraising ventures centered on Europe, Japan, and North America. My private network (with Sally's blessing) included her business contacts, and I developed my own contacts in all the obvious foundations supporting education internationally.

Embracing the challenge, our home hummed as the center for this vast outreach. The work closest to my heart revolved around regular visits to educational programs our organization funded in African countries. Treated as a celebrity both for my anti-apartheid activism and my efforts in the educational realm of—as I expressed myself—"Africa's children," I found this ironic. I was still a pariah in my own country.

Paul asked how I could work day-by-day in such abject conditions.

I answered, "Sometimes the pervasive poverty, dire need of the children, and despair, especially in the refugee camps, overwhelms me. But I understand we are both fortunate to visit places I never thought would be in my life and others I'd only vaguely heard of such as Kampala, Kigali, Lagos, Abidjan, Bamako, and Ouagadougou."

In truth, I thrived in the African heat, dust, and flies. In the refugee camps, I loved being surrounded by ragged children while sitting on a makeshift chair reading to them from a book of *Aesop's Fables* or some other classic with an interpreter at hand, her impromptu remarks generating gales of childish laughter. Sometimes I'd share with Paul, "I'm living my dream."

This status changed decades later in 1994, when, after a momentous and historic election, Nelson Mandela's ANC became the first truly democratic government of the country. In July 1994, I was invited by the Office of President Nelson Mandela to attend the inaugural celebrations.

On that day, at the Union Buildings in Pretoria, once the proud and imposing outpost of the far-flung British Empire, the winter sky was a deep blue. The air shuddered as South African Air Force fighter jets thundered in salute formation over the elegant arc of the red-hued brick buildings. Behind the dignitaries and seated guests (we among them), hundreds of thousands of people packed Union Square and the streets lining the processional route for President Mandela's motorcade. Several speeches were delivered by the new president over several days, in which he always mentioned the Freedom Charter and the debt all South Africans owe to those who died in the struggle. Each time he did so, I dabbed at my eyes with a tissue, remembering Daniel's collegiality in 1960. Warmth and appreciation greeted me from so many Black and White attendees at the inaugural dinner.

Toward the conclusion of one dinner party when Paul and I were exhausted but happy and content, two older men—one White and one Black— both with hair-tinged gray, strode smiling toward us, albeit one with a notable limp.

I almost leaped into Daniel Molefe's hug. The other man hung back. I assumed he waited to greet me.

"Trevor Lewis." He extended his hand.

I looked at him quizzically, his name familiar.

"Miss Lann?"

"Miss Lann? Rosie?" I responded perplexed as I struggled to fit his name and face. Suddenly I remembered what Jaco had told me. "Trevor Lewis, Rosie's accomplice and one of the drivers in the Mbabane exploit." Trevor Lewis who had broken down in interrogation and torture and named Rosie.

We shared a brief conversation. Then, holding Daniel by the hand, I brought them to meet Paul. We listened as Daniel and Trevor shared snippets of each other's roles in the Mbabane escape. We raised our champagne glasses to toast one another. This reminded me of the night Rosie and I met at Alan Paton's house meeting in January 1960, when Black and White mingled and drank, an illegal and subversive activity.

Soon after, Trevor excused himself. A distinguished older woman arrayed in full regalia of Xhosa royalty walked to Daniel's side, and he introduced his wife. After several minutes of pleasantries, other guests corralled the Molefes.

As he turned away, Daniel spoke *sotto voce*. "The solemn vow. Intact?"

I nodded. "And with you?"

Molefe nodded.

"Sobukwe . . . the Prof?" I asked, "He's not here?"

Daniel shook his head, "Sadly, he died . . . in 1978, in Kimberley, still under house arrest. Lung cancer. He's currently a forgotten man . . ."

I patted Daniel's arm. Without speaking we knew what the other was thinking: The Prof will never be forgotten.

We stared into one another's eyes for a long moment. I broke the lengthening silence. "You must both come and visit us in France when you are in Europe."

Daniel, a new appointee by Mandela to a senior position in the foreign affairs department, bent his head in acknowledgment. "Count on it. We'll make every effort."

Our welcoming and generous hosts in Johannesburg, Jaco and Pauline Malan, along with their adult daughters, husbands, and many offspring in tow, made our reunion so special. We attended several Weisz and Minthof afternoon tea gatherings, in addition to dinners.

Jaco drove us around the city and suburbs. As we neared Hillbrow, he asked if I would be uncomfortable driving past The Fort. I expressed no qualms, just a faint uneasiness tinged with curiosity. Jaco told us of the Mandela government's plans to keep many of the cell blocks intact as monuments to the past.

"On another section of the site will arise, out of remnants of other buildings, a glass-encased block housing the Constitutional Court, the highest court in the land." Thoroughly satisfied with this idea, I thought it a brilliant stroke of political symbolism.

Loeriebos, rebuilt after the fire by the Weisz family to my original architectural specifications, was now rented to a family with young children. My desire to see my home again drove me to arrange with the renters a time to visit *Loeriebos* with Paul. Sculptured gardens thrived, containing only indigenous plants and trees. Much of the veld area survived, but with many more walking trails named and maintained. Weaverbirds still darted, hadidas nested, and the pervasive scent of eucalyptus floated on the air. I was so pleased.

After the inaugural celebrations and family visits in Johannesburg, we flew to Plettenberg Bay and *Milkwood* for a week. *Milkwood,* untouched by time with the same "old world ambience" I remembered, had remained a family retreat for generations of Weiszes.

Plett, the once sleepy village, was now an ever-growing holiday venue bustling with fast-food outlets and condo buildings fortunately situated nearer the village and not on Robberg Beach. The small town was unrecognizable from when I was last there in 1960. Robberg Beach was still mainly unspoiled; no houses were permitted on the sand dunes running almost the entire length of the beach to Robberg Peninsula. Clusters of condos were situated in proximity to the one access path onto the green-gray peninsula, the very path previously hidden by a small caravan park, which now boasted more low-rise condos.

From a distance, Robberg appeared untouched. Much older now, but still fit enough after long walks every day in Carcassonne, we both ventured forth on a brilliant sunny winter's day to hike Robberg, just as Sally and I had done so many years earlier when I didn't think I would ever return.

An attendant in the National Parks uniform manned the new parking ticket booth and issued warnings about the tides and not venturing too close to path edges. He glanced doubtfully at us, as if questioning if we knew what we were attempting, an older couple on a six-mile hike around Robberg.

I smiled. "I grew up here. I know Robberg like this—" I held up the palm of my hand.

He saluted and waved us in.

Muttering annoyance about the tarred and ticketed parking lot, I complained, "Can't anyone leave well enough alone?" The trails from the parking lot to The Gap were now maintained and railings inserted into the rocky ledges with the most precipitous drops. The "improvements" pleased me since they only extended to The Gap. I then stopped muttering and morphed into a somewhat elderly mountain goat. I moved blithely and with joy on the narrow descent to The Point. I *did* remember every step and left Paul far behind.

After a glorious hike, we emerged many hours later sweaty and thirsty but safe at the parking lot. I told Paul, "This time, sweetheart, is truly the last time I'll hike Robberg. So many, many memories. Robberg is one of the special places on the planet."

Paul agreed. I was relieved we had both hiked without incident, and that Paul said the peninsula met his expectations. Back in the village, we enjoyed tea and scones at a trendy, coffee house in a new open-air shopping mall opposite the old jail where Sargent Dawid Myburgh had presided before he died many years earlier.

Describing images in the rearview mirror can be nostalgic and in a way cathartic, but change being inevitable, I agreed with Paul.

Yet, I transcribed those recorded conversations during which he was a gracious, if unwilling, participant. I placed them inside a manila folder in the old canvas gym bag in the wardrobe.

Paul's writing career burgeoned after *In Search of Dying*. His success grew into a flurry of activity in the mid-1960s and into the 1970s that produced a series of popular mystery novels, since faded from interest.

In Search of Dying, his first and only effort at autobiography, evoked many emotions for him—familiar and unfamiliar—including gratification for its generally positive critical reception and substantial sales and overwhelming shame and guilt at exposing himself, friends, and family to voyeuristic attention.

In 1961, once we settled safely in France, the besiegement in my final weeks at *Loeriebos* by the psychopath Hennie Van Niekerk intrigued him.

After many months of immersing himself in research on psychopathology and hours of interviews with the cooperative Interpol agency in nearby Toulouse, he created his protagonist, Damon Ellis, an intrepid, British-born, Interpol detective specializing in psychopathology. With the publication of each book, Damon Ellis's reputation in the fictional Interpol community grew (as did Paul's readership) with his ability to solve every psychopathic murder mystery he encountered. Each book was set in a different city from across Europe and sub-Saharan Africa.

While I attended to matters in various places pertaining to my education outreach, Paul wandered those same cities, towns, and rural villages, sat and read in public libraries where available, and visited police stations writing fervid notes for his next book. His books were popular in the murder-mystery genre, as much for the mystery as for the international locales that hopefully transported readers—along with Damon—to little-known and often exotic destinations.

During the fecund period, Paul said. "My commitment to writing is eroding the precious time I want to spend with you."

He wrote less and less. When I retired after twenty years as a roving deputy general secretary, he stopped writing . . . a decision neither of us ever regretted. I am pleased that now the novels are slowly being reissued, and there are even talks of a movie deal featuring Damon Ellis, the lone-wolf specialist detective. I think Paul would be pleased, too.

As instructed often by Paul that when he died, I must search in the back of the bedroom wardrobe. There, in a dark corner, lay the faded canvas gym bag I had brought from *Milkwood* after our South African sojourn at the time of Nelson Mandela's inauguration. It was flattened by the weight of forty-something years of old shoes. About to toss it aside, I recalled a vague memory. Forty-six years earlier, this bag was placed in my bedroom wardrobe at my home, *Loeriebos*, in Rivonia, Johannesburg. When I hoisted the bag, it settled with a familiar heft in my hands. This very bag contained my toiletries and other essentials preparing for the moment I might be detained by the security police. Later, I had sequestered Rosie's letters and the transcriptions of Paul's recordings.

Perhaps Paul placed other documents in it, too. I struggled to open the clasp, but it broke away from the fraying cloth. Placing my hand into the bag, my fingers encountered a legal pad with many pages covered in my handwriting . . . sprawled writing so scattered, it was scarcely legible in numerous places. I had worked at a frenetic gallop when I had arrived at Plett to find some peace after my time in The Fort. Until that moment, I had forgotten about this record of my prison experience.

Stuck to the legal pad was a note from Paul.

I know I shouldn't have, but I have read every piece of paper in this bag. I am horrified once again, reading this firsthand account of your incarceration and interrogation in

The Fort. But you are also blessed, my darling, by so much love in your life and of your ability to give and receive love. When you read this note, I will be dead.

My one regret—I never met Rosie.

As ever, yours, Paul.

After I sorted through Paul's possessions, I came to a decision. I wanted to spend my last years at *Loeriebos*. I made the arrangements to return home.

Paul and I had been together for all those years, until that final time when death parted us—but not our hearts.

Liv Weisz,
Carcassonne, 2006

BIOGRAPHICAL NOTES ON HISTORICAL FIGURES

(Notes sourced in part from Wikipedia)

ROBERT MANGALISO SOBUKWE (1924–1978)

Robert Sobukwe was born on December 5, 1924, in a small Graaff-Reinet township adjacent to the historic Cape Dutch, Karroo town. The local Methodist mission gave him financial help to attend Healdtown, a Methodist boarding school for Black boys, where he proved to be an exceptional scholar.

In the late 1940s, he attended Fort Hare University College in the Transkei, the only Black tertiary educational institution in South Africa, and was elected president of the Students' Representative Council. At Fort Hare he joined the African National Congress (ANC), the organization formed in 1912 to fight for Black inclusion in governing South Africa. He helped found the ANC Youth League with among other founders, the young Nelson Mandela. In the early 1940s, the Youth League challenged the moderate policies of older ANC leaders. Together they developed a Programme of Action—the kernel principle—proactivity and not reactivity in response to the newly elected

Nationalist government's continued implementation of laws entrenching White *baasskap*—superiority.

In the mid-1950s, Sobukwe challenged the ANC's policy of allying itself with anti-apartheid organizations of other races, namely Whites and Indians under the umbrella of the ANC. In 1959, he led a breakaway faction from the ANC and formed the Pan-African Congress (PAC). Sobukwe was elected the first president.

Sobukwe's rationale for rejecting cooperation with White and Indian anti-apartheid groups lay in his belief that centuries of White supremacy conditioned Whites to be dominant and Blacks to be submissive. Blacks thus needed psychological independence. He admitted some Whites were intellectual converts to the African's cause, but, because of their material benefit from apartheid, they could not completely identify with the PAC cause. He argued that only Blacks themselves could achieve real democracy.

These ideas drew much from the "Africanist" philosophy articulated some years earlier by Ghanaian President Kwame Nkrumah, and Sobukwe's fellow ANC member, Anton Lembede. Sobukwe understood the danger that this stance may become anti-White, rather than more precisely the anti-White supremacy position. He frequently stated that even though Blacks must be independent of the influence of sympathetic Whites, ultimately loyalty to Africa was the crucial requirement for citizenship in a liberated South Africa. Whites and Indians would have full rights, so long as they viewed themselves as Africans and accepted majority rule.

On March 21, 1960, at the launch of the PAC anti-Pass campaign, Sobukwe gave himself up for arrest at the Orlando Police Station. Initially imprisoned at the Awaiting Trials Block at The Fort prison in Johannesburg, in May his sentence condemned him to three years in prison. At the end of·his sentence the government enacted the General Law Amendment Act empowering the Minister of Justice to detain a political prisoner indefinitely. Sobukwe was sent to Robben Island (an island off the Cape Town coast) for a further six years of detention.

In 1969 released from Robben Island, he joined his family in Kimberley where he lived under a twelve-hour house arrest order. Because of the ban on the PAC, he could not partake in any political activity. By correspondence courses, he earned both a degree in economics from the University of London and a law degree and established his own law office in 1975.

Several American universities offered him teaching posts, but the apartheid government would not let him leave the country.

On February 27, 1978, in Kimberley, he died from lung cancer.

HENDRIK FRENSCH VERWOERD (1901–1966)

Hendrik Verwoerd was born near Amsterdam, Holland on September 8, 1901. A few months later his parents immigrated to South Africa. He read psychology and sociology at Stellenbosch University and from 1925 studied for doctorates in these disciplinstherein Germany and the United States.

Verwoerd was tapped as a member of the White supremacist, Afrikaner secret society, *Die Broederbond,* an anti-Black, anti-British, and anti-Semitic body. Founded in 1919 its goal was to establish an Afrikaner-led Christian-National republic and to make the Afrikaner South Africa's master race. In 1936 Afrikaner nationalists founded *Die Transvaaler,* a daily newspaper published in Johannesburg, and asked Verwoerd to edit it. He used it to campaign for Afrikaner unity based on clearly defined

Broederbond principles. He virulently opposed "British-Jewish" imperialism. Like most Afrikaner nationalists, Verwoerd fought against South Africa's participation in World War II. Those who supported the war effort and Prime Minister General Jan Smuts accused Verwoerd of using *Die Transvaaler* as an instrument of Nazi propaganda.

The 1948 general elections brought *Die Broederbond* to power. Verwoerd contested and lost a parliamentary seat. But, *Broederbond* leadership headed the government, and it imposed its apartheid policies on the country. Later Verwoerd accepted a seat offered to him in the Senate.

In 1950 Verwoerd became Minister of Native Affairs. An advocate of segregation, he abolished the institutions set up for the representation of Black South Africans and planned to slowly transform the Black reservations into autonomous states (Bantustans) that would federate with South Africa. Year after year he placed before Parliament legislation to bring every aspect of Black life under his control.

In 1958 Verwoerd became Prime Minister. In response to his iron-fisted policies; insurrection, protests, strikes, and riots occurred in both the rural and the main industrial areas. Verwoerd's responded to these actions with more bans, banishments, arrests, and the enactment of increasingly harsh laws. On April 9, 1960, David Beresford Pratt fired two bullets into Verwoerd's head. He recovered to win, in October1961, a Whites-only referendum by a slim majority and to proclaim South Africa a republic.

Dimitri Tsafendas, a parliamentary messenger, stabbed and killed Prime Minister Verwoerd on his front bench in the House of Assembly on September 6, 1966.

HELEN SUZMAN (1917–2009)

Helen Suzman was a long-standing parliamentarian and anti-apartheid activist. In the 1960s and early 1970s she spent thirteen years as the lone parliamentary opposition to the apartheid government. Her penetrating scrutiny of apartheid legislation and defense of human rights and the rule of law in the face of obdurate and erosive attacks by the apartheid government earned her a worldwide reputation as a defender of democracy. During the "dark years" following the Sharpeville Massacre, she single-handedly kept the vocabulary of democracy alive in parliament. She also used her parliamentary privilege to visit political prisoners on Robben Island (the only parliamentarian to do so) and forged unbreakable ties with Nelson Mandela, the future President of the New South Africa.

Suzman, born on November 7, 1917, in Germiston worked for the Supply Board during the World War II and then lectured in Economics at the University of the Witwatersrand.

In April, 1953, Helen Suzman was first elected as the United Party's (UP) Member of Parliament (in the House of Assembly) for Houghton constituency. In 1953 Suzman and eleven other members of the UP resigned from the party and in August that year formed the new Progressive Party (PP).

In the general election of 1961 Helen Suzman became the only PP candidate to be elected to parliament, the first person since 1910 to be elected by South Africa's White minority on a platform explicitly rejecting racial discrimination. Suzman remained the PP's sole elected representative for the next thirteen years.

When Suzman visited Nelson Mandela and the other prisoners on Robben Island, state security officials warned her about associating with "opponents" of South Africa. After his release from prison Mandela and Suzman established a warm camaraderie.

Suzman spent a total of thirty-six years in parliament, resigning in 1989. She was one of eleven veteran activists appointed by F.W. de Klerk in December 1993, to sit on the Independent Electoral Commission to oversee the transition to majority rule. Awarded twenty-seven honorary doctorates from universities across the world (including Oxford, Cambridge, Colombia, Harvard, Witwatersrand, and Cape Town). Twice nominated for the Nobel Peace prize, Suzman became an honorary Dame Commander of the British Empire (DBE) in 1989 and was presented with the United Nations Human Rights award in 1978. She remained outspoken until her death. The Helen Suzman Foundation was established to honor her enduring human rights legacy.

Helen Suzman died in Johannesburg on January 1, 2009, at the age of 92.

ALAN PATON (1903–1988)

Alan Paton was born in Pietermaritzburg, Natal in 1903. He became the principal of the Diepkloof Reformatory for young (Black) offenders from 1935–1948. After the World War 2, he toured correctional facilities across the world. On the tour, he began work on his seminal novel *Cry, The Beloved Country* that he completed over the course of his journey, finishing it on Christmas Eve, 1946 in San Francisco. It became a huge international best seller.

In 1953 Paton founded the South African Liberal Party (SALP) that offered a multi-racial alternative to the apartheid government of the National Party. He remained the president of the SALP until its forced dissolution by the apartheid government in the late 1960s, officially because both Blacks and Whites comprised its membership. Paton's passport was confiscated on his return from New York in 1960 and not returned for another ten years. In New York he had received the annual Freedom Award.

Paton retired to Natal where he lived until his death in 1988. He wrote many other works, both fiction and non-fiction. He is honored in New York's Hall of Freedom of the Liberal International Organization.

DAVID PRATT (1907–1961)

David Beresford Pratt, a socialite and gentlemen farmer, became a long-term member of the Witwatersrand Agricultural Society. Prior to his assassination attempt on Dr. Verwoerd at the Rand Easter Show on April 9, 1960, he stood close to the Prime Minister on several occasions.

Pratt claimed he shot at the epitome of apartheid. The day before the shooting, he saw about a hundred prisoners being packed into a police van. He hated apartheid and felt strongly that someone must do something to end it. At the Rand Easer Show he decided to sacrifice himself to accomplish this.

Eventually found to be "disordered and epileptic", on September 26, 1960, he was detained at Pretoria Central Prison "to await indication at the Governor General's pleasure."

On October 1, 1961, he "hanged himself" while an inmate and patient at Bloemfontein Mental Hospital.

CHIEF ALBERT JOHN LUTHULI (1898–1967)

Albert Luthuli died in 1967 under mysterious circumstances on an abandoned railway line near his home in Stanger, Natal. A banned person then, he could not meet with more than one person at a time. Luthuli and Robert F. Kennedy forged a relationship when Kennedy insisted on meeting with Luthuli in Stanger during his brief South African visit in 1966.

Luthuli defied his ban and led the resistance nationwide in the immediate aftermath of the Sharpeville Massacre. Elected president of the African National Congress (1952–1960), Luthuli became the first Black South African to be awarded the Nobel Peace Prize (1960).

LAURIE GANDAR (1915–1998)

Laurie Gandar, a South African journalist, encouraged investigative reporting in South African journalism. He became the crusading editor-in-chief of the *Rand Daily Mail* during the late 1950s and 1960s. He played a pivotal role in the anti-apartheid movement using his editorial clout as a bully pulpit to fight for human rights, especially the right of free speech and economic equality. He helped expose the appalling conditions in prisons with Black inmates. These series of articles in the late 1960s brought him into head-on clashes with the apartheid government.

BENJY POGRUND (1933–)

A South African journalist and activist, Benjy Pogrund remains well known for his anti-apartheid reporting during the 1960s at the *Rand Daily Mail* newspaper in Johannesburg. Pogrund endured harassment by the Security Branch: the revocation of his passport, his several trials, and one imprisonment. He left South Africa for London in 1985 when the *Rand Daily Mail* closed. Currently he lives in Israel.

SIR HAROLD MACMILLAN (1894–1986)

Harold Macmillan was born on February 1, 1894, in London, England and died on December 29, 1986, at Birch Grove, Sussex. He was the British Prime Minister (1957–1963) and served in the House of Commons (1924–1929; 1931–1964).

PRESIDENT PAUL KRUGER (1825—1904)

Paul Kruger (Stephanus Johannes Paulus) was born on October 10, 1825, in the Steynsburg district. When the Great Trek started in 1836, he joined the trek party of Hendrik Potgieter, and later settled on a farm at the foot of the Magaliesberg in 1841. After the death of his first wife and child, he married Gezina du Plessis, with whom he had seven daughters and nine sons. Kruger started his political career as a Commandant General in the Boer Army and soon thereafter became the Vice-President of the Transvaal Republic. When the Transvaal was annexed by the British, Kruger took leadership of the resistance movement.

When the first war of independence (First Boer War) against the British broke out in 1881, Kruger was instrumental in negotiating Transvaal's independence under British sovereignty. In 1882, he became the President of the Transvaal Republic, a position he held until 1898, before the outbreak of the Anglo-Boer War (Second Boer War).

As British forces advanced on Pretoria, Kruger left the capital of the Transvaal and was given refuge in Europe. He settled in Clarens, Switzerland for the last six months of his life where he died of heart failure on July 14, 1904. His remains were returned to South Africa and he was buried in the Pretoria Church Street cemetery on December 16, 1904.

PRESIDENT GENERAL LOUIS BOTHA (1862-1919)

Louis Botha was born near Greytown in Natal in 1862. The son of Voortrekker parents he was raised on a farm in the Orange Free State. He was educated at the local German mission school.

A Boer general and statesman, he became leader of the Transvaal Republic's army in the Second Anglo-Boer War (1899-1902). From March 1900, he was one of the architects of the Union of South Africa established in 1910. His vision of South Africa included both British settlers and Boers. Botha was a leading figure in the Paris Peace Conference at the end of World War I. A great man of action, he was renowned for his simplicity, humanity, quick wit and good nature.

He is buried in Heroes' Acre, Pretoria. -1924

PRIME MINISTER JAN SMUTS (1870-1950)

Jan Christian Smuts, who became South Africa's second Prime Minister in 1919, was born on the farm Bovenplaats near Riebeeck West in the Cape Colony. Smuts had a distinguished political career as an international statesman and a general in the South African Army. He also participated in the Second Anglo-Boer War (South African War). He was re-appointed Prime Minister in 1939-1948. Smits was a signee at the Treaty of Versailles in Paris at the end of World War 1.

Throughout his career Smuts received many decorations, honors and awards. His house at Doornkloof is preserved as a museum, while his birthplace was declared a historical monument in 1955. Smuts has also been honored with statues including one in Durban, Cape Town and in Westminster, London.

Prime Minister Jan Smuts died on his farm Doornkloof, near Irene close to Pretoria, on September 11, 1950, after suffering a coronary thrombosis and several heart attacks.

PRESIDENT CHAIM WEITZMANN (1874–1952)

Born in the village of Motol, near Pinsk, in the Russian Pale Settlement, where Weizmann attended a *chedar*, he was one of fifteen children of a timber merchant. At the age of eleven he entered high school in Minsk. Weizmann studied Chemistry at the Polytechnic Institute in Darmstaat, Germany, and at the University of Freiburg, Switzerland, where in 1899 he was awarded a doctorate with honors. In 1901, he was appointed assistant lecturer at the University of Geneva and, in 1904, senior lecturer at the University of Manchester.

Weizmann's first Zionist steps began at an early age, and from the second Zionist Congress onwards, he was a prominent figure in the Zionist movement. In 1901, he helped found the Democratic Fraction within the Zionist movement.

An international statesman, he travelled widely, including visits to South Africa, speaking of the need for a Jewish homeland. On the international stage he and South African Prime Minister Jan Smuts had a warm relationship.

Weizmann died on November 9, 1952, after a long and painful illness. His grave was situated, at his own wish, in the garden of his home in Rehovot, Israel. Weizmann was survived by his wife Vera, and by his elder son Benyamin. His younger son, Michael, was killed in air action during World War II. His writings include an autobiography, *Trial and Error* (1949), which has been translated into several languages.

ABOUT THE AUTHOR

JANET LEVINE was born in Johannesburg, South Africa. Levine is an author, educator, and nonprofit entrepreneur. She has lived in the USA since 1984, both in Boston and in southwest Florida.

Levine has decades of published writing experience both as a book author and a freelance journalist. She is the author of five published works, including the 2022 release *Reading Matters* (Armin Lear Press). Others are *Know Your Parenting Personality* (Wiley 2004); *The Enneagram Intelligences* (Greenwood Publishing Group 1999) nominated for the 2002 Grawemeyer Education Award; *Inside Apartheid* (Contemporary Books 1988); *Leela's Gift* (Lulu, 2010) and available in several editions. Her books have been reviewed in

The New York Times Book Review, The New York Review of Books, The Yale Review, and many other publications both paper and electronic. Her books are translated into several languages.

Levine has published prolifically in magazines and professional journals as a writer both in her native South Africa and the United States. She is a book reviewer for the online *New York Journal of Books*. Her work has appeared in *The New York Times Sunday Magazine, The Sowetan* (in South Africa, the only White journalist to have a column in a Black newspaper, 1978-1981), *Boston Globe, Boston Phoenix,* and many online journals and magazines. She was interviewed by Terri Gross on NPR's Fresh Air and has appeared on all major TV outlets.

Levine has many years of experience as an educator and presenter. From 1986-2014 she taught in the English department at Milton Academy in Massachusetts. In 2014, she retired from her teaching career to concentrate on writing. Levine leads talks, workshops, and programs internationally on the Enneagram, reading and writing, and, occasionally, current events in South Africa. An anti-apartheid activist, she is an expert on South Africa and South African politics.

Levine was twice elected (1977 and 1982) to the Johannesburg City Council to represent the Progressive Federal Party. She was a member of many anti-apartheid organizations. Levine is the founder and leader of several successful non-profit organizations both in South Africa and the United States.

ACKNOWLEDGMENTS

My first thanks are for my agent, Maryann Karinch, who guided me through inevitable publishing travails. For that and for generally being an impassioned supporter of this book, she has my enduring gratitude. Thanks to my first readers, my son and advisor, Roger; and Alice, Antony, Bernice, Effie, Ellen, Malinda, Margery, Merri, Michele, Nan, Rose, and Sandy.

Many thanks to Lorraine Fico-White, my editor through several years and versions of this book, for her patience, perseverance, and attention to detail.

Thanks to the editors and staff at Armin Lear Press.

This book was written over several years. Thanks to now sadly deceased Tom, and still very much alive, Regina, for the frequent loan of their summer home over this time, a writing sanctuary.

Thanks to my extended family for inspiration and the hope that this project would one day be completed and published. Without our lifelong interactions the book would never have been written. Special thanks to my long deceased maternal grandfather and my more recently deceased mother. They kept our family stories alive.

Lastly, but most importantly, and never least, I want to acknowledge the innumerable interactions, experiences, sacrifices, fortitude and triumphs I share with my comrades and companions, in the long struggle for freedom and human rights in South Africa. I honor all those who were tortured, and those who gave their lives for freedom. Liv's story is not my story, but all our story.

CPSIA information can be obtained
at www.ICGtesting.com
Printed in the USA
BVHW031409270423
663156BV00007B/433